LIVERPOOL LAMPLIGHT

LIVERPOOL LAMPLIGHT

Lyn Andrews

HEADLINE

First published in 1996
by HEADLINE BOOK PUBLISHING

10 9 8 7 6 5 4 3 2

British Library Cataloguing in Publication Data

Andrews, Lynda M.
    Liverpool lamplight
    1. English fiction – 20th century
    I. Title
    823.9'14 [F]

ISBN 0 7472 1568 5

Typeset at The Spartan Press Ltd,
Lymington, Hants

Printed and bound in Great Britain by
Mackays of Chatham PLC, Chatham, Kent

HEADLINE BOOK PUBLISHING
A division of Hodder Headline PLC
338 Euston Road
London NW1 3BH

For my dear friends Jan and Mal White, who live in Grimsby, Ontario. I wish I could see you more frequently, but thank God for telephones.

Lyn Andrews
Southport, 1996

PART ONE

Chapter One

1938

'Mam, our Joe's at it again! I saw him up the road.' Katie Deegan slammed the shop door behind her, her brows drawn together in a frown, her lips set in a line of annoyance.

'Oh, Jesus, Mary and Joseph! That lad will be the death of me, and me with the shop full! Get back behind this counter, Katie, quick as you can while I go and see what's up now.'

Molly Deegan took off her flowered print pinafore and handed it to Katie. Since Molly was a big woman, and her eighteen-year-old daughter had a different build entirely, it rather resembled a tent on Katie and she pulled a face as she wrapped it around her, wishing now she'd never opened her mouth. 'Where's me Da?' she called to her mother, who was apologising to her customers while making her way towards the door.

'He'll be in soon and so will our Georgie. This is just what I don't need right now! God stiffen him! Where exactly did you last see the little get?'

'Running out of Coyne's Undertakers with that gang of hooligans he calls "me mates". They all ran off together. Now, what do you want, Mrs Maher?' The question was asked in a quieter, more respectful tone.

Mary Maher pursed her lips and nodded in Molly's direction. 'I don't know what's gorinto kids these days. Only last week you had to cart your Francis off to Stanley Hospital, didn't yer, Ellen?'

Ellen MacCane nodded her agreement. 'If I've told 'im once I've told 'im an 'undred times about climbing on the jigger walls. Still, a broken wrist will keep him out of trouble for a while.'

Katie hoped they weren't going to engage in a long catalogue of the faults and misdeeds of Vinny Maher and Franny MacCane. People at the back of the shop had started muttering and were getting impatient. Mam would have her life if she came back and found the shop still full of the original customers.

'What can I get you?' Katie urged.

Mary turned her attention to her shopping. 'I'll take three of your

3

mackerel, a pound of soft cod's roe, and has yer Mam any fresh rabbits left? We'll have a pie termorrer. I'll cook it tonight, the kitchen mightn't get so hot. God, it's murder havin' to keep the range going full blast to cook stuff in the oven, especially in this weather.'

There were nods of genuine agreement.

'I think so, I'll have a look in the larder.' Katie leaned across the white marble slab behind the glass of the shop window where early that morning Molly had arranged the fish she'd brought home from market. It was always so tastefully done, Katie thought, with sea shells and parsley and crushed ice which was replaced at dinner time. Somehow the striped canvas awning outside, that protected the window and its contents from the sun, gave the shop a professional air others lacked. She picked out three of the fish, their silver and dark gun-metal scales shimmering, trying to find ones that were all the same size. It was the end of the day so it wasn't an easy task. She placed them on a sheet of paper on the counter.

'Will they do? Not as much choice, I'm afraid.'

Mary nodded and watched as Katie weighed out the pound of soft cod's roe.

'That's great, luv.' She said approvingly.

In summer the rabbits were kept in the dark cool larder, which was off the back kitchen, which meant Katie had to leave the shop unattended. It didn't worry her, she knew nothing would be stolen in her absence. Molly Deegan's regular customers weren't like that. Of course you got the odd 'chancer' but there was always someone like Mary Maher there to confront the would-be thief.

As she walked into the living room, Katie saw Georgie hanging up his coat. At nineteen he was the eldest and worked for the British and American Tobacco Company, or the B & A as it was known locally. He earned good money, most of which he saved, and got cheap cigarettes which he sold because he didn't smoke, adding the profits to his savings. Mam often asked him what he was saving it all *for*? So that when he died he could get his name in the paper as a millionaire?

'Oh, do me a favour, Georgie – get a rabbit out of the larder and bring it into the shop for me,' Katie wheedled. 'There's a crowd out there all waiting to be served, and our Sarah's still bad with that migraine headache.'

He looked at her, annoyed. 'I've only just got in from work. Where's Mam?'

'Gone out looking for our Joe again. Oh, come on, please?' She sighed. 'I don't know why Mary Maher and the like don't shop earlier. Mam's up at the crack of dawn to get to the market.'

'They're all looking for something cheap, something that won't keep until tomorrow.'

4

'Mam doesn't have stuff like that . . . You know as well as I do, Georgie Deegan, that she's famous around here for her good, fresh fish. Everyone knows they'd have to pay twice as much if they went to the likes of Coopers or the big shops in town.'

'Well, things she'll let them have a bit cheaper because she's soft-hearted and tired,' he answered belligerently. 'It's the end of the day and I'm worn out.'

Katie glared at him. Worn out. Him. He might not be very tall but he was broad and fit. She was the odd one out, very slightly built unlike Sarah who was quite tall and sturdy too. Sarah hated her build which she'd inherited from her Mam, but whenever she complained about it, Mam would say she should thank God she hadn't been born afflicted or deformed in any way. She was a fine strapping girl. She hated being called 'strapping', too. She said it made her feel like a cart-horse.

'I'm just as worn out as you,' Katie insisted. 'I've been working too and our Joe's taken the deliveries instead of Sarah.'

Some of her mother's customers were infirm, and would send a shopping list with a neighbour. Sarah would then wheel out the old bike from the back of the lean-to in the yard, put the order in the basket on the front and deliver it. On Saturdays when she served in the shop all day, her younger brother Joe earned his pocket money by doing the deliveries. He didn't mind. None of his mates had bikes and he often gave them rides on the crossbar or let them sit behind him, legs sticking out dangerously.

'Well, it's part of her job, not mine.' Georgie sat down at the table, opened the *Echo* and began to scan the pages, completely ignoring his sister.

Katie unceremoniously shoved past him towards the larder. 'Oh, I'll get it myself! There's half of Chelmsford Street out there in the shop and Mary Maher wants a rabbit, but don't give it another thought. Read your paper.' She shot a scornful look at Georgie. 'I should know better than to ask you to lift a finger. Lord Muck thinks that after a day's work it's his right to be waited on hand and foot.'

Although slight in build she was quite strong. Her dark, naturally curly hair didn't need a perm or the sheer torture of trying to sleep with a headful of curling pins or papers as Sarah had to do. Her mother always said that Katie's brown eyes were the mirror of her soul, but Katie herself thought they were the mirror of her mood.

They were glaring at her brother now as she went into the pantry. Georgie was arrogant, overbearing and unscrupulous, and always had been! It was really only her Da who kept him in his place. He'd often answered Mam back, but in such a way that it didn't sound like downright insolence.

5

She herself had spent the last eight hours in the bottling room of Moorehouse's lemonade factory in Lytton Street. It was a boring job, particularly as the noise the bottles made meant conversation was almost impossible. Even though they all went out to work, except for Sarah who helped their mother, they were expected to take a turn serving in the shop. Officially it was only open until seven, Molly then insisted that every surface be washed down, the remaining stock moved to the larder, placed in trays and covered with the remaining ice. Buckets and implements for crushing the ice were stored neatly under the slab. In reality it was frequently after ten before the door was locked, as people often 'popped in' for a bit of 'something' for supper. They were open seven days a week, from eight-thirty until late, and they were always busy. The only one who didn't take a turn at serving was Joe, who had to be supervised all the time, otherwise he'd be trick-acting with his mates.

Just then, the back door from the yard into the entry was thrown open and Katie looked up out through the window. 'You'd better shift yourself, Georgie, Da's home.'

As she went into the shop and placed the rabbit down on the counter to wrap, the door opened and her Mam appeared with a face like thunder, dragging an untidy, yelling ten-year-old boy by the ear.

'I'll swing for him one of these days, so help me God I will. You'll come to no good, Joe Deegan. You'll end up on the gallows in Walton Jail!' Each prediction was accompanied by a hefty belt across the legs.

Molly turned to her customers, who were all standing taking in the spectacle, avid to know what the lad had been up to now.

'You try to do your best for them and what do you get?' Molly panted. 'Nothing but trouble, heartache and dog's abuse. Well, meladdo, your Da's home and you're for it!'

Before she had time to disappear into the living room beyond the shop and thereby deny them all the details of the latest misdemeanour, Mary Maher caught Molly's eye. 'What in the name of God has he been doin' now, Molly girl?'

'Just the usual, Mary, annoying and upsetting half the neighbourhood,' the woman replied grimly. 'First it was into Coyne's. They just happened to have in a bereaved – a *posh* bereaved – family who could have taken their business elsewhere, when meladdo opens the door, runs in and bawls, "Have yer any empty boxes, Mister Coyne?"'

Katie tried hard to hide her smirk. Coyne's was the most prestigious undertakers in the area.

'Can you imagine it? Carrying on like that! I caught up with him and his mates, including your Francis, Ellen, coming out of Adaire's. Not content with sending Jack Coyne's blood pressure sky-high and nearly losing him an important client, he goes into Miss Adaire's Wool

6

and Baby Linen shop and tells her he's got something really interesting to show her. He got it in school, he said, from the Nature Table.' Molly cast her eyes to the ceiling. 'As if there's any such thing as "Nature" around here! Well, you know what she's like. She's that gormless she'll believe anything. So he puts a matchbox on the counter and opens it. I guessed what he'd done the minute I heard the screams. He'd stuffed a dead mouse inside. Amelia Adaire nearly had a flaming heart attack on the spot! Last week he did the same thing to that Miss Prescot who has the stationer's shop further down Stanley Road.' Molly again raised her eyes to the ceiling. 'Mother of God, what did I do to deserve him?'

'Well, I blame the wireless,' Mary sniffed. She was a thin woman with slightly hunched shoulders and what appeared to be a permanent headcold which made her eyes watery.

'You haven't got a wireless,' Ellen cut in, smarting that Francis had been involved – and more to the point – that Molly had publicly announced the fact.

'*And* the pictures and all this building of bomb shelters and talk of war,' Mary went on.

'Well, luv, we *have* got a wireless,' Molly said grimly, 'but meladdo won't be listening to it for a while, nor will he be going to the cinema. And he definitely won't be sitting down comfortably either, after Bill gets through with him. It'll be hanging on the back of trams next, then pinching sweets and then God knows what else! Katie stay out here while I see your Da. Then our Georgie can shift himself and give a hand or we'll get no tea until midnight!'

Business always slackened off from six to seven, when most people were at home having their tea. That night, after they'd all eaten their own meal, only being interrupted twice, Molly issued the list of chores.

'Georgie, have a look at that block of ice wrapped in sacking at the back of the larder. If it's too far gone I'll have to get more in the morning. Stack the fish boxes and give the yard a good hosing down. Oh, and while you're at it put up more fly papers under the lean-to. With this weather, they're a damned nuisance.

'Katie, get the steps and a bucket of hot soapy water and wash down those green and white wall tiles by the door. I was going to get Sarah to do it but she still can't raise her head off the pillow without feeling sick.'

'Ah, Mam! I hate doing that, it makes my hands go all red and dry and I'm going out. I'll look a mess.'

'Well, it's got to be done and the sooner you get going the sooner it'll be finished. Then give the floor a good sweeping and a mop over with Jeyes Fluid.'

7

Katie knew it was useless to argue. She had made plans to go to the Olympia Theatre on West Derby Road. It was cheaper than the Hippodrome – only threepence instead of sixpence – and the show was just as good. She was going to meet Josie Watson and Violet Draper, girls she worked with at Moorehouse's who lived in the adjoining streets. Resigned to being late, she departed into the shadows of the shop.

After washing the dishes and leaving them to drain in the wooden rack, her mother at last sank wearily into a chair and passed a hand over her forehead. It was the first time she'd sat down since dawn.

'A long day, Moll?' Bill asked as he stood up. It was easy to see where Georgie, Sarah and Joe got their height from, Molly thought as she'd done a thousand times before. Her husband was over six foot and broad too.

Molly smiled at him and nodded.

He poured her a cup of tea.

'God, you could stand a spoon in that, Bill, it's stewed to death.'

'I'll make us a fresh one. What about meladdo up there?' He jerked his head in the direction of the ceiling. Joe had been chastised and given a good talking to, which in his opinion was punishment enough. Molly was not as forgiving.

'He can stop up there. I'm fed up running around the neighbour-hood apologising to people for him. I've a good mind to go and see Father Macreedy and tell him that that lad isn't fit to serve on the altar at Mass. Scaring people half to death, being disrespectful to the bereaved and the Lord alone knows what else. A nice way for an altar boy to carry on, I must say! What's going to become of him I daren't think.'

'I know he's a handful, but it's only divilment.' Despite his build, Bill was a softly spoken man whose words and direct, piercing gaze had far more of an effect on the offenders in the family than all Molly's yelling did.

'Divilment for the time being, but who knows what it will lead to?' She fretted. 'He's so easily influenced. If I could only keep him at his books, Bill. He's clever, much cleverer than the girls and our Georgie. Oh, our Katie's sharp, she'd make a good businesswoman, but there's a difference. I want a trade for him – something technical. Something that will stand him in good stead.'

'Our Georgie's not got a trade, luv,' he reminded her.

'Georgie doesn't need one; he knows he'll get the business when we're six feet under and pushing up the daisies.'

As if on cue, their elder boy stepped in from the yard, his tasks completed.

'Are you off out tonight, son?' Bill asked.

8

'I don't know, Da. I might go out for a drink with the lads for the last half hour.' That way he'd only have to buy one round.

Molly glared at him. 'You're not old enough to drink.'

'Oh, leave him, Moll, he doesn't get much pleasure out of life and you've got to admit he doesn't waste his money.'

No, he's too tight-fisted, Molly thought, although she didn't say it. He must give the moths a terrible fright whenever he opens his wallet! Georgie was altogether too fond of acquiring and hanging on to money, in her opinion.

'Neither do we waste our money,' she said firmly, 'but until he's twenty-one it's against the law to drink. I'm not having the coppers banging on my door and hauling him off. This is a respectable house. We're a good Catholic family.'

Any further comment was cut short by the clanging of the shop doorbell. As Katie was still in there no one made any attempt to get up.

'I just hope it's a customer and not Amelia Adaire or Jack Coyne with a copper in tow!' Molly sighed.

Katie came through, clasping the mop and bucket, followed by Josie Watson, a pale girl with soft light-brown hair and large appealing grey eyes that always looked slightly startled.

'It's Josie, she's early. I told her I wouldn't be ready until half-past seven.'

'Just put those in the scullery then, and go and get yourself ready. Sit down, Josie,' Molly said comfortably. 'How's your Mam, luv? I haven't seen her in the shop much lately.'

The girl blushed, her eyes downcast but she glanced at Georgie from beneath her lashes.

'She's not been too well, Mrs Deegan. She's had one of her turns.'

'Oh, I'm sorry to hear that, Josie,' Molly concentrated on pouring herself a cup of freshly made tea. One of Florrie Watson's 'turns' was usually brought on by utter exhaustion. No wonder with six kids, even though the three eldest were working. The younger ones were still at school. Terribly house-proud, that was Florrie's problem. She half-killed herself keeping their small house spotlessly clean and tidy – a virtual impossibility with eight people living in it. Then there were the clothes and linen to be washed, starched and ironed, to say nothing of the shopping and cooking. Florrie was a fool to herself, Molly thought.

She liked Josie though. She was a quiet girl, a bit on the shy side but with no common or forward ways. She'd often heard Katie say she was a hard worker and clever with her hands. She could sew and knit and make cushion covers, rag rugs and even curtains. Molly wished her own daughters were that gifted. Neither of them could even take up a

9

hem, and as for knitting! Well, Sarah had once made a scarf. An uneven affair it had been, some bits wide and some bits very thin. She'd used odd balls of wool that Amelia Adaire sold for a halfpenny. It had kept Sarah occupied all winter, but by the time it was finished it was so long it would have looked well on a giraffe. Mind, it wasn't all their fault, Molly admitted guiltily to herself. She'd never had the time to teach them. Her business took up most of her waking hours. She would be the first to admit that she hardly had a minute to herself.

They'd rented number 72 Chelmsford Street, just off Stanley Road, for years. The rent included both the shop and the living accommodation, which comprised three bedrooms upstairs, and a big living room-cum-kitchen with a large cast-iron Stanley range that needed blackleading every day. There were comfortable chairs and a sofa, all with spotless, lace-edged antimacassars. The big dresser took up one wall and was arrayed with the dishes that were in use every day, its polished cupboard doors reflecting the flames from the range. On the back wall, under the stairs, was a glass-fronted cabinet that held the good china and glass. Over the high mantelshelf was draped a red chenille cloth edged with a fringe and covered with bric-a-brac. But in pride of place and carefully taken down and dusted each week, was a statue of *The Infant of Prague*, the child Jesus clad in the robes and crown of a king.

Beyond was a fair-sized back kitchen. Shelves were fixed all around the walls and to the left was the pantry or 'larder' as it was more commonly known. There was a big sink and a wooden draining board, two mesh-fronted food presses and the dolly tub and scrubbing board.

Molly had worked hard to build up the business and her effort, determination, her fairness and good judgement had paid off, even during the terrible years – not so long ago – when half the country was unemployed and soup kitchens had been set up in church halls and assembly rooms.

She went to the Queen's Square fish market herself every morning and was well-known there and greatly respected. In the early days, when she was just starting out, Jackie Woodward, one of the less scrupulous dealers, had made the mistake of giving her the ends of yesterday's catch but charging full price for them. It was a ruse he never pulled again. He never ever wanted to experience the scathing, outraged portrayal of his character to which Molly Deegan's tongue had treated the entire market.

She bought the best produce within her budget, not in great quantities, but she also sold rabbits which were purchased from a very reliable source. She was far from a 'soft touch' but she had a kind heart. Quite often Joe or Sarah would be sent, at night, with a parcel of fish they'd not managed to sell that day to someone in their neighbourhood who she'd heard was down on their luck. She'd never see a child in the street go hungry, even if it was only some apples or pears she thrust into their hand.

Bill was a carter, with his own horse and cart, and was out in all weathers. Like his comrades, he used to tie sacks around his shoulders to protect him from the worst of the rain, wind and snow in winter, but Molly had been down to Greenberg's, the naval outfitters in Park Lane, and bought him a good heavy oilskin coat and a sou'wester like sailors wore. There was no sense at all in leaving yourself open to arthritis and rheumatics, not if you had the cash for decent clothes to keep out the weather.

Accidents were frequent: icy roads in winter; goods not properly loaded or secured; collisions with motor vehicles; and skittish horses that bolted. Two years ago, Bill had had a lucky escape. He'd been at the King's Dock waiting for a load, when he'd been hurled backwards from his seat as Bessie, the most even-tempered animal they'd ever owned, reared up in fright when a bale of cotton had suddenly fallen from the deck of a ship on to the dockside. She hadn't been the only horse to shy. One of the iron wheel-rims of the cart beside his had gone over Bill's forehead and he'd nearly lost an eye. Had the cart been loaded and the driver less skilful, he would have been dead. He still had a large contusion above that eye which the doctor said would be permanent, but Molly thanked God it hadn't affected his sight. All in all, she thought, as her eyelids grew heavy with contented weariness, they hadn't got too much to complain about.

Georgie's eyes, in contrast, were wide open. He was sitting staring at Josie who was blushing furiously under such direct scrutiny. She wasn't a bad-looking girl, he thought coolly. A bit pale when she wasn't blushing, but a good worker – and she was shy, which in his book meant biddable. There'd be no backchat from Josie the way there was from their Katie. He pitied the man who got her – he'd have to take a firm stand from the start, but then he and Katie were always at loggerheads. She was a bit too sharp, was his sister, and you had to be damned clever to pull the wool over her eyes for long, although he sometimes managed it.

'Where are you off to then?' he asked.

'Oh, we're going to the Olympia. There's a good few turns on. We're meeting Vi Draper there. Well, she's actually meeting someone.'

'She's got a feller then?' Molly asked sharply, her sleepiness dismissed. She was always keen to keep track of what her daughter and her friends got up to when they were out.

'Maybe I shouldn't have said anything.' Josie was confused and the colour in her cheeks deepened.

'Oh, don't be daft Josie,' Katie said. 'Everyone knows she's been sweet on that Jack Milligan from work. He's "Maintenance".'

'Does "everyone" include her Mam?' Molly probed.

'Even her Mam,' Katie answered, tucking her hair under her hat and observing the effect in the large, gilt-framed mirror on the wall. 'So it's no big secret, Josie. You seem frightened of your own flaming shadow sometimes.'

'Less of the language in this house, Miss, or it's the back of me hand you'll get, eighteen or no eighteen.'

'Sorry, Mam.'

'All right, get off with the pair of you then and don't be late back.'

As Georgie helped his father count out the day's takings from the old jug they kept under the counter, he thought again of Josie Watson. He might just ask her out on Saturday night . . .

'She's a nice, quiet, steady girl, that Josie,' Molly remarked to Bill as he checked the ten-shilling notes, silver halfcrowns and florins, and the copper coins that Georgie passed to him. She cast a sideways glance towards her eldest son. He'd be twenty soon and wasn't even walking out with anyone. At his age, she and Bill had been engaged.

'I was thinking, Mam . . . maybe I'll ask her out on Saturday night. What do you think?'

'I'd do that, Georgie,' she said approvingly. 'She comes from a hard-working, decent, clean family. You could eat your dinner off Florrie Watson's front step and woe betide any of her kids who walked into her lobby with dirty boots on.'

There were a series of thuds from upstairs.

'Can't he come down now, Mam?' Georgie interceded for his brother.

'No, he flaming well can't, but you can take him a cup of tea and a butty.' The fact that she'd relented was due to the sudden vision of a budding romance between Georgie and little Josie Watson. She could see it all in her mind's eye. That was one match she would certainly not discourage.

Chapter Two

Autumn hadn't lasted long this year, Molly thought as she pegged out the washing on the line in the yard. There was a definite nip in the October air, a hint of the sort of sharpness that was present on a frosty December morning. The outside walls were whitewashed and reflected the light, so the yard always looked clean and bright, winter or summer. The sky was a pale greyish-blue, with ribbons of white clouds trailing across it, but the sun was low and its rays held little warmth. Still, the clothes should all be dry by mid-afternoon, she decided optimistically. Then, after tea, the three of them, herself, Sarah and Katie, would take turns in ironing the mound of clothes and bedding. Bill and Georgie would have to see to any late customers.

It was a miracle she got the washing done at all, but on Mondays she was always up extra early to light the fire under the copper boiler in the small wash-house in the yard before she went to market. She considered herself lucky in having a wash-house; many women had to take their washing down to 'the bag-wash', as the public wash-houses were known. Those women considered it almost a social function and spent the day jangling, speculating and joking. That way the drudgery could be laughed away for a few hours.

Molly wanted none of that. Her business was private and so was her linen and her family's underclothes. She'd often heard the derogatory remarks made by Mary Maher about the state of some people's washing.

It wasn't easy to keep it spotless and white around here. Maybe in the country perhaps, where there were no smuts, dust and all kinds of muck pouring from factory chimneys. She and most of her neighbours often skinned their knuckles to the bone on the corrugated metal wash-board. Then it was a good pounding and pummelling with the posser, a sort of pole that looked as though a three-legged stool had been attached to it. Then came the endless rinsing, and finally everything was soaked in the water that contained the 'Dolly' blue bag to give it all a bluish tinge that was supposed to make it all look brighter. Then came the folding and the mangling and the pegging out. It took almost the entire day and meant that Sarah had to look after the shop and make a pan of scouse for supper. It was no wonder women with big families were always on their knees by the end of the day and then the men came home, expecting a hot meal on the table before they had a wash and went down to the pub for a pint, if they could afford it. No, life for women was far from easy, and giving them the vote had done nothing to better their lot as far as Molly could see.

At least the breakfast dishes were all neatly piled on the draining board. It was one of her rules that the table be cleared. Sarah was pouring hot water from the kettle into the sink.

'I'll do those, luv. You put your shop pinny on and open up for me.'

Sarah smiled with relief. She hated washing up. The harsh 'Aunt Sally' liquid soap left her hands red and roughened. None of her friends had what could be called 'beautiful' hands, for they all worked in the factories or shops along the dock road. It must be very offputting for a lad to get hold of your hand and find it was like grasping a piece of sandpaper, Sarah thought dreamily. Not that any lad had ever held *her* hand.

She finished tying the strings of the all-enveloping apron. 'Mam, do you think our Georgie will ever get around to asking Josie Watson out?' She asked. 'She's round here often enough and our Katie says she fancies him. She must be out of her mind, I reckon, but it's her life and I suppose it takes all kinds.'

Molly plunged the dishmop into the hot water and attacked the first plate. 'He's certainly taking his time about it,' she agreed. 'You can be too cautious, you know, I told him. It was months ago when he said he might ask her out. If he doesn't shift himself soon she'll up and off with some other feller who's not so slow off the mark. But there's no moving him, he does as he pleases.'

Sarah thought her Mam sounded annoyed. 'It would be nice to have a wedding in the family though, wouldn't it?' she said wistfully.

Molly rubbed hard at a stubborn stain on the plate. 'It would be nice to have the money to pay for it too, and if you don't go back and mind the shop there'll be no money for anything, never mind weddings.'

When Sarah had gone, Molly carried on with her task but her mind was on other things. Yes, it would be nice to have a wedding – maybe next year. She liked Josie and she fully approved of the whole Watson family. Fred was lucky enough to have a steady job, Norma and Brenda worked at Tate's, and Florrie knocked herself out looking after them all. Yes, Georgie would get a good bargain in Josie. He just needed a push or some kind of a jolt. He certainly had enough money to take the girl out. She suspected he had enough to take her to somewhere as posh as Lewis's Red Rose Restaurant, but that was something he'd never do. Her son was a born miser and where he got that trait from, she couldn't imagine. Still, she'd better get a move on. Bill was coming home for a bit of dinner today while he left Bessie at the smithy to be shod.

'That animal wears out more shoes than the whole of Everton Football Club or the other lot across the park,' he always complained.

'Except that she does about fifty miles a week and God knows how many hours, and they do an hour and a half, and with a ten-minute break in the middle,' she always replied dryly. Bill supported Everton while Georgie and Joe were Liverpool supporters. She never cared much about who won what, but it was a source of some very heated arguments in the kitchen on a Saturday night, arguments usually ended by Bill pulling rank over his sons. He was a good father, she thought fondly, as she stacked the last dish. No, she had no complaints.

The shop was busy later as the women finished the weekly wash and came in for something for tea, usually only a few of the small selection of vegetables they carried to use in a pan of scouse: 'blind scouse' if they weren't fortunate enough to have the remains of a Sunday joint to boil them up with. Molly was enjoying a rare uninterrupted gossip with Mary Maher, her only customer at that moment, when the shop doorbell rang briefly.

It was Mr Catchpole, who travelled all the way in from Kirkby, to deliver the rabbits, as he always did three times a week.

'My motto is "country fresh is always best",' Molly always laughed, 'and "straight from the sea to the slab".'

'They'll be easier to keep fresh now, ma'am,' he remarked. 'The weather's getting much colder. We'll have snow before Christmas, you mark my words.'

Molly paid him willingly: she'd sold four dozen in that week alone and there was never any need to examine the produce.

'Well, I've never known you to be wrong yet about the weather,' she smiled as she counted out the coins.

'Aye, well, I hope I'm wrong about that feller Hitler, ma'am.' He shook his head sadly. 'I remember the last lot, when we were fighting Kaiser Bill.'

'I don't take a lot of notice of politics, but that was different. At least he was . . . well, Royalty, I suppose. This feller Hitler is only a house-painter! And have you seen the cut of him? He looks like Charlie Chaplin!'

'That's as may be, but he's Chancellor of Germany now. In charge of the whole kit and caboodle and he's a powerful speaker, so I've heard. He wants an Empire too and he'll do his damnedest to get his hands on most of ours.'

'The man's a raving lunatic if he thinks that. Mind you, he looks mad. I've seen him on the Pathé News at the pictures, and he's a strutting little runt of a windbag,' Molly said tersely.

'I'll give you that, ma'am, but Napoleon Bonaparte was a strutting little runt, too, and look at the trouble he caused!' The elderly man shook his head and sighed heavily as he left.

'Who the hell was he talking about? I've never heard of anyone called Nap . . . Napoleon,' Mary Maher asked, when she was sure he'd gone.

'How do I flaming well know! I'll ask our Joe when he comes in from school. They're supposed to teach them things like that. Sarah, when you've got a minute, luv, take those into the larder.' Molly nodded her head towards the rabbits tied in braces that now hung from the rail behind the counter.

They never closed for lunch, so when Mary had left, Molly told Sarah to go and put the kettle on.

'You have yours and I'll just have a cuppa until your Da gets in.'

She checked the window display and spread out the haddock, herrings and dog fish, the latter known as Rock Salmon, the cod and the Manx kippers. She decided to replenish some of the crushed ice although in winter it didn't melt as quickly. She went through into the kitchen.

'Mam, what's up?' Sarah asked.

'Nothing, luv. I just need a bit more ice.'

She half filled a galvanised bucket and went back and began to scoop up the ice that was melting, then she moved the fish to one side and wiped the slab, then she replaced them and the ice. The bucket of water and slushy ice she carried to the shop door to empty it in the gutter. Mr Catchpole was right, she mused, it certainly was colder today. And she feared he might be right about that Hitler. The Council had been building shelters and they'd all been issued with gas masks, horrible rubber things that made you gag. More planes were being built, and across the Mersey in Birkenhead at Cammell Laird's shipyard there was great activity. The only good thing you could say was that there were more people now in work. But there seemed to be unrest everywhere; even in London that Mosley and his Blackshirts were strutting around while the police did nothing . . . !

Suddenly she looked up and was startled to see their Georgie racing down the street towards her, his legs and arms going like pistons. Her hand instantly flew to her mouth. Oh, God! Something was wrong!

He was gasping for breath as he clutched her arm. 'Mam! Mam! It's me Da!'

A cold fear began to creep over her. 'What's wrong? What's wrong with your Da? Georgie, for God's sake, tell me!'

'I . . . I . . . was in me break. I'd just been selling some cheapo fags when I saw Da coming up the road.' He paused for breath but Molly caught him hard by the shoulders and shook him.

Georgie was regaining his composure. 'He waved to me and I just started to go over to him when a bloody fire engine came around the corner, going hell for leather with no bloody bell clanging to warn people. Mam . . . Oh Mam, he didn't stand a chance! It all happened so fast. The fire engine tried to slew across to the other side of the road, but Da was tossed in the air and flung right across the road and up against the factory wall. Bessie was screaming and trying to get up even though all her legs were broken and bleeding and there was a big gash in her side, so big you could see her ribs.' His face was deathly pale.

Molly was appalled. 'Oh, Mother of God! Is . . . is . . . ?'

'They shot her,' Georgie replied.

'I'm not talking about the bloody horse, you damned fool! Your Da . . . where's your Da?'

'They took him to Stanley Hospital. I said I'd come and tell you.'

Molly ran back into the shop and took a halfcrown from the jug under the counter.

'Mam, what's wrong?' Sarah's eyes were round with fright.

'You stay here, don't move! I'll send our Georgie back.' Molly was at the door again.

'MAM!' Sarah screamed at her mother who looked back over her shoulder.

'Your Da's had an accident – he's in Stanley Hospital,' she flung back, rushing down the street after Georgie.

There wasn't sight nor sign of a tram but Georgie managed to flag down a lorry and asked the driver to help. After hearing the few grim details the man nodded.

'Mam, come on, get in. This feller's going to give us a lift there. I'll give you a leg up.'

'Here, missus, take hold of my hand and I'll pull yer up.'

All the way to the hospital, which wasn't far and could have been reached on foot in ten minutes, Molly's lips moved in silent prayer, her rosary clasped in her hands. 'Oh Holy Mother, don't let him be badly hurt. Please, please, don't let him die. Oh, Blessed Infant of Prague, hear me now. Oh, Bill! Bill!' The pleading became a repetitious refrain in her mind.

Georgie, pale and drawn, looked straight ahead. He couldn't get the sights and sounds of the accident out of his head. The ear-splitting crash of the collision, the terrible screaming of the fatally-injured horse and the awful dull thud as his Da's body had hit the wall then crumpled up in a heap. Then the arrival of the police and the

17

ambulance, and amidst all that confusion, the single shot that had rung out and silenced the awful screaming of poor Bessie.

The lorry driver's voice broke into his thoughts. 'Right, lad, we're 'ere. Help her Ma down, I've got ter get ter the docks.'

Molly was so stunned she just held out the halfcrown.

'Keep yer money, missus,' the man said with rough kindness. 'If 'e's bad off 'e'll not be workin' for a while. Good luck to yer.'

Georgie nodded his thanks and, uncharacteristically, held out a packet of Players Navy Cut cigarettes as a token payment. The cigarettes were accepted.

Molly hated hospitals. That smell of ether and carbolic combined always made her stomach heave, but there was no time for such thoughts now. She *had* to find Bill. She *had* to see him. She caught the arm of a Sister who was walking rapidly through the Casualty waiting room.

'My husband! Bill . . . William Deegan. Where —?'

The woman's expression softened a little. 'The man who has just been brought in? A collision with a fire-engine, I believe?'

Molly nodded, tears stinging her eyes, a sick fear gnawing at her guts. No, she just wouldn't let herself think the worst! She wouldn't care how badly injured he was, as long as . . . Thank God money was no problem. There was the shop and she had a bit saved.

'Follow me. The doctor is with him now.'

If there was a doctor with him, surely that was a good sign? The heels of Sister's black lace-up shoes tapped loudly as they followed her along a corridor. At least to Molly the tapping sounded loud. She couldn't speak. She clutched Georgie's arm tightly, feeling that if she were to let go, she would fall. Bill had got over his other accident, thank God. When she'd reached the Royal Infirmary which had been the nearest hospital at the time, he'd looked terrible, but he'd pulled through. He was strong and healthy, was her Bill.

The Sister pulled aside a curtain that divided the row of cubicles. 'This is the man's wife and son, Doctor.' Her voice was clipped and respectful but there was a note of compassion in it too.

Molly couldn't see all of him, for the doctor was leaning over him, but Bill's trousers were torn and one of his boots was missing. How could he have lost it? It was a stupid, irrelevant question that passed quickly from her mind. Her heart was in her mouth. What was the doctor hiding from her? She was a strong, capable woman not given to hysterics, so why didn't he stand up straight and look at her, let her see Bill?

After what seemed like an age he did turn towards her. 'I'm very sorry, madam, but—'

'It's Deegan, Mrs Deegan and that's my Bill,' she interrupted. Now

18

she could see him properly and he didn't look hurt at all. He looked as though he was simply asleep or unconscious. Georgie had got it wrong, Bill was all right! Maybe concussed, she thought, as hope and relief surged through her.

'Then, Mrs Deegan, I'm very sorry to have to tell you that Mr Deegan is dead. He was dead on arrival. His neck had been broken. He wouldn't have suffered: it would have been instantaneous.'

She felt as though he had slapped her hard across the face. Then she felt clammy and sick.

'I think perhaps some smelling salts and then a little sedative, Sister. Mrs Deegan is in shock.'

Georgie and Sister led her back out into the Casualty waiting room and sat her down. She hadn't fainted, the smelling salts had worked quickly, but now she wished she'd sunk into that black oblivion. Now she had to face it. The shock. The horror. The cruel trick her mind and Fate had played on her. Letting her think he wasn't hurt, raising her hopes and then snatching everything away. Her rosary was in one of her pockets and she grasped it so tightly that the metal crucifix cut into her hand, but she didn't feel it. She must pray. Pray for Bill's soul. Pray to the Holy Mother. Tell her beads. *Holy Mary, Mother of God. Holy Mary, Mother of God.* She must pray. Pray. Pray.

Sister turned to Georgie. 'You'll stay until the formalities have been completed?'

Georgie looked horrified. 'Me? You mean me?'

'Yes, young man, I mean you. Unless of course you have any older brothers or relatives that can be contacted. Your mother is in no fit state to do anything. She must be taken home, given a sedative and then helped to bed.'

'Well then, I'll have to take her home, won't I?' he snapped. He too was shocked. No one here realised that he'd *seen* it. That it was *his* Da lying back there.

Sister glared at him. She wasn't used to being spoken to like that, not even when the person concerned was in a state of shock. 'I will send a Medical Orderly and a nurse with her in an ambulance. I also believe you were a witness, so the police will want to question you.'

Before he had time to retort that he wasn't staying for anyone, the double doors burst open and Katie ran in, hatless and with her coat flying open, revealing the overall underneath.

'Mam! Oh God, Mam! Mary Maher got a copper to phone Moorehouse's and the girls had a whipround for a taxi for me . . .' She looked from her stunned mother to her pale but mutinous brother and finally the Sister. 'Is . . . is he . . . ?'

Sister nodded. 'I'm afraid so.'

All the terrifying uncertainty that had built up almost to an hysterical pitch on the journey burst forth, and sinking to the floor, Katie buried her head on her mother's lap and sobbed as though her heart were breaking. Unconsciously, Molly stroked her daughter's dark curly hair.

Unfortunately, scenes like this were all too frequent in the hospital, Sister thought, but calm and commonsense must prevail.

'Right, young man, if you will sit over there until the police arrive, a nurse will bring you a cup of strong sweet tea.' She bent and touched Katie on the shoulder. 'Are you capable of seeing your mother home, dear? In an ambulance, of course. Doctor has recommended a sedative, I'll send for it now.'

Katie nodded and wiped her eyes with the back of her hand. It was impossible to believe. 'And . . . and what about Da?'

'That will depend on you . . . the family. We will lay him out in the mortuary, but perhaps you might want him at home.'

Katie nodded. 'We . . . we'll take him home.'

Her words seemed to bring Molly out of her trance-like state. 'Send for Ma Edgerton and Father Macreedy, Katie. I'll not leave him here unshriven.'

Katie nodded, fighting back the sobs. 'Mam, his soul will have gone straight to Heaven. He . . . he was a good, kind man.'

'I know, but he still must have the Last Rites.' Molly stood up, a little unsteadily and Katie caught her arm and held it tightly, the tears still falling unheeded down her cheeks.

'Can I sit with him, Sister, please? Just until the priest arrives. After that, I'll take him home.' She felt calmer now. Katie's raw grief and suffering had made her drag her mind away from the awful truth that would take days, weeks, maybe even months to sink in.

Sister looked at Molly with respect. 'Are you certain about this, Mrs Deegan? You know, shock can take many different guises. It affects people very diversely.'

'I'm sure. I'll be all right when we're home.'

With some difficulty Katie was persuaded to leave her mother in the small cubicle. Molly was holding Bill's hand while tears slid down her face and over and over in her mind she asked God why? Why her Bill? A good Christian man, a dear man going home to his family for a bite to eat. Why him? In his life he'd never done anyone harm. She could find no reasonable answer but clung to her faith that taught that all reasons and mysteries would be revealed on the Last Day.

Katie went and found her brother who was sitting with his head in his hands. She put her arm around his shoulder.

'Are you all right, Georgie?'

He raised his head and nodded. 'I've got to stay here until the bloody coppers arrive.'

She didn't want to ask him, but she *had* to know.

'Did . . . did you see it?'

'Yes, that's why I've got to bloody well wait!'

'Stop swearing! Da's lying in there . . .' she couldn't get the word out. 'Was it . . . quick?'

He nodded.

'Does our Sarah know?'

'Only that there was an accident, I think.' No one seemed to be even remotely interested in him. He felt sick with shock, but all they'd done was give him a cup of tea and an aspirin and told him to wait. And you could trust the bloody coppers to take the statements of the fire bobbies first and then all the other witnesses before they got around to him. When he looked up, Katie had gone.

Bad news always travels fast, and by the time Katie got home, the front curtains of all the houses in their street were drawn tightly across the windows as a mark of respect for Bill Deegan's passing. All the neighbours were out, standing in shocked little groups, whispering. They looked at Katie with pity as she passed but she didn't even notice.

Sarah was white and trembling, and clutching the edge of the counter for support.

'Mam told me to stay here. Oh Katie, is it true? They're saying there was a terrible accident with a fire engine, and that Da . . .' She choked on a sob.

Katie put her arms around her. 'It's true. There was an accident. Da's dead, Sarah. His neck was broken and . . . they had to shoot poor Bessie. Georgie's at the hospital and they've sent for Father Macreedy. Then . . . then we'll have to get Ma Edgerton and someone will have to go for our Joe.' Her head was beginning to pound and she felt vaguely dizzy. 'We'll close the shop. You fetch Ma Edgerton and I'll go to the school.' She could now hardly see for tears and each movement increased the thudding in her head, but she picked the harder errand for herself. Sarah just wasn't up to it. She wouldn't be able to find the right words to say to a ten-year-old lad. But could *she*? There was no easy way out of this predicament.

'Oh Katie, we'll never see him again,' Sarah sobbed, and Katie's thin veneer of calmness shattered. The thread of courage snapped and she clung weeping to her younger sister, sharing shock and grief.

Chapter Three

Three days later, the curtains of the houses in Chelmsford Street were drawn over again and the neighbours, dressed in black or simply with black armbands, according to their means, stood on the edge of the pavement as the funeral cortège passed. The sky was an ominous grey but as yet there was no rain. A strong wind whipped up the litter in the gutter, twisting and whirling it into small eddies.

Coyne's, always greatly respected by Molly who said they were just a cut above all the other undertakers, had been very helpful and very deferential towards the widow's wishes.

Two official mourners in tailcoats and tall silk top hats, carrying ebony canes, walked in front of the horse-drawn hearse, the gleaming dark coats of the horses witness to many hours of meticulous grooming, their leather bridles and harnesses to hours of polishing. The black plumes attached to their headbands bent before the gusting wind, as though bowing in respect for the man whose body they were taking first to the church, then to its final resting place in Kirkdale Cemetery.

In the second carriage Molly and Katie appeared outwardly calm and self-contained, but Sarah sobbed quietly. All three wore full mourning. Black coats, dresses, stockings and shoes, small hats with veils that covered their faces and dropped below their shoulders.

In the third carriage sat Georgie and Joe; the young lad's eyes were red and puffy and he was still sniffing. The brothers wore black suits, white shirts, stiff collars and black ties. Georgie had on a black Homburg hat, and Joe a black and grey tweed cap. Bill's brother, Alfred, whom no one had seen in years and who had looked down on his brother's family for the same length of time, sat bolt upright, gazing stonily at the faces of the people who had gathered in the street.

Among them, of course, were Mary Maher and Ellen MacCane, both of whom had been towers of strength. Ellen had served in the shop, helped by her two girls Rosie and Cissie, after they'd come home from work, and Mary Maher had gone with Katie to buy the mourning clothes at Blackler's, for Molly hadn't felt up to it and Sarah just dissolved into tears when anything about the arrangements was

22

mentioned. It was Mary and Ellen who had made all the sandwiches, and with money provided by Molly, had bought the small meatpies and the pigs' trotters that were such a delicacy, as well as the fancy cakes and fruity 'Sally Lun' and, of course, the drink.

They had set it all out on the table in Molly's big living room. Glasses, some borrowed, now stood in neat rows on a crisp white tablecloth with bottles of whisky, rum and gin, beside those filled with sherry and Madeira wine. The food was covered with clean damp tea-towels to stop the sandwiches curling up and becoming dry.

Mary and Ellen wouldn't go on to the cemetery; they were returning to the shop to be ready to serve the thick, home-made pea soup as the mourners arrived back. As Mary said, 'It's a cold, miserable place, that Kirkdale Cemetery, even on a good day weather-wise, and today is horrible.'

The day after Bill's death, Joe had gone back to school. Mr Parry, the Headmaster of St John's, had called to express his sympathy and told Molly that it would be better for the lad to carry on as usual, to try to maintain a modicum of some sort of normal life, and Molly had agreed. She seemed to be living life in a daze, her movements wooden. Nothing seemed real at all. Nothing. She woke each morning and for the first few seconds, didn't remember. Then reality would hit her. Bill was dead. She'd never turn and see his head on the pillow next to her own ever again.

She had no heart for seeing to food and drink. Arranging the Requiem Mass with Father Macreedy had been bad enough, choosing hymns and passages from the Gospels. In the end she'd been so upset and confused that the priest told her he would pick something suitable on her behalf. Bill Deegan had been a good parishioner, a good Catholic and a member of the Catholic Men's Confraternity. A man with no enemies and only goodness in his heart. His soul would have gone straight to Heaven.

As the procession made its way up the aisle of St John's, Katie saw Josie Watson and Vi Draper turn and half-smile at her. A sad sympathetic smile. She couldn't return it and besides, they wouldn't be able to see her face clearly beneath the veiling, but she was grateful for their support. They must have taken a couple of hours off, so their wages would be short this week. It was good of them.

Georgie also saw the smile and didn't think twice about returning it. Josie looked away in confusion while Vi glared at him. Fancy giving Josie the eye like that – and with the church full, too! She'd never liked Georgie Deegan. Oh, he wasn't bad-looking but he was mean-spirited and miserly, yet her friend was desperate to be asked out by him.

Throughout the Mass, with Father Macreedy wearing the black chasuble – the cape-like vestment with the large white cross on the back – and with the heavy, sickly-sweet smell of incense filling the church, all Katie could think of was that she'd never hear her Da's voice again. Never hear him laugh or joke or scold in his quiet but severe way. Over the years would she even be able to recall it as clearly as she could now? Beside her, Sarah was still sobbing; the sound was grating on Katie's raw nerves and she could see it was affecting Mam and Joe too. She leaned towards her sister.

'For God's sake, Sarah, stop it!' she hissed. 'You're upsetting Mam and Joe and we don't want any hysterics. Have some dignity! Da wouldn't want you to be carrying on like this.'

'I can't help it. I'm not like you,' her sister gulped.

Katie sighed wearily. 'Yes, you are. I'm upset too, but just try to think that Da is in Heaven now. He's happy and he wouldn't want us crying and carrying on.'

At this, Sarah's sobs gradually diminished, much to everyone's relief.

None of them remembered much about the actual burial; their shocked and grieving minds mercifully blanked that part of the day out. Molly held Joe close to her, his face pressed hard against her coat, the sobs wracking him.

'It's all right, luv, your Da's in Heaven now,' she soothed. 'That's not really your Da down there. Hush now, lad.' She tried desperately to believe her own words of comfort.

All Katie could remember was Father Macreedy pressing the damp cold soil into her hand and then she'd let it fall through her fingers into the open grave.

They all turned and left, shepherded by the priest before the gravediggers began to shovel the earth down on to the coffin. Everyone hated to hear that sound, so the men always waited until the bereaved were well out of earshot.

'Merciful God, you must all be starved! Get your coats off and some of this pea-whack down you.'

Mary Maher relieved Molly of her coat and veil while Ellen handed out the bowls of steaming soup.

Katie had thought she wouldn't be able to get a single crumb past her lips, but surprisingly she was hungry and began to feel much better with some hot food inside her. Mary had decided that the two girls were old enough to have a glass of Madeira wine to help steady their nerves. She noticed that Georgie had already helped himself to a fair-sized tumbler of whisky. Someone would have to keep an eye on him, she thought grimly, or he'd be roaring drunk and a disgrace to his Mam and his Da's memory before the day was out. Then her eye fell on Bill's brother who was standing a little apart from everyone else and who was obviously a wealthier and more educated man than Bill had been.

Mary made a concerted effort to moderate her strong accent. 'Excuse me intruding, like, but well, could you keep an eye on meladdo there? He's making too free with the hard stuff an' he's not used to it. The last thing poor Molly wants is him falling down drunk.' She jerked her head in Georgie's direction.

Alfred Deegan paused for a minute then nodded. He'd always considered that Bill had married beneath himself, but Mary Newsham as she'd been then, had proved to be a good wife and mother. Perhaps he would take an interest in the lad. Discuss his prospects, try to keep him relatively sober.

For the most part he succeeded, but it wasn't easy. The lad was surly and uncooperative until the family business was mentioned.

'Oh, I've got big plans for this place,' Georgie boasted, flushed and emboldened by the drink.

'Indeed?'

'Aye, Uncle Alfred, I have. As well as fish and game, I'll have groceries, milk, patent medicines, sweets, newspapers and cigarettes – all under one roof. I'll sell everything.'

'I don't think the owners of those specific businesses in the area will take kindly to that, lad, but I can see the sense in it.'

'Who cares about them? If people can get all they need without running up to the Maypole Dairy or down to the newsagent, or along Stanley Road to Pegram's for their groceries, Deegan's will grow. We'll all get rich.'

'Very admirable, but does your mother know about these plans?' Alfred was beginning to find the youth's arrogance hard to take.

'Oh, I'll manage Mam.'

Katie, standing behind her brother, had overheard the whole conversation. 'You'll not start mithering Mam about anything, Georgie Deegan. You're not going to take advantage of her.' She looked up at the uncle she'd only seen twice in her life, and addressed him directly.

'Uncle Alfred, Mam's always been the one who coped and took care of everything, and she will be again. She won't take a back seat just because . . . Da's gone.' She glared at her brother.

Alfred Deegan could see all the makings of a family brawl brewing. 'Well, I'm sure she will and if I'm to get back to Manchester today, I'm afraid I'll have to be leaving soon.'

Katie roused her Mam enough to thank Bill's brother for attending the funeral, considering the distance and all.

'It was the least I could do, Mary. And you have a champion in this lass here.' He turned to Katie. 'You take care of your mother, young Katie. You do understand what I mean?'

Katie flashed a quick glance in Georgie's direction before nodding. She'd never heard her mother called by her baptismal name before. It sounded very odd and out of place.

'Just remember, my dear – bullies are invariably cowards. Stand up to them and they'll back down.'

'I will, Uncle. Our Joe will get your hat and coat and will I walk with you to the tram-stop?'

'No, that won't be necessary,' he smiled graciously. 'I would say you are needed here.' At least he's managed to crack his face, Katie thought. For most of the day it had looked as though it had been carved out of granite.

But there was no need to keep her eye on Georgie. Mary Maher had removed all the bottles of spirits.

'An' if he starts, Ellen, I'll lay him out flat, so help me God!' Mary said as she locked the whisky in the sideboard.

'Ah, take no notice, Mary. It's all talk. He's a right bucket-gob is that one,' Ellen commented acidly. Mary wasn't a big woman but one unexpected hefty swipe from her would indeed lay Georgie Deegan flat on his back. 'Though the way he's carrying on, I can see Katie taking a swipe at him before long.'

'They'll all feel better after a night's sleep. It's just nerves and grief,' Ellen replied sagely.

On Sunday, two days after the funeral, as Katie had cooked the meal, Sarah coaxed Molly to at least sit at the table with them.

'What are we going to do about the business, Mam?' Georgie asked confidently. He appeared to have no feelings of grief, or else he was hiding them well.

Katie was instantly on her guard, remembering her uncle's words of warning. 'What do you mean by that, Georgie?' she demanded.

'Well, I'm the man of the house now, so to speak, and it's only right that I give up at the B&A and do full-time here. Take over all the buying and so on, too.'

Molly raised her head, for the first time in a week, there were signs of animation in her eyes.

'While I'm still fit and well, I'll see to the business. It's *my* business, Georgie: I built it up. Your . . . your Da had his own business. If you want that, I'll not mind.'

Georgie hadn't expected this. 'But Mam, you're still shocked and —'

'But she's still got all her wits about her and she'll need them with you,' Katie chipped in.

Georgie ignored her. 'It's not right for you to be getting up in the middle of the night to go to the fish market. How will you get there now, anyway?' Bill had always taken her on the cart and brought her home with the crates.

'She can get a lift from any one of a dozen people. She's well known and respected!' Katie persisted.

Molly sighed heavily. 'You're more use to me bringing in a steady wage, lad, and keeping an eye on our Joe.'

'So, I'm to get no part in the business?'

'I didn't say that. I'll make provision for all of you, in time.'

'Oh Mam, don't start thinking and saying things like that!' Sarah cried, bursting into tears.

Katie rounded on her brother. 'Now see what you've done. Everyone's upset again – except you! Why don't you clear off down to the pub and upset them. They'll all buy you a round, out of sympathy, and that's something you're good at, Georgie Deegan – taking. But you're flaming useless at giving.'

He pushed back his chair so violently that it made a protesting screeching noise on the lino. 'You've got too damned much to say, Katie Deegan!'

'Oh, clear off and give us all some peace,' she yelled at him.

Molly shook her head after the front door had been slammed shut. 'I don't want you all fighting like this.'

'It's him, Mam. Even at the funeral he was spouting off to Uncle Alfred about how he wants to turn the shop into some kind of department store. All he cares about is money. Money and the power to lord it over people.'

Molly shook her head sadly, thinking that Bill's death had not only robbed her of a supportive loving husband, but now seemed to have caused some kind of animosity between her elder son and daughter. She could only thank God that Sarah was too quiet and that Joe was too young to get involved in what, if she wasn't careful, would be a family split. That thought alone seemed to give her courage. Bill wouldn't want anything like this, so it was up to her to put a stop to it now before it got completely out of hand. She must pull herself together and keep them all under control, just as Bill had done.

Georgie moodily kicked a small stone down the street, looking neither to right nor left, deep in his own thoughts. He'd been so sure that Mam would agree to him taking over the business. If it hadn't been for their bloody Katie . . . He didn't know just how much she'd heard of his conversation with Uncle Alfred – in fact, he wasn't sure he could remember all of it himself – but obviously she'd heard enough to stop him becoming what he considered himself now to be – the rightful head of the family and the business. Of course, he could always get another horse – Da's cart was still in the coalyard around the corner – but that would mean sitting out in all weathers and humping sacks and boxes and bales on and off the cart all day. And anyway, motor lorries were on the streets in larger quantities now. The days of the horse and cart were numbered. No, he didn't want to take over from Da. He could sell the cart along with the contracts Da had had, for surely Mam didn't intend to drive herself to the market and back? She didn't even know how to hitch the animal up to the cart.

He was so engrossed in his thoughts that as he turned the corner into Stanley Road he almost collided with Josie Watson.

'Georgie!'

'Oh, I'm sorry, Josie. I was just . . . well . . . thinking.'

'How is your Mam?' This was the first opportunity she'd had to talk to him alone for ages.

'Oh, she's not too bad.'

'Time heals,' Josie said simply. She paused, pleased that she'd managed to say just the right thing. Not too gushing, not too gloomy.

'I'm bloody sick of hearing that one, Josie!'

She blushed, distressed at his rudeness.

'Sorry. Is your Katie coming back to work tomorrow?'

He shrugged. 'I suppose so. I couldn't care less what our Katie does.'

'She's been a good friend to me, Georgie. If it hadn't been for her, I'd never have got my job or made all the friends I have. I'm too . . . quiet, like, to speak up for myself.'

Georgie studied her. What she'd said was true, and she wasn't a bad-looking girl either. If he started to take her out it would please Mam, put him in her good books again, and maybe in time she'd relent about the business. After all, it *was* his. He was the eldest, but more to the point, it wouldn't half annoy Katie.

'Josie, are you doing anything tonight?'

'Tonight!' Her heart began to race. He was going to ask her out at long last. 'No. No, I'm not going anywhere.'

'Then will you come out with me?'

'Where to?' Her eyes were shining.

'Where would you like to go?' He hoped it wasn't anywhere that would cost him too much money.

'Well, I don't know. Could we go on the ferry to New Brighton? I don't mean actually *do* anything there, just walk and look at things.' She wasn't going to jeopardise any future outings by asking to be taken to the theatre or to a cinema. A sail on the ferry and back, with a bit of a walk in between would do her fine. Then maybe he'd take her to the cinema next time. If there *was* a next time.

'Great, I'll call for you at about seven then.' He shoved his hands deeper into his pockets and walked away.

Josie stood staring after him, her face radiating happiness. She'd get home now and wash her hair and press her good skirt and blouse and maybe Norma would lend her her new handbag. Oh, it was a dream come true! Katie and Vi both made fun of her for being so mad about Georgie, but she didn't care.

Josie almost danced along the pavement. Six hours! In just six hours she would be going out with Georgie Deegan!

Chapter Four

'Mam, do you think he'll ever get around to marrying Josie?' Katie asked thoughtfully, whilst drying the dishes after tea. Georgie's meal was set between two plates perched on top of a pan of water to keep it warm. These last couple of weeks he'd often been late in from work. 'Overtime,' he informed Molly. 'You've got to get it while it's going.'

Molly was finishing her cup of tea and Sarah was in the shop. Joe, as usual, had disappeared before anyone could send him on errands or make him sit down at the table and do his homework.

The evenings were getting lighter now and the sunlight of spring 1939 filtered through the window in the back kitchen and made strange silhouettes of familiar objects that hung on the opposite wall.

'Oh, I don't know, love. He's all set here, he knows which side his bread is buttered on all right. He gives me his keep and that's all he has to pay out – and he's got no responsibilities.' Molly sighed, heaving herself to her feet.

'She's too eager,' Katie complained. 'I keep telling her to be more – well, off-hand with him. Not rush to get ready to go out whenever the fancy takes him to call and see her on his way home. It's a waste of breath, though. She won't take any notice.'

Molly nodded. Josie would make a good wife but she feared that the girl would be easily browbeaten by their Georgie.

Katie finished the last plate and placed it neatly on top of the pile, then went out and hung up the tea-towel to dry in the yard.

When she returned Sarah was in the back kitchen, looking pale and uneasy.

'What's up with you?' Katie asked.

Sarah bit her lip.

Katie became impatient. 'Oh, now what's the flaming matter? Where's Mam?'

'In the living room. It's our Joe.'

Katie's impatience turned to annoyance. Didn't Joe have poor Mam persecuted and her hardly over the shock of losing Da! Christmas had been terrible. They'd tried so hard. She and Sarah had put up the paper-chains and holly and filled Joe's stocking, using the money her

Mam had given them for the bits and pieces. And they'd bought gifts for each other, but it had all been so awful. People, customers and neighbours, had all meant well but it was upsetting. Each time someone forgot their tact and left the shop calling 'Happy Christmas' she'd felt the pain and loss again. New Year hadn't been much better either. Everyone was out in the street and in other years they would have been too, even Joe. All the church bells were ringing and there had been the cacophony of fog horns and ships' whistles blasting from all the craft on the river.

'Just come out for "Auld Lang Syne" Molly luv,' Mary Maher had urged sympathetically. 'Things will get better in the New Year.' But Molly had refused; they all had.

And now Joe was causing problems again. If he would only stick at his books, Mr Peel had told Mam, he'd have a chance at a scholarship to Saint Francis Xavier's College – and who knew where that would lead? Somehow or other they'd find the money for the uniform and the books. But no, Joe was stubborn and just downright stupid some-times. She'd often asked him if he wanted to end up like most of the men in the neighbourhood – dockers, carters, labourers – all decent ways of earning a living, but breaking their backs in any kind of weather for a pittance and often being laid off.

'What's he done now?' she demanded.

'It's bad.'

'How bad? Don't just stand there looking like a flaming lemon and saying daft things like "It's bad". What's bad?'

'Well, there's a scuffer in there with Mam.'

Katie's eyes widened. 'Holy Mother of God! Has he been pinching things?'

'I don't know! All I know is that the scuffer marched in the shop holding our Joe by the scruff of his neck. I ran in the living room for Mam and she told me not to go back in there.'

'Where's our Georgie?'

'He's round at Josie's.'

'Are you sure, Sarah?'

'Yes, she said he was going round there to see her on his way home. She called in to see if we had any dabs left. She got some earlier but doesn't think they'll be enough. Mrs Watson didn't have enough for their tea.'

Sarah sat down on the hard wooden chair that stood by the back door and Katie leaned against the sink.

'So, there's no one in the shop?'

'No.'

Katie gnawed her bottom lip. Someone should be in the shop. If anyone came in and found it empty there would be all kinds of rumour

31

and speculation, for someone was bound to have seen that young hooligan being dragged home by the police. And besides, something might get pinched. Mam probably hadn't even brought in the jug with the takings in it.

'I'm going out the back way, Sarah. I'll run up the jigger and round the front. We can't just leave the shop empty.'

'Then I'm coming with you.' Sarah had no wish to be present when her Mam, Joe and maybe even the scuffer came into the room.

'No, you stay here. When I see the scuffer leave I'll come back through.' And before Sarah could object she was gone, leaving both the back door and the yard door open behind her.

Cissie MacCane was standing in the shop, looking around mystified. 'Where've you been? I've been standing here for five minutes. I've shouted "Shop" twice and rattled the doorbell.'

'Sorry, Cissie, I had to dash around the back.'

'Didn't I see your Joe coming down the street with a scuffer?'

Although caught by suprise, Katie put on a mocking, scornful expression.

'Our Joe – with a scuffer! Are you mad, Cissie, or do you just need glasses. Mam would kill him! God, he'd have had to have committed murder for a scuffer to yank him home. Now, what can I get you?'

Cissie sniffed. She was a pale, thin girl with dark, lank hair who did have poor eyesight and seemed always to be squinting. 'Mam said have yer got any bits left? Doesn't matter what kind, she'll make a pie.'

'A pie, Cissie?'

'Yeah, it's not bad. She puts a birrof milk an' arrowroot in it for a sauce, like, and then bakes it. Me da's on late finish so we've all got ter wait for our tea anyway otherwise 'e goes mad.'

'Right then, let's see what we've got.'

Cissie sighed. 'Our Rosie's been laid off again, yer know. I never know from one day to the next iffen I'm going ter get me cards.'

Katie took the proffered coins. 'Well, if it's any consolation, I hate my job, Cissie, I really do.'

'Why? It's a pay-packet at the end of the week, isn't it?'

'I know, but it's so flaming boring, and the noise gives you a headache.' Hearing the sound of voices from the back room she didn't go on to enumerate her complaints. 'But you're right, Cissie, it's a job. Tell your Rosie I'm sorry.'

'Tarrah then.'

'Tarrah and thanks,' Katie replied, only just in time. The voices had become louder and the door opened. Katie turned and gazed up at the policeman. He looked huge but then they all were. 'Would you mind, sir, if . . . if . . .'

32

He looked down at her. She was a pretty enough girl but with a determined set to her chin.

'If what?'

She took a deep breath. 'Well, Mam's only just getting over Da's death and you know what they're like around here. Could you, I mean *please* could you go out the back way – just for Mam's sake? We've always been an honest, decent, hard-working family, sir.'

'I know. This has been my beat for nearly two years now. I knew your Dad – honest as the day is long, Bill Deegan. A great pity, his accident. And a pity his sons aren't as honest.'

She sighed with relief that he seemed sympathetic, but then jerked her head in the direction of the back room. 'What's our Joe done now?'

'I think you'd better ask your Mam, girl, or maybe your older brother.'

'Our Georgie?'

He shrugged and she knew she would get no further information out of him, but at least he had turned and gone back into the living room.

At that same minute, Mary Maher's youngest lad Vinny came in for a tub of Southport potted shrimps. Katie eyed him suspiciously, as he was one of Joe's best mates. 'That's pretty exotic for you, Vinny, isn't it? Come into money then?'

He was indignant. 'I earned it. Some feller give me tuppence for helpin' him along the road with a big sack of wood blocks he had. Me Mam said I could spend a penny an' save a penny.'

'So why potted shrimps of all things? Why not sweets?'

'Because I aint never 'ad potted shrimps, not in all me life, an' I want ter know what they taste like.'

She put some into a bag and took the money, then stared at his departing back. He obviously had nothing to do with whatever it was that Joe had done.

Sarah came out, white-faced, her eyes like those of a frightened rabbit.

'What's he done?'

'I don't know. He won't say.'

Katie pushed past her and stormed into the living room. Molly was slumped at the table, her head in her hands, while Joe stood by the range. He was obviously frightened but stood mutinously with his hands thrust deep in his pockets.

Katie's first concern was for her mother. 'Mam, are you all right?'

Molly looked up, her eyes suspiciously bright. 'God give me strength, girl, but I don't know what I'm going to do with him.'

She sounded so weary, miserable and upset that Katie's fiery temper flared up.

'All right, you little get! Just what have you done? And don't think standing there like that as if butter wouldn't melt is going to fool *me*. I'll flaming well batter you until you tell me!'

Joe said nothing.

'I'm going to ask you one more time.'

'I'm saying nowt.'

She lunged out and grabbed him by the tuft of hair that was always standing on end no matter how much wetting and brushing down was done to it. She slapped him hard across the cheek with the flat of her hand. 'I'm not having you upsetting Mam like this! Do you hear me, Joe Deegan?' This time it was the other cheek that took the full force of her hand.

Joe yelled with pain and tried to twist away from her, but she hung on tightly to his hair.

'Right, Mam, get his clothes together, I'm taking him to the Kirkdale Homes. They can have him. He'll learn to behave there. He'll get no decent food or clothes from them. You'll have to scrub out toilets and corridors and you'll have to wear that horrible uniform and everyone will know that you've been thrown out of this family. Go on, Joe Deegan! Get out that door!' She shoved him bodily across the room towards the back of the house.

Molly was on her feet. 'Katie, stop it! He won't tell me. He won't even tell the police, so why should he tell you?'

'Because I mean what I say, Mam.' Katie's voice shook with rage. 'I'm not joking or just saying it to frighten him. He's not going to upset you *ever again*. This time it's too much. Out that door he goes and he never comes back! Go and get his stuff together, Mam.'

Joe suddenly broke down and began to cry, great noisy gulping sobs. He'd held out against them all, even the scuffers and that took some doing, because Georgie said his mates would cut his ears off and his tongue out if he told, but the terror of being disowned, locked away in what people said was a terrible, grim orphanage worse than prison, and the sheer conviction in his sister's voice broke his resolve.

'He made me do it! He *made* me! He said his mates would cut off me ears and cut out me tongue!' he sobbed.

Katie looked at her mother, mystified. 'Who said?'

Joe was sobbing so loudly he was unable to answer.

'Mam, what did the scuffer say? Why did he bring him home?'

'"Loitering with Intent", was what he said.'

'Intent to do what?'

'I don't know, Katie. It was all to do with illegal games of Pitch and Toss, he wouldn't tell me any more. He said a CID man would come later on to see us.'

'Oh, God!' Katie cried, the thought of the grim ruthless men of the

34

CID who reputedly had their own set of merciless rules, terrified her.

'Mam! Mam, don't let her take me to the 'omes! I'd sooner go with the scuffers!' Joe clung like a limpet to Molly, who hadn't the heart to distance herself.

Katie had calmed down a little. 'Joe, for God's sake will you tell us what this is all about, then we might be able to help?'

Joe sniffed and Molly handed him a handkerchief from the dresser. How she wished that Bill were alive.

'I . . . I just had to stand on the corner, an' they told me if I saw a scuffer coming I was to whistle three times.'

'Stand on which corner?' his sister demanded.

'Tillard Street, on that bit of wasteland.'

'Who told you? Who said they'd cut your ears off and your tongue out?'

Joe buried his face in Molly's pinafore. 'Our Georgie and Tommy Kelly and Pug Mahoney.' The names were muffled but they were familiar.

Katie looked at her mother, her lips set in a grim line, her eyes dark with anger. 'You see, Mam? Our Georgie's a liar and a cheat, I've known it all along! Even when we were kids and you gave us money to go out for the day, he always managed to trick us out of it, one way or another. That's what all the fights and arguments between us were about. He'd pay his tuppence for the ferry-ride and we'd have to sneak under the ropes or hide in the crush of people while he hung on to our fares. I got caught once; I was terrified. I had to wait until the ferry came back and he had to pay up even though I'd not gone to Seacombe. I made sure he never got my money again but he often took our Sarah's, if I wasn't there. He's no good, is our Georgie.'

'Don't say things like that about your brother, Katie!'

'But it's true, Mam. He's been using our Joe as a look-out for a Pitch and Toss game! God knows how long this has been going on. Overtime, my flaming foot! Frightening the poor kid so badly he wouldn't even tell the police. Gone to Josie's, he says. Just wait till I see him!' She was shrugging on her coat.

'Where are you going?' Molly demanded.

'I'm going to Josie's – and if he's not there, then when that feller from the CID comes asking questions, I'm going to tell him the bloody truth!'

'Katie! Stop! Our Georgie wouldn't get mixed up with that crowd of no marks.'

Katie ground her teeth in frustration. 'Oh, Mam. When will you realise he's no good! Look at the state of our poor Joe, he's terrified out of his wits.' She put her arm around her young brother. 'I'm sorry I belted you, Joe, I really am. But I just thought you were upsetting

Mam for no good reason. I wasn't really going to take you to the Homes, I promise. I'm going now, don't panic.'

As the door slammed Joe looked up at his mother. 'I was scared, Mam. Honest to God, I was so scared!'

'It's all right, lad. No one's going to hurt you, not while I'm here.' Molly smoothed down the tuft of hair that Katie had recently yanked so hard. There were tears in her eyes. Oh, Holy Mother, help me! she prayed. Why did you take my Bill?

'Come on, Joe, lad, we'll have a cup of tea and some biscuits. Your Mam's here and no one's going to lay a finger on you.'

Katie rushed down Chelmsford Street, totally ignoring the greetings of the neighbours she passed, all of whom looked at each other questioningly, eyebrows raised.

When she got to number 3 Becket Street she hammered on the front door until it was opened by a terrified Josie.

'Katie? God Almighty, you've nearly bashed a hole in the door! What on earth's the matter?'

'Where's our Georgie?' Katie demanded.

'He's gone home.'

'Stop lying for him, Josie. The CID will be round at our house soon. He's been using our Joe as a look-out for Tommy Kelly and Pug Mahoney's Pitch and Toss games, and our Joe was dragged home by a scuffer. Now, *where is Georgie*?'

Josie's eyes grew rounder with fear. 'Honest to God, he's gone home. He *was* here but he's gone. See for yourself.' She caught Katie's arm and pushed her down the lobby and into the kitchen.

'Where's your Mam and Dad?'

'Da's not home yet, he's on late shift, and Mam's just nipped down the street to see Maureen Cassidy who's having her baby.'

'And I suppose all the others have gone out living it up and the kids are out playing hide and bloody seek?'

'Katie,' she pleaded, 'Georgie wouldn't do anything like that. He might have a bit of a bet on a horse, once in a blue moon, but he'd not get mixed up with that lot.' Josie was trying hard to sound convincing, for two hours ago Georgie had arrived in the Watsons' yard, breathless, his face red and damp with sweat from his exertions. He'd sent one of her young sisters into the house for her and told her that if anyone, anyone at all came asking questions, she was to say he'd been here, with her, ever since he finished work. She'd started to ask him why but he'd just caught her by the shoulders and said, 'If you really love me, Josie, do as you're told!' She'd nodded her agreement but had pursed her lips.

'What's the matter?' he demanded.

36

'Well, if you *do* love me we could get engaged soon and then married in . . . August?' She held her breath, amazed at her own audacity. She'd been thinking about it a lot lately and now it had just sort of 'popped out'. She knew it was the best chance she had of getting her way. He paused, startled, his mind clearly thinking rapidly. Then: 'Yes, yes, that's what we'll do, Josie,' he said finally. 'I promise.' And then he was gone, running down the jigger.

Katie wanted to scream at her friend. 'I know those two, they spend more time inside Walton Jail than out of it! Open your bloody eyes, Josie, and see Georgie for what he is!'

Two spots of red appeared on Josie's cheeks, making them look like those painted on Dutch dolls' faces and her expression changed.

'You've never got on with him, Katie Deegan, not since you were kids. You don't understand him, but I do. I love him and he loves me and we're going to get married.'

Katie fumed at her naiveté. 'Oh, look up there in the sky, Josie, there's a pig flying around the chimney-stack! He's just playing you along. He'll never marry you, he's too mean and selfish.' She stormed down the lobby and out into the street. He had the perfect alibi in Josie. She was such a trusting little fool!

When she got back, Georgie was sitting in the chair by the range, the chair where Da had always sat, reading the *Echo*. Without a word of greeting to her mother or Joe, she walked over to him and snatched the paper out of his hands.

'What the bloody hell's the matter with you?' he snapped, jumping to his feet and towering threateningly over her.

'You know damn well what's the matter. We've had the police around here. A scuffer dragged our Joe home but he wouldn't say anything because he was so terrified of you and your so-called "mates"! I know what you've been up to, and when that CID bloke comes around, I'm going to tell him all about you, Tommy Kelly and that Pug Mahoney and your little games.'

A red flush spread upwards from Georgie's neck and anger flashed in his eyes. 'Tell him what?' he hissed, his face an inch from hers. 'There's nothing *to* tell. I've been at Josie's – I went straight there after work. We had things to talk about.'

'Like your engagement? Your wedding? How much you love her?' Katie jeered. She turned to Molly. 'That's what she's just told me, Mam. She's so flaming blind she's protecting him! He knows he could go to jail so he's promised Josie everything she wants, and has terrified the life out of our Joe, and he doesn't care about shaming us all. Oh, I wish Da were here. He'd give him the hiding of his life!' She felt so useless and frustrated. Emotion bubbled up inside her until she felt she would burst if she didn't *do* something. She looked around and her gaze alighted on the rolling pin that Molly had left by the range to dry off. Before anyone could stop her, she went for Georgie, swinging it in a wide arc.

'Katie! Katie for the love of God, stop it!' Molly yelled.

Both Sarah and Joe began screaming; Georgie was calling her a string of names at the top of his voice while trying to protect his head with his arms.

'Mam! Mam! Get her off me, she's mad! She's round the bloody bend!'

Fortunately for Georgie the combined efforts of Molly, Sarah and Joe succeeded in restraining her. Georgie quickly yanked the rolling pin out of her hand and held it behind his back. She'd only bruised his arms but he was shaking. If she'd caught him just one blow on the head he'd have been floored or his skull might have been cracked. He swallowed hard. He'd never expected his own sister to do something like that. You couldn't fool her for long, she wasn't afraid to speak her mind and she had a temper – but he'd never thought Katie would carry on like this.

Molly quickly took the situation in hand. 'Joe, get yourself upstairs. Homework then bed, and if the police want to speak to you I'll come up and get you. Go on, lad. Good night, God bless. Sarah, put the kettle on – we all need calming down. And you two, well your Da will be turning in his grave at the carry-on out of the pair of you! Katie, sit there and you, meladdo, over there, well away from her and me.'

They all did as they were told and for a few seconds silence reigned in the room, except for the sound of the water in the kettle beginning to boil.

Molly folded her arms over her ample bosom. 'Now, were you at Josie's and did you promise to marry her? I want the truth because if you've been lying to her, using her, it will break her heart and so help me God *I'll* brain you with that rolling pin here and now.'

'I *was* at Josie's and *yes*, we're going to get married in August.' The price of Josie's loyalty was high but he had no choice. It was an engagement ring now and a wedding in August. That would guarantee she'd say she was with him all the time the Pitch and Toss game was going on while Joe was supposed to have been keeping watch. That scuffer must have been watching his brother for a few days.

'Then why was our Joe hanging around Tillard Street, terrified out of his wits by you telling him that Tommy Kelly and that Pug feller would cut him up?' Katie interrupted.

He brazened it out. 'How the hell should I know? There's always a gang of lads, our Joe, Franny MacCane, Vinny Maher messing about on street corners, climbing and swinging on the lamp-posts. Maybe Kelly did tell him that to scare him away. I don't know.'

Katie was on her feet. 'Our Joe doesn't tell lies like that. You're a liar, Georgie Deegan! You've been playing Pitch and Toss and for how many nights? "Just on your way home" or "calling in to see Josie" or "working overtime"! It's money again, isn't it? Just pure greed. So how much did you win?'

Molly's nerves snapped. 'THAT'S ENOUGH, THE PAIR OF YOU!' she shouted. 'I'll have no more of this! If and when this CID bloke comes, you'll all tell the truth, do you hear me?'

Georgie picked up the newspaper again while his sister glared malevolently in his direction and Sarah, white and shaken, handed out the cups of tea.

He came at nine o'clock, a big, burly man in a dark suit, a tweed overcoat and a rather battered Homburg hat. He curtly introduced himself and showed them his Warrant Card, but then, to their astonishment, he said nothing. He just stared at each one of them in turn – a long, level, searching look. Katie quailed before it and Sarah clutched her hand tightly. Neither of them had ever seen such hard, cold eyes. He frightened them and they'd done nothing wrong.

He got out a notebook and glanced at it. 'Your son, Joseph Deegan, was apprehended at ten minutes to seven on the corner of Tillard Street and Fountains Road. He's been seen there on several occasions and could not, or would not, give any explanation as to why he was there or what he was doing. There was also a distinct sound at the time. That of boots on cobbles – running.'

'He's not eleven years old until next month,' Molly began in Joe's defence.

'That's old enough for a Reformatory Institution,' he interrupted.

'He wasn't doing anything wrong. I know he should have been in doing his homework, but since his Da died, well . . .' Molly spread her hands in a helpless gesture. 'You can go and see his Headmaster, Mr Peel, at St John's School. He's a good lad and he's got brains. He could get a scholarship, Mr Peel told me so himself.'

There was silence while the policeman weighed up Molly's explanation. 'I'll see this Mr Peel tomorrow. Maybe this little episode will keep his mind on his schoolwork.'

Inwardly Molly sighed deeply. Thank God! Thank God!

'And now you, George Francis Deegan.'

Beneath that cold serpentine gaze Georgie quailed too but the consequences if he told the truth didn't bear thinking about. He'd probably be found floating in the Mersey with his throat cut.

'Where were you tonight between six p.m. and seven-thirty p.m.?'

'I finished work at six and then called in to see my girlfriend, Josie Watson. We've decided to get engaged. We're going for the ring on

Saturday and getting married in August. We wanted to talk about . . . all that.'

Katie glared across the room at him. Oh, poor, silly Josie. Was she really so blind that she couldn't see him for what he was?

'Can this Josie Watson vouch for all that?'

'Yes.'

'So, what time did you eventually get home?'

'About half-past seven, maybe five minutes later, wasn't it, Mam?'

Molly had lost all track of time and nodded wearily, longing for the support Bill would have given her.

Katie couldn't stay silent any longer.

'It wasn't as late as that. Maybe a quarter past seven.'

'And how do you know that?'

'Because I went round to Josie's myself after the other policeman left. Our Joe was upset and so was Mam.'

'And was he there?'

'No. Josie said he'd just left to go home. That I must have missed him.'

'And did she tell you about this wedding?'

Katie nodded. There was nothing else she could do. Georgie was going to get away with it all. The gambling, the lying, the worry for Mam, the terrifying of Joe and promises to Josie that she was sure he would wriggle out of. Even if he didn't, he would make Josie's life hell because he certainly didn't love her.

'I'll be calling on this Josephine Watson then. Address?'

'Number three Becket Street,' Molly supplied, thinking in dread of Josie's Mam, hard-working, uncomplaining Florrie, opening the door to such shame and trouble.

The note book was snapped shut and once again they were all raked in turn by that cold sceptical gaze, Katie knew he didn't believe any of them but without proof he could do nothing.

'Then I'll be on my way.' He turned at the door that Sarah had opened for him and looked back at Georgie. 'I won't forget, lad, and there'll be a lot of eyes in this city watching you. You won't see them but they'll be there.'

When Molly came back into the living room Sarah was in tears but her son and other daughter were scowling at each other.

'He'll get you, Georgie, they always do! They're not like the uniform scuffers,' Katie said vehemently.

'He won't and he won't need to. I've done nothing. Anyway, on Monday I'm going down the Pool to sign on for the Merch. I'll need money to get married with, won't I?'

'You're going to go away to sea?' Molly cried out, stunned. This plan to get engaged, join the Merchant Navy and then get married in August was too much to take in.

40

Katie laughed sarcastically. 'Oh, he thinks he's so clever, Mam. He's got it all worked out. You see, he won't be here for any more police visits. He'll be away from Kelly and his mates because you can bet your life he's taken a few bob off them. He'll get his keep and he'll not be bothered with poor stupid Josie, just keep her happy with lies about saving up. Well, I for one think it's great. At least *we* won't have to put up with him either! Just make sure he leaves you an Allotment, Mam. If he gets taken on as a steward or a waiter he'll receive plenty of tips, he's that two-faced and smarmy. It'll be "Yes, madam" and "No, madam" and "Anything you require, madam" just as long as "madam" tips well.' With that she marched out of the room and pounded up the stairs.

Molly looked sadly after her elder daughter. Maybe it *was* for the best, Georgie going away. Tempers would cool, memories might fade . . . She never again wanted to experience what she had been through this night.

After Mass on Sunday, Josie was blushing and smiling as she showed everyone the ring she now wore on the third finger of her left hand. Georgie stood beside her looking bored and embarrassed. The ring was a small diamond solitaire and it had been bought at Brown's at the bottom of London Road. A very good jewellers, Josie emphasised, to the large group of well-wishers who surrounded them.

'I wonder how much that cost him?' Vi Draper said to Katie as they stood apart from the main group. 'You'd need a flamin' magnifiying glass to see the diamond.'

'Well, whatever it cost – and you can be sure he won't have dug very deep in his pocket – it's going to cost Josie plenty in sadness and misery in years to come. I wonder if she's owned up to lying for him in confession. Did you see she didn't go to Communion? Oh, honestly Vi, she's so besotted! She must know what she did was wrong but she still can't see him for what he is.'

'Well, she's not going to believe anything you say about him, is she? The pair of you have been arguing hammer and tongs since you were kids.'

'Can't you talk to her, Vi? You know what he's like and she *is* our friend. I don't want her to get hurt.'

'Me? She wouldn't believe the daylights out of me either. I've called him enough names in the past. Look, Katie, if she wants to throw her life away that's her affair. She can't say she hasn't been warned.'

The other girl sighed, still anxious and unhappy for her friend who in a few months would become her sister-in-law. 'All I can say then is thank God he's not going to be around much.'

Vi looked mystified. 'What d'you mean?'

'He's signed on with Cunard as a waiter,' Katie explained. 'He's sailing next Wednesday on the *Ascania* – going to Canada, Montreal. Like a fool, Mam said she'd save his Allotment as they'll need money for the wedding and furniture, though I'm damned sure he's got pounds stashed away somewhere. He *must* have, Vi. He never spends a penny.'

'Where will they live – with you? There's almost enough bodies for a football team in Josie's house. I don't know how they all manage.'

'No, Mam said they'll be able to rent a house, thank God. She'll keep her eyes open nearer the time. You hear all sorts of things working in a shop.'

Vi suddenly pulled a face. 'Oh God, Katie, I've just realised – we'll have to be bridesmaids. It'll be like leading a lamb to the slaughter, or following it in this case.'

Katie grimaced. 'I'd not even thought about that. Oh, let's get away from here. Let's go for a long, brisk walk. I'm depressed enough as it is without all that!'

Chapter Five

The whole Deegan family went down to the Pier Head to see Georgie off on his first trip aboard the *Ascania*. Joe was given the morning off from school as it was a custom to wave off a new seafarer. Katie was the exception. She'd be happy to lose a morning's pay, she told her mother, to mind the shop, but not to see him off.

'I wish you two would stop all this bitterness.'

Katie sighed deeply. 'Mam, I know him for what he is, that's all. He's a cheat and a liar and he's ruthless – even if he *is* my brother!'

Molly shrugged on her jacket and straightened her hat. 'I want to hear no more talk like that, Katie Deegan. Josie is coming round after work with Florrie to get this wedding organised so I don't want you making accusations or casting slurs on our Georgie's character, do you hear me?'

Katie nodded. You helped your friends, she thought. You went out of your way to do them favours, and Josie *was* her friend – but the only favour she could do for Josie was to stop her marrying Georgie. And if she tried to do that, all she'd get for her pains would be vigorous condemnation from all sides and she'd lose Josie's friendship into the bargain.

While the others went off to the *Ascania*, she served the few customers who came in, answering their queries as to why she was there instead of Molly and Sarah. With a smile nailed to her face she replied: 'Our Georgie's away on his first trip. They've gone to see him off, so I'm minding the shop.' At half-past eleven it began to get busy and she was having a hard time coping when her mother and Sarah came to relieve her, having come in the back way.

'He's gone then?' Mary Maher called, sniffing a cod steak to check its freshness.

'Thank God!' Katie muttered under her breath.

'Aye, he'll be away for just on three weeks, but she looks to be a good sound ship.'

'"Speed an' safety" – isn't that what they say down the Cunard Building?' Ellen added.

'Well, I'm all for the Safety bit. The speed doesn't bother me.'

'It would if you were an emigrant going to Canada to make a new life.'

'Well, he's not, so what can I get you, Ellen?'

'The usual, Moll. Have they set the date yet?'

'Oh, aye, Saturday the twenty-sixth of August.'

'Josie and her Mam are coming round tonight to discuss it all.' Sarah's eyes danced with excitement.

Molly glared at her. This was private family business, not something to be gossiped about on every doorstep from here to the Rotunda.

'I'm off, Mam,' Katie interrupted diplomatically. 'If I hurry I'll be back for the afternoon start.'

'You'd better tell Vi to come round tonight, Katie, but a bit later than usual,' Molly called after her daughter's disappearing back.

Josie and Florrie arrived after tea. Josie's eyes were bright with excitement but her mother, who sat casting her eyes appraisingly round Molly Deegan's clean, comfortable living room, was not so enthusiastic about the affair. The reason was quite simple. Florrie Watson didn't like Georgie Deegan. Oh, he came from a respectable family and one that seemed to lack for nothing. Nor should they, for the shop was a little gold mine and three of Molly's kids were working, although she guessed that Sarah didn't get much in the way of a wage. According to Jimmy her youngest, the young lad, Joe, was reputed to be clever, but he was also a bit of a hooligan and hardfaced with it – except at home.

Molly seemed to read Florrie's mind. 'Well, we're all here now so I'll put the kettle on and we can get down to the arrangements. I've sent our Joe upstairs to do his homework and the girls will take turns in dealing with any customers. Have you seen Father Macreedy?'

Florrie settled herself in the armchair near the range. She was a small, stooped woman whose features and demeanour showed all the signs of hard, unrelenting work and constant childbearing, although her youngest was now nearly nine.

'We went last night, after our Josie here had said her goodbyes to her fiancé. We're down for ten o'clock Mass on Saturday the twenty-sixth of August.'

'Isn't that a bit long for people to go without food or drink? It'll be dinner-time before they sit down for the wedding breakfast.'

'He's already got one wedding in for nine so we had to settle for ten. We could have had eleven, but I thought that was too late.'

'You couldn't expect people to fast for that long, Florrie, especially Josie. She'd be passing out at the altar steps with hunger and nerves. It's all right for the clergy, they'll have had their breakfasts after the first Mass.' Molly handed Florrie a cup of tea in one of the best cups from out of the glass cabinet. The bone-china teaset was being given an airing especially for the occasion.

'I've made a list of our guests,' she went on, 'there's not many, just immediate family. Bill's brother Alfred, if he accepts, that is, and a couple of Georgie's mates, and Katie and Sarah's friends.'

Florrie nodded and sipped her tea. It tasted quite different in a real china cup, she thought. Obviously Molly was showing off; on the other hand it could be a sign that Molly considered her to be a proper guest. She decided to opt for the latter.

'Well, there's my lot and Fred's brothers and their wives, that's fourteen. Then there's our Hilda and Katie an' their 'usbands, and our Jack and Robbie and their wives – and what will we do about the neighbours?'

'Jesus, Mary and Joseph! At the rate we're going, Florrie, half of Kirkdale, Everton and Anfield will be coming!'

Although it was customary for the bride's parents to pay for everything, Molly knew the Watsons had little money to spare. With eight mouths to feed, life wasn't easy for Florrie. 'I'll pay for the food,' Molly said now. 'I can get most of it at trade price. I think a help-yourself style would be best, as there's no real facilities in the church hall, except for making tea. Our Georgie can pay for the flowers, the church and organist and the cars. I'm having none of this walking up there with everyone out on their doorsteps jangling and making remarks.'

Florrie nodded; it was a very generous offer. 'We'll pay for the church hall, the cake and something for the toast.' She paused, biting her lip. 'I was wondering about the drink . . . ?'

Molly had been expecting this. 'We'll get two half-barrels of ale and a couple of crates of stout and light ale. Can you manage some port and lemonade for the women?'

Florrie nodded. 'Thanks, Molly. It's going to be hard enough to rig the three youngest out, the rest of them can buy their own gear and God knows what I'll be able to manage. The borrowed finery of Becket Street probably, although I might get a new hat.'

'I'm paying for my dress and veil. I've been saving up,' Josie added proudly.

'So, who are you going to have as bridesmaids?' Molly refilled the tea cups and offered a plate of Jacob's Assorted Cream biscuits.

'I don't want any small ones and I'm not having any kids under eleven. I don't care what anyone says, they're nothing but a nuisance,' Josie announced firmly, the vision of her younger siblings causing havoc uppermost in her mind.

Florrie tutted while Molly raised her eyebrows. This was virtually unheard of, but she had to agree with Josie. Kids at weddings were nothing but flaming nuisances. Running around screeching, getting under people's feet. Stuffing themselves with food and then being sick and having to be taken home.

'And you can imagine how that piece of news is going to go down in our house,' Florrie said irritably.

'What are you going to do about your Jimmy, Daisy and Betty? You can't not have them,' Molly enquired.

'She'll have them,' Florrie Watson said grimly, 'and if anyone can't get someone to mind their kids they can bring them too. I'm not havin' a family war on me hands, nor all these rules and instructions from Madam here!'

Josie ignored her mother but it had been worth a try. 'So, our Brenda and Norma, Katie – and Sarah.'

Flushed with delight, Sarah replied that she'd be made up to be a bridesmaid.

'And Vi Draper,' Josie finished.

'So, that's five,' Molly said, thinking about the size of Georgie's bill for the flowers.

'It's going to be like a May procession,' Katie whispered to Sarah out of the corner of her mouth. Sarah glared at her; she thought it all sounded lovely.

'Have you decided what colour you want us in?' Katie queried.

'Well, I thought our Brenda and Norma could wear blue, and you and Sarah could have pink, and Vi could wear yellow . . . sort of lemon-coloured, like.'

Katie looked at her in open astonishment. 'God, Josie, we'll look like a walking flower border!'

'I know it's usual to have all the same colour, but I want something . . . different.'

'It'll be that, all right.' She hated herself in pastel colours. They looked well on Sarah but she preferred the deeper, richer hues. 'Well, it's your day, so pink, blue and lemon it will be.'

'Mrs Frost in Sessions Street is going to make them. She's very reasonable. I could make them myself but I'd be that nervous I'd ruin them and waste your money.'

'What are we to wear on our heads?' Sarah asked eagerly.

Josie blushed. 'Er, picture hats, with flowers and ribbons around them.'

Everyone in the room turned disbelieving eyes towards her.

Florrie at last managed to speak. 'Hats! Picture hats! You never said a word to me about flaming hats!'

'They'll cost a fortune.' Katie had been with Josie when they'd seen the large-brimmed, flower- and ribbon-strewn hats in Val Smith's window in Church Street. They were far too ostentatious and expensive for bridesmaids to wear – unless, of course, the wedding was in the Pro-Cathedral and the bridesmaids came from Childwall or Allerton, the posh suburbs.

'No, they won't. Mrs Frost told me you can buy just the stiffened shell bases from the millinery wholesalers and either dye them or cover them and trim them yourself. I'm going to do that.'

She would do it well too, Katie thought. Josie was clever with her hands. It was a natural gift she had.

'I'm going to have white, yellow, pink and blue flowers in my bouquet, and all of you can have white and the appropriate colour to match your dress.' Josie looked very pleased with herself. She'd spent so many happy hours planning all this, mulling it over in every detail and she knew exactly what she wanted. She was a little hurt that Georgie didn't take the same interest; after all, it was his wedding too.

'All that is women's stuff. Your mam and mine will get it organised,' he replied off-handedly when she'd broached the subject. She'd bitten her lip, for he sounded as though he really didn't care.

Georgie wasn't exactly what she would call a 'romantic' person. There were never any flowers or sweets, but then lots of lads considered it 'soppy' to be seen in public with such things; it usually meant creeping up the back jiggers with the gifts under your jacket in case anyone saw you. She'd heard her Mam say that all the flowers she'd ever had from her Da had been bent and broken.

Yes, Georgie was the type of lad who didn't show affection, in public, but she had to admit there weren't any really passionate moments in private either. Still, he wouldn't respect her if she carried on the way some of the girls at work did. It would be so different after they were married. It was all she wanted from life. Georgie, a nice little home and then a baby. One thing she was certain of was that she wasn't going to have six of them like her Mam had, but that, too, was something she wouldn't have to worry over for a few years.

Katie made another pot of tea while her Mam and Florrie sat at the table making lists as Josie and Sarah launched into a highly animated conversation about wedding dresses, veils, headdresses and hymns. So absorbed were they that only Katie heard the shop doorbell ring. Going through, expecting to see a customer, she found instead her friend Vi.

'I think I've got them a place to live,' Vi said excitedly. 'Mam told me there's one in Stour Street coming empty soon. The family are emigrating to Canada, apparently.' Vi paused for breath and stared hard at the other girl. 'Well, what's up with you? You've gorra face that would stop a clock. I thought you'd be made up to see the back of your Georgie.'

'I am. It's the wedding.'

47

Vi's eyes widened. 'Holy God! It's noroff, is it?'

'No, it's just what she wants us to wear.'

Vi peered over her shoulder at the door to the living room and lowered her voice. 'Tell me the worst.'

'Their Brenda and Norma in blue, me and our Sarah in pink and you in lemon and with hats to match. Picture hats with ribbons and artificial flowers stuck all over them.'

'Oh, Jesus, Mary and Joseph! We'll look as though we belong to three separate weddings and I hate yellow! And what's wrong with just a circlet of flowers or even a comb with a couple of flowers attached to it?'

'That would have suited me too, but our Sarah's egging her on so we'd better get inside. Don't for God's sake start raving about how you hate yellow, but tell them about the house instead.'

The table was now littered with sheets of paper and Josie was in raptures over the dress she'd seen in Blackler's and the fact that she wouldn't have to walk to the church as many brides did. She would go in a big shiny car provided by Mr Coyne, who did weddings as well as funerals.

'Vi thinks she's got you a place to live,' Katie announced before Josie could drag the conversation back to hats and dresses and cars.

'Where?' Florrie demanded.

'Stour Street. The O'Haras are going to Canada.'

'I know Maude O'Hara vaguely,' said Molly. 'She's a clean-looking woman who sometimes comes in the shop. Is it a whole house or just rooms?'

'Rooms. Front parlour, front bedroom and share the kitchen.'

'How much?' Josie asked, her cheeks glowing, thrilled at how well everything was going.

'Nine and six a week.'

Florrie was outraged. 'For two rooms and shared kitchen! We only pay that for our entire house.'

Josie bit her lip. It *was* a bit on the high side and Georgie might put his foot down and say it was too expensive.

'It'll be a start, Josie. It's furnished, sort of.' Vi looked at Katie for encouragement.

'Well, if it's furnished I can't see what anyone's moaning about and as Vi says, it's a start. You can buy your own things bit by bit and look around for a cheaper place.'

Josie was encouraged. She'd really wanted a nice little house, but she knew it was a lot of people's dream as well. The city was overcrowded. They were overcrowded at home. At least she and Georgie would have more privacy than many other young married couples did.

48

'We'll take it,' she said, ignoring her mother's expression. 'When will it be free?'

'In two weeks. Mam knows more about it than I do. I'd go and see her, Josie.'

'And who's going to pay the rent until you move in?' Florrie demanded. Although her husband Fred and her three eldest kids were working, she found it hard to make ends meet and without Josie's wage it would be harder still. She'd counted on that weekly sum until August; it would have helped to pay for the wedding.

'Well, I can, I suppose.'

'Don't be daft, Josie. How can you save up for your dress, turn up your keep *and* pay rent?'

Josie stared at Katie in disappointment. She was right, she couldn't manage all that.

Katie turned to her mother. 'Our Georgie's left you an Allotment, hasn't he? He can pay the rent with it.'

'It's only six shillings a week.'

It was on the tip of Katie's tongue to retort that he certainly wasn't hurting himself with what he'd left her, but she bit back the words. 'Then when he gets home he can change it to nine and six.'

Molly nodded. 'In the meantime I'll make up the difference myself.'

'That's dead good of you,' Florrie nodded thankfully.

'Mam, he's only got a bit saved up and he's going to have to pay for the flowers and everything.'

'Every young married couple start off broke, Josie,' Florrie said tersely. 'It takes years to build a home, doesn't it, Molly? The trouble with you young ones now is that you want big posh weddings and houses and furniture. I walked to church and I didn't have a fancy wedding dress, just a plain costume and a nice hat and I lived with yer Da's Mam and Dad for five years before we got that place around the corner – by which time we had four kids.' Florrie rose. 'Talking of which, we'd best be off or my three youngest will be squabbling and half-murdering one another, to say nothing of the mess they get the place in.'

'You know, Florrie, a bit of dust and a few mucky footmarks never did any harm. Put your feet up now and then and let them all take a turn.'

Florrie sighed. 'It's good of yer to think like that, Molly, but the truth is I couldn't stand the mess and the nagging. I'd go mad.'

Josie turned to Vi. 'Will you tell your Mam we'll take it, and I'll go down to see the landlord with the first week's rent on Friday. Georgie's money mightn't be through by then and I don't want to miss it or have anyone else get there before me. The money will be like a promise, I suppose. Good faith, like.'

'There's no need for that, Josie. Even if it's not through, I'll pay the rent,' Molly stated firmly, having caught the look of alarm on Florrie's face.

When they'd gone, Molly gathered up all the lists and put them in a dresser drawer.

Vi settled herself on the sofa cushion that Josie had just vacated. 'So who's going to pay for these frocks and furbelows?'

'We are, I presume,' Katie answered, pouring Vi a cup of tea.

'Well, that's a birroff, isn't it? We've gorra pay for an awful frock and an even worse hat that we'll never wear again and in fact that we wouldn't be seen dead in – *iffen* we had the choice. I hate yellow and she knows it! Why can't you wear yellow, Katie? It suits you.'

'I don't know. I suppose she wants all the sisters in the same colour.'

Sarah frowned. 'It's Josie's day. It's not fair of you to be making fun of her and I think we'll all look very elegant and different.'

'Oh, we'll look different all right. We'll look like a flaming rainbow. Thank God she's not having their Daisy in red and their Betty in green too.'

'That's not at all nice, Vi Draper,' Sarah said heatedly.

'Oh, shut up, Sarah. Honestly, what a palaver!'

'Well, there certainly won't be much style about it all,' Vi added snootily. She was always nicely dressed. Her clothes were cheap but she had a knack of wearing colours that toned with her blue-grey eyes and natural blonde hair, and she'd smarten up things with bits of cheap jewellery.

'I think our Georgie will hit the roof when he hears about paying all that rent and not living there. But maybe he'll decide to move in before the big day,' Katie added, thinking of the peace and quiet that move would bring.

'What for? He's at sea most of the time and Josie can't live there on her own.'

'She could take half that tribe of sisters and brothers with her, give their Florrie a bit of a breathing space for a while,' Molly suggested half-jokingly.

'But they'd only have to move back again in August.'

The conversation was cut short by the appearance of Joe, his hair sticking up, his fingers covered in ink. 'Have they gone? Can I come down now?' he asked.

'Wash those hands first or you'll go putting ink on everything. Have you finished?'

He nodded.

'He'll have rushed it and then spent the time reading daft comics. I saw him swop with Vinny Maher for a bundle of cigarette cards,' Sarah informed them smugly.

'I heard that an' I haven't rushed it! It was Geography with maps an' rivers and things; it takes ages.'

'I'd get used to it, for you'll have plenty of work like it next year. Mr Peel is determined you're going to get that scholarship and so am I.'

'Aw, Mam! I don't want to go to SFX. I won't see me mates and I'll get skitted something soft wearing a uniform and that daft cap!'

'You're going to get a nice lot of practice looking daft soon,' Katie said seriously. 'Josie says you're to be a pageboy and wear a sailor suit and shoes with big silver buckles on them.'

All the colour drained from Joe's face as he thought of his mates. 'Mam! Mam!' It was the only word he could get out.

'Now stop that, Katie. Josie said no such thing. You'll just wear your Sunday suit and your best boots.'

Katie, Vi and Sarah collapsed in a fit of laughter.

'Oh, you should have seen your face, Joe Deegan!' Vi screeched, wiping her eyes.

Joe glared at them all and turning, ran back upstairs.

Chapter Six

When Georgie Deegan got home from his maiden voyage, during which he had been horribly seasick for the first four days, before finding his sealegs, he was quite pleased with himself. He'd made thirty shillings in tips, his 'pay off' money was in his pocket and he'd not spent a penny in the Pig and Whistle, the crew bar. Nor had he bought the small gifts all the other members of the crew seemed to have purchased for their kith and kin.

This present-giving at the end of every trip was a custom he didn't hold with, a total waste of hard-earned money, in his opinion. And the work had been very hard indeed. Up at five, scrub a portion of deck, lay his tables for breakfast, wait on, clear his tables and set them for lunch, all before he could get a breakfast himself. Then it was lunch and afternoon tea and dinner and more scrubbing of decks.

It was a Saturday so he expected to see Josie, Sarah and Joe waiting for him when the ship docked.

It was Josie he saw first. He began to wave, then realised that she was alone. A nice homecoming this, he thought irritably.

Josie pushed her way through the crowd and flung her arms around his neck.

'Oh, Georgie! Georgie! I've missed you so much. What was it like – was it awful? Were you seasick? Did you make any mates?'

He disentangled himself after kissing her briefly on the lips. 'If I can get a word in edgewise, Josie, it was damned hard work. Going out, the weather was terrible and yes, I was sick and no, I didn't make any new mates, but apart from that . . .' He shrugged.

'Did you go ashore in Canada?' she asked eagerly, clinging to his arm as they walked towards the tram.

'I had a bit of a look around.' He hadn't gone into the cities of Montreal or Quebec. 'All docksides look the same,' he said with an air of experience. It was a comment he'd picked up from one of his colleagues.

'Did you bring anything back?'

'Like what?'

'Oh, I don't know. Souvenirs, things like that.'

'No. Some of the other blokes did, but it's a waste of money, especially as we'll have so much expense soon.' If Josie had one fault it was a tendency to be wasteful, he thought. What point was there in spending money on tatty souvenirs, bits of wood and glass and fur?

She pushed aside her disappointment. No doubt in future, when they had their own home, he'd bring her ornaments and other knick-knacks.

When they arrived home, after walking arm in arm up the street to the welcoming greetings of the neighbours, the table was all ready, set for dinner.

'I'm home, Mam, and all in one piece,' he announced.

Molly embraced him. 'You look well on it, son.'

'Oh aye, they feed you well enough. Mind you, there's this system where you have your own chef and he sees you right. But you have to pay him, otherwise you get all kinds of rubbishy leftovers, and we have to eat standing up.'

'Well, you can sit down now, your dinner's nearly ready,' Molly told him. 'It's nothing exotic though – just steak and kidney pie, your favourite. We'll have ours then I'll fetch Katie in from the shop; there should be a bit of a lull soon. Did you tell him the news, Josie?'

'No, I waited until we got home.'

'What news?' Georgie looked suspiciously at his mother and his wife-to-be.

'The wedding's all fixed up,' Josie said excitedly, 'and we . . . we've got a place – rooms in Stour Street. A front parlour, a front bedroom and we share the kitchen. It's great, Georgie, really it is. The rooms are bigger than these, it's lovely and clean and bright being at the front of the house and it's furnished too. Well, there's a sofa and a table and chairs and a few mats in the parlour and a brass bed and a chest and a bit of a wardrobe in the bedroom. The other things we'll get as wedding presents, I suppose, and we can buy our own stuff, in time.'

He was taken aback. 'How much is it?' It hadn't even crossed his mind that she'd want a place of her own. He'd assumed Josie would move in here, that Mam would share with the girls, or Joe, and he and Josie would have the other bedroom. It was a bit high-handed of Josie to take it on herself to go and find furnished rooms without consulting him.

'Nine and six a week, but it *is* furnished.'

'Nine and six a week! A week, not a month!'

Josie's bright, excited expression disappeared at the anger in his voice.

'And we've been paying the rent for two weeks. I used your

53

Allotment. You'll have to increase it,' Molly stated flatly, annoyed at her son's parsimony and the hurt look on Josie's face. 'She's been down and scrubbed it out from top to bottom, even the kitchen and the privy.'

'You used my Allotment money to pay for these . . . these rooms and without even asking me!' Georgie was outraged by his mother's statement.

'There wasn't time. I told you I'd save it for you – well, I did better than that. You've got a nice place to live.'

'But Mam – nine and six a week!' He was still stunned and angry.

'Well, where did you think you were going to live? At Florrie's? You can't swing a cat in that house, they're all packed in like sardines now.'

'I thought we could live here.'

'Well, you can't. Having your own place is the best start to a marriage. It's something I never had nor Florrie either, so stop your moaning and sit down and eat your dinner.'

'I don't want it. Put it in the oven, I'll have it later.'

Molly glared at him. She'd made the pie specially and now poor Josie was on the verge of tears. 'Where do you think you're going now? You've hardly got a foot over the doorstep,' she said angrily.

'Down to the pub.'

'Which one? You're not very welcome in most of them. You'll have to spend some money, or "waste" it, I should say!' Molly called after him. It was the nine and six rent. He'd banked on living here to save money. She was furious. If he'd had none at all and a poor wage, she would have welcomed them both, but he had plenty. It was money again. It was always money with their Georgie.

On his way out he almost collided with Katie. She could tell from his face there had been a row, just as she'd known there would be, as soon as the rent was disclosed.

'I see "Happiness" is home then and you've told him the good news about the rooms in Stour Street?' she said as she walked into the kitchen.

'Don't you start, Katie, for the love of God,' Molly snapped. 'Come on, luv, take no notice of him – he'll get over it.' She put her arm around Josie's shoulders as the tears spilled down the girl's cheeks.

'I . . . I thought he'd be pleased and . . . happy.'

'He's never happy when he's got to spend money,' Katie said acidly, taking the pie from the oven and helping herself. 'The face on him, you'd think he'd been asked to rent the Town Hall.'

Molly shot her a warning look. Josie was upset enough without Katie adding to things.

'I suppose he said he couldn't afford it or something like that?'

'Not outright,' her mother said.

'He thought he could live here, didn't he?'

Josie nodded.

'I knew he would. Still, you've forced his hand, Josie and you'll not regret it. You'll have a lovely wedding and a nice home and you can buy bits and pieces yourself, as you'll still be working. And he'll be away so you won't have to feed him,' Katie said, her mouth full.

'Don't talk with your mouth full, Katie Deegan!' Molly reproved her daughter before turning to Josie.

'Take my advice, love, and put whatever you can afford into the Post Office Savings and don't tell him. It's always a good thing to have a few shillings of your own put by, for presents and suchlike. And over the rent and Allotment you'll just have to put your foot down very firmly.'

Josie shot her a wary glance. Neither Molly nor Katie knew that secretly she was a little bit afraid of Georgie. She just wanted a peaceful, orderly life. There were always rows going on in the Watsons' house, always had been and probably always would be, and she wanted to get away from that.

Looking from her mother to her future sister-in-law, Katie suddenly remembered what her Uncle Alfred had told her at Da's funeral. 'Uncle Alfred said something that stuck in my mind.'

'What?' her mother asked, pouring the tea.

'That bullies are invariably cowards.'

'What's that got to do with anything, Katie?'

She shrugged. 'Mam, our Georgie is a bully. You put your foot down with him now, Josie, or he'll bully you all your life.'

'Oh, stop all this!' Molly said, exasperated. 'What a morning! When you've had that, Katie, will you go and get Georgie's best suit from his wardrobe? It must stink of mothballs. I'll hang it in the yard to get rid of the smell, then it will be ready for tonight.'

'What's going on tonight?' Josie asked, her eyes still watery.

'He'll be taking you out, of course,' Molly said firmly.

'But he never said. He's down at the pub.'

'Well, he won't be there long. He'll not put his hand in his own pocket. When it's his turn for a round, they won't see him for dust.' Katie changed the subject. 'Where's our Joe?'

'Still doing the deliveries. He should be in soon.'

'Right, I'll go and get the suit.'

Molly went to join Sarah in the shop, leaving Josie alone for a few minutes. She didn't want to go home and have to face her Mam and tell her that Georgie had gone mad over the rent money. She'd carried on so much about their 'flat' as she called it that her Mam had told her that if she mentioned Stour Street again she'd clock her one. And now it felt as if all her pride and happiness had been trampled on.

Everything was going wrong.

Georgie hadn't unpacked his kitbag so Katie dragged it upstairs and threw it on the bed. Why wouldn't Josie listen to all their warnings? Didn't this latest episode give her a hint of how tight-fisted he was? Even Mam had advised her to keep some money for things like birthday and Christmas gifts. He certainly wouldn't be happy to pay for them with Josie working. He'd keep her short and every penny would have to be accounted for. She sighed at what Josie would have to put up with, but then, she supposed, she wasn't besotted with him.

She opened the wardrobe and roughly yanked his one suit off the rail. The trousers fell from the hanger and ended up in a crumpled heap on the bottom of the wardrobe.

'Oh, damn!' Now she'd have to refold them, making sure the creases were in the right place. As she pulled them out, one leg caught on something and she scrabbled about with her fingers trying to release the cloth without tearing it. Peering down to get a closer look, the noticed that one of the boards that formed the wardrobe's base had a raised ridge, a bit like a wooden handle. Curiously, she lifted it up. There was a space underneath. Listening to make sure that no one was coming up the stairs, she poked her hand inside and drew out a bag of some sort. Katie sat back on her heels, emptied the contents into her lap and gasped with astonishment. There was a roll of notes and a small pile of gold sovereigns. Methodically she counted it all. Forty-seven pounds! Forty-seven pounds and he'd slammed out to the pub because of a piddling nine and six a week rent! She knew Mam was helping out with his share of the cost of the wedding. She'd always suspected that he had money stashed away somewhere and she'd known he'd won money from those two hard cases Pug Mahoney and Tommy Kelly. But there was enough here to completely furnish a house and pay for a grand wedding! She sat staring at it for a few minutes then she put it all back.

Sarah's voice came floating up the stairs. It made her jump. 'Mam wants to know if you're going to be much longer with that suit?'

'I'm coming now,' she called. What should she do? Tell Mam? Tell Josie? Tell them both? They'd all accuse her of prying, of rooting around in his personal things. No, she wouldn't say anything, but she'd certainly tell *him* when the right opportunity arose. She was fuming with rage as she went down the stairs, thinking of the way he'd treated Josie. Never a bunch of flowers or a box of chocs. Never a decent night out – usually they went for long walks in Stanley Park or for a sail on the ferry to New Brighton. And the paltry little brooch he'd bought Josie for the birthday . . . Katie thought of all the

Christmases when he'd given them cheap trinkets, with maybe tobacco or some hankies for Da and a bag of glass marbles and some sweets for Joe, and all the time he possessed – a fortune!

The opportunity to confront him arose when he came in at ten o'clock that night. Georgie had been out with Josie; he'd been sullen with everyone but had grudgingly taken his fiancée to the Rotunda, no doubt in the cheap seats. Mam had gone to bed and so had Joe. Sarah was round at her friend, Lizzie Wharton's house and was due in any minute now. Katie had urged Mam to go to bed, saying she'd wait up, hoping to save her sister from a telling off. But when the door clattered open, it was Georgie who walked in.

'Oh, it's you. I thought it was our Sarah.'

'That's a nice greeting, I must say.'

She didn't answer, too busy thinking. Did she have enough time to tell him what she'd discovered, or would Sarah walk in right in the middle of it? She decided to risk it.

'I suppose you took Josie a box of chocolates and paid for the most expensive seats?' she said sweetly.

'Don't be so bloody sarcastic. How can I afford things like that? I'm getting married, remember.'

'Oh yes, and you've done nothing but moan about it, yet I know Mam is helping out with the cost.'

He faced her squarely; there was something in her expression he didn't like. 'So?'

'You've got a bloody nerve, Georgie Deegan! Upstairs, there's forty-seven pounds hidden in the bottom of your wardrobe and you're still taking money off Mam! You've complained for years about how hard up you are, how your wages were a pittance and you couldn't afford this or that. You didn't even buy Josie a decent ring, but then of course you couldn't, could you? People would want to know where you got the money from. You never give her any kind of a treat. Not a meal out or a visit to the theatre in the best seats. No, a flaming ferry-ride that costs you less than a shilling! I knew you had money and you won more off Tommy Kelly. I just *knew* it!'

His face was purple with rage. 'You've been through my things! My private things!'

'By accident. Mam asked me to get your suit and the trousers fell off the hanger on to the wardrobe floor.'

He was shaking with temper now. 'You've always had too much to say for yourself, Katie Deegan. You've always been the one to snoop and pry.'

'So, what are you going to do about it, then? Tell Mam? Tell Josie? You might be able to bully her but not me because basically you're a coward. Uncle Alfred pointed that out to me on the day of Da's funeral. What were you going to do with it? Turn this place into a smaller version of Cooper's?'

He could have strangled her, so great was his rage. He raised his arm.

Katie held her ground and looked up at him defiantly. 'Go on, belt me! I told you I'm not frightened of you.'

He remembered the episode with the rolling pin. 'It's a good thing I'm back at sea in two days,' he spluttered.

'Great, you can make even more money, can't you – and no one will miss you, except poor Josie.' She was openly sarcastic.

'I'll get the better of you one day, Katie Deegan, so help me God I will.'

'He's the last person Who'd help you. "Money is the root of all evil" – isn't that what Father Macreedy says?'

He couldn't control himself. 'Oh, go to hell!' he yelled before bounding up the stairs two at a time.

'Oh no,' she called after him, 'it'll be you who'll go to hell, Georgie, unless you mend your ways.'

She heard the back door open softly and Sarah crept in looking anxious.

'It's all right, they're all in bed, including Scrooge,' Katie told her. 'Thank God he's only home for two days and then he won't be here to annoy us for another three weeks.'

'Have you had another row with him?' Sarah asked.

'Sort of,' she shrugged. 'Oh, you know our Georgie and me, like oil and water. But I just wish to God I could get Josie to change her mind.'

'Oh, give over Katie! He's not *that* bad and she loves him and he loves her, in his own way.'

Katie shook her head. 'You're wrong. There's only one person he loves and that's himself. Come on, let's go up, we're due for early Mass too.' Suddenly she thought of Mam getting up at five o'clock to go to the market, and of how her Da had been out in all weathers. Mam didn't need to get up early at all. With the money Georgie had, they could pay someone to deliver each day. How could he have treated his parents so callously? He was cold-hearted, greedy. He was different from the rest of them; where he got it from she didn't know. What she *did* know was that from now on, she would have to be on her guard. Georgie was cunning and he'd do her a bad turn if the opportunity arose.

Chapter Seven

Josie didn't know which was worse. The nervousness, the excitement or the exasperation. What's more she was hungry. She would take Communion during the hour-long Mass, so she'd had nothing to eat or drink since midnight. Neither had anyone else, but that knowledge didn't do much to stave off the empty, slightly nauseous feeling in the pit of her stomach. She hadn't slept very well either and as she looked out of the window at a clear, bright blue sky and already blazing sun she thanked God not only for the weather but for the fact that her wedding was to be at ten o'clock, before the real heat of the August day set in.

Even on an ordinary day the Watsons' house was overcrowded. Today it was bursting at the seams with people. Not just her immediate family but her aunts and uncles as well. There was hardly room to move in the bedroom she shared with all her sisters. She, Norma and Betty slept in one of the two iron-framed double beds, while Brenda and Daisy slept in the other. They usually swopped over from time to time as two occupants in a bed was infinitely preferable to three. Under the window was a big seaman's chest in which all their clothes were kept, and this arrangement caused many an argument, with the adage 'First up, best dressed' often proving the truth. There was a mirror on one wall, and on the wall over the beds a cheap, badly carved crucifix.

Her wedding dress hung on the back of the door, covered in tissue paper, along with her veil and headdress. Josie's dress was of white taffeta, with long tight sleeves that ended in a point, and a high neck trimmed with lace. The skirt was not very full but she didn't mind that; the two-foot-long 'fishtail' train made up for it. But how on earth were they all going to manage to get dressed? This was just one of the problems that nagged at Josie's aching head. Her Mam had driven her mad over the past week, insisting on a thorough house-clean and the distempering of the walls in the parlour.

'I'm not having our Hilda and Imelda making remarks, nor our Jack and Robbie's wives neither,' Florrie had stated grimly when they'd all complained about the upheaval. When Florrie cleaned a room it meant that every piece of furniture and all mats and ornaments were moved out and then put back, one by one, after being polished, wiped or dusted.

'Florrie, in the name of God, who's going to notice? And anyway, the reception is in the church hall, not here,' her long-suffering husband had remarked.

That had been the wrong thing to say entirely.

'But they'll all be coming here before going to church.'

'Why can't they go straight there?' Fred had demanded.

'Because it's not done. We'd be talked about – and anyway, *I'll* know it's all been cleaned and the parlour has been distempered!'

He gave up.

They always took turns to get a wash in the kitchen and there were usually at least two of them in the room at the same time, bickering and jostling each other, but today Josie had been given priority and privacy. Brenda had stood with her back against the kitchen door to protect her, although the privacy hadn't lasted long. Even now Brenda and Norma were becoming overexcited as they got dressed with a great deal of giggling.

Norma stuck her head out of the window. 'It's hot out there already. We're all going to be sweating like pigs by the time we get to the church.'

'Well, at least you won't have to walk,' Josie said irritably. Molly had specifically promised that Georgie would pay for cars, that the bridal procession wouldn't have to trail to church on foot, so she'd expected a big shiny car to come and collect her.

Georgie had refused point blank.

'Why can't we walk?' he said. 'Everyone else does. I thought you girls all loved to show off in your fancy gear.'

'But I wanted our wedding to be special. Your Mam and me think it's common to have to walk.' She was close to tears.

Katie had come into the room just then and had seen the tears in Josie's eyes.

'What's the matter now?' she demanded.

'Nothing,' Georgie replied belligerently.

'I wasn't asking you,' Katie snapped back. 'What's wrong, Josie?'

'Oh, not much really. I . . . I'd sort of set my heart on being driven to church in a car, one like Mr Coyne has, but it was just a daft notion.' She tried to sound offhand. She had to be loyal to Georgie.

'Oh, I see. Lover Boy won't cough up the money, is that it?'

There was a silence. Josie looked down at her hands and fiddled with her engagement ring. Georgie glared at his sister and Katie met his stare unflinchingly. All that money stashed away yet he wouldn't pay for a car to make Josie's day perfect. She'd worked so hard, had

Josie, doing the hats, overseeing the dressmaking, sorting out what her Mam should wear, ordering the flowers and helping her Mam, Molly, Mary Maher, Ellen MacCane, and all her bridesmaids to set out the tables in the church hall and decorate it with the pink, white and blue crêpe paper-chains that Sarah had made.

'You'll have a car, Josie, and it'll be one of Mr Coyne's best,' Katie promised. 'I'm sure our Georgie will see sense when I've had a word with him or Mam.' It was blackmail but she didn't care. Josie was her friend and she wasn't going to let her brother's penny-pinching ways spoil Josie's big day. Probably the one day in her life when she'd be the centre of attention and attraction.

Josie had got her car.

'In the name of all that's holy, what's going on in here?' Josie's Auntie Imelda poked her head around the door.

Josie felt like crying. This was just what she didn't want – people coming in on top of them, even though Imelda was her favourite aunt.

'There's just no room. We've got to climb over the beds to get to the mirror and it's not easy in these long frocks,' Norma informed her.

'Right, you two, take all your stuff and go into Jimmy's little box-room.'

'We can't do that, it's too small – and anyway, there's no mirror in there. Mam won't let him have one because he'd be sure to break it and no one wants seven years bad luck!' Brenda exclaimed.

'There's no one in there now except your Mam and our Hilda. I've chased Jimmy downstairs; your Da can see to him, he's down there fixing his collar and tie. The buttonholes are in the living room or the kitchen. The flowers are under the slab in the larder with wet newspaper over them, and I've told those three little hooligans that I'll murder them one by one with me bare hands if they so much as touch them. Go on with you and tell yer Mam to come in here. I'm going down to see that our Henry doesn't get stuck into those bottles of ale yer Da forgot ter put out of sight. It's a warm day and they'll look like Manna from Heaven to Henry, but I'll kill him if he has a single drop and shows me up by not being able to go to Communion.'

Josie sat down on the bed she shared with her sisters and smiled tearfully, but with affection at her aunt. A few seconds later, Florrie came in and put her arms around her.

'Come on, luv, this is your big day and our Imelda's got everyone under control. I thought I was going mad down there until she arrived.' Florrie wore a navy and white spotted dress, navy shoes from T. J. Hughes in London Road, and a borrowed navy handbag. Josie had made her hat. She'd covered it in white muslin and trimmed it with navy ribbon and Florrie thought she looked the bee's knees. She was, after all, the Mother of the Bride and people would notice her because of that.

Carefully, Florrie helped her daughter on with her dress and then Josie sat on the edge of the bed while her mother brushed and combed her hair and placed the half-circle of white wax flowers over it and arranged the veil around her face. There were tears in Florrie's eyes as she urged Josie to stand up.

'Come on, luv, give yer old Mam a twirl. Yer look gorgeous! If it wasn't for the fact that I'd mess up everything, I'd give you a great big hug.'

Heedless of all Florrie's efforts, Josie threw her arms around her. 'Oh Mam, I'm so happy! Do I really look great?'

Florrie disentangled herself and adjusted her hat. 'You do, and he'll be made up with yer!'

Things were almost as hectic in Chelmsford Street. The Deegans' shop was closed for the day. 'For once they can go elsewhere for their fish,' Molly had announced when Georgie asked who they were going to get to stand in.

It had been decided that because there would be so many people at Josie's house, Katie and Sarah would get ready at home and that Vi would come around too. Their dresses and hats were all hanging in the biggest bedroom. They'd collect their flowers from Josie's house later on.

'It must be sheer murder over there, it's bad enough here,' Katie commented as Vi fastened up her dress at the back.

Sarah, who was ready, sat watching the two older girls. She wished she had their confidence, their outgoing natures. Even in the shop she never felt comfortable with people she hadn't known all her life. When she'd left school, she'd said she just couldn't cope in a factory or a big, strange shop, which was why she helped Mam. She didn't earn as much as Katie, but then she didn't expect to.

The pale pink dress with its full skirt and puffed sleeves suited her, Vi had said so, and that was high praise indeed. She put on a little lipstick, not so much that her Mam would notice, and would have liked to have dabbed just a bit of Bourjois 'Soft Peach' rouge on her cheeks, but that was definitely out of the question. She had placed the large-brimmed hat so it was straight on the back of her head but Vi had taken it off and replaced it, bringing the brim well down on her forehead and tilting it to one side. Now it looked much better.

'Now at least it doesn't look like a halo,' Vi had giggled, and Sarah had wished she had Vi's style.

'God, I look as though I've got jaundice!' Vi exclaimed as Katie placed the pale yellow hat over her friend's naturally blonde hair.

'Come on, stop that.'

'I do, I bloody do. I hate yellow! I never wear it.'

'Well, you will today, so stop swearing, shut up and keep still while I get the hatpin in. One move and it'll stick in your head.'

'There's not much use fussing with our hair; it'll look a flaming mess by the time we get these oversized dinner-plates off our heads!'

Sarah tittered excitedly. 'Do you think we'll meet anyone?' she asked.

'We'll meet all Josie's bloody relations as well as half of Anfield and Everton by the sound of it, *that's* who we'll meet,' Vi replied, now in the process of putting Katie's hat on at the right angle.

'No, I mean . . . anyone special.'

'You mean lads, Sarah, so say so. It won't bother me, Jack's coming on later to the do.' Vi looked at Sarah kindly. 'But maybe Josie's got a couple of nice cousins we don't know about. One for you, Katie, and one for you, Sarah.'

'Fat chance of us getting anywhere near a feller with Mam watching our every move. I mean, it's not as though we were just ordinary guests. Dolled up like this, she can't help but see us.'

'What harm is there in having a chat or a bit of a dance with a lad?' Vi demanded, trying not to look at herself in the mirror. She was certain that any stranger seeing *her* would be sure to call an ambulance immediately and she'd be carted off to Stanley Hospital. She *hated* bloody yellow.

'None, just so long as it's only one dance or one chat, and providing she likes the look of them. If she doesn't, well . . .' Katie smiled at her sister. 'It's a pain isn't it, Sarah, but today we're all going to enjoy ourselves and you never know – we just might meet someone!'

Sarah blushed furiously.

'Now look what you've done, she's all embarrassed,' Vi scolded laughingly. 'Sarah, you've gorra be a bit more pushy. Don't just sit with all the ould ones. Even if you don't know any of Josie's relations, if they look nice, go up and talk to them, introduce yourself.'

'Oh, I couldn't do that, Vi! I . . . I'd just die!'

'And we'll all be dead if we don't get a move on and go on over to the bride's house. Although I'll feel such a fool traipsing up the road dressed like this. You know what Dennis MacCane and Paddy Maher are like. I dread to think of the remarks out of them.'

The service was beautiful, Sarah thought as she, like most of the females in the church, wiped away a tear. Josie looked gorgeous. Different and sort of transformed, really pretty. Georgie looked handsome but solemn, as he was supposed to look, she thought. She hadn't minded the walk from Chelmsford Street to Becket Street, after all. Lots of people had called out to them – nice things, and they'd received plenty of whistles too. She'd just ducked her head and tried not to blush too much. Vi had started off by grinning back but halfway there her shoes had begun to pinch and her smile to disappear.

The ride to church in the car, although very short, was exciting, too. None of them had ever been in a motor car before. Sarah sighed inwardly with pleasure. It had all been perfect. The sunlight streaming in through the stained-glass windows, throwing rainbows of light over the altar and the congregation, Father Macreedy in his white and gold vestments, the flowers, the music and the smell of incense that always made her feel so calm . . . If she ever got married it would be like this.

While Josie Watson had been busy becoming Josie Deegan and promising to 'love, honour and obey' her husband, and Georgie Deegan had been promising 'for better or for worse, for richer or poorer' and with all his worldly goods to endow her – something he was a bit uneasy about – a group of neighbours had been collecting up the bowls of jelly and trifle and plates of sandwiches, bridge rolls and assorted pies, and were setting them all out in the church hall. Molly had given them each a bottle of sherry for their trouble.

Everyone tucked in, although Jimmy Watson had his hand slapped and received a threatening look from his Mam for grabbing at a roll before Father Macreedy had said Grace.

The happy couple were toasted in Yates's best Australian white wine, known as 'Ozzy Whites' and then the men got down to the serious business of the day: discussing football, racing, their jobs or lack of them, and the state of things in Europe. Their throats were eased, of course, by a pint or two of ale. The women of both sides formed similar groups to discuss housing, husbands, kids, rationing, prices and all ailments and operations that had been experienced and were considered relevant.

Josie was listening carefully to her Auntie Hilda's household tips but Katie, Sarah, Vi, Brenda and Norma were getting restless.

'Racing, recipes and relations. I'm bored to death!' Katie said, pulling a face.

'All weddings are like this,' Brenda announced gloomily. 'I thought your Jack was supposed to be coming, Vi?'

'He is, but seeing as he's not related to anyone at all he's just coming for the evening, like.'

'After he's been to the first footie match of the season, you mean. That's what's the matter with most of that lot,' Brenda jerked her head in the direction of her father and uncles. 'They couldn't go. Me Da said if he'd realised our Josie was going to get wed today, he'd have changed it to last Saturday.'

'My Jack's not gone to no football match, Brenda Watson.'

'Isn't there anything we can do?' Norma asked to save an argument starting.

'Well, I'm going home to get this hat off and do my hair,' Katie announced firmly.

'Mam will kill you!' Sarah's eyes were wide with fright.

'No, she won't, not if we ask in the right way and not if we *all* ask.'

They agreed it was worth a try. Katie was elected to speak to Molly and Florrie since it was her idea.

'Mam, Mrs Watson, we were thinking that it might be a good time for us bridesmaids to go home for a bit. Take off our hats, do our hair, and poor Vi's shoes are killing her. We won't be long, honestly.'

Molly looked at Florrie, who simply shrugged. Mrs Watson felt completely worn out. She was past caring, now the important bit of the day was over.

'All right, but don't go missing for hours and no acting the goat on the way home.' Molly turned again to Florrie. 'You know, I've been thinking and watching that lot.' She indicated the group of men. 'The rate they're going, the ale will have run out by six o'clock. Suppose we tell them they can go to the match, so long as they don't pop into the pub on the way back, either to celebrate or drown their sorrows, as the case may be.' She was glad now that Bill's brother Alfred had been unable to attend, although he'd sent a nice clock for the happy pair. He wouldn't have fitted in with this lot!

Florrie sighed and looked to her sisters for support.

'Oh, let them go, Flo,' Imelda replied. 'They're nothing but a damned nuisance most of the time, worse than kids, and we don't want to be having to send out for more ale, because by midnight they'll all be paralytic and *I'm* not trying to drag him home in that state.'

Within the space of ten minutes the room was cleared, except for the bride, her female relations and her mother-in-law.

After an hour and a half, Josie had become a little bored, but by the time all her bridesmaids arrived back, followed by some of the men who had withdrawn their support for their chosen team after being a humiliating three down at half-time, things began to liven up. Then Ernie, Fred's brother, was persuaded to play the piano and Fred himself said he'd go home for his accordion. Shortly afterwards the rest of the men and boys arrived back, followed by the 'evening guests', and Molly declared the knees-up officially under way.

'Thank God for a bit of excitement,' Vi said as Jack Milligan arrived and she dragged him on to the square of linoleum that served as a dancefloor, to join Josie and Georgie who had done one turn around the middle of the floor on their own.

'They're not going to play stuff like this all night, are they, because if so I'm going home,' Jack complained. He preferred bebop and swing to the old tunes being played by Fred and Ernie.

'Don't be daft, it's just for Josie and old misery guts there.'

Sarah was asked to dance by one of Josie's cousins – a third cousin, he explained in an earnest sort of way. He was gangly and his hair was plastered down with some sort of oil that smelled sickly and he was rather spotty. Neither of them spoke and she was glad when the dance was over.

'Ugh! He was horrible,' she hissed to Katie.

'I can see that. Why did you say yes?'

'I didn't want to be rude, but what will I do if he asks me again?'

'Tell him your feet are hurting, or you've got a headache, or Mam said only one dance per feller. Use your imagination.'

Katie had scanned all the male company to see if there was anyone of interest, but there wasn't. 'It looks as though we're going to be wallflowers, Sarah,' she said. 'Never mind, we can just sit here and watch people making fools of themselves. It'll be a laugh. Brenda said when her Uncle Norm has had a few pints he's a scream. That's if her Auntie Hilda will let him be.'

'Our Georgie doesn't look very happy.'

'He won't be. He's had to put his hand in his pocket.'

'Oh well, he'll be back at sea on Monday.' Sarah nudged Katie. 'That lot down there seem to be a bit rowdy.'

'Which lot?' Katie craned her neck.

'Him in the uniform.'

'Oh God, that's Mickey Mac! "Bucket-gob" he's known as. He's one of Josie's lot. Fancies himself, he does,' Vi informed them, having sat down with Jack at their table.

'Oh aye, all mouth an' trousers! Thinks he's Admiral of the Fleet 'cos he just joined up. God knows why he joined the Navy, he gets seasick on the ferry to Birkenhead,' Jack said disparagingly.

The voices were getting louder and suddenly the level of conversation in the room dropped. An argument now seemed to be going on between Georgie and Mickey Mac.

There was silence now and Mickey's voice carried clearly. 'Goin' back ter sea on Monday, are yer then? Waiting on tables, that's a tart's job,' he jeered.

'I don't see any bloody medals or gold braid on your uniform,' Georgie retorted.

'At least I'm a proper sailor. A mat . . . mat—' he gave up on the word matelot, 'on a warship norra bloody pathetic liner!'

66

'Yeah, and we all know how bloody great you are on ships. Can't even go over the water without turning green. You should have joined the Army – or wouldn't they have you because your mouth's too big?' Georgie sniggered.

This was too much for Mickey. Fired up by drink and Georgie's insults, he lunged out and caught the other man a blow on the side of the head.

With a roar of pain Georgie retaliated and bedlam reigned, with the women screaming and the men yelling and shouting until Fred Watson, his brothers and brothers-in-law, pulled the protagonists apart.

'You save your bloody fighting for when it matters, Mickey!' Fred roared.

'Aye, and the way things is goin', that might be sooner than yer think. Anyway, what the hell's wrong with yer, beltin' a feller on his weddin' day!' John Watson demanded.

'He's got no manners and never has had,' Florrie piped up, mortified by Mickey's behaviour.

'No, he's been dragged up,' Imelda agreed tartly.

'It's a good job me Mam's not here. She'd have somethin' ter say ter youse two!' Mickey shouted defiantly.

'Who *is* his Mam?' Vi asked Brenda.

'Me Da's cousin. She's a right one. No one speaks to her an' he's a bastard.'

They all looked shocked.

'I'm not swearing. He is a bastard. God knows who his Da is, 'coz no one else does.'

'Well, no wonder he carries on like that. It must be awful for him, the shame and everything . . .' Sarah's voice died away as they all turned and stared at her.

'Oh, God! You haven't gone and fallen for *him*, have yer?' Vi asked, horrified.

'No! I was just trying to be kind.'

'Well, don't waste your time, he's not worth it. Best place for him is in the Navy. They'll soon sort him out.'

Josie and Molly were fussing over Georgie who had a cut above his eye which was bleeding copiously. Molly was all for taking him along to Stanley Hospital to have it seen to, but Georgie wouldn't hear of it, especially as a tearful Josie was insisting hysterically that she must go with him. Her place was by his side now, she kept repeating. She was so upset that Katie and Vi went and virtually dragged her to their table, sat her down and made her drink a glass of port.

'I could murder him! That . . . !'

'Well, who asked him or did he invite himself?' Vi enquired, trying to calm Josie down.

'I think he invited himself. I *know* Mam wouldn't have asked him. I'll never forgive him for the things he said to Georgie, and today of all days!'

'Don't upset yourself, Mrs Deegan, the whole day's been great. Don't let the likes of that no mark spoil it,' Katie urged.

Josie suddenly smiled. It seemed to hit her for the first time that day that she was indeed now Mrs Josie Deegan.

Over at another table, Molly pursed her lips and looked at Florrie, whose face was set in grim lines of disapproval.

'I'm sorry about him, Molly. He wasn't invited.'

'And I can see why,' the other woman answered sharply.

'No one in the family has much to do with him or her, our Doreen. She's got another kid, a girl – Joanie. They live down Scottie Road, not that I'm being a snob.'

'Well, it's a fine way to start married life, I must say.'

'They'll be all right, Molly. Our Josie's a good girl. There'll be no trouble from her.'

Molly's expression softened. 'I know, Florrie. In fact, I think she's too good for our Georgie.' She nodded, as Florrie's eyes widened with surprise. 'Aye, and him me own son. Call your Norman over and we'll both have another port and lemon, or would you prefer stout?'

Chapter Eight

Georgie had sailed and was almost in sight of the coastline of Newfoundland on 3 September when the news came over the ship's radio that Britain was at war with Germany. He felt a shiver go down his spine. The Germans had large numbers of submarines – U-boats, they called them – which could sink a merchant ship without even being seen on the surface. Later, as they entered the Gulf of St Lawrence, they were informed that that was exactly what had happened to the Glaswegian merchant ship *Athenia*. One hundred and twelve lives had been lost. Again he felt that shiver and for the moment thanked God they were in safe waters. But they had yet to go home. They had to sail back across that seemingly never-ending mass of grey water – with the added danger of the U-boats. He felt sick at the thought.

Molly was one of the few in Chelmsford Street who had a wireless set – a big, brown Bakelite one that was installed on a shelf in an alcove by the range. On the day war was declared, Mary Maher, Ellen MacCane and their husbands came in and the two men between them moved the wireless into the shop so more people could come in and listen, even though it was a Sunday. Florrie and Fred came around too. It only seemed right, their Josie being married to Georgie.

They all stood and listened to the doleful voice of the Prime Minister, who had promised them 'Peace in our Time' such a short while ago, tell them: 'This country is now at war with Germany.'

They remained silent, trying to digest the news, while the bright autumn sunlight filtered in through cracks in the window blinds. The older men were remembering the Great War, the one everyone said would end all wars. The women, too, recalled the uncertainty, the shortages, the terrible tragedy of the decimation of the battalions of the King's Liverpool 'Pals' Regiment on the Somme, tragedies they'd thought never to have to face ever again. And this time the war would be brought right to their doorsteps. Ordinary people had already been bombed in their own homes in Spain.

After the King's speech to the nation in the evening, Josie clung tightly to Florrie's hand, thinking of Georgie. Sarah and Katie had their arms around Molly's waist, while Joe looked bewildered.

When the news was broadcast about the *Athenia*, the first unarmed merchant-ship tragedy, Josie's tears verged on the hysterical and Molly got out her rosary. All they could do now was pray. Pray that the *Ascania* would make her way home to Liverpool safely.

The entire population of Liverpool waited tensely. They waited for the sirens to wail, the planes to come, the bombs to drop. They were all prepared. Gas masks, Anderson shelters, public shelters, children evacuated to the country where they'd be safe . . . and then nothing happened, except the blackout.

At sea, and there were so many Liverpool men amongst the crews of the passenger liners and cargo ships, things were not so calm. On 18 September 1939, *HMS Courageous* was sunk, with the loss of 500 lives. At the end of October, the *Royal Oak* was sunk at her moorings at Scapa Flow with the loss of 800 men. Mickey Mac had been on the *Royal Oak*, and although everyone who was at the wedding had been disgusted at his drunken outbursts, they still felt a sense of shock and loss.

And then the government called up all men over the age of twenty.

'What'll our Georgie do, Mam?' Joe asked Molly.

'Stay in the Merchant Navy, I suppose. It's no picnic, as it's a reserved occupation, for where do you think our food comes from, lad? But at least it's not the Army. It's always the poor bloody Tommies who fare the worst. Cannon-fodder, they are.'

'I wish I was twenty,' he answered gloomily.

Molly rounded on him. 'Don't you dare go saying things like that, Joe Deegan! Haven't I just told you what they are! Bloody cannon-fodder – and there were too many who lied about their age the last time. Too many boys died – aye, boys! Only fifteen and sixteen years old. I've enough to worry about with our Georgie, without you wishing you were twenty.'

Her words didn't lift his mood. At least he could have been evacuated, Joe thought frustratedly. It would have been great to have gone somewhere in the country, by train, with your mates and your gas mask and suitcase. He wouldn't have been whinging and moaning like a lot of them did. But Mam wouldn't let him go.

'If we're going to get bombed, we'll all be together,' she said firmly and repeatedly to Mr Peel's urgings.

At first it had been great not to have to go to school, but after a while it became boring and besides, kids were coming back because there hadn't been any planes or bombs. St John's was open again and Mr Peel told Mam he'd put Joseph's name forward for the scholarship;

now it was work, work, work. Mind, it wasn't much fun when he got to play out. You couldn't see a single thing. You fell over the kerbstones, tripped over tramlines, walked into lamp-posts, got knocked over by bikes, cars and other vehicles whose headlights were hooded, so street-games were out of the question. It was inside playing Tiddlywinks or Snakes and Ladders. No, so far this war had been a bloomin' big disappointment.

Josie wouldn't admit it, not even to herself, but she was becoming very disenchanted with marriage. It certainly wasn't what she had envisaged. Georgie was away most of the time and she worried herself sick about him. She refused to listen to any news on the wireless and wouldn't buy a newspaper, but she still couldn't banish the war from her mind. It was all people talked about.

She was at work all day with Katie and Vi and the other girls, but when she got home to Stour Street it was so lonely. She kept things spotless, but with only herself there the place didn't get messed up. Sometimes she went round to see her Mam but there was too much noise. Brenda and Norma were always bickering while Betty, Jimmy and Daisy were busy scrapping. She sometimes thought the house resembled a zoo and wondered how she had stuck it. She couldn't understand how her Mam and Dad survived.

She could go to Molly's and some nights she did, but the relationship between herself and Katie was different now, and she didn't really have that much in common with her mother-in-law. No, life felt very miserable and drab and empty.

In mid-November she was walking home from the tram-stop with Katie, who surprised her by asking her what was the matter.

'Josie, you've got a face like a wet week and have had for the last month. What's the matter? Is it our Georgie?'

'Yes. No. I mean, I worry about him but it's *different* being married.'

'Of course it's different, it's supposed to be. You know, the Happy Ever After bit?'

Josie didn't reply.

'So there's no Happy Ever After bit?'

'Yes! Yes, most of the time when he's home it's great, it's just . . .'

Katie could guess what was wrong. 'Money – that's the problem, isn't it, Josie?'

'Well, that and a lack of company. It really *is* different. You can't do things, go places like you did before – that's if . . . if you did have the spare cash.' She felt guilty complaining, but after all, she'd known Katie all her life.

'Oh, now I see why you're miserable. How much Allotment does he leave you?'

'Ten shillings.'

Katie had stopped walking and was peering at Josie in the gloom. 'A week?'

'No, a trip.'

'A TRIP! A BLOODY TRIP!'

'For God's sake, Katie, don't let the whole flaming neighbourhood know! He said I've got my wages, and seeing that I've only myself to feed . . .'

'But the rent is nine and six a week, Josie, and we only earn one pound and ten shillings. How in the name of God do you manage on a pound and sixpence?'

'I saved up in the Post Office, like your Mam told me to do. Georgie doesn't know but he's always telling me to save up, not waste money, and I try to add a few shillings to it to have something put by for things of our own, but what with Christmas coming . . .' She burst into tears.

Katie put an arm around her friend. 'Now look here, Josie, you're coming home with me. I won't let you go back to those empty rooms. I'll bet you've had no fire for weeks either.'

'I don't want to be disloyal, Katie. I *do* love him and when he's home, it's great. He's never been one for treats, I knew that before I married him.' Josie wiped her eyes with the back of her hand.

'What you didn't know was that he's the biggest skinflint this side of the Mersey and that he can damned well afford to pay for the rent and everything else.'

Josie still rallied to defend him. 'Georgie says he's saving for the future, for a place of our own. I mean *really* our own. He wants to buy a house.'

'He's mad! People like us don't buy houses, but maybe he thinks *he* can.' She called to mind Georgie's conversation with Uncle Alfred at her Da's funeral. Georgie was more likely to be saving up to expand the shop when the war was over.

Both Sarah and Molly were in the kitchen when the two girls arrived home. These days the shop closed early. Molly had blackout curtains on the window and the door, but fish was getting scarcer and she was finding it hard, these pitch-dark winter mornings, to get up and walk to the corner of the street where Jem Cargill would pick her up.

'Set another place, Sarah. Come on in, Josie, and sit by the fire, luv. You look frozen stiff.'

'And so would you, Mam, if you were living in cold rooms with no money for coal, food or anything else.'

72

Molly stared hard at Katie. 'What do you mean by that?'

Katie had taken off her coat, hat and gloves. 'Go on, Josie, tell Mam how much Allotment he leaves you.'

Josie huddled close to the range. 'Ten shillings.'

'A trip, Mam, not a week!'

Molly was incredulous. 'Never! How does he expect you to manage on that?'

'He . . . he says I have my own wages.'

'Yes, and you're trying to keep body and soul together with those. Does your Mam know?'

Josie shook her head. 'I feel so guilty. It's like betraying Georgie. I shouldn't be talking about our private affairs to people.'

'We're not just "people", Josie. You're part of this family now. When's he due home?'

'Early next week, I hope. I get so worried about him. Those convoys are so slow and when I'm on my own I imagine all kinds of awful things happening to him.' Her lips quivered.

'Right, then you're to come here for your tea after work every night and I'm going down to meet him when the *Ascania* docks. You go to work; at the rate things are going, you young ones are going to have to go into munitions, like we did in the last war. Now sit down at the table the pair of you, tea's almost ready.' Outwardly Molly was calm; inwardly she was seething. He'd left that poor girl to live on her wages and ten bob a trip. No wonder she hadn't been looking very well lately. She had suspected that Josie might be pregnant; now she knew the depressing truth.

The following week, the remaining ships of the convoy limped across the Bar and into the Mersey. It was freezing cold, the wind so bitter it brought tears to Molly's eyes, but she didn't move to seek a more sheltered place. She wanted to stand and wait where he could see her plainly.

It was another hour before he got ashore.

'Mam! What's the matter? Why are *you* down here? You must be frozen!'

'I'm not half as frozen as that poor little wife of yours, with no money for coal or to keep body and soul together. Get over there under the archway, out of the wind. I've a few things to say to you, Georgie Deegan!'

It was a long time since he'd received such a tongue-lashing but he stood and took it all, albeit not in total silence.

'She gets good money,' he said sullenly when Molly confronted him with the pittance he gave Josie.

'You call thirty shillings a week good money? I certainly don't!

She'll get better wages in munitions, but that doesn't mean you can give her even less. She'll have to go out to Kirkby for a start, so there's more tram and train-fares. I just don't understand you, Georgie. You've got this . . . this obsession with money.'

'I need to save, Mam. What if the ship gets hit? We lost four on the way out and one coming home. What will she do for money if I'm killed or maimed?'

Molly crossed herself. She was superstitious about such things.

'That's not the point at all, son. I've never forgotten that copper coming around to us about you gambling, or the carry-on and complaints out of you over the wedding expenses.'

'She shouldn't have told you. It's not right, her running to you with tales!'

'She didn't. It was our Katie she told only last week on the way home from work.'

Georgie grimaced. That was even worse. Bloody Katie again, and she knew how much he had stashed away, too.

'So, from now on, meladdo,' Molly concluded, 'you'll pay the rent and you'll give her enough for coal and gas and electric. She's said she'll feed and clothe herself out of what she earns, she insisted on that. I wanted you to fork out for that, too. It's a husband's responsibility. If there wasn't a war on she wouldn't be out at work at all. Have you got no pride? You know what people would say about you – that you couldn't provide properly for your wife. Well, I'm not having anything like that said. I've got *my* pride even if you haven't! Now get home, light a fire and have the kettle on when she comes in. And it wouldn't hurt you to take her to the pictures either.' Molly noted the grim set of his lips. 'And if you say one word or even worse, lay one finger on that girl, you'll have me, Florrie, Fred and all her uncles to deal with.' Tugging the knot in her headscarf to tighten it, Molly turned and walked purposefully away towards the tram-stop.

Georgie stared after her. In the name of God why had he ever married Josie Watson? It was all their Joe's stupid fault. His bloody day-dreaming had left him with no option except to throw himself on Josie's charity. Some bloody charity . . . Well, she could go and whistle for a night out! If he was going to have to spend good money on coal and light and all the rest, then they'd bloody well stay in and reap the benefit. He would sit and read the newspapers and she could do what the hell she liked.

Chapter Nine

With the danger from the U-boats ever present, quantity, quality and variety of produce was getting harder and harder to keep up. Even in peacetime, it was difficult in winter, Molly thought, but this year there seemed to be even less choice. She said a quick prayer of thanks to the trawler crews who had at least managed to get some fish in for Deegans' shop, mainly herring and cod. There was no haddock, plaice, sole, dabs, bass, rock salmon or even mackerel. The shellfish was non-existent: no shrimps from Southport, none of the Dublin Bay prawns people bought at holiday times. The large sheds were not brightly lit and Molly peered into the gloom, nodding and exchanging greetings and remarks with the traders and buyers, all of whom she knew well.

'You've not got much, Albert Dun,' she said to one of them, picking up a small cod.

'Neither has anyone else, luv. You know what it's like in winter at the best of times. They lost one Manx boat, "Mona's Isle", you know. Her nets caught on the rigging of a U-boat. Dragged to the bottom with all hands.'

Molly crossed herself. 'God have mercy on them.'

Albert Dun nodded. 'The convoys are what's bringing in the basics – wheat, oats, meat and soon it'll be arms, weapons, steel and petrol.'

'Well, there hasn't been much happening that I've noticed. Except at sea,' she added, thinking of what Albert had just told her about the 'Mona's Isle'.

'Don't you listen to the news, girl? Don't you know we've got one hundred and fifty thousand troops in France now and that the first Canadian lads arrived yesterday? You never know, it might not be as bad as some people have been forecasting.'

'Our Georgie says it seems like the Merchant Navy are the only ones that are having a rough time of it. He says they're just like sitting ducks out there on the Atlantic and you'd need the speed of the *Queen Mary* and the new one, the *Queen Elizabeth*, to outrun those bloody U-boats.' Molly broke off and attended to the business in hand. 'Well, seeing as your stuff seems to be the best of a bad bunch, Albert, you'd better give me a box of cod – or codling, more like, and four boxes of herring. They always go well. Have you heard that sugar and meat are on ration now? We'll all be shutting up shop the way it's going.'

'Aye, Christmas won't be the same this year,' Albert Dun remarked as he packed more ice into the boxes of fish.

'Christmas will never be what it was for me without Bill,' Molly said quietly.

He nodded. 'I'm sorry, luv, I'd forgotten.'

'That's all right – there's plenty like me in this city and there'll be more if this war goes on.'

He looked around and caught the eye of one of the porters. ''Ere, Bob! Will yer give Mrs Deegan a 'and with this lot. Me back's playing up something awful with this cold and damp.'

Molly knew Bob Goodwin. He was a pleasant lad and a hard worker, and he always had a cheery word. She'd never seen him lose his temper yet.

'Have you got the same lift as usual this morning, Mrs Deegan?' he asked as he effortlessly stacked her purchases on his trolley.

'Aye, Mr Cargill will be waiting for me by the entrance. I can't see there being a Christmas Rush this year can you, lad?'

He shrugged. 'Except there's never much call for fish, is there? Except for kippers or salt fish for breakfast. But one of my mates at the fruit and vegetable market says there'll be no oranges to put in the kids' stockings this year. Anyway, I've been called up. I'll be with the King's Lancashire Regiment.'

'When will you have to go?'

He grinned. 'They've been dead good, given me Christmas and New Year's Day off. I've got to report on the second of January.'

'Where to?'

'Warrington.'

'Well, you won't be that far away from home, will you?'

'No, but I'll have to get passes and I've heard they don't give them out too often, like.'

They were out of the sheds now and had almost reached the gates that led out on to the road when suddenly, without any warning, Molly's feet went from under her as she slipped on a patch of black ice. Instantly Bob was on his knees beside her and Jem Cargill climbed down from his cart.

'Are you hurt, Mrs Deegan?' Bob asked.

Molly was more shocked than hurt. 'I . . . I don't think so.' Then as both Bob and Jem tried to get her to her feet she winced, 'It's my foot or my ankle.'

Bob examined it gently while she leaned heavily on Jem's shoulder. 'Can you put any weight on it at all?'

Molly tried but gritted her teeth and shook her head. 'I think it's only sprained but it needs strapping up.'

Jem looked perturbed. 'She can't go to the hospital on me cart – and what about all our stuff?'

'That'll keep, Mr Cargill. It's certainly not going to go off in weather like this.'

'Look, Jem, you get off home,' Molly said faintly. 'Drop my stuff off. I'm not going to no hospital. Our Katie can bandage it up and with a day's rest it'll be as right as rain.'

'How will you get home?' Bob looked very concerned. Mrs Deegan was a heavy woman and she'd taken quite a bump. She must be shaken up too.

'Get me a taxi, lad, please? Go on, I've got the money.'

'But you still have to get in and out of it. You know you should just call in at the hospital. You have to pass it on the way home anyway.'

'Call in! Listen to him. Have you ever been in the Casualty Department in the Stanley?'

'No, but they won't be busy at this time in the morning, surely.'

Molly sighed. She could see she was going to have to agree. 'All right then, I'll "call in".'

He disappeared, leaving her supported by Jem. When he came running back he had his coat on and his cap.

'Where are you going?' Jem asked.

'I'm going with Mrs Deegan. The boss says it's all right.'

'You'll lose pay, lad, and your Mam won't be too happy about that, not with Christmas almost on us.'

'Mrs Deegan, I don't mind.' Bob sounded almost indignant. 'If it were my Mam I'd want someone to look after her and see her home safely.'

Molly stared at him, deeply touched. He was a good lad, a real good lad.

The Casualty Department at the hospital was empty except for a young nurse who was half-asleep but who livened herself up when Molly hobbled in, leaning heavily on Bob Goodwin. The girl went off to find a doctor who duly arrived, manipulated the foot and pronounced it 'sprained'. He then left the young nurse to strap it up, and departed with the instruction to 'rest it as much as possible'. Rest? Molly thought. Oh, it was all right giving advice out like that but she had a living to earn.

'Right, lad – is that feller still outside?'

'He said he'd just park up. He can't waste his petrol, so nothing will go on the meter. I'll go and find him.'

'That's good of him.'

'Well, there's not much chance of him getting another fare at this time of day, and he knew he'd get his money.'

Both Sarah and Katie were waiting anxiously at the shop door. Behind them, Molly's purchases had been dumped on the floor by Jem but neither of the girls had picked anything up, they were too worried.

'Mam, are you all right? Mr Cargill said you'd had a fall and gone to Stanley Hospital.'

'Wouldn't you just know he'd say something like that, the flaming old fool. Yes, I did fall, and I have been to have it seen to. It's only a sprained ankle, so don't fret, you two. They strapped it up and it will be fine by tomorrow.'

Sarah helped her mother through into the living room, sat her down and pulled a low stool over for her to put her foot on. 'I'll make us some tea.'

Katie and Bob had followed. 'It must have shaken you up, Mam. A cup of strong, sweet tea is best.'

'Will you all stop fussing! I'm all right but give this lad, Bob Goodwin he is, a cuppa and a large slice of that Dundee cake. He's lost a morning's pay bringing me home.'

Katie made the tea and then went upstairs to get Joe up for school. She'd liked this Bob Goodwin from the minute she'd seen him, and for him to have forfeited his pay to bring Mam home meant he must have a nature that matched his looks.

While she made the beds, almost tipping Joe out of his and ignoring his complaints, she wondered why she had felt instantly drawn to Bob. He was quite tall but of a slim build. His hair was a reddish-brown and waved naturally, and his blue eyes had been full of concern for Mam. As she passed the dressing-table she caught sight of herself in the mirror. What a mess she looked! She quickly brushed her hair and put on a little lipstick, not much, she didn't want him to think she was in any way brazen. She stared at her reflection. She'd only known Bob a few minutes so why was she even thinking like this?

When she went downstairs again he wasn't there and she felt a pang of disappointment. 'Where's he gone?'

'He's in the shop, He insisted on helping our Sarah with the produce.'

'He seems nice . . . and thoughtful.'

'He is. His Mam can be proud of him. Do you know what he said when I told him I'd manage just fine on my own? He said if it were his Mam he'd want someone to look after her.'

'What does he do?' Katie began absentmindedly tidying away the cups and newspapers.

'He's a porter.' She scrutinised Katie's face. 'I don't think they earn very much, but it's a job. Anyway, he's been called up.' She decided to change the subject. 'We'll have to go easy now on the sugar, it's going on ration along with meat.'

But Katie wasn't really listening; she was trying to think of a reason to go through into the shop before she had to leave for work. Luckily she didn't need an excuse, for Bob came through just at that moment, smiling and rubbing his hands.

'Well, that's done. All shipshape and Bristol fashion in there. Can I wash my hands? I don't want to be messing anything up, everywhere's so . . . nice.'

'In the back kitchen, I'll show you.' Katie indicated that he should follow her, realising as she did so that her heart was acting very oddly, beating in a jerky manner. She put the towel they used for 'dirty work' on the draining board.

'Are you the eldest?' he asked, soaping his hands vigorously with a bar of reddish-coloured Lifebuoy soap.

'No, our Georgie is. He's married and he's in the Merchant Navy, on the convoys. Mind you, we all get more peace now he's not living here.'

'Oh, I see.' Obviousy she didn't get on with her brother, Bob thought, but then that was nothing new. She was a pretty girl; her expression was soft and pleasant and the corners of her mouth tilted upwards. The sign of a sunny nature, his Mam always said.

'Where do you work?'

'Moorehouse's, bottling lemonade, but that's going to end after Christmas. We're all going to work in munitions out at Kirkby – we've volunteered.'

'All?' he asked, drying his hands and turning his full attention to her.

'Me, our Sarah, Josie – my sister-in-law – and Vi Draper, my friend.' She turned away and began to wipe around the sink so he wouldn't see the colour rising in her cheeks.

'Do you go out much, Katie?'

Her heart almost stopped. Was he going to ask her out?

'Oh, a bit, usually to the pictures, sometimes to the Grafton at the weekend. Ma said you've been called up.'

'Yes, but I don't go until January, and then it's only to Warrington and that's not very far away, is it?' He was smiling at her and she grasped the edge of the draining board, almost giddy.

'I know I've only just met you, but time is so short and everything. Would you come out with me, Katie, on Saturday?'

For a second she couldn't speak, then she swallowed hard and nodded.

'Where would you like to go?'

Remembering what Mam had said about him not getting much of a wage she thought quickly. 'I don't mind – you choose.'

'Let's go dancing, then we can get to know each other better.' He could hold her close too, he meant, and that was something he very much wanted to do.

'Are you sure?'

'I'm certain. What time shall I pick you up?'

'About half-past seven? By the time the tram crawls along there it will be almost eight and it really doesn't get going until then.'

'What about your friend – Vi, was it? Will she be upset or annoyed?'

'No, she's courting steady, like.'

They both stood in silence, just staring at each other for a few seconds.

'You know, in a way it's been worth it to lose a few hours' pay,' he said finally. Then he smiled and her heart turned over.

'I daresn't say it was worth it Mam fell, but . . . well, if she *had* to fall it was great that it was you who brought her home.'

'I'll see you on Saturday then, Katie.'

She smiled, her eyes dancing, her cheeks flushed as they went into the living room.

'You get off now, lad, and here's something for your trouble.' Molly held out an envelope.

'Oh no, I don't want paying, Mrs Deegan!'

'You lost money and your Mam won't be very happy about it. Take it, Bob, I insist.'

Reluctantly he took the brown envelope from her and stuffed it in his pocket. It would pacify Mam, but he would have been more than willing to listen to her complaints, just to have met the lovely Katie Deegan.

'How will you manage for the rest of the week? Could Mr Cargill bring your fish home? I could always buy it for you, providing there's anything to buy,' Bob offered diffidently. 'See that no one fobs you off with rubbish just because you're not there in person.'

'Would you?'

'Of course. I'll go and see Mr Cargill on my way home. Ask him to come around and you can make some arrangements about the money.'

'Your Mam must be right proud of you, lad.'

He just shrugged and smiled, said goodbye and was led through the door into the shop by Sarah.

'He's very nice. He – he's asked me out on Saturday, dancing,' Katie informed her mother as she carried on getting ready for work. She always met Josie and Vi at the tram-stop.

'And are you going?'

80

Katie nodded happily. Seeing a troubled look cross her mother's face she frowned. 'What's the matter with him? You like him, you said he was a decent, thoughtful lad.'

'I *do* like him and he *is* just that – decent and thoughtful.'

'So?'

'He lives on Netherfield Road.'

For a minute Katie looked puzzled, and then her eyes widened and she bit her lip.

'Yes, he's a Protestant, Katie. Good family, I hear – church-going, but members of the Orange Lodge.'

The light went out of Katie's eyes but then she set her chin determinedly. 'Well, there's nothing wrong in just going dancing, is there? There's no one on the door saying "Catholics this side only" and "Protestants that side only".'

'No, there's no harm at all. I just wanted you to know that nothing can ever come of it, Katie. He'll not turn his religion and I know you won't, so "friends" is all it can be.'

From feeling so light-headed, Katie's spirits now plunged to the depths. It was true: Mam was right. The Orange and the Green had never mixed in Liverpool. There were often near-riots between the two factions on St Paddy's Day and the 'Glorious' Twelfth of July. She picked up her gas mask in its cardboard case and slung it over her shoulder with the strap of her bag. Suddenly she felt thoroughly miserable.

'And you're going out with him?' Vi said as they stood at the tram-stop.

'Yes. Like I said to Mam, there's no harm in going to a dance.'

Josie looked irritable. 'It's what it leads to, Katie.'

Vi backed Josie up. 'She's right.'

'Well, I'm going!' Katie said vehemently.

Josie said nothing; she didn't feel at all well. In fact, she hadn't done for a few weeks and she was late with her period. Very late. She was almost certain she was pregnant and it was alarming and a bit frightening. She'd have to go and see her Mam, Florrie'd know about these things. She'd certainly had enough practice. Josie wondered how Georgie would take it. They had been married so little time and she'd got nothing around her in the way of furniture that was their own, just a few pounds in a Post Office book – and what would she do without her wage?

Vi, in her usual careless way had now dismissed the implications of what Katie was telling her. 'Oh well, if you *are* going, what'll you wear?'

'Probably that sage-green dress with the black trim.'

'That colour doesn't suit you, I don't know how come you bought it. Emerald green, apple green – yes, but sage! It's too dull and plain-looking. It's the sort of colour me Mam wears.'

'I liked it!'

'What else is decent?'

Katie mentally riffled through the garments that hung in her small wardrobe. 'Not much. I suppose I could wear that white blouse and red skirt. The blouse doesn't look bad when it's been starched and ironed.'

Vi considered this. 'It's better than that sage green. I'll lend you a pair of red earrings and a string of red beads. They're only cheap but it will dress it all up a bit, like. Why don't yer meet Jack and me inside, we're going this week. We'll have a laugh.'

'Thanks, Vi.'

Vi nudged her and jerked her head slightly in Josie's direction. 'Is she all right?' she whispered.

'Josie, are you all right?' Vi said aloud. 'You're very quiet and you don't look at all well.' Vi rarely beat about the bush.

'Thank God, here's the tram,' Katie announced. Josie was probably just cold.

To both their surprise, Josie shook her head. 'I feel awful . . . Oh God – I think I'm going to be sick!'

'Vi, you get the tram,' Katie said rapidly. 'I'll see to her. If you get in before me, tell them I'm following on – it's a sort of emergency.'

Josie was now a sickly green colour, had clapped a hand over her mouth and was swallowing hard.

'She's pregnant! I bet she's pregnant!' Vi called from the platform of the tram.

Oh, trust Vi, Katie thought. She might just as well have shouted it from the top of the Liver Buildings. Jesus, Mary and Joseph, what a morning!

'Come on Josie, I'll take you to your Mam's,' she said, gently taking her shivering friend's arm.

Saturday was the day before Christmas Eve, and Katie and Joe had gone for the Christmas tree.

'I hope it's going to be better than last year,' Joe said as they carried it into the living room.

Sarah was in the shop and Molly was sitting on a stool doing the ironing.

'Mam, you're supposed to be resting that foot.'

'I am.'

'You're not! You're up and down like a yo-yo.'

'Oh, stop fussing and go and see if Sarah needs a hand,' Molly said.

'I really don't know what I'd have done without that Bob's help,' she repeated for the umpteenth time.

'Mam, can we do it all up?' Joe was only interested in the Christmas tree.

'When our Katie comes back. Until then you're not to touch a single one of those ornaments. Some of them are so old they're almost antiques.'

Business wasn't very brisk, so from time to time Sarah came through to help with dressing the tree and putting up the paper-chains and the holly that had come fresh that morning.

'Doesn't it look gorgeous,' she breathed when everything was finished.

'It does, you've worked hard. Katie – you'd better make an effort with yourself if you're going out, while I get on with some tea.'

'Mam, I'll do it.' Sarah was insistent. She herself was going round to Lizzie's later on although she wished she was going to the Grafton with someone as handsome and as nice as that Bob Goodwin, even if he was a Protestant . . .

Bob was prompt, but it was raining when he and Katie stepped out into the street, and Katie pulled a face. Now her hair would frizz and she'd spent ages doing it, getting it to look just right.

'Come on, put the brolly up and we'll make a run for it and hope there's a tram coming along Stanley Road,' Bob laughed, catching her hand and pulling her along beside him.

They were both out of breath and giggling when they finally boarded the tram and collapsed on to the long seat by the door.

The conductor looked highly amused. ''Aven't the pair of yez 'eard? Them Olympic Games is over, or are yer practisin' for the next lot – iffen there *is* a next lot?'

Katie was beyond caring about the state of her hair now.

'Two to West Derby Road please.' Bob fished in his pocket for the fare.

'As the Registry Office don't stay open all night now for them wanting ter get wed,' he said facetiously, 'are yer goin ter trip the light fantastic at the Grafton then?'

'Too right we are.'

'Then I 'ope it keeps fine for yer. It's all right for some. There's others 'ave gorra work. Midnight I finish, bloody midnight!' he muttered as he moved down the tram.

Vi and Jack were waiting inside for them.

'What happened to yer? Yer look like something the cat dragged in.'

'Hasn't she got a nice, tactful way about her?' Katie said to Jack.

He grinned. 'It's all part of her charm.'

'We had to run for the tram and in case you hadn't noticed, it's chucking it down out there.'

'What do you want to drink?' Jack called as Vi dragged Katie in the direction of the Ladies' cloakroom and Bob promised to find them a table, preferably on the balcony which was a good vantage point to see what was going on on the dancefloor below.

'Don't ask daft questions. The usual – port and lemon.'

'Well, don't be in there all night.'

'There's been so many rumours. Is Josie pregnant?' Vi whispered as Katie combed her hair, trying to reshape the curls by twisting and combing strands around her finger.

Katie nodded. 'Yes. She's made up, or she would be if she wasn't so sickly. So are Mam and Florrie too, but—'

'But no one's told yer dear brother yet?'

'No. How can we, when he's not due home until the end of next week – we think. The Merchant Navy've stopped telling us things like that now and they won't tell you when they're going to sail either.'

Vi crossed herself. 'Please God he makes it 'ome then. Right, let's go and find those two Romeos before they kop off with some of the right floozies yer get in here sometimes.'

It was a wonderful night. They won a spot prize, a small basket containing three precious oranges, and Katie laughed delightedly as Bob pulled her towards the stage to collect it. Oh, he was so nice and such a good dancer. They seemed to have so much to talk about, too, and when he had one arm around her waist and the other holding her hand, she felt as though she were floating on a cloud of sheer happiness. She knew now that she *must* love him. She'd never felt remotely like this before, and she was sure that there would never, ever be anyone else for her. She hoped he felt the same way.

He held her hand and squeezed it a couple of times, and smiled fondly down at her on the way home, and when they reached the backyard door he opened it for her and then kissed her gently on the lips and held her to him.

It was pitch dark in the jigger. No one would see and carry tales, so she nestled closer to him. He kissed her hair, then her forehead, then the tip of her nose. She was feeling so ecstatic that when she felt the movement of his head, she closed her eyes, raised her face and kissed him. Finally he drew away from her.

'The minute I set eyes on you, I knew I loved you, Katie Deegan.'

'I felt the same. I . . . I love you, too.'

They clung together but this time it was she who drew reluctantly away.

'I'll have to go or Mam'll be out calling me. She'll have heard the door open.'

'When will I see you again?'

'I don't know.'

'Tomorrow?'

She sighed heavily, longing to say yes. 'I was planning to stay at home with Mam,' she whispered. 'You see, Da's only been dead just over a year.'

'I understand, Katie, really I do. Can I come round for an hour on Christmas night?'

'Yes. Oh yes, that would be great.'

She closed the yard door and listened to his footsteps as he walked up the entry, then she went into the house, her eyes bright, her cheeks tinged with pink.

A scene of total confusion met her eyes. Mam was sitting by the range with a face like thunder. Sarah was on her hands and knees, but there was no sign of Joe. Lying on its side amongst the debris of shattered baubles, strands of tinsel and tiny broken red candles, lay the Christmas tree.

'Don't tell me . . . our Joe!'

'I went out for a few seconds, just a few seconds to Mary's. I was feeling down in the dumps with both you and Sarah out. I'd no sooner got sat down than in comes their Vinny looking as guilty as sin.

'After Mary had clocked him one, he told us what meladdo upstairs had done. Apparently he'd made a new star for the top – didn't like the old one. Climbs on the chair, couldn't quite reach and fell over, bringing the whole flaming lot down with him! Look at it! Some of those ornaments belonged to your Da's Mam. I'd treasured them for years and that little get smashes them to smithereens in seconds.' Her voice broke.

Katie went and put her arms around Molly. 'Oh Mam, he didn't mean it – he's just dead clumsy. Maybe it's time we got some new ones anyway.'

Sarah decided to help. 'You've got to admit, Mam, that some of them were looking a bit tatty. Why don't I go along to Great Homer Street Market tomorrow and buy us some new ones? Don't get upset with our Joe please, Mam. It's Christmas.'

'She's right, Mam,' Katie said gently. 'I'll go with her.' Nothing could dim the emotions that were bubbling up inside her, of goodwill to all men – or boy in this case.

Molly looked at them both and smiled tiredly. 'What would I do without you two?'

Chapter Ten

He came on Christmas Day but in the early evening, armed with a small bottle of sherry for Molly and a cake of Cusson's perfumed soap for Katie.

'It was the last one they had, I was lucky to get it.' He looked a bit embarrassed.

She was full of dismay because she had nothing to give him, and as she saw him out later on, she confessed as much.

'I didn't expect anything,' he said tenderly. 'Just *seeing* you was enough, Katie.'

She went to see him off at Lime Street Station on Tuesday morning, the day after New Year. She'd lose a morning's pay but she didn't care. Their farewells were necessarily rather constrained because his parents and sisters were there, too. The Goodwins looked respectable people, tidily dressed and quiet. She smiled shyly at them as Bob introduced her, but they didn't smile back. They certainly weren't the monsters she'd built them up to be in her mind, but they didn't stay to talk to her after he'd gone through the barrier and was lost to sight amongst the crowds of men all in uniform.

Bob had promised to write as often as he could, and get home soon, too, but he didn't hold out much hope of that.

He did write, amusing and loving letters. She read the funny bits out, but it was the bits she omitted that worried Molly.

'Mam, we *are* friends,' she insisted when Molly boned her about the relationship; at the end of February, Bob wrote to say he'd be home at the weekend, but only on a forty-eight-hour pass.

'But it's getting to be more than that, girl. I can see it in your eyes and in your voice when you read his letters – to say nothing of the look on your face when you knew he was coming home.'

'Mam, I'm trying, really I am, but what can I do?'

'Put a stop to it now, luv, before things get more involved and you both are badly hurt. Think about it.'

She promised she would, but she found it harder and harder. Josie and Vi were no help, either. Josie, still sickly and listless, thought she was completely mad and had little sympathy nor interest, come to that. All she could think about was how awful she felt and looked, and the upsetting fact that Georgie didn't seem overjoyed at the prospect of becoming a father. She'd said as much to Florrie.

'He's only twenty-one himself, Josie, just a lad. It's a big responsibility, especially when he's facing danger nearly every day of his life.'

'Mam, I'm not twenty until next month and *I'm* the one who will have to do all the looking after it and the housework and everything else, on my own.'

'Well, isn't that what you wanted?' Florrie demanded. 'I seem to remember you going on and on in raptures about your "lovely little flat", and how you'd like to be a "real" family. Well, now you will be, so stop moaning and put a brave face on things. The sickness will go, believe me. I was like that with both our Brenda and Norma. And for God's sake try to smarten yourself up, Josie, at least when your Georgie comes home. After all he's been through, the last thing he'll want to see is a washed-out, sloppy-looking wife who does nothing but whine. I had six kids, madam, and I had to manage on my own. Your Da was out working all the hours God sent to keep us, yet our house was always spick and span, and I scrubbed my step and brushed our bit of pavement like everyone else.'

After that talking-to, Josie had gone home and cried all afternoon, but she had made an effort when Georgie got home and he seemed to appreciate it.

Vi, in the lucky position of having fallen in love with a boy who had served on the altar of St John's when he was a lad, was more concerned for her friend.

'Look, Katie, it must be hard. I know how I'd feel if my Mam told me to give Jack up, but—'

'Vi, I know you mean well, but you can't possibly understand.'

'Well, you're not going to see much of him anyway,' Vi concluded reasonably. 'Only the odd weekend here and there until he goes overseas. You could let it just . . . fade out naturally.'

The other girl knew there was a lot of sense in what Vi said. That would be one way to do it, but not the easy way.

'Don't get me wrong,' Vi said hastily. 'I like him. He's a great bloke and Jack says so too. It's obvious we all get on well as a foursome.'

'Can't we just keep it to that – a foursome?' Katie interrupted.

'It'll be a twosome soon, just you and me. Jack's going to Portsmouth next week for basic training, then it's a battleship or a cruiser or a corvette or some other kind of damn ship.'

Her friend managed a smile. 'Then we'll both be in the same boat, if you get what I mean?'

Vi managed to laugh but inside she was afraid. Afraid for Jack's safety and for Katie's predicament. Mixed marriages were rare and the couples were usually completely cut off and ignored by their families. Sometimes the girl's Mam would come round and visit, but not often. And then when the kids arrived there was more trouble. Which religion to bring them up in? But if Katie *did* marry Bob Goodwin, in the eyes of the Catholic Church it wouldn't even be recognised. She'd be living in sin and any kids would be branded illegitimate, so that narrowed things down a bit. Better to be baptised a Protestant than branded a bastard, was Vi's view, although she knew it wouldn't be everyone's.

When Georgie came to visit his mother after he got home, he was alone. Josie was lying down; she wasn't at all well, he informed Molly.

'Don't worry, son, it'll pass. Give her another month and she'll be blooming.'

'Blooming enormous,' Katie grunted. 'She's put on weight like nobody's business.'

Molly sighed at her tone. She personally felt sorry for Josie; her daughter-in-law was having a rotten pregnancy. She now had more days off work than on, and it seemed soon she'd have to give up altogether. She'd have stopped work long ago, except for the war. The girls were all in munitions now. They worked shifts and the journey was long and often cold and miserable. The trams only went as far as Fazakerley terminus; from there you got the train that ran direct to the factory. The work, too, was messy, smelly and dangerous. But at least Sarah, Vi, Josie and herself were on detonators, which wasn't as bad as some jobs where your skin turned yellow and your hair went green or you could get your fingers, or worse, blown off . . .

Molly turned to Katie; this was no time to be making remarks like that. 'It's only fluid. You carry a lot of fluid when you're in that condition.'

'I hear you're getting serious with that Bob Goodwin from Netherfield Road,' Georgie remarked accusingly.

'So? I write to him and go dancing with him when he gets home, which isn't very often.'

Molly drew in her breath. Josie must have spilled the beans to Georgie and from the look on his face he was spoiling for a fight.

'He's a bloody Orangeman!' he spat.

'He's not! His family are, but he doesn't walk with the Lodges, he doesn't even own a bowler hat, and anyway they're decent-living people, the Goodwins – which is more than can be said for a lot of Catholic families in this city!'

'Mam's told you it's got to stop.'

Katie's cheeks began to burn. 'No, she hasn't. She's *advised* me – it's not the same thing at all.'

'Well, *I'm* telling you to get rid of him. I won't have a bloody Orangeman in this family!'

Katie turned on him, her eyes flashing. 'You'll mind your own bloody business, Georgie Deegan. I'll go out with whom I like and I'll marry whom I like.'

'Oh no, you won't! You'll not disgrace us by marrying the likes of *him*. I'll break every bone in your body first.'

'Just try raising your hand to me, and see who comes off worst! Mind your own flaming business! At least Bob's prepared to fight for his country, unlike you. Skulking off in the Merchant Navy, sailing with battleships all around you, with blokes like Jack Milligan on board to protect you. Why didn't you join the Royal Navy like him, and leave the convoys for the older men?' she taunted.

He was purple in the face with fury. 'My service to this country is just as dangerous, just as important. At least Jack Milligan and the rest of 'em have weapons to fight back with – big guns, depth-charges and armour plating to protect themselves. We're just defenceless merchantmen with maybe one piddling anti-aircraft gun bolted to the deck. Three thousand miles of ocean there and three thousand back. Eight ships we lost this time, Katie, two of them tankers. They just erupted into huge balls of fire; those men never stood a chance. Do you know what it's like to have to watch that, and not be able to do a single bloody thing to help? No, you bloody don't!' His voice rose to a near-scream of frustration, then he paused to calm down. 'And we lost another two in the Western Approaches – ten ships in all, and that wasn't bad! Those bloody wolf-packs just lurk under the water and wait. They know we've got to come in that way to get to port. So don't you say the men of the Merchant Navy are bloody cowards! There's men in the service who fought in the Royal Navy in the last war. We're no cowards!'

'I never said *they* were,' Katie wasn't quite so self-assured. 'I asked you why *you* hadn't volunteered to go and fight.'

'Well, this is just like old times, isn't it?' Molly said acidly. 'A pair of scrapping dogs, always at each other's throats. Well, that's enough of it. You're only home for a couple of days, Georgie, so I'm not standing for it. I don't want to hear another word about ships, guns or religion out of the pair of you. Do you understand me?'

They both nodded silently, Georgie tight-lipped and still red-faced. Katie went out into the yard and sat shivering on an empty upturned apple barrel, rather than stay in the same room with her brother. His words about Bob had shaken her, though. It was the first time anyone close to her had voiced such bigotry outright, but she knew it wouldn't be the last. In fact, if she were to continue to see Bob, in the end whole streets of people she'd known all her life would turn against her and it would be the same for him. Could they survive such isolation, such hatred? Only time would tell, because now she knew that if he asked her, she'd marry Bob Goodwin or stay a spinster for the rest of her life.

She was deep in thought but looked up, startled, when Jimmy Watson threw open the yard door with such force it shook on its hinges.

'What's up with you?' Katie snapped. 'You've nearly demolished the bloody door.'

'Is Georgie 'ere?' he gasped. 'Me Mam sent me ter tell 'im to go 'ome now – Josie's been took bad – an' for yer Mam ter go too.'

Katie rushed back indoors with a breathless Jimmy following. 'Georgie, you'd better get home quickly,' she said rapidly, 'Josie's been taken ill. I don't know what with, I don't know anything more except that Florrie is already on her way there.'

Georgie went pale but snatched his cap from the dresser whilst Mam slapped on a hat and started shrugging into her coat.

'Will I come too?' Katie demanded.

'No. You and our Sarah stay put until I come home. Florrie and me and him should be able to manage. Didn't they say *anything* about what was the matter?' Molly quizzed Jimmy.

'No. I think I 'eard 'im say blood, but me Mam shoved me out so quick that I didn't hear any more.'

'Oh, no! Oh, Holy Mary, Mother of God!' Molly prayed aloud.

'Mam! Mam, what *is* it?' Georgie demanded.

'It looks as though she's losing it! On second thoughts, you stay here and keep your eye on meladdo there and our Joe. Katie, Sarah, get your coats on and bring every towel you can find plus all the old newspapers we've got.'

Sarah's mouth dropped open and she started to tremble.

'Mam, let Sarah stay here,' Katie said quickly. 'Georgie can come with us. He'll not be much use but at least he'll *be* there.'

Molly took one look at a screaming, agonised Josie and the scarlet-coloured sheets, and told Katie to go for Dr Birch. Payment wasn't even given a thought at times like this. Nor would she allow Georgie to go into the room.

'Can't I do something, Mam? Boil water or things like that?' he begged. His wife's screams had unnerved him.

'There'll be no need for boiling water, lad. Warm to clean up with, but . . .' Molly shook her head sadly. 'You could tidy up a bit down here before the doctor comes – and he'll need water and soap to wash his hands and a decent towel, if you can find one.'

It was all over by the time Dr Birch arrived. He took Josie's pulse, gave her a perfunctory examination, glanced at the aborted foetus and shook his head.

'I'm afraid, Mrs Deegan, that you've lost your baby,' he said gently. 'I'm very sorry. I'll inform the District Nurse and she'll keep an eye on you, but your mother and Mrs Deegan, Senior, seem to have coped admirably and I can't see that there will be any complications. I'll leave you something to calm you down, make you sleep. You must have rest, plenty of rest.' He turned to Florrie. 'If she starts to haemorrhage, send for me immediately,' he said in a low voice.

Florrie nodded.

It was Molly who took the tiny blood-covered thing and wrapped it up in a towel. Miscarriages were not rare and neither was infant mortality. Josie was lucky, in a way – she could have gone to term and had a stillborn child. That was far, far worse. All the hours of agonising labour and nothing at the end of it but heartbreak.

'I'll take it up to the hospital, Florrie. I . . . I can't do the alternative, then I'll call to see Father Macreedy and ask him to say a few prayers.'

Florrie nodded again, the tears trickling down her cheeks. The alternative, to flush it away here, was too dreadful. The hospital would 'dispose' of the tiny body of her grandchild. Molly, she noted, had avoided using that clinical word: it would have been her first grandchild too.

'Will I come with you?' Katie asked when her mother emerged from the bedroom. She and Georgie had been standing on the landing, waiting, and for once she felt sorry for her brother. Obviously, in his own way, he did love Josie. He'd been in such a state he'd been shaking all over. She didn't know that the trembling was a recent legacy of war; that it always started when he heard screams and cries of agony from anyone.

'No, luv. But you can go in and help Florrie to clean up, although we've coped with the worst. Then when Josie's clean and comfortable, Georgie can go in.' She patted her son's arm. 'I'm sorry, lad, I really am, but it wasn't to be and maybe it's for the best. I think that maybe it's God's way of not letting a poor little baby come into the world deformed and having to suffer all its life.'

When Katie went into the bedroom she gritted her teeth and wondered how Josie could have been in a worse state. Trying to ignore the pile of blood-stained bedding in the corner of the room, she helped a silently weeping Florrie to wash Josie and pull a clean nightdress over her head. Her Mam and Florrie had already changed the bottom sheet, placing a rubber one beneath it, provided by Mrs Bennett who rented the other rooms in the house. At Florrie's request, Katie asked her brother to go down into the yard and bring up some old bricks, or anything he could find to raise the bottom of the bed. Josie was half-asleep already, as Katie bathed the sweat and tears from her friend's face and gently brushed out her tangled hair.

'She's so pale,' she whispered, tears on her own face. '*Will* she be all right, Mrs Watson?'

'With the help of God she will.'

'Shall I take those?' Katie nodded at the pile of linen.

'No, luv, you've done enough. You're only a bit of a girl to be having to do these sort of things. I'll see to them. You'd better send Georgie in now before she goes out altogether.'

Katie felt more tears prick her eyes. Poor, poor Josie. 'She's the same age as me, Mrs Watson. Just a bit of a girl.'

Molly was already home when she got back to Chelmsford Street. Sarah was crying quietly but her mother just sat staring as though in a trance, her rosary in her hands.

'I'll put the kettle on,' Katie said. 'Everything over there is as right as it can be. I just hope our Georgie looks after her properly. Where's our Joe and Jimmy Watson?'

'I sent them out to play,' Sarah sniffed.

'I expect they're round at Mary's or Ellen's,' Molly said wearily.

'So most of the neighbourhood will know soon. Oh Mam, she looked so pale and sort of . . . small. Like a doll.'

'She's never been what you'd call robust.'

'I just keep thinking of that poor little mite . . .' Sarah added, still wiping away her tears.

'Now stop that, girl, or you'll have us all in hysterics!' Molly's voice was firm. 'It's God's will, and who are we to question it?'

Sarah gradually calmed down, the room falling into silence for a while until it was interrupted by boys' voices and the barking of a dog. Joe, Jimmy Watson and Vinny Maher all trooped in, dragging with them an over-excited brown and white Springer spaniel.

'Jesus, Mary and Joseph! What's that?' Molly cried.

'It's a dog, Mam.'

'I can flaming well see that! Whose dog is it?'

'We don't know. It was running around in the jigger, I think it's lost and it's hungry.'

'And *I* think you can take it straight back where you found it. Oh, this is all we need, Joe Deegan! Get it out of here!'

'Aw, Mam,' he pleaded. 'It's lost.'

'Then take it out and look for its owner. The dog's a spaniel and probably has a pedigree as long as my arm.'

'Is it valuable then, Mrs Deegan?' Vinny asked eagerly, thinking there might be some chance of a reward.

'How should I know? Very probably, you don't see many of those around here. Try Miss Adaire or Mr Ayres, the grocer on the corner of Foley Street – they're the only two people I can think of who would be daft enough to buy a pedigree dog and then lose it. If you have no luck, take it into the Police Station.'

'If we can't find its owner, can we keep it, Mam?' Joe pleaded. 'I've got a name for it already – Rags.'

'Joe Deegan, if you, your mates and that animal aren't out of that door in two minutes, I'll kill the lot of you with my own bare hands. Get it out NOW!'

They all scattered, Joe crestfallen, the other two set on getting a reward.

'Isn't that all we need? Him wanting to keep a flaming pedigree dog.' Molly gave a huge, trembling sigh. 'Sarah, luv, be a good girl and pour me another cup of tea and see if there's any aspirin in the dresser drawer. I've got a splitting headache. It's been a long, black day that would test the faith of a Saint.'

Chapter Eleven

Josie made a slow recovery. She felt tired and depressed all the time. It was the depression that was the worst. Weeks, then months slipped by and still she hadn't the energy or inclination to go back to work.

'It's only to be expected, with Georgie away and you never knowing when he'll be home or leaving again. Oh, what a mess the country's in.' Florrie pursed her lips and shook her head.

'Mam, I don't care. I'm not interested in what kind of a state the country's in. I just want to know that Georgie's safe and that he'll always be safe.' Her eyes filled up with tears.

Florrie was really concerned. 'Oh Josie, if I could promise yer that, luv, I would – but I can't! The war is something we've all got to live with. No one wanted a war, except them Nazis, but there was no choice. We certainly don't want them over here, bossing us about. Why don't I go into town and see if I can get two tickets for that new American picture that's coming to the Gaumont? The one with Vivien Leigh in it – *Gone with the Wind*. It's all the rage. A ticket for you and one for Katie. It would cheer you up.'

Josie shrugged half-heartedly. 'It's always late when Katie gets home.'

'No, it's not, luv. It depends which shift she's on. I'll get them for when she's on earlies.'

As she spoke there was a knock on the door and Florrie got up to open it.

It was Molly.

'How is she today?' Molly mouthed the words.

'You're a bit better today, Josie, aren't you?'

Josie barely moved her head in agreement.

'I was just saying, Molly, that I'd go into town and try to get tickets for that picture *Gone with the Wind*.'

Molly looked perturbed as she sat in the armchair opposite her daughter-in-law. 'I've heard it's very romantic, but—'

'But what?' Florrie demanded, hoping the other woman wasn't going to pour cold water on the idea. Josie needed company. She needed to be taken out of herself. Couldn't Molly see that Josie needed something to do, to give her life some purpose – even if for the moment, it was only an outing to the cinema.

'Well, there's all sort of things in it. Civil War. Death, a lot of death. Soldiers and families and a little girl and there's also . . . well, it would depress you even more, Josie, luv.'

'How come you know so much of the story?' Florrie demanded, indignant at seeing her idea having cold water thrown over it.

Molly didn't want Josie to go and see a film in which Scarlett O'Hara sees her four-year-old child killed, and also suffers a miscarriage.

'Amelia Adaire told me. I got the whole lot on the way home from town, in detail. Apparently she's read the book, too – you know what she's like when she gets going. I think she put most of the women on the bottom deck of the tram off it, too, but anyway then I heard that the queues for tickets are miles long and we have enough queuing to do these days.'

Florrie was still indignant but she had to accept that if the picture was only going to upset Josie further it would be a waste of time and money.

She tried another subject. 'I was reading in the paper this morning that after that fiasco in Norway and the arguing in Parliament, Mr Churchill is to be Prime Minister.'

'Well, I hope he's better than old Chamberlain,' Molly replied grimly. 'Peace in our time, my flaming foot!'

'This Winston Churchill says he's going to tell us the truth. Straight out, no wrapping it up in fancy words or ignoring things. He said in the paper "I've got nothing to offer except blood, toil, sweat and tears." Well, you can't get much plainer than that, can you?'

Molly looked uncertainly at Josie. It was a grim message but the girl didn't appear to understand. 'Josie, did you hear what your Mam said? We've got hard days ahead and I think it would be better for everyone if you went back to work.'

'To work?' Josie seemed mystified. 'Me?'

'Yes, you, Josie. Every pair of hands is needed. You're fit and well now, just a bit depressed which is only normal, isn't it, Florrie? It'll go when you get back to the factory with the other girls.'

'She's right.' Florrie backed Molly up, glimpsing a way to drag her daughter back from the abyss of depression. 'Hard work never hurt anyone yet and you'll enjoy the company. Ask your Katie to tell them she'll be back on Monday.'

Josie didn't speak, just stared at her mother. Oh, maybe it would be the best thing. She still felt weak, but she'd have something to occupy her mind and she'd have her wages again. Georgie had had to increase the amount of money he left her and at least having her own wage

95

again she could save more. So far she'd only managed to buy a set of pans and a few odd dishes at Ray's in London Road.

'Well?'

'All right, Mam, I'll go back on Monday.'

Florrie nodded her approval and then suddenly noticed the bandage on Molly's leg.

'What's up with yer leg, luv?'

'That flaming dog bit me. I tell you, Florrie, I should be called "Harpic" because I must have been clean around the bend to let our Joe keep it.'

No owner had been traced for the spaniel, although the police had kept it for a week. Then Joe and Sarah had begged and pleaded with their mother to let them have it. It would be put down, otherwise – pedigree or no pedigree, the Station Sergeant had stated. 'It's a police station we're running, not a flaming zoo!' he'd added.

'Oh, please, Mam? They'll kill it,' Sarah had urged.

'An' Vinny said their kid told him they 'ave a glass tank with an 'ole in it for their head an' they gas them!'

'Ah Mam, you can't let them do that to the poor thing!' Sarah had tears in her eyes.

'Oh, all right – but I'm not having any mess in the yard. You take it for walks on a leash and clean up after it, I've enough on me plate,' she said. It was a decision she soon regretted.

'I'll admit it did surprise me, you keeping it,' Florrie nodded now. 'We never found out how it came to be roaming around the back jiggers.'

'Well, I've got a good idea. The damned thing is so inbred it's mad, raving mad. I reckon whoever owned it had had enough and just dumped it. I wish to God I could dump it too. I've told our Joe, if it goes for anyone else, that's it. Out it goes, one way or another.'

Molly gingerly patted the bandage on her leg and winced. 'It was like a flaming circus in our back yard,' she told the other two women. 'No one could get near the wash-house, let alone the privy. Jem Cargill finally managed to get it cornered with a chair, like they do with wild animals at Chipperfield's. I don't know what set it off but it was foaming at the mouth, Florrie! I tell you, you could see the whites of its eyes. Then our Sarah came out and it seemed to calm down. She's got it even dafter the way she treats it, but anyway it quietened down and I thanked Jem and he went home. Our Sarah was sitting on the back step stroking it and talking to it and it seemed dead placid, like. But then as I went into the back kitchen, didn't the bloody thing go for me? Bit me on the leg. Well, I'd had enough, Florrie, so I battered it with the carpet-beater.'

'Didn't that set it off again?'

'No, it got under the table and sulked. It wouldn't even come out for our Sarah, despite madam crawling on her hands and knees after it. It's more damned trouble than it's worth.'

'Don't you think you should have Dr Birch take a look at your leg? Bites can get infected, you know.'

'No, it's not that bad,' Molly confessed. 'I've had far worse – it's just a scratch really. I washed it straight away and our Sarah bandaged it. It doesn't hurt, just throbs a bit now and then. Are you going to the Novena at St Mary of the Angels, Fox Street, tonight?'

'I am and you should come too, Josie,' said Florrie bossily. 'It won't do you any harm to say some formal prayers for a Special Intention. Your 'usband's safety.'

Josie nodded her agreement sullenly. She'd get no peace otherwise, and maybe a formal novena – specific prayers to a specific Saint said at a specified time or day – might work.

Florrie and Molly rose together. 'Do yourself up a bit, luv, it'll make you feel better,' Florrie advised.

'You mean it'll make *you* feel better, Mam.'

Florrie glanced at Molly. At last Josie's voice had a bit of light and shade in it now. 'I'll come round for you at seven, then,' she said. 'Bye for now, luv.'

Once outside Florrie turned to Molly.

'I'm so glad you came round. I've been trying to get her to do *something* for weeks.'

'She'll be all right now, Flo,' Molly said comfortingly. 'Once she's back at work with the girls she'll be right as rain, which is more than can be said for the state of the country! God Almighty, now isn't the time for the flaming politicians to be arguing and falling out. Thank God we've got someone down there in London with a bit of sense at last.'

Florrie drew her shawl closer to her body. 'I tell you, Molly, they're like kids, that lot in Parliament. Give the running of the country over to us women and we'd soon have it sorted. I wonder sometimes if they could win an argument, let alone a war, but we're stuck with them now – all of 'em.'

Both Katie and Vi welcomed the news that Josie was going back to work. They called to see her on their way home.

'It's better than sitting here on your own,' Katie said cheerily. 'We get *Music While You Work* now over the tannoy system and *Forces' Favourites*. It's great.'

'It's still shifts, though. I hate shifts,' Vi complained.

'It's better now that the evenings are lighter, Vi. At least we're not going or coming home in the dark. I got so fed up with tripping over things, my shins were black and blue, and God alone knows how many pairs of stockings I've ruined.' Katie looked down at her legs to see if there was any proof left.

'Me Mam said she's fed up to the back teeth with queuing. There's hardly any time left in the day for everything else, the house is a real tip. And as for the flaming blackout curtains, she's mithered to death with Tommy Rigby, the warden. He's always yelling and bawling at people. That bit of power has gone straight to his head. He thinks he's God. One day someone will thump him and I wouldn't put it past me Mam to have a go at 'im with the yard brush.' Both girls tittered appreciatively at the thought.

'I suppose we're lucky really,' Katie said ruminatively. 'The papers are full of the fighting in Belgium and Holland, and I'm sure Bob's going to be sent overseas soon.'

Vi sighed. Jack was on board *HMS Victor*, a cruiser on convoy duty. 'Then she'll know what real worry is, won't she Josie?' she said. At this, Josie's face crumpled.

'I thought we came around to cheer her up, not depress her?' Katie admonished. 'Josie, guess what? Vi's going to teach me how to make a frock.'

'I'm going to *try*, but we both might need your help, Josie. I'm all right at sewing braid and bits of ribbon on things to smarten them up, but I've never tried a whole frock. I've borrowed a Butterick paper pattern from one of the girls in work but I don't want to waste good money and coupons on material by making a right mess of it.'

'I'll help you,' Josie said quietly. 'There's not much to it really, if you follow the instructions. Are you going to do it by hand?'

'What do you mean?' Katie looked puzzled; she knew so little about sewing. Her mother sent all their mending, patching, turning-up hems and the like to a little old Irish lady who didn't charge much. It was easier than having them try to cobble things, she said. Katie caught an equally puzzled glance from Vi.

'By hand or on a sewing machine, you pair of idiots,' Josie explained.

'Who's got a sewing machine?' Vi asked.

'My Mam has.'

'Josie, we can't all go round to yer Mam's, now can we? She'd murder us. We'd have the place all messed up,' Vi stated, as though she were explaining something to a small child.

Katie interrupted: 'And you know what she's like about that.'

'Well, we could bring it around here,' Josie suggested. Vi was right. Her houseproud Mam *would* go mad if they invaded the place and left pins, cottons, bits of material and paper patterns all over the place.

'How?'

Josie's brow furrowed as she searched for a solution. 'I'll ask Uncle Ernie and Uncle Norm to stick it on a handcart and bring it round.'

'Would they mind? I mean, they're both going hell for leather down at the docks all day and I bet the last thing they want is to be shoving a sewing machine on a handcart around the streets.'

'They won't mind, Vi – and even if they do Mam will have a few words in the right ears.' Josie smiled knowingly.

'You know, that's the first time I've seen you smile for months,' Katie stated, delighted. 'Here, you don't reckon there'd be enough material left over for a turban, do you?'

'Katie Deegan, what on earth d'you want a matching turban for?' Vi looked appalled. 'We have to wear the flaming things for work and that's bad enough. You should see the way I have to brush my hair to get it halfway decent to go out after I've had a turban on all day!'

'You could make a bag to match,' Josie suggested. 'You know, one of those little drawstring ones, and you could cut the brims down on the hats you wore for the wedding and make strips of bias to trim them with. You'd have a nice outfit.'

'That sounds dead complicated. *Bias?* I've never even taken up a hem.' Katie was looking dubious.

'My hat's yellow,' Vi complained.

'Get a dye from Compton's, the Ironmongers on Stanley Road, and dye it green.'

'Won't the blue-bag do? Blue and yellow make green, don't they? Can't I just dip it in after Mam's finished doing the whites?'

Now it was Josie's turn to explain patiently: 'Yes, Vi, yellow and blue *do* make green – but the blue-bag isn't strong enough. Besides, if you get caught out in the rain it'll run and a nice sight you'd look then. Where are you going for your material?'

'We thought Blackler's or T.J.'s.'

'T.J.'s used to have some Miss Muffett prints. They'd look nice for summer, or gingham – that always looks fresh. I'll come with you,' Josie said excitedly. 'It'll be great to have something new to wear when Georgie gets home, and it won't cost much either.'

Katie looked at Vi with relief.

'Well, thank God she seems to be getting back to normal,' she said, once they were out in the street. 'Mam's been worried to death and so has Florrie. Mind you, I didn't see our Georgie doing much worrying last time he was home.'

They linked arms companionably.

'Some men don't,' Vi shrugged.

'And some do. When Bob was on his last leave, he said he thought Josie looked terrible. Thinner and drawn and ten years older.'

Vi sighed. Who was she to tell Katie to give him up? There was a war on. Who knew what would happen to the men? Or girls, too, for that matter . . .

The sewing party was well under way. Material had been bought, the pattern pinned on and then cut out and they were all at the tacking stage. The Singer treadle sewing machine stood in one corner of Josie's living room, with a cloth over it when not in use. Florrie had declared she'd be glad to see the back of it, as someone was always catching their foot or big toe on the cast-iron treadle. It would give her more room and would be one less item to dust and polish.

They all complained bitterly at the precious coupons they had to hand over for the material, because Josie had persuaded them to get an extra half yard to use for other things.

'Oh, stop moaning. It'll be useful, you'll see.'

'You mean for bias trims or bags?' Vi asked, looking pained. She'd calculated that she might just have enough coupons left for a single pair of precious stockings, if she could find someone with a pair to sell, that is.

'Well, actually, I had a sleeveless bolero in mind. They look really nice over plain frocks or blouses.'

'Oh, for heaven's sake, Josie,' Katie groaned, 'let's just get the frocks done first before we tackle anything else, especially boleros!'

Josie was delighted that her own dress at least was finished by the time Georgie came home. Vi's wasn't, but then Vi had more clothes than either herself or Katie.

'It only needs a bit of finishing off,' she'd consoled Vi.

When Georgie walked into the room she'd thrown her arms around his neck, crying, 'Oh, thank God you're home! I know you can't let me know, but . . . oh, it's great!'

After he'd kissed her and disentangled himself from her embrace, he slung his kitbag down on the floor. It was extremely heavy, being half-full of tinned food. He'd take some round to Mam later, but he was going to keep the rest. He'd decided that with the risks he took, he was entitled to make some money on the side. Blackmarketeering was against the law, but what was a few tins here and there?

'Well, you certainly look better, Josie.'

'Oh, I am. I'm back at work and Katie, Vi and me have been making summer frocks. Mine's finished so I'll be able to wear it when – if – we go out.'

'Great. We'll go to Otterspool, have a nice walk along the front there.'

It wasn't what she had in mind, nor was it a 'nice' walk. The place was known locally as 'The Cazzy' or the cast-iron shore because of the amount of old scrap there was along it. Mind you, it had been cleared of all that now, so she'd heard, as every bit of scrap metal was needed for tanks and planes. It still didn't appeal to her though.

'What about Calderstones Park?' she suggested. 'It's very pleasant there, so I've heard. The people who live in that area are dead posh.'

He kissed her forehead. 'OK – why not? We're as good as any of them. I'll wear me best suit and you can dazzle 'em with your new frock.' At least his wife was clever at things like sewing, Georgie thought, and she did always look neat and respectable without costing him a fortune either.

Josie smiled up into his face, happy again for a while.

Katie was far from happy; she had begun to be worried about her Mam. She'd noticed Molly limping a week ago, but when she asked what was the matter, Molly told her it was just a bit of stiffness and sometimes cramp. But now Mam didn't look well at all.

'When I came in, she was sitting on the sofa and she looked terrible,' Sarah informed her. She and Katie were on different shifts, this particular week, and had barely had a chance to catch up with each other.

Katie resolutely made up her mind. 'Then I'm getting the doctor in, right now. I don't care what she says. And I'll pay him too. In fact, I'm not even going to tell her I'm sending for Dr Birch.'

Molly wasn't very pleased at all when Dr Birch arrived.

'There's nothing wrong with me, Doctor. Our Katie had no business sending for you. Dragging you down here for nothing!'

'Well, seeing as she did, let me have a look at you.'

Molly reluctantly let her chest and heart be listened to through his stethoscope, and replied curtly to his questions. 'I'm just a bit off-colour, that's all. That flaming dog had a go at me of course. But I bathed it well.'

He examined the wound which was healing. 'Well, that seems to be fine. If it continues to bite I'd seriously consider having it put down.'

'I will, it's flaming mad. I reckon it's too inbred but I'd have murder with our Joe and Sarah if I said it was going on a one-way trip to the police station.' Molly sighed and smiled wryly. 'Kids and animals.'

Dr Birch nodded understandingly as he straightened up. 'Just off colour, Mrs Deegan, I agree.'

'She's off-colour, all right,' Katie interrupted, less than reassured.

Molly ignored her. 'Doctor, there's a war going on. I've a son on the convoys and I know you've got a lad in the RAF, so let's worry about them and not about trifling ailments that are probably due to getting older. Now, how much do I owe you?'

'Nothing, Mrs Deegan.' The doctor put away his stethoscope.

'We'll just treat this as a social call, shall we? I really can't see much wrong. Slight rise in temperature, leg a little stiff. Could be a touch of rheumatism. It's been damp, lately.'

'No, I insist. I always pay my way,' Molly said, wincing as she put her shoe back on. 'I believe that the labourer is worthy of his hire, and your time and experience are precious.'

'Then just two shillings for the house visit.' He wished more of his patients held her views.

'You really are sure there's nothing seriously wrong?' Katie asked as she showed him out, seeking reassurance.

'She's worried – like everyone else is – and she's run-down, working too hard – like everyone else is. I could give her a tonic, but would she take it?'

'No, she's too stubborn. She'll say *that's* a waste of money as well.'

Dr Birch raised his hat and left, but Katie still wasn't altogether happy.

Georgie's visit was greeted with cries of delight and relief by Molly and Sarah.

'Now perhaps you'll buck up, Mam. She's not been well,' Katie informed him.

'What's the matter, Mam?'

'Nothing, but madam there called the doctor out. He's a good man, Dr Birch, he didn't want to charge, but I insisted. How are you, son?' She embraced him tenderly. 'I go every week to the Novena at Fox Street for you and so do Josie and Florrie.'

'I'm all right, Mam, just tired. You can never sleep properly at sea – it's murder on your nerves. But Josie's much better now, the weather's warmer and we're going out to Calderstones tomorrow.'

'That'll do her good. Did you manage to get anything?'

He grinned and placed two tins of cooked ham, two of corned beef and one tin of peaches on the table.

'Is that all?' Katie demanded.

'Yes. it's becoming harder and harder to get stuff in now.' There were four tins of corned beef at home, concealed in a drawer beneath his underclothes until he could find a proper place for them. With luck, he'd build up a stock, and then he'd need someone to sell the goods for him. Someone he could trust and who wouldn't ask too many questions . . .

'Oh, peaches! Peaches!' Sarah gloated.

'They're for Christmas, luv. They're not to be opened until then.'

'Oh, Mam!' both girls cried, but Molly was adamant. 'I said Christmas and I mean Christmas.'

On Georgie's way out, Katie caught his arm and drew him down the yard to the far back door. 'Mam's really not well, Georgie. She put that "bright as a button" act on just for you.'

'Well, what's the matter with her? I thought she looked all right.'

'She's got a terrible colour and she keeps sitting down, as though she were about to faint. And that leg is still stiff.'

'But Dr Birch said there was nothing wrong, didn't he?'

'I know, but she was annoyed and wouldn't really tell him anything. He gave her just a brief examination and then said he could give her a tonic, but he couldn't force her to take it. You know what she's like, she'd only pour it down the sink.'

'She's right, it would be a waste of money.'

'I think we should get a second opinion,' Katie said bravely. 'Arrange for a specialist to come and see her.'

Georgie stared at his sister in amazement. 'Are you stark raving mad? Do you know how much those fellers up in Rodney Street charge – that's if they'll come at all!'

'It's *Mam*, Georgie. I don't care how much it costs.'

'Well, I do and she will too. She'll go bananas!'

'Too bad. I'm going to go and see Dr Birch and ask him to recommend someone.'

'And all you'll get from him is a flea in your ear! He's said there's nothing wrong and then you, an ignorant bit of a girl and dead hardfaced too, go and ask for a second opinion! A flaming specialist, too!'

'So what! We're doing the paying, at least our Sarah and me will, you won't have to put your hand in your pocket!'

'Go on then, waste your money – but I bet he throws you out when you go round there demanding specialists from Rodney Street to come out to Chelmsford Street!'

Chapter Twelve

Georgie's prediction was right. She'd gone to the surgery on Stanley Road and waited until Dr Birch had seen everyone else. She herself wasn't ill; she'd come to see the doctor about her Mam, she explained to the poker-faced receptionist.

He welcomed her in and told her to sit down, and all the time her insides felt like ice. His genial expression changed abruptly when she swallowed hard and asked would it be possible for someone else to have a look at Molly? She was sure, certain that there was something really wrong. Even the fact that Georgie, her brother at sea, was home couldn't dispel it. Mam looked awful and she was just dragging herself around. Every chore was a terrible effort. She'd said a few times now that her legs and arms were stiff.

'You have the audacity . . . the sheer insolence, to sit there and imply that my diagnosis is wrong, young lady?' snapped Dr Birch before she'd had a chance to explain exactly how her mother had deteriorated.

'No! No, Dr Birch, it's not like that at all!'

'It looks very *much* like that from my point of view! Your mother is a healthy woman, always has been. She's had good food and plenty of exercise all her life. She recovered amazingly well after her confinement with your brother Joseph and she wasn't a young woman then. At her age it's not unusual to have a bit of rheumatism in the joints. Life is not easy for anyone these days. She has your elder brother's safety to worry about, a business to run, you and your sister to think about, to say nothing of Joseph and the hopes she has for his chance of a place at St Francis Xavier's College. If her nerves are not all they should be, is it really so surprising?'

'I know all that, Doctor, but I just *feel* that there is something else terribly wrong.'

'Like what? Do you have a Degree in Medicine that you've neglected to tell anyone about? Or perhaps psychic powers? I don't think Father Macreedy would look on anything of that nature with much favour.'

He sounded so scornful that by now she was almost in tears. 'I don't know anything about special powers, but it's my MAM! I told you, she's started to complain about feeling stiff in her arms and legs and she's having more cramps – really bad. She tries to hide it, but at night I've heard her moaning in pain. In the day she just passes them off as having slept awkwardly or been in a draught, but I've seen her taking aspirin and she hardly ever takes pills.' She could see by the expression on his face he was taking no notice of what she was telling him. 'Don't you understand? Please, please, help!'

He stood up. 'There's the door, Miss Deegan, close it after you and don't come wasting my precious time again or insulting my intelligence, integrity or profession. If I thought your mother needed another opinion, she would have one!'

Tears slipped silently down her cheeks as she left the surgery. Maybe she was wrong and Georgie was right. Oh, how she prayed that he was . . .

She had to pass St John's Church on her way home to Chelmsford Street so she went inside for a minute. It was cool and the perfume of lilac blossom hung heavily on the air. She went up the side aisle to the rail in front of the altar to Our Lady, and knelt down. She crossed herself slowly and looked up at the statue. The Madonna was dressed in a long white robe over which was a blue mantle that covered her head. Beneath her bare foot a serpent lay crushed and vanquished. Her hands were stretched out, palms upwards and there was a beatific smile on her gentle face.

'Oh, Holy Mother, Mary, please don't let there be anything seriously wrong with Mam, and if there is, let her get better. We've lost Da, so please don't take Mam, too. However would I manage without her? Please, Holy Mother?' She said a decade of the rosary, then stood and lit a candle, placing her penny in the box. She genuflected before the main altar and then walked slowly down the centre aisle.

Vi came round to ask if she could borrow Katie's white handbag. Jack was taking her to the Empire, no less!

Her expression changed when she noticed the tears in her friend's eyes. 'What's up?'

Katie told her.

'He *must* be right,' Vi pointed out. 'He's very clever and he's had years of being a doctor. And, like he said, your Mam is worried about everything and everyone, and she's not getting any younger. We forget that our parents are getting on – that they're middle-aged.'

'I know, but she's not well,' Katie's voice trailed off. 'I suppose I'll just have to believe him.'

'You will, luv. You *must* or you'll drive yourself mad.'

Katie managed a smile. 'So, the Empire, is it? Mixing with the high and mighty now, are we? I don't suppose you know when they're due to sail again?'

'No, I don't – and I don't want to know either, although I suspect they have some idea. Jack said it's getting worse now. They're losing too many ships and men and precious cargoes.'

Katie nodded; she read the newspapers. 'Well, go on out and enjoy yourself. Our Sarah will be in soon and our Joe has masses of homework. I just hope he gets that scholarship! It'll do Mam the world of good if he passes.'

'Oh, he'll pass it all right,' Vi told her. 'He's a real little clever clogs on the quiet. Bone idle, of course, but he'll do well for himself, Katie, without either you or your Mam worrying over him.'

After she'd gone, Katie felt more reassured. Vi was right. She *had* to believe Dr Birch or she'd drive herself mad.

It was nearly dawn the next morning when she woke with a start, but not knowing why. She'd not slept well at all, Molly's deteriorating health firmly entrenched in her subsconscious mind. Twice during the night she'd got up and gone to her mother's room. Each time she'd crossed to the bed and looked down at Molly who lay perfectly still, her eyes closed. Each time Katie had leaned over to reassure herself that her Mam was breathing. She had been, but in a shallow sort of way. It didn't seem to be distressing her so after a few minutes Katie had gone back to bed but she'd still tossed and turned and worried. She sat up, wide awake. Sarah was still fast asleep in the other bed. Was it a noise – an unfamiliar sound that had woken her? She listened hard but the house was silent and there was no movement in the street outside. It was even too early for the milkman. For no apparent reason, Katie felt cold, icy cold. There was something wrong. *Something very wrong.*

She got up and opened the door quietly so as not to disturb Sarah, then crept along the landing to Molly's room. She'd left the door slightly open after her nocturnal visit so she would hear if Mam called out. She stood for a few seconds peering into the half-light of the room before she realised that her mother was awake.

'Katie, I can't move, luv. My legs, back, arms and shoulders.' Her breathing was very laboured.

'Don't speak, Mam, save your breath. I'm going to get our Sarah to get the Doctor.' Katie's heart was hammering against her ribs with fear. Mam was paralysed, that's why she had appeared to be sleeping peacefully when she'd checked during the night. Oh, she'd *known* something was very wrong and all this time everyone had ignored her.

She shook Sarah frantically. 'It's Mam, Sarah! Mam's very bad. She's paralysed. Go to Dr Birch,' then she changed her mind. This was *his* fault. 'Go and phone for an ambulance, tell them to be quick, it's very urgent.'

'Oh, God! Katie she's not going to die is she?' Sarah cried out, sheer terror in her eyes.

'Just GO, Sarah. Please. Run, but on your way back knock for Mary Maher.'

Before Sarah could reply Katie had dashed out of the room.

Joe was standing on the landing rubbing the sleep from his eyes.

'What's up?'

Katie caught him by the shoulders and shook him.

'Get dressed and get down to the church. Tell them to come quickly. Mam's very ill. Go on, hurry up.'

Fear filled Joe's eyes as Katie's words sunk in.

As he fled back to his room Sarah, feet bare and pulling a dress over her head, shot down the stairs. Katie went back into Molly's room.

'Mam, Mam can you hear me?' she pleaded.

Molly's eyes opened and she tried to smile.

'Our Sarah's gone for the ambulance and Mary Maher. I've sent our Joe for the Priest but you'll be fine, Mam. You *will* once they get you to hospital. You can't give up. You've always been strong. You've always been a fighter. They'll all be here soon, Mam. Just hang on, please?'

Molly's throat had constricted and her words were disjointed. 'Sarah and . . . Joe . . . look . . . after.'

'Don't, Mam. Save your strength.' Katie pleaded.

'Georgie . . . don't trust . . . Georgie.'

Molly's jaw had locked, she couldn't speak. She was barely breathing.

Katie began to cry. 'Mam! Mam don't die. Don't leave us alone. I can't manage without you. I can't, not with the war as well.'

Sarah ran breathlessly into the room and clung to the brass bedstead.

'The ambulance is coming, Katie. From Stanley Hospital it will be here any minute. Mrs Maher's on her way too.'

Katie looked up at her and shook her head. 'Our Joe's gone for the priest.'

'No! She can't die.' The younger girl sobbed. 'She'll get well once she's had Extreme Unction, the last rites, lots of people do.'

Katie took both her mother's hands in her own. They were stiff, the fingers rigid. Molly was still breathing but the sound was very faint and intermittent.

Through her tears, Katie glanced at her sister and knew that, from now on, she would have to look out for Sarah. 'Go and get the things ready,' she whispered. 'A bowl of water and a clean white cloth, the candles and the crucifix. Put them all on the little table in Joe's room, but bring it in here first.' All the time she was speaking she could feel her Mam slipping quietly away. She could feel the life ebbing from the hands she clung to so tightly, as though by such pressure she could stop death's progress.

When Sarah had left, she turned back to her mother and she knew that Mam had gone. She was alone now. They all were. Her Mam had gone to her rest and to join Da, that's what she'd have to tell Joe. She laid her cheek against Molly's. It was warm but she knew the soul had gone. 'Oh, Mam! Mam!' She grieved brokenheartedly. 'I loved you so much! Why didn't you say you were ill? Why would no one listen to me?'

Father Macreedy anointed the body with sacred oil, the eyelids, lips, the nose and ears, the hands and feet, while Katie and Sarah clung together and Joe buried his head in the shawl Mary Mayer had thrown around her shoulders. The tears fell down Mary's face too. Molly Deegan had been a good friend and neighbour for many long years, and she was shocked by the suddenness of her death. Her face was grey and drawn with sorrow.

When he'd finished, the priest laid his hand on the heads of all Molly's children in turn and prayed to God to give them strength to bear their grief.

Paddy Maher had been sent for Georgie and Josie, just as life in the street was beginning to stir in the morning sunlight.

There seemed to be people in and out of the house all day, Katie thought dazedly. Ma Edgerton, Florrie and Fred Watson, Brenda and Norma. The MacCanes, Miss Adaire, the two other priests from St John's, neighbours, friends, customers. She wished they would all go away – except Vi. She just wanted to be alone, to have some peace to sob out her grief.

Eventually Vi took her hand and led her into Joe's room. He was downstairs with Jimmy Watson, Vinny Maher and Franny MacCane, none of whom knew what to do or say to comfort him.

'Oh Vi, why would no one listen to me? I *knew*!' Katie wept. 'I *told* them all! Our Georgie, Dr Birch – but no one would listen to me!'

'What was it, Katie?'

'Tetanus, they said. A kind of poisoning from that dog-bite.'

'Where is that sodding lunatic of an animal?' Vi's voice was harsh.

'Paddy Maher took it to the police station and told them to put it down. Vi, what am I going to do now? How will I manage? You know what our Sarah's like.'

'She's much better since she started in munitions, Katie. She'll be all right. I promise you she will.'

'And Joe? How can I get him to take that scholarship now?'

'Stop worrying about things like that, luv. There will be time for all that . . . later.'

'Oh Vi, I wish . . . I wish Bob were here. I miss him so much!'

Vi took her friend in her arms and held her while she sobbed, her own tears falling down on Katie's dark curls. No matter how much the poor girl wanted her boyfriend to comfort and console her, the last person they needed in this house right now was Bob Goodwin. His religion alone would cause an eruption of anger borne of grief and shock that she dreaded even to think about, but she couldn't say that to Katie.

'He'll get a bit of leave soon. It's all going to be all right. It is, honestly!' Vi tried to sound convincing but knew it was impossible. She, too, was shocked and upset.

Eventually everyone departed, except Vi and Jack, Georgie and Josie. The funeral arrangements would be made by Georgie and Uncle Alfred. Father Macreedy had sent a telegram and Uncle Alfred had phoned the presbytery to say he would come over the next day.

'He'll want the best of everything. It'll cost a fortune,' Georgie said glumly.

Katie raised her head from Vi's shoulder and looked at him with red puffy eyes. '*She'll* have the best. She deserves it.'

Georgie was annoyed. 'Did I say she wouldn't?' He got to his feet and began to pace up and down. 'I've a good mind to sue that bloody Birch feller!' he brooded. 'What kind of a doctor does he call himself? He's not fit to be treating people – should be struck off. Nothing wrong with her! He could give her a tonic! He can't even spot the signs of tetanus poisoning.'

This was too much for Katie. She struggled to free herself from Vi's embrace. '*You've* got a mind to sue him? YOU! *You, Georgie Deegan!* But you sneered at me, remember? You said I was a fool! And now YOU want to sue. Well, you won't, because it won't bring Mam back. I should never have listened to you. I should have just gone and got another doctor. Gone up to Rodney Street myself, but no, YOU said there was nothing wrong! Between you, you and Dr Birch killed our Mam. His mistake was bad enough, but *yours* was worse! A waste of money, you said! If you'd have backed me up and paid out, then Mam might be alive now.'

Vi caught hold of her. 'Stop it! Stop it, Katie! It's not right! Do you think she'd want you screaming at each other and her lying upstairs hardly cold? No, she wouldn't, so hush and you, Georgie Deegan, keep your opinions about suing to yourself. No one wants to hear them!'

She paused, relieved her words seemed to have sunk in. 'Do you want me to stay over tonight, Katie?' she offered quietly.

The other girl nodded. Vi would help to keep them all calmer. Herself, Sarah and Joe.

Georgie got up and took Josie's hand. 'Then we'll be off.'

'I'll walk with you,' Jack offered, picking up his hat and kissing Vi lightly on the forehead.

When they'd gone, Katie turned to her friend. 'Do you know what she said to me, Vi . . . when . . . before . . .'

'What?'

'She said, "Look after our Sarah and Joe, but watch *him*. Watch your back with Georgie".'

Vi nodded. He wasn't anyone's idea of a loving son or husband, except Josie's – and surely even she must be having her eyes opened now. He was sly and crafty and he always had been. Had Katie agreed, he'd have tried to sue Dr Birch, if he thought there'd be any money to be made from it. Money, which if he had backed Katie up and paid for a specialist, could have saved Molly Deegan's life . . .

Vi made a mental note to write to Bob Goodwin in the morning to ask him not to go rushing for compassionate leave to attend the funeral, it would only cause trouble, but that Katie would need his support when it was all over.

The day that Molly Deegan was laid to rest with her husband in Kirkdale Cemetery, the war news was as bad as it could be. The German Army had overrun Holland, Belgium and northern France, and the British Expeditionary Force had been compelled to retreat. They'd fought their way to the coast of France, to a small town called Dunkirk, and now there was nowhere else for them to go except back to Britain. But between them and home lay the Channel. Every available ship was called on to sail across to evacuate them and the French troops who'd fought alongside them.

No one in Chelmsford Street thought much about the disastrous situation, at least that day. Curtains were closed, people stood lining the pavement all the way to the church, which was packed with neighbours, friends and customers. Georgie and Josie followed the hearse in a black car with Alfred Deegan, who wore a morning suit, a white stiff-winged collar and black tie, and carried a silk top hat. In the next car were Katie and Sarah, wearing the black outfits and veils they'd worn for their father's funeral, together with Vi and Joe.

Although flowers were expensive, there were wreaths for Molly from people they barely knew. There'd been collections in the streets around the neighbourhood to pay for them. Molly Deegan had been greatly respected.

Vi had her arm around Joe's shoulder. The young lad looked pale and bewildered as though he didn't know where he was going or why, and he clung to Vi like a limpet. Ever since Mam had died and Paddy Maher had taken Rags to the police station, he'd been riddled with guilt. He was the one who'd brought the dog home. He'd begged and pleaded to keep it, although it had been mad, as Mam kept saying. It was such an unpredictable animal – you couldn't trust it. It would lick your hand one minute and snap at it the next. Sarah seemed to be the only one it had taken to. So it was his fault that Mam had died.

He'd gone to Father Murray in tears and told him the sad tale, yet when he'd finished there was no tirade of wrath or condemnation. Instead, Father Murray said: 'It wasn't your fault, son, any of it. You must believe that. God wanted your mother, Joe. She'd earned her eternal rest and peace, and He works in mysterious ways. The dog was immaterial and its temperament wasn't its fault. Go home, lad, you've nothing to blame yourself for. Don't feel guilty.' But he did.

Next to Joe at the graveside stood Katie, fighting back a wave of panic and grief. This was even worse than Da's funeral had been, she thought: the crowds at Mass, many of them weeping, the cemetery and the open grave . . . Father Macreedy with the black stole around his neck over his starched white surplice, sprinkling holy water on top of the coffin where Mam lay. No, not Mam, just the empty shell of her body. Her spirit lived on, her soul was with God.

It was a dream. A nightmare, it had to be. Katie couldn't breathe. Soon she would wake up and everything would be back to normal, she thought feverishly, but as the earth was pressed into her hand and she heard the awful sound of the first sod falling on to the coffin, reality struck her. It *wasn't* a dream. She would never wake up. Things would never be the same, ever again. A cry of utter anguish broke from her lips.

The small reception at Lyon's, in the Old Haymarket which faced St John's Gardens, was paid for by Uncle Alfred, who was staying at the Stork Hotel in Queen's Square until tomorrow. It was a quiet affair, that broke with the tradition of having the 'funeral tea' at the deceased's house.

The room was very warm but the conversation-level was no louder than a buzz. Alfred had made sure everything was conducted with a decorum that was sometimes missing from Catholic funerals. Alfred Deegan was a man of some standing and wealth, shrewd, studious and meticulous, totally unlike his brother Bill, except for a streak of generosity and a sense of fair play. Katie was grateful for his solid support throughout.

Vi had made her drink two glasses of sherry, and now her head was beginning to thump.

'Vi, I feel awful,' Katie said shakily. 'I've got a terrible headache.'

'It won't be long now, luv. People will soon start to leave.' Vi looked around at the small groups, the priests in conversation with Uncle Alfred, the Mahers and MacCanes looking awkward in these rather grand surroundings. Then there was Josie's family, including Fred and Florrie's sisters and brothers. Joe was sitting in a corner, still tearful and bewildered, whilst his mates were tucking unrestrainedly into the food.

'Vi,' Katie blurted out, 'I'll have to leave, get out for some air. I can't take this any longer!'

Vi looked around helplessly, trying to catch Jack's eye. He was deep in conversation with one of Mr Coyne's drivers. Finally she managed it and he excused himself and came to her side.

'Katie's not well, Jack,' she hissed. 'She's got to get some air.'

Jack tried to catch Georgie's eye. 'We ought to be going anyway, Vi. We're supposed to be aboard in half an hour. I didn't want to have to tell you just yet.'

'You mean you're sailing today?'

'Everyone is. There's hundreds of thousands of men stranded on the beach at Dunkirk, with their back to the sea and the Germans advancing on them with heavy artillery and tanks. Things are very bad, Vi.' He put his hand on her arm. 'I'm sorry to have to say all this right now, luv.'

With an effort Katie pulled herself together and went over to her uncle.

'How are you?' Alfred asked solicitously. The girl looked awful. She was deathly white and drawn, her eyes red from weeping. His heart went out to her. Of all his brother's children he liked and admired her the most, but she'd have to fill Molly's shoes now and that was no easy task for such a young woman. On the other hand, times were bad. Unlike Katie, he'd taken in today's news: if the men of the Expeditionary Force were not evacuated the country would be facing invasion with no army to defend it. Maybe in the end, as Churchill had warned, they would have to fight on the beaches, the landing grounds and in the streets . . .

'Uncle Alfred, can you— I mean . . .'

Jack had followed her over.

'What she means, sir, is can she leave? She needs some fresh air as she's not feeling well, and I'm afraid Georgie and me will have to go now, too. We sail in half an hour's time for Dunkirk. Could Mrs Maher see Sarah and Joe safely home?'

Alfred and Father Macreedy conferred and then the priest cleared his throat loudly. The small private room became silent.

'I know you'll understand that the Deegan family have all had a long, emotional and exhausting experience, and that Jack and Georgie must board their ships, they're needed desperately. So, on the family's behalf I'd like to thank you all for your kindness and your prayers, and Mr Alfred Deegan for his support and generosity.' He raised his right hand and made the Sign of the Cross over the assembly, and all heads were bowed.

'May Almighty God, the Father, the Son and the Holy Ghost, be with you now and for ever, Amen.'

Then he and Father Murray went to make the arrangements for Sarah and Joe.

Finally, Katie managed to stumble outside into the fresh air. 'Oh Vi, I thought I was going to pass out in there.'

Vi looked worried. 'I thought you were, too. Deep breaths now. Jack, you take hold of one of her arms, I'll have the other.'

'There's a tram. If we're quick we'll catch it,' Georgie announced, hoisting his kitbag, which had been left with the receptionist, on to his right shoulder, with his free hand taking Josie's arm and hurrying her across the road.

They caught the tram but it was full, so they stood for the few stops they needed to travel. There were no dry or humorous remarks from the conductor when he saw the uniforms and kitbags, and the pale, worried faces of the three girls. He waved away the money for their fares that Jack held out.

'Keep it, lad, the Corporation can afford it. I know where yer goin'. God go with yer and bring them home safe! We'll be back one day, Gerry won't have it all his own way for ever.' Over the heads of the passengers he motioned the driver to proceed to their destination without stopping. There wasn't room for anyone else anyway.

Even though she was still dazed and heartsore, Katie couldn't help but gasp along with Vi and Josie when they reached the Pier Head. The river was always busy but they'd never seen such a sight before. From Birkenhead, Seacombe, New Brighton and the lighthouse at Perch Rock across to the Prince's and George's Landing Stages, the Victoria and Trafalgar Docks, right along to the Gladstone Dock, the river was packed with ships. Liners, cargo vessels, dredgers, tugs, luggage tenders, Royal Navy ships of all sizes, the Isle of Man and North Wales boats, the Dublin and Belfast ferries, the ships of the Coast Lines that carried passengers and freight around the coast of Britain, fishing boats, private sailing yachts and the Mersey ferries.

'Oh God, is it really *that* bad?' Vi gasped.

'Half of those ships will take a couple of days to make it down to the Channel, but they've sent out everything that floats from all the

south-coast ports and from those in Bristol and South Wales too,'
Georgie said, his face set.

Josie threw her arms around him. 'Oh, take care, take care! Please,
Georgie. We . . . I . . . couldn't face—'

'Anything else,' Vi interrupted hastily, clinging to Jack. 'You, too,
Jack Milligan – take care of yourself.' She kissed him. 'Now go on, the
sooner you go the sooner you'll be back.'

Jack and Georgie kissed them all and then pushed their way towards
the landing stage, where the *Ascania, Andania*, the *Empress of Britain*
and *Empress of France*, the *Lady of Man, Manx Maid, King Orry* and
St Tudno were alongside, black smoke pouring from their funnels,
ready to cast off.

Suddenly the air was filled with the noise of steam whistles; the
buildings along the waterfront seemed to shake with it. The deep-
throated bellows that issued from the liners, the less strident ones of
the cargo ships and dredgers, the bellicose ones of the ferries, the odd
'Whoop, Whoop' of the naval ships and the mournful sound of the
fog-horns too told all those watching that this comparatively small
armada was ready to sail.

With tears pouring down their faces, the three girls clung together
while all around them men cheered and whistled and women wept
silently or sobbed brokenly.

At last Vi managed to steady her voice. 'They'll be back. They'll be
all right.' She wiped her eyes. 'Come on, if we stay here any longer
we'll never get home, the traffic will be murder.'

Vi insisted on going home with Katie, so they left Josie on the corner
of her road. The streets were deserted. Silent, dusty and empty in the
sunlight.

Ellen MacCane was sitting in the living room with Sarah. There was
no sign of Joe.

At the sight of Vi and Katie, she got up. 'I'll go now, luv. Your
Joe's with our Franny at Mary's house. She says she'll keep him
overnight, if that's all right an' if he wants to, of course?'

Katie nodded her head wearily. 'Thanks, Ellen.'

'I'll put the kettle on. Have you any aspirins?' Vi asked.

'In the drawer of the dresser. Mam always . . .' Katie choked on a
sob. She gazed around her. This wasn't 'home' any longer. It felt
different, with both of her parents gone. She looked over at the chair
by the range, Da's chair, and remembered the day Georgie had been
sitting there when she'd snatched the newspaper from his hands and
then gone for him with the rolling pin. Flashes of memory, images,
came and went with no kind of pattern or sequence. Mam's face when
Joe had demolished the Christmas tree. The look of pride when

Georgie had married Josie. Then Georgie again sitting in the chair this morning, deep in thought or sorrow or both. Was it only this morning? It seemed to have been a hundred hours ago.

Vi was in the kitchen; Katie could hear the kettle begin to whistle as it boiled on the gas ring. She wiped her eyes and got up and went into the room.

'Go and sit down – I'll bring it in,' Vi fussed. 'I've found the aspirin, so you can take a couple with your tea, an' if you don't mind I'll have one meself.'

Katie stood there in the familiar room, and her gaze was suddenly and inexplicably drawn to the sink.

'What's the matter now?' Vi asked.

Katie didn't answer. Instead she bent down and pulled back the bit of curtaining, moving the tins of Brasso, Zebbo for black-leading the range, the bleach, bottles of 'Aunt Sally' liquid soap and cans of Jeyes Fluid.

Vi bent down beside her.

'For God's sake, Katie, what's up now? What are you doing? What are you looking for?'

Katie sat back on her heels; her eyes, that a few seconds ago had been dull and dark with pain, now blazed and in their depths were tiny pin-pricks of fire.

'Mam's cashbox and the other tin box she kept her jewellery in – they're gone,' she said in shock. 'He's taken them! He's taken it all, Vi. He must have stolen the key. Mam always wore it around her neck on a chain and I know Ma Edgerton wouldn't have touched it. She wouldn't know what it was for, but *he* did! He took it from around her neck while we were all too shocked to even think straight. He's gone off with everything, Vi!'

Vi sat down on the flagged floor beside her friend, not knowing what to do. Then she took Katie's hands in her own.

'He'll be back,' she said gently, 'and you'll feel stronger then. You'll have me as a witness, too.'

'He . . . he stole it! He took it from her before she was even cold, as she was lying in her shroud!' Rage and grief combined and the words stuck in her throat.

Vi felt anger and disgust rising in her. 'God will make him pay for it, Katie, He will!' What kind of a son was he, to steal like that? she thought in horror. To coldly and calculatingly take a key on a chain from around his mother's neck. And he couldn't say he didn't want it to be buried with her; the boxes under the sink could have been levered open. Maybe he had a right to remove it, but he also had a duty to tell them all what he'd done and to share everything. Molly had left no will.

115

'He'll pay for it,' Vi promised her. 'He'll rot in hell, Katie, never fear. One day he will. And God help poor Josie, being tied for ever to a swine like that!'

Chapter Thirteen

In a determined, dogged and almost miraculous way, and by ships of every size and shape, most of the British and French soldiers were evacuated and saved from annihilation on the beach at Dunkirk. The Prime Minister had told them over the wireless, that Britain and the troops of her Empire would fight on alone, now that France had fallen.

They were huddled around the set in the living room, with Mary Maher and Ellen MacCane, to hear Mr Churchill promise that they would fight the enemy on the beaches, the landing grounds, the fields, the streets and hills. That they would never surrender. Even the King was practising shooting with a revolver, he told them; if necessary he would die at the Palace, fighting. The Queen refused to leave the Palace or the country with her daughters, unlike many wealthy women who were fleeing to Canada and America.

'An I 'ope she puts all the nobs ter shame!' Mary Maher said grimly. 'She's got more money than all of them put together, but she's not up and running off like them.'

'Nor His Majesty either,' Ellen added, with pride in her voice. 'We've got half the kings and princes from over there, over 'ere. There weren't many of *them* practisin' ter shoot or sayin' they'd die fightin'. I'm only glad that the one who married that Simpson woman and abdicated isn't King now. Weak 'e was, and weak 'e still is. Well,' she finished in a matter-of-fact way, 'there's only us now, so we'll 'ave ter gerron with it.'

Despite all the shortages and the queueing, Mary and Ellen both managed to spare a few hours per week to help the Deegans keep their shop going. Jem Cargill obtained what he could for them in the way of stock, and when the girls' shifts overlapped, one of the two older women or even Joe would go behind the counter. Business wasn't very good even though fish was still coming in from the Isle of Man and the west coast of Scotland. Trawlers from Eire, a neutral country, also brought in their catches, although it was usually to Holyhead, the nearest port from Dunlaoghaire. But catches were often small and days and times were irregular. Mr Catchpole didn't come as often now. He didn't have much time to go shooting rabbits since he was working his own land like every other farmer. Most people were now growing their own vegetables in their gardens or on the allotments, where prize dahlias and chrysanthemums usually flourished.

So far, Katie had received five letters from Bob – loving, consoling letters in which he said how desperate he was to get some leave, but because she wasn't his wife or even his fiancée, he couldn't get to see her on compassionate grounds.

'Those letters'll fall to bits and you'll 'ave ter glue them together the way you're going,' Vi predicted, as she watched her friend read them time and time again.

'I know every word off by heart, Vi, but somehow just to know that his hand has held the pen and touched the paper seems to bring him closer.' Katie even slept with the letters under her pillow.

Vi sighed deeply. 'I wish I got letters from Jack. He writes and posts them whenever they get to a port, but it takes ages, so I have to go weeks an' weeks without a word from him.'

'I know, Josie is the same and you've both got the worry of them being out there. At least Bob's still over here, and not far away in Warrington,' she replied.

Katie had fully expected that both Jack and her brother would return home after the evacuation. She was planning to have it all out with Georgie, but so far there had been no sign of them. The last letter Josie had received had been posted in Quebec. Obviously they'd sailed with a convoy from Southampton.

Josie was very upset when Katie went round to see her.

'Are you sure about this Katie?' she asked, horrified. 'It might have been moved or something . . . for safety.'

'Safety! Where to? We've searched all over the house, the yard and the shop, Josie. Your husband's taken it all right. Georgie's definitely stolen it.'

Josie bit her lip. 'He *is* the oldest and everyone was upset.'

Katie didn't pursue it; she could see her sister-in-law was nearly in tears with anxiety. 'I still don't think he should have left us without any money,' was all she said. 'The rent's got to be paid. We don't own the shop, Josie, and there's only mine and our Sarah's wages and what bit we get from the shop when we manage to get any fish.'

'I've still got a couple of pounds in the Post Office that he doesn't know about,' Josie offered.

'No, luv, keep it. It's *your* emergency money,' Katie replied wearily.

Joe had passed his scholarship, but they could never afford to send him to St Francis Xavier's now. He was delighted, of course, when

Katie told him that, unfortunately, they just couldn't find the cost of the uniform and the books. Joe wanted to carry on his education with his mates, not go to some fancy college where they all wore a daft uniform and probably spoke in posh accents.

'I'm letting Mam down, she really wanted him to go, Sarah,' she said when she'd broken the news.

'She'd understand, Katie.'

'If *he* hadn't gone off with everything, we could have managed. Now he's ruined our Joe's chances of a good career.'

Sarah had just shaken her head sadly.

But all thoughts of Joe and Georgie vanished on a bright sunlit July evening when the back door opened and Bob stood there looking smart and handsome in his uniform.

With a cry of surprise and delight, Katie threw herself into his arms. 'Why didn't you let me know? Why didn't you write? Oh, I can't believe you're here, really here!'

He kissed her for a long time and she clung to him, the weariness, the anger and grief of the last month banished.

'How long have you got?' she asked when they finally drew apart.

'Thirty-six hours, not long. Oh, I wish I could have come sooner, my love. I knew you'd be going through hell, what with your Mam and then him legging it off with everything.'

She took his hand and drew him into the living room. Sarah was at work and so was Josie; fortunately she and Vi were on the same shift. Only Joe sat reading a tatty comic borrowed from Vinny. He looked up as they came into the room.

'Here, make your name Walker,' Bob instructed him, 'an' I'll give you a tanner to scarper.'

'A tanner?' Joe was indignant.

Bob dug into his pocket. 'Oh, all right, a shilling. Now hoppit for a few hours – there's some things I want to talk about with your sister.'

Joe smirked, pocketed the money and disappeared into the yard.

'You should have made him take the sixpence,' Katie said sternly. 'You're too generous and I don't want him getting any of our Georgie's ways.'

'He won't, and it was worth it.' Bob smiled as he drew her down on the sofa and held her in his arms.

She laid her head against his chest and gave a long sigh. 'Oh, I've missed you so much. I'm worn out most of the time, what with going to market with Mr Cargill, the journey to work, the work itself, the shop, the housework and the queueing, but I still think of you all the time.'

'I think of you, too, luv. Any word or sign of your Georgie?'

'No. Josie had a letter posted in Canada, but that was nearly two weeks ago. I couldn't believe what he'd done, Bob. I still can't sometimes. *I* was too upset to even think about anything like keys or Mam's bits and pieces.'

'You were, he wasn't. He's cold, calculating, ruthless and utterly selfish, Katie.'

'I know. I've always known it, but no one else would believe me. Even now Josie insisted he only took the things for safekeeping, and that when he gets home everything will be shared out. But it won't, of course.'

Bob stroked her hair. If he ever got his hands on Georgie Deegan, he knew what *he'd* do to him. But for now, there was something more important he had to do.

'I came home to ask you something, Katie, something important.'

She looked up at him, her dark brows drawn together, a question-ing look in her eyes.

'Think hard before you answer, luv. In fact, you don't even need to give me an answer at all yet. You see, it's a big decision.' He took both her hands. 'Will . . . will you marry me, Katie Deegan?'

She didn't stop to think, the words bubbled out. 'Yes! Oh, yes! I'll marry you, Bob! I love you so much.'

'You realise what it will mean?' He looked solemn.

She nodded. 'Yes. We'll both be . . . outcasts.'

'Can you stand that?'

'I've lost my Mam and Dad and everything they worked so hard for,' she said sadly. 'Yes, I can stand it. I don't care about anyone else, just you.'

'It may not be so bad, what with the war and me being away . . .'

'Away where?' she asked, with a feeling of dread.

'We haven't been told yet, but there are rumours going around that it will be North Africa.'

Her heart dropped, and tears sprang to her eyes. 'When?'

'The first week in August, but don't worry, they'll give me leave before then, to get married! It will have to be at Brougham Terrace though, Katie.'

She nodded slowly. The Register Office. Legal in the eyes of the law but not in the eyes of her Church, and she couldn't, *wouldn't*, for the sake of Molly's memory, get married in his church. She realised, too, that he wouldn't agree to be married in St John's, and anyway there wasn't time. It would mean he would have to change his religion entirely, and there would be hours of instruction to be undertaken for that. Besides, she'd never ask him to become a convert, not just so they could get married. That wasn't what it was all about.

As he held her in his arms, she struggled with her emotions. Mam would have been broken-hearted, if she had been alive and so would

Da. In fact, they'd probably have forbidden it altogether. As it was, she'd have to face the wrath of Father Macreedy and the denunciation of the Catholic Church, then the condemnation of everyone she knew, probably even Sarah and Vi and Josie.

'I know what I'm asking of you, but I love you and I'll be going off to fight soon.'

She placed her fingers over her lips. 'Don't! I love you, Bob, and I don't care what anyone says, not even Father Macreedy. We'll worry about them all when the war is over. Have you told your Mam and Dad?'

'No, not yet, but there's going to be one almighty row when I do, and if I get thrown out, can I stay here until I have to go back?'

She nodded. Would it always be like this? she wondered sadly. He knew what faced him too. Was it really such a sin? They shared the same God, after all. Did it matter that their prayers and hymns were different; they were all addressed to Him. Inwardly she sighed. Oh, it mattered a great deal in this city.

When Bob had gone she sat in the still-gathering dusk waiting for Sarah to come in. Joe would be with Vinny or Franny and anyway he had no interest or opinion about her love-life. She could visualise the scene at Bob's house, though. The angry words, the hurt disbelief, the condemnation, pleas, threats, and the utter rejection. She knew it wouldn't be long before he was back. She and Sarah could sleep in Mam and Dad's room; he could have Sarah's bed.

However, when the door did open, it was neither Bob nor Sarah but Vi.

'I've just seen Bob Goodwin,' she said excitedly. 'Did you know he was home, Katie?'

'Yes. What . . . what did he say, Vi?'

'Not much, only that he was going to the pub for a quick drink before he came here.'

Katie nodded and sighed. He'd told his family, then. 'We're going to get married, Vi,' she said bluntly.

Vi's eyes widened. 'Oh, Holy God! Katie, do you really know what you're doing? Do you know what'll happen?'

'Yes, but he's going overseas soon, and I love him, Vi, and he may never come back. What if I said no, and he was killed? I . . . I couldn't take that, not after Mam.'

'You're going to have to take a lot more than that, girl. Insults, threats, they'll cut you dead – people you've known all your life.'

'I know. Will you turn your back on me, too, Vi? I know Josie will because of our Georgie.'

Vi looked at her friend with pity in her eyes. In any other city or town, it wouldn't be so bad, but here in Liverpool in the areas they lived in, it was going to be more terrible than the war in some ways. 'No, I'll not dump you or cut you dead. You're my friend and no religious bigots will make me see otherwise. I'll stand for you and if Jack's home, he'll stand for Bob. And I want to help you with your outfit, flowers – anything. Mam will carry on like a lunatic but I don't care. You're my friend and always will be.'

Katie looked at her gratefully. 'I suppose I'll have to leave here, find somewhere else to live,' she said quietly.

'Why? He'll be away and your Sarah couldn't cope on her own – she's just not capable or strong enough. And she certainly can't manage your Joe.'

'But I don't want either her or Joe to be involved because I'm still living here.'

'Your Joe couldn't care less and if any of the other lads start, he'll just thump them. Your Sarah will do as anyone tells her, she's that daft. I'll tell her she's to keep her mouth shut and ignore people, and if she can't do that then she can go and live with your Josie.'

When Sarah did get home, tired and sticky with the oppressive heat, she was surprised to see Bob and Vi in the living room, but before she could speak Vi gestured that she be seated.

'You'd better sit down, Sarah, we've something to tell you,' she instructed. She'd already asked Katie if she wanted her to leave when Bob had arrived, his lips set in a thin line.

Bob himself was emotionally drained. He'd had a horrendous few hours. He would never have believed that his normally quiet father would have known some of the words he'd used to express his opinion of both Katie and her religion. His mother wept quietly as his father ranted and cursed, while his sisters went white with shock – but none of them had said a single word. Finally, Bob had lost his temper and told his father he could go to hell, that he'd never set foot over the doorstep again and that if he were killed in battle, the old man could wallow in guilt until the Lord felt it was time to call him – and probably reject him for his lack of Christian charity.

'Get out then! Go crawling to your Papist whore!' was his father's reply.

Bob turned, his hand on the doorknob. 'Whatever happened to "Love thy neighbour"? There's not much evidence of that in this bloody house!' The dishes on the dresser shook as he slammed the door behind him.

Between them, Bob, Vi and Katie explained the news to Sarah. At first she couldn't take it in, but as the possible repercussions began to dawn on her, she felt numb with dread.

'What about me?' she whispered.

'You don't have to be bridesmaid. Outside the house you needn't even speak to me, and if you'd feel more comfortable with Josie then you could go and live with her,' Katie answered quietly.

Sarah shrank further into the chair. 'Oh God, what's our Georgie going to say?' she cried in horror.

'He's got no right to say a single thing – not after what he's done, Sarah, and besides I don't give a damn for him and I'm not frightened of him either!'

'She won't need to stand up to him. If I'm here and he starts, I'll give him the hiding he deserved long ago,' Bob informed them grimly.

Vi shook her head sadly. 'Oh Katie, what a mess. What a bloody way to start married life.'

Katie gripped Bob's hand tightly. 'I don't care, Vi. I'll have Bob and . . . you.'

Chapter Fourteen

Bob soon went back to his training camp at Warrington, and after Katie had gone to see the parish priest, accompanied by Vi, the news became public knowledge. There were arguments with Mary Maher, Ellen MacCane, Florrie Watson and with Josie, too. Customers began to look in the window of the shop to check it wasn't Katie serving before they came in. Because they needed the money, Joe served at the times his sister would normally have taken over.

Sarah had spoken timidly to Jem Cargill about the buying.

'We won't mind if you feel you can't go along with the arrangement because of our Katie. We'll understand.'

'I don't give a bloody damn who your Katie marries,' the man told her firmly. 'As it happens I'm an atheist – don't believe in God. All religion does is set neighbour against neighbour – and what kind of a God lets people kill and maim in His name? No, the arrangement stands, girl.'

It was the very worst moment of Katie's life when she and Vi were shown into the parlour of the presbytery by Father Macreedy's housekeeper, Mrs Conlon. A widow woman who took her duties seriously, she nevertheless smiled as she showed the girls in. She liked Vi's mother, Mrs Draper, and had respected and admired Molly Deegan.

Father Macreedy got up from his chair. He was smiling a welcome, and the book he'd been reading was placed face downwards on the seat of the chair. The girls looked around swiftly. On the other side of the fireplace was a sofa, while a large picture of the crucifixion hung above the mantelpiece.

'Kathleen and Violet! This is a nice surprise now. Come in and sit down, the pair of you.'

'I . . . I think we'd rather stand, Father,' Vi replied.

'Right then, what is it?'

'I . . . I'm going to get married, Father, on the twenty-fourth of August.'

'Well, wait now until I get my diary. It doesn't seem so long ago that I married your brother and little Josie Watson.' The priest crossed to the large table covered with a bias cloth and began searching amongst the books and papers there.

'Father, please . . . wait.'

He looked up, puzzlement in his eyes.

'It won't be here,' Katie blurted out. 'It will be at the . . . the . . . Register Office.' Before he could reply she plunged on: 'I'm marrying Bob Goodwin, he's a Protestant.'

They both waited, heads bent, for the explosion of wrath. The silence dragged on until Katie finally raised her eyes. The priest was looking at her as though she were some creature from Hell.

'I love him,' she said simply.

At last Father Macreedy found his voice. 'More than you love your God?' He turned to the picture and pointed with a quivering finger at the figure on the cross. 'Can you look at that, at Christ Who suffered and died a terrible death for you, and still tell me you love this *person* more?'

'Yes, but it's—' She got no further.

Father Macreedy's fist crashed down on the table. 'It will be no marriage, do you understand that? You will live in sin and your children will be unbaptised. If they die, their blameless innocent souls will be denied Heaven. They must stay forever in Limbo because the stain of Original Sin has not been washed away by the Sacrament of Baptism. That's what you'll condemn them to, and if they live they will be unrecognised, outcasts in a Catholic society. Who will befriend them and who will befriend *you* in your times of need? You'll be denied the Sacraments also. You'll be denied the blessed reward of a place in Heaven with your parents. You'll be damned,' he thundered, 'unless you reconsider and tell this man you love your God and your Catholic Faith more than him!'

Katie was sobbing quietly and although she too was shaking, Vi felt a sense of injustice and defiance rising in her.

'You always taught us that God was a God of love and compassion, Father,' she began hesitantly. 'Not a vengeful God Who would deny us Heaven. If Bob Goodwin dies fighting for his country, fighting against evil for us, will he go to Hell just because he is a Protestant?' Vi was getting into her stride now. She pushed to the back of her mind what her parents would do when they found out she'd been so brazen as to argue with a Priest of God. 'Didn't Jesus say "Greater love hath no man than he lay down his life for his friends"?'

Father Macreedy's face was puce and a pulse beat in a vein in his neck above the white clerical collar.

'Don't you dare to stand there and quote Christ's words to me, Violet Catherine Draper! Get out, the pair of you! You will beg God's forgiveness for your insolence and pride in Confession, Violet, and as for you, Kathleen Elizabeth Deegan, think deeply about the way your parents, God rest their souls, would have felt about this. Get rid of this man or you will not be welcome in this church ever again!'

They were both trembling and in tears when the housekeeper let them out, a far different expression on her face than that with which she had greeted them.

Vi pulled herself together. 'Hush, that's the worst over, Katie.' Although she sounded confident she knew inside what kind of reception she would receive when she got home. Without doubt, Father Macreedy would put on his biretta and be round to see her parents so quickly it would make your head spin.

'It was what he said about . . . babies, Vi – And Mam. I . . . I could stand the rest. I know God won't deny me Heaven, not really, but—'

'Don't think about babies and Limbo. You're not even married yet, so don't torture yourself about it just now.'

Katie's sobs diminished a little. 'Oh Vi, you shouldn't have said anything.'

'I know. I'll get half-killed when I get home because Father Macreedy'll be round there like a flash or he'll send for them. But I couldn't help it. It's not fair. You *do* love God and you love Bob, but it's not in the same way, and I'm sure God understands. He *must*. Oh, why can't everyone be the same religion!' Vi cried in frustration. 'Haven't we got enough fighting on our hands already?'

Vi had been a tower of strength since that day, Katie thought, her heart full of gratitude. Her friend was still black and blue from the hiding she'd received from her Da, but she'd held her ground at home and refused to desert Katie. When her Da had started ranting and raving again, her Mam had surprised them all by turning on him.

'Oh, in the name of God, shut up, Bernie! I'm sick of all this. We should just be thankful that it's not her who's going to marry one of them. At least Jack Milligan is a good Catholic boy.'

'Look – if Katie Deegan's Mam and Da had been alive, this would never 'ave 'appened!' These were Bernie Draper's final words before he'd slammed out to the pub.

In preparation for the wedding, Vi and Katie had pooled their clothing coupons plus Sarah's. The two friends went to town and bought a nice ivory-coloured two-piece costume and a small cream and brown hat from Blackler's. Josie had resolutely refused to have anything to do with it. When Vi asked her if she would make Katie a dress, if they bought the material, she refused point blank.

'I could never do that! Georgie would go mad.'

126

'You mean you *won't* because you're terrified of him!' Vi snapped back. 'He's a bully, Josie, and unless you stand up to him, he'll give you a dog's life, so he will.'

Josie's expression hardened. 'You can mind your own business, Vi Draper. It's *my* life and it's *my* marriage.'

'Suit yourself,' Vi replied.

Josie felt angry, but deep down she knew Vi was right. She was still loyal to Katie in her heart, but she didn't have the same courage and determination as her friends.

Vi could lend her a nice brown handbag and Sarah a pair of cream shoes, which just left Katie lacking some gloves.

'Do I really need them?' she asked Vi, when all avenues had been explored and no solution found.

'Well, I don't suppose they'll report the fact that you didn't wear gloves in the society columns of the local papers.'

'We've no more coupons and there's no one else we can ask,' Katie fretted.

'Of course there is,' Vi stated, having suddenly had a brainwave.

'Who?'

'Your future husband.'

Katie smiled. She tried always to think of him, and not the terrible pronouncements of Father Macreedy. She hadn't been to Mass since that traumatic confrontation.

'And you'll get two days in Llandudno in a hotel.'

'It's only a guest-house.'

'It's more than your Mam and mine got, or Josie either. Can you imagine Scrooge paying out for a guest-house?'

They were all three of them laughing when the shop doorbell rang.

'I'll go, they'll rush off out again if either of you go,' Sarah said hastily. After work she stayed at home more now, rather than have to face the neighbours, although it was implied that she wasn't speaking to her sister.

'You'll look great, Katie, you really will!' Vi was enthusiastic. 'There's a lot of brides now not having the traditional long white frock with all the trappings. It's the war, see. People can't get stuff.'

'She won't look great for anything.'

They both turned to see Georgie standing in the doorway, behind him a white-faced Sarah.

Vi looked at her friend then back to Georgie. 'Is Jack home, too?'

'Yes. You'd better get yourself round there and explain your part in this fiasco and you won't find him so amused.'

'Jack Milligan wouldn't spit on you if you were on fire, Georgie Deegan. You're a coward, a liar and a thief!'

'Go on, Vi. Go to see Jack. I can manage *him* on my own.'

With an anxious glance, Vi picked up her bag and went out the back way.

'So?' he demanded, taking off his cap and throwing it on the dresser.

'So what?'

'You're not going to disgrace this family and Mam and Da's memory by marrying a bloody Orangeman!'

His sister faced him, her eyes blazing. 'You can go to hell! I'll marry who I like! And before you say anything else, Georgie Deegan, where's Mam's cashbox and all her jewellery? You left us without a penny. While we were breaking our hearts you were busy taking the key from around her neck, and her still not cold! You're . . . you're worse than a grave-robber!'

'That money is mine.' His voice was hard, assured. 'I'm head of the family now, and Mam would have wanted it this way. You didn't expect me to leave it all for anyone to pinch, did you?'

'*You* were the one who pinched it! It should have been shared out fairly between us all! And where's the box containing her gold earrings and chains?'

'In my safekeeping, and this is now *my* business!'

'And just who is going to run it? Our Joe? I don't think they'll let you off from the convoys just to run a shop, somehow. Oh, wouldn't *that* look well to the neighbours?'

'*No, Mrs Maher, they don't need me to bring in petrol for tanks and steel for weapons or the wheat for bread. I have to stand all day in the shop, you see!*' she jeered, shaking with temper. 'And you'd do it, too, wouldn't you, while Jack and Bob are out in the thick of it!'

He grabbed her by the wrist. 'You listen to me, girl,' he hissed, 'you're not marrying that bleeding Orangeman and dragging this family's name in the mud. Josie told me what Father Macreedy said.'

She jerked her wrist away. 'I thought she would. The stupid fool's got no taste and no guts, otherwise she wouldn't have married you!'

Sarah was sobbing quietly in the background.

'You're *not* going to marry him!' Georgie bawled.

'I am!' she yelled back.

'You can't! You're not twenty-one yet, and you need my permission!'

It was as though he'd slapped her in the face. She gasped and drew back. He was right! Oh, why hadn't she or Vi or someone thought about that?

He smiled grimly. 'That's put a stop to your gallop, hasn't it, girl? So you can get all that gear off, and sit down and write and tell him it's all off, then get round to Confession!'

She stood quite still and watched him leave, the way Vi had gone, through the back door.

'Oh Katie, I'm sorry! I'm so sorry!' Sarah sobbed. 'I couldn't get in to warn you! He pushed past me and I knew from his face that Josie had told him.'

'It's all right, luv. It wasn't your fault. Don't get upset.' She took off the hat and sat down.

Sarah sat beside her, her hands over her face, rocking gently to and fro and still sobbing. 'Oh, I wish Mam was here and Da . . . and that everything would be just like it was, with no war . . .'

Katie hugged her sister. The initial shock was wearing off. 'So do I, Sarah, but life's not like that and one day you'll meet someone, and then . . . well, you'll know what love is.'

Sarah raised a tear-streaked face. 'No, I won't. Who'd want me? I'm plain and shy and afraid of everything!'

'You're not, silly girl. When you're dressed up you look lovely, and you're much better now since you went to work in the factory. Look at all the people you know.'

'I could never be like you, Katie. I couldn't face Father Macreedy or the neighbours . . .'

'You probably won't have to. At least, I hope you won't.'

'What will you do now?'

'I don't know, but whatever our Georgie says, I'm going to marry Bob.'

Sarah looked alarmed. 'But they'll know you're not twenty-one and they'll need proof of permission . . . or something.'

Katie's mind was slowly going over everything. Sarah was right: they would need 'proof of permission'. Who, apart from Georgie, was there to give that permission? Then a smile slowly crossed her face.

'I'm going to Manchester, Sarah,' she announced. 'I'm going to see Uncle Alfred.'

'Uncle Alfred? Why?'

'He's Da's brother,' Katie explained. 'He's older than Georgie and if he'll give me permission, then Georgie can go to hell.'

'But what if he won't?'

'I won't know that unless I ask. Oh Sarah, stop being so miserable. You've got to fight for things in this world, if you want them badly enough.'

The journey was long and tedious. She'd often heard people say it wasn't that far to Manchester, but that was before the war. The train kept stopping for half-hours at a time, and there didn't seem to be any explanation at all. The third-class carriage, which was all she could afford, was stuffy and packed. Even the corridors were full of people sitting on cases or kitbags. There seemed to be a lot of soldiers on the train.

When she finally arrived at Manchester's Piccadilly Station, she asked how to get to Wythenshaw – and that entailed another tedious journey by tram.

Her exhausted arrival at Uncle Alfred's solid red-brick Victorian house coincided with tea-time, and she was anxious about how she would get back to Liverpool.

She pressed the doorbell and finally it was answered by a gentleman of her uncle's own age, very soberly dressed.

'I've come to see my Uncle Alfred.'

'And you are, miss?'

'Katie Deegan. My Da was Uncle Alfred's brother.'

He indicated that she should step into the hall and she did so, looking around curiously. Uncle Alfred must be quite well off, she thought. Da's voice came clearly into her mind.

'He's a clever one is our Alfred, a head-worker; he could have gone far but he's a loner – and he's going a bit odd, eccentric like, these days. Gets a bee in his bonnet and there's no shifting him. I seem to remember him having a row with the parish priest over a church boiler, of all things. He's attended another parish ever since . . .'

Her uncle worked in a bank or some other kind of office, that much she knew. They really hadn't seen much of him over the past few years – until the funerals, that is.

She was beckoned towards a door.

'Good grief, it *is* you, girl.' Alfred Deegan had half-doubted Squires, his gentleman's gentleman of twenty years standing when he'd told him who was at the door.

'Oh, I'm so glad to get here at last. I left Liverpool at half-past nine this morning.'

'Have you eaten, my dear?'

'Not for ages.' Suddenly Katie realised how famished she was.

'Something substantial, Squires, please, and a pot of tea.'

Alfred motioned her to sit down and she did so gingerly, perching on the edge of a leather-padded chesterfield. The blackout curtains were pulled tightly across the window and although she didn't glance around her, she knew it was a comfortable room with good furnishings. He'd obviously been reading the newspapers. *The Times* and the *Manchester Guardian* were spread out on a side table.

'What on earth's the matter, Katie, that you've come this far and without letting me know? I'd have driven to the station to collect you.'

'I . . . I didn't think. It's . . . our Georgie,' she confided.

Her uncle's eyebrows drew together in a frown of disapproval. 'Now what's he done?'

'Well, after the funeral, after everyone had gone home, I suddenly remembered Mam's cashbox. She kept it under the sink.'

'Good Lord. Did she not use a bank?' He was astounded. Molly had seemed such a sensible woman.

'No, she was funny like that,' Katie explained with a half-sob. 'She kept the key on a chain around her neck, and . . . and she had a lot of gold earrings and chains in another box. Our Georgie took them, Uncle Alfred. He went to Dunkirk and then I don't know where afterwards, but he took that key from Mam when she was lying upstairs, hardly cold.'

Alfred leaned forward. He'd never liked the lad. He was arrogant, cunning and uncouth. 'Go on.'

'He left us with nothing, just mine and Sarah's wages to pay the rent. The shop is hardly doing any business, we can't get the stuff. It's only the Manx and Irish boats that come in now. Mr Cargill brings us what he can from the market, but it's not much.'

He fleetingly wondered if she had come for money. 'He's home now?'

She nodded.

'And you confronted him.' He knew the girl had spirit; she was like her mother.

'He said it was his. He's the oldest, you see, so he thinks he's entitled to it and the business as well. He's the head of the family now, but it's not that, Uncle Alfred. I could have managed with just . . . that.'

'So, what is it?' He waited patiently for his niece to explain herself.

'Oh Uncle, you're my last hope! I don't know who to turn to, but I don't think you'll be very happy when I tell you what I've come for, and I wouldn't blame you. Father Macreedy ordered me out of his house.'

'Good God, girl! What on earth have you done?'

She took a deep breath. 'I . . . I want to get married, but Bob . . . he . . . he's a Protestant. They live in Netherfield Road and his family – well, they belong to the Orange Lodge.' She swallowed hard and plunged on. 'He's been thrown out too, but he's going overseas soon and I might never see him again.' Then sheer exhaustion, coupled with the tension of the last weeks took hold of her and she began to sob.

Alfred Deegan wasn't used to having young women sitting weeping on his sofa, and he didn't know what to do. Clumsily, he passed her his handkerchief. 'Come on now, Katie.' His voice was gruff. 'Pull yourself together.'

She tried. 'Because I'm not twenty-one until next February, Georgie won't let me. He won't give his permission.' She dissolved again into tears of abject despair.

Alfred Deegan drew himself up. He was not in favour of the match at all. Mixed marriages seldom worked out well and he could imagine what the priest had said to her – probably threatened her with excommunication; some of them were very radical about such things. Some were even contrary over new and more efficient heating boilers for their churches! She'd also probably had to cope with the condemnation of her friends, and had more than likely been ostracised by her neighbours. He looked at the girl closely. She was young to have coped with so much. The deprivations of war, the essential but dirty and often dangerous munitions work. The loss of both her parents – a shattering enough blow to anyone – and a blackguard for an elder brother. Alfred was beginning to equate his nephew Georgie with the obnoxious Italian dictator, Benito Mussolini. But the lad – Bob hadn't she called him – must have some backbone to confront the equally bigoted attitudes of his own family, friends and neighbours, apart from shortly being sent overseas to fight and maybe die. And to go willingly, as so many hundreds of thousands had done.

He himself had seen action in the last year of the Great War, so he knew what these lads faced. He also viewed his nephew's service in the Merchant Marine as cowardly. His place would be filled voluntarily – by a man unfit or too old for active service, freeing Georgie – young and fit – to join the Army, Navy or Airforce.

Squires entered, bearing a tray.

'Squires, my niece has spent all day travelling from Liverpool,' Alfred announced. 'She's upset and exhausted, and she can't possibly go back tonight. Make up a bed in one of the spare rooms, please.'

Katie got up. 'I can't stay, Uncle Alfred. They'll be worried sick about me at home.'

'Sit down. I insist. Is there no one who can be contacted by telephone to take a message?'

'Only the Presbytery, and—'

He nodded his understanding. 'I'll send a telegram then.' Seeing the look of alarm on her face he added quickly, 'It's the only way, unless you want them to worry?'

She looked at him trustingly.

'Right then. Squires will attend to it. The telegram to read "Safe and Sound. Back tomorrow. Katie." Agreed?'

She nodded.

'Now eat your supper while I find my fountain pen and some of my writing paper.'

'Writing paper?'

'Yes. I think we'll start like this.'

To Whom it may concern,

I, Alfred Deegan, the brother of William Deegan and therefore the Uncle of Miss Kathleen Deegan, do claim Guardianship of her until she reaches her majority, being her oldest living relat-ive. Her parents being lately deceased.

In such a capacity I do freely give my permission for her to marry . . .

He paused. 'His name?'
'Bob Goodwin.'

Mr Robert Goodwin.
Signed by my hand on this day the 18th August 1940.

He felt a glow of satisfaction spread over him. That would be one in the eye for that arrogant pup of a nephew, and for Father Macreedy. He disliked zealots of all kinds but particularly those within the clergy who had no conception that the words 'tolerance' and 'humility' should apply to them.

Katie couldn't take it in, in such formal language. 'You mean, you really mean, that . . . ?'

'I do. You have my permission, if not my entire blessing. Now finish your supper, girl, then you must have a good night's rest. I myself shall take you to the station in the morning, and you will travel back first class.'

Chapter Fifteen

They were all waiting for her when she got back to Chelmsford Street. She'd expected Sarah and Joe and *him* but not Josie. Obviously she was on late shift, like Sarah.

Georgie got up out of the armchair. 'Where the hell do you think you've been? Our Sarah's been worried to death,' he snapped.

'But *you* weren't? Anyway, she should have got a telegram, so don't go telling me lies, Georgie Deegan.'

'Disappearing, sending telegrams and you know how people feel about them, especially in wartime. And it arrived late at night.'

'I'm not standing here arguing with you, I haven't got time. There are things to do.' She looked closely at Josie, who seemed paler than usual – and that was saying something. 'Josie, are you all right? You don't look very well. Should our Sarah tell them you're not going in today when she gets to work?'

'No, she won't!' He looked warningly at Sarah. 'Just mind your own business, Katie.'

'I'm pregnant,' Josie informed her with a half-smile. In one way she was glad; in another she was afraid. Afraid of what had happened last time. The agony, the sense of failure and guilt and afterwards the awful depression. But Mam had told her to put all thoughts of that out of her mind completely. This time she'd be fine and she'd go full term.

'Oh, that's great! I'm made up for you, Josie, I really am. Does everyone know?' Katie was deliberately ignoring her brother.

'Only family. Mam says I should get as much rest as possible, particularly now, at this stage. I really shouldn't be going to work,' Josie glanced furtively at her husband, 'but there is a war on, we're desperately needed.'

'Did you hear that? She should be resting but she won't take time off.' Georgie's tone was sanctimonious. He didn't agree with Florrie and her theories. Rest! Resting cost money and as Josie had said, there was a war on. 'Josie's responsible, not like you going jaunting all over the country and telling no one.'

'I wasn't jaunting and our Sarah knew where I was going *and* what for.' She opened her shoulder bag and pulled out the letter in its unsealed envelope. 'This!' She threw it across the table at him.

Georgie's eyes narrowed suspiciously as he took the envelope. It was of very good quality paper. He drew out the single folded sheet of cream velum and looked at the professionally printed address on the letterhead. Uncle Alfred. So that's where she'd gone! He scanned the lines of neat copperplate writing and as he did so his temper increased. The bitch! The sly little bitch! She'd gone to Manchester and probably told their uncle a pack of lies.

'What kind of a tale did you spin him to get this? That Bob Goodwin is a Catholic and I just don't like him and have forbidden you to marry him out of spite?' He cruelly mimicked a whiny female voice.

'No! He knows Bob's a Protestant. I told him the truth, all of it. About how you had taken the key from around Mam's neck, and her not cold. Stolen from your own mother and left us without a penny. How you came back bragging you were head of the family, and that the money and the business are yours and that you've forbidden me to marry Bob.' Katie's eyes narrowed. 'He doesn't like you, Georgie. He doesn't like you one little bit because he can see right through you. He knows what you are and what you'll sink to, to get your own way.' She wasn't completely certain of her uncle's depths of mistrust, but she wasn't going to let Georgie know that.

'And you're *not* the head of the family. He is, he's Da's brother, the only relative we have alive. He's given his permission so there's nothing you can do about it.' And before he could reply she snatched the letter from him, in case he tried to destroy it.

She could see he was having trouble controlling himself.

'He even offered to come over and give me away, but I said it was too much trouble. The trains are terrible, it takes hours, but he said if I needed him he'd come. He paid my fare home, first class, and drove me to the station himself.'

Katie turned to Josie who was sitting clutching her handbag tightly and biting her lip, and her voice softened. 'He asked after you, luv. He said I was to tell you that he wishes to be remembered to you, and for me to thank you for the letter you sent him for that nice clock.'

Josie smiled. 'It *is* a nice clock. Everyone admires it.'

'But I suppose he'll give *you* something far grander and dearer because you went creeping to him,' Georgie sneered.

'No, he won't. I told him I didn't want anything; he'd given me the thing I most wanted in the world – this letter.'

Georgie turned to his wife. 'Come on, you've work to go to. There's nothing else to keep us here.'

'Josie, look after yourself,' Katie called as the pair left. He'd convinced everyone, including Josie herself, that she was working for the war effort, but Katie would lay a pound to a penny that it was the extra money he was interested in, so he could add to the haul she'd found. By now he must have nearly a hundred pounds! If Mam had been here to back Florrie up, Josie wouldn't be dragging all the way out to Kirkby and standing long hours on her feet.

When Katie recounted all her news, Vi was delighted. She clapped her hands together.

'God, how I'd love to have seen the look on his face! You know you're dead devious you, Katie Deegan. I'd never have thought of that in a hundred years.'

'You need to be flaming devious to keep up with that get. He's as cunning as a fox. I knew he'd try to do something else to stop me, so I said Uncle Alfred had offered to give me away but that I'd refused. I said he'd come over if I needed him – I just had to telephone. He'll think twice now before interfering, will our Georgie.'

'You know, Katie, I think it's you who should be in charge of the country, we'd soon win the war! Can we go ahead with all our plans now?'

Katie nodded and laughed with sheer relief.

On the morning of her wedding day, Katie studied her image in the mirror critically. 'Does this blouse *really* go, Vi?'

'It goes great with that cream suit, and the ribbon on your hat matches it.'

'Oh Vi, I'm so nervous!'

'Every bride is. Don't you remember how terrified Josie was?'

'I wish . . . Oh, in a way I wish Mam was here and could see me and sort of help me along.'

'She *can* see you, luv, and I'll bet there's no flaming bigotry in Heaven. She'd be proud of you, they both would.' Vi didn't think it was the moment to refer to Bob's being a Protestant. 'Here, let me pin these flowers on your jacket.' Her eyes were suspiciously bright and Katie felt tears start to well up in her own.

'We're a fine pair,' Vi grinned weepily. 'This is supposed to be a happy day. Come on, or we'll be late and he'll think you've changed your flaming mind or that the clergy at St John's have kidnapped you, locked you in a dungeon and thrown away the key.'

The wedding party took the tram to West Derby Road and Brougham Terrace. Jack had agreed to stand for Bob, but not without some coaxing from Vi.

'I thought he was your mate?' she'd demanded. 'That we're all mates together? If you knew what Katie's been through and him, too. For God's sake, Jack, it's wartime! There are more important things to fight over than flaming religion. Look at the state London's in.

136

Thousands left homeless and women and kids killed in their beds! Half the city gone up in flames. It could happen here, God forbid, and all you can think of is what Father Macreedy will say!'

Put like that, he was unable to argue.

The Register Office room itself was austere, but Katie hadn't expected anything different. With quiet solemnity they both repeated their vows after the Registrar. Bob placed a gold ring on her finger, the Marriage Certificate was signed, and then it was all over. Katie felt slightly hurt and disappointed. They'd both given up so much, gone through so much that she felt it could have taken a bit longer and been a bit more dignified. The man hadn't even smiled genially, just gave a sort of grimace really, as he wished them happiness. To him they were just another soldier and his girl getting married.

The ceremony over, they went off to the Gregson's Well pub on the corner of Cobden Street to have a celebratory drink before Bob and Katie got another tram to the station to go on their honeymoon to Llandudno. A honeymoon that would be over all too soon.

It was a little sore and embarrassing at first, but she soon lost her inhibitions in his arms. Each moment was so precious that she treasured each kiss, each touch. She loved him with her whole being, not just 'with my body I thee worship' as she'd promised that morning. That evening, after their meal, they walked along the promenade. The beach was covered with wooden spikes and rolls of barbed wire and notices that warned of the danger of mines.

'There's no getting away from it, is there?' she said with dismay.

'I'm afraid not, luv,' he answered, pulling her closer to him.

'Still, it's a very nice place. Sort of pretty and peaceful with the mountains behind.' She swallowed hard; just two days was all they had. Oh, she knew her Mam and Mrs Draper and Josie – in fact practically everyone she knew – never went anywhere on honeymoon, but at least all the others had known they would have plenty of time to spend together. After tomorrow, God alone knew how long it would be before she saw Bob again.

They stopped and looked up at the cliff known as the Great Orme and then across the wide bay to the other craggy outcrop, the Little Orme, the breeze ruffling her dark curls and the setting sun still warm on her face.

He bent and kissed her softly on the lips. 'I love you, Katie Goodwin, and I always will. No matter what happens, remember that. You're my wife . . . you're mine now – for ever.'

They began to walk back towards the guest-house, slowly, so slowly. Each minute a memory to be cherished.

★ ★ ★

She waved him off from Lime Street. As his wife, this time she was able to kiss and hug him publicly, smiling through her tears as so many other girls and women were doing all around them. But this time there were none of his relations there and she knew he felt hurt. She had half-hoped that his mother at least would have come.

'Take care of yourself! Don't go being a hero.'

'I'm not the stuff heroes are made of, Katie. I'll just do as I'm told.'

With a shudder she remembered what her Mam had said about the soldiers of the Great War, that all they'd been was cannon-fodder. She hugged him again. 'Come home safely, and please will you write?'

'I promise. You look after yourself, luv.'

She clung to him again for a few minutes, then drew away. She waved frantically until the train had gone, bending slightly to the left between the high walls whose bricks were covered with the soot of a thousand coal-fired engines.

As she walked out into the sunlight and looked across at St George's Hall with its magnificent but soot-blackened portico, she felt so alone. People were hurrying past her up and down the steps, and the pavement along Lime Street was quite crowded, but she had never felt so lonely in her entire life.

The war went on relentlessly. London was bombed again and again, and half the population now slept in the Tube stations for safety. In the skies, fierce fights took place betwen the planes of the RAF and the Luftwaffe. Throughout September, October and November 1940, German Dornier bombers flew over the Mersey, giving the city, the docks and the shipyards on the other side of the river, their first baptism of fire.

In October, what later became known as the Battle of the Atlantic began. Both Josie and Vi wore worried expressions all the time. Gone were Vi's carefree ways. These days it was hard to get her to even smile, and now Katie knew exactly how she felt. Letters were slow arriving; when they did, they'd already been opened and read by the Censor, with words, even phrases and whole sentences blacked out.

The loss of shipping was horrific. The convoys, so vital to keep the country fed and armed, took ages to arrive. The zig-zagging tactics used in the Great War were effective to a point, but delayed their progress. They travelled at the top speed of the slowest ship, which made many an old sailor long for the twenty-seven and twenty-eight knots of the old and new Cunarders.

The brand new *Queen Elizabeth* had sailed in complete darkness from Greenock and had outstripped her Naval escorts, arriving in New York two days ahead of them. She'd also astounded and in-furiated one U-boat captain who'd heard her on his Sonar and couldn't believe his luck. There was no other ship in the world of 82,000 tonnes, or as prestigious. His excitement was short-lived as she left him trailing far behind, his torpedoes wasted. The two Cunard *Queens* were now safely in New York and being fitted as troop-carriers.

Even ships carrying women and children were attacked and sunk. When the loss of 306 children on the *City of Benares* was announced, it almost broke the hearts of tough, hardened Liverpool dockers.

On hearing the news, Fred Watson turned to his mate, his eyes full of tears. 'I waved those kids off,' he told the other man, his voice trembling. 'One little lad whistled to me an' I thought, Yer 'ardfaced little sod – yer'll do well over there, but I waved and whistled back. I wonder where he is now, the poor little nipper? He was only as old as our Jimmy. Christ Almighty, Alf! What kind of people deliberately kill kids like that?'

In Chelmsford Street the Deegans had an Anderson shelter that took up most of the back yard, but their neighbours either went to the public shelter or sat huddled under the stairs or even the kitchen table that had been reinforced by the Council by means of a metal covering.

Thank God, since the raids had started, nearly all the neighbours had thawed towards Katie. As Mary Maher said, sensibly: 'All that will get sorted out after the war. For now, let's just get this over. We could be killed in our beds any day, so what's the use of arguing over religion?'

'Christmas 1940 isn't going to be much of a celebration, is it?' Vi said glumly to Katie as they trudged home one day along Melrose Road. The bomb damage from raids in November made sections of tram-track still unusable.

'Well, the last two haven't been what you'd call great in our house,' Katie answered flatly. She'd received a letter from Bob yesterday, and had gathered from the tortuous, roundabout way he'd written to avoid everything being blanked out, that they were on the move and that he'd been under attack. She'd felt sick when she read it. She knew from the newspapers that there was fighting in North Africa between Montgomery's 'Desert Rats' and Erwin Rommel's Afrika Corps.

'Look, why don't we all try and really make an effort? I'm sure if we scout around a bit we can get things together. Come up with new ideas, like,' Vi suggested.

'All of us?'

'You, Sarah, Josie and me, and I suppose Jack and even old Misery Guts if they're home. Josie told me yesterday she'd had a letter from him telling her she shouldn't be so friendly with you. But she just shrugged it off – we'll try and drag him along too if he's back. We'll start by getting some tickets for the Empire as a real treat. Josie's the one who's clever with her hands and ideas, and she's a great cook – she can rustle up a special meal.'

'Vi, she's knitting baby clothes in her spare time and she hasn't got much of that,' Katie pointed out. 'She shouldn't be working – you know as well as I do that it's only because she's threatened to turn up and stand at the gate all day that she's still there.'

'Oh, we'll all muck in and help. I wasn't suggesting she do *everything*. And your Sarah can get out the old decorations and make a couple of new Christmassy signs.'

'How?'

'All she'll need is some cardboard and paint. Joe can paint the cardboard red and then she can paint *Happy Christmas* or *Gloria in Excelsis Deo* on it and we'll stick it up over the fireplace.'

'Jesus, Mary and Joseph! Vi, I wouldn't let our Joe loose with a paint-brush! He and tins of paint are best kept well apart.'

'Sarah can do it all herself, then. I just thought it might keep him out of mischief.'

'Huh – it'd take more than that. In fact, I'm going to put his name down for a messenger boy. They've got lists in the police stations, and with the ARP Wardens too. He can do something useful for a change after school and at weekends.'

When telephone wires were down and electricity supplies gone, boys on bicycles proved invaluable in taking urgent messages to the emergency services, and Katie didn't see why Joe shouldn't be doing his bit. Mam and Da would have expected it.

Josie was none too enthusiastic about the trip to the Empire, thinking of what Georgie had said about not associating with Katie in his letter. Deep down she was relieved he didn't look like being back for the planned treat.

'It's a bit expensive,' she said nervously.

'I'll pay for you if you don't want to tell your dear husband about it,' Vi said in exasperation. 'God, Josie, we earn two pounds ten shillings a week now, more than we ever earned before and there's hardly anything to spend it on. A five-shilling seat isn't going to break the bank.'

'No, *I'll* pay,' Katie insisted. 'We all deserve a treat and you more than us, Josie.'

'My Aunt Hilda's given me some new recipes,' Josie confided. 'One's for Christmas pudding, using carrots and other things instead of candied peel and currants and sultanas.'

Katie pulled a face.

'Well, it'll be better than having no pudding at all, won't it?' Josie replied with some spirit.

'Let's pool our coupons and see what we can get in the way of meat. It won't be a turkey, God knows, but let's make an effort.'

They planned to have the meal at Chelmsford Street, and Vi was going to come around a bit later.

'I'm not exactly going to be missed, not with six of us at home, and anyway I've given you half my coupons. Mam's still ranting and raving about that. She's cursed me up hill an' down dale. She doesn't half go on sometimes, it's a wonder me Da doesn't go and live in the pub!'

They'd bought tickets for the evening performance at the Empire for 21 December and Josie had scraped together the ingredients for a pudding. Sarah said Jem Cargill would get them sprouts and potatoes. Katie and Vi had promised to scour all the shops and markets on Christmas Eve and queue half the night if necessary, for a bit of meat of any kind.

The night before their outing they all got off the tram together. With a lot of persuasion, some bribery, some lies and some luck, they now all worked on the same shift. Katie didn't like to even think of what Joe got up to when he was on his own after school, but she'd given him a good talking to and threatened to send him to Uncle Alfred if he got into trouble. Although his name and that of Vinny Maher, Franny MacCane and Jimmy Watson were on the Warden's list, they hadn't been called upon yet.

'We're nearly all set. It's going to be a good Christmas this year,' Vi said determinedly.

'I've even made some paper doylies for the table from some old sheets of blotting paper I found at the back of the dresser drawer,' Sarah announced proudly.

'Won't they look funny, what with all the writing on them?' Josie asked.

'No, I've got a bottle of red ink. I'm going to dilute it, soak them in it and let them dry out.'

'Well, just watch nothing wet or runny gets put on top of them otherwise they'll ruin Mam's best white cloth.'

Josie turned to them. 'I've unpicked all the wax flowers from my wedding headdress. I thought I'd wire them separately and stick them in a small bowl or basket with a bit of red ribbon for a table decoration. I could put a candle in the middle. Can I use some of the red ink, Sarah? I'll try and dye some of them, or maybe cochineal would be better . . . It might not—' The rest of her words were drowned out by the rising wail of the air-raid siren.

'Oh, God Almighty! Sarah, run on ahead. Grab the kettle and the cups and our Joe, and get in the shelter. If I've got time I'll fetch the blankets and the little stove. Run, Sarah! Run!' Katie and Vi grabbed

Josie's hands and began to hasten up Chelmsford Street, pulling her along with them. When they reached home they could hear the familiar drone of enemy planes.

'Josie, get in the shelter and you, Vi. I'm going to nip inside for the blankets and the paraffin stove.'

'Oh, to hell with them, Katie, there isn't time – and anyway we'll only be out there for a while. The Jerry planes never stay long. They'll bugger off home in half an hour.'

'Well, I'm going for the blankets. It's freezing in that shelter.'

Sarah and Joe were already settled on the two long bunk-type benches that doubled as beds which ran the length of each side of the shelter.

'Move up, Joe, Josie needs more room.' Vi handed Josie a blanket. 'Here, luv, put this around you.'

'There's more of them than usual,' Joe announced with interest. He, like every other boy in the city, could distinguish the planes and guess at their number. 'It's just the usual Dorniers though, nothing new.'

'Oh, shut up! Haven't you got a comic or something? Every time I see you, you've got your head stuck in some sort of rubbish.' Although afraid herself, Vi could see that Josie and Sarah were looking fearfully at Joe.

'I was only saying, like,' Joe said huffily.

'We'll sing,' Katie suggested.

'What?' Josie asked.

'Everything we know.'

They did, but when after two hours the raid still wasn't over, they were hoarse and now all scared to death. Each blast made them clutch at each other and when one was so close that it shook the shelter, they all finished up on the floor, their arms over their heads.

'Somewhere near must have got a direct hit,' Vi said, getting up and praying that her family were all right. She knew her Mam would be worried to death about her.

Sarah was almost hysterical. 'I think we should pray! Let's say the Rosary.'

Josie looked fearfully at Katie.

Vi forestalled any comment from Josie. 'Does it matter if it's a Catholic God or a Protestant God? He's still God and we need Him! And if it gets any worse you'd better gerron your bicycle and go and find a warden to see if he needs messages running, Joe Deegan.'

'No! He can't go out in that!' Sarah cried.

'Other lads are out there,' Vi said.

With her stomach churning from fear, Katie nodded. 'Vi's right, Joe. They'll need you too. Get Vinny and Franny on your way.'

All the cockiness had gone from Joe's manner. He was scared. In fact, he was terrified, but if he didn't go and the Warden sent for him, it wouldn't look good to his mates. His face was pale in the candlelight as he dissapered into the night.

'Oh, Holy Mother of God, look after him,' Sarah said quietly.

'Look after us all,' Katie added.

The raid went on for nine and a half hours. It was the worst night they'd ever known, but when the All Clear sounded at half-past three in the morning and they finally emerged, they all breathed a deep sigh of relief. At least no houses around about appeared to have been damaged.

'I'll just go and see mam. She'll be out of her mind with worry about me,' Vi called as she ran up the yard.

Joe returned, his face streaked with dirt and sweat and tears. His hair was plastered to his head beneath the tin hat that he wore. He'd never thought that war was really like this. Like the terrible things he'd witnessed during this endless night. He was tired, heartsore and sickened. But he was safe and he was home.

'Will we still be going to the Empire?'

Katie looked at Josie with some impatience. 'Of course we will, *if* it's still standing. The Germans can send as many bloody planes as they like, I've paid five shillings for my seat and I'm going. After all our hard work I'm not letting bloody Hitler ruin my Christmas!'

The talk next day at work was all about the raid. Everyone was tired out. There were tales of homes demolished, personal treasures destroyed . . . and there were some faces missing at break-time. But the four girls tried to cheer everyone up with the hope and excitement of their Christmas outing.

After work they travelled home through the rubble-filled streets, changed into their best clothes, nipped out and caught the tram, and were seated in the five-shilling seats waiting for the curtain to go up, in plenty of time. The atmosphere was cheerful, the noise from the audience an expectant, excited buzz.

Joe had been promised a treat on Christmas Eve – anything within reason – so he was quite content to be with Vinny at Mary's house, making paper-chains from old newspapers which they'd painted over with red ink. Neither of the two boys had said a word about the raid the previous night, but to look at her younger brother's closed-in face, Katie could guess that he'd seen some terrible sights – things no lad of his age should ever be exposed to. She shivered, then pulled herself together. It was so lovely here, so warm and friendly, the atmosphere so exciting. She'd enjoy this evening if it killed her.

The orchestra was tuning up rather discordantly when they heard the rising wail of the siren.

'Oh, no! Not again,' Katie cried, more angry than afraid.

'What will we do?' Sarah pleaded, biting her lip, naked fear in her eyes.

'What we'll all do, girl, is stay put. Sod 'em!' a man in the row behind said loudly. He was answered by cries of, 'Aye! Sod 'em!' 'Bloody Jerries,' one shrill voice yelled. 'They bombed our chippy last night and me Mam's still livid.'

'We should go to the shelter,' Josie's eyes too were full of fear.

'Well, no one's moving by the look of it,' Vi shrugged and the orchestra burst into life with the opening music of the show: 'Strike Up the Band'.

The musicians played as loudly as they could and the audience joined in with the songs sung by the artistes on the stage, but it was impossible to drown out the noise of the planes and the earth-shuddering explosions that shook the building.

Katie looked up to see the enormous chandelier that was suspended from the centre of the high ceiling, swinging alarmingly to and fro, and flakes of plaster began to drift down like snow on to the heads of the audience. She gripped Sarah's hand tightly while Vi had a firm grip on Josie's. Suddenly it seemed to be the only way they had of fighting back – to show their defiance by singing and to keep on singing.

She hauled Sarah to her feet and Vi pulled Josie up with her as the whole audience stood and sang 'Land of Hope and Glory' and 'Rule Britannia' at the top of their voices. They'd gone to 'We'll Meet Again' and then the National Anthem which they'd kept on singing until the All Clear sounded and everyone streamed out in an orderly way, on to Lime Street.

The sight that met their eyes stunned them all. The whole city looked as though it was on fire. They could see the buildings of the waterfront etched clearly against the fiery orange sky, so obviously the docks had taken a hammering again, but there across the road – only yards away from them – St George's Hall was ablaze. Huge tongues of flame leapt upwards into the night sky, as though seeking to reach and destroy the creators of their plight.

The crowd could feel the searing heat on their faces. Fire engines were already converging on Lime Street, their bells clanging, and within minutes the hoses began to play on the fire that was destroying the Assize Courts. All over the city, infernos were raging. Engines from the entire county had been summoned, as fire crews fought to save the city's most beautiful and treasured building.

Vi finally managed to speak. 'Oh, God in heaven! How are we going to get home?'

'Walk,' Katie replied firmly and the others nodded. They were all shaken and tearful. It looked like a picture of the end of the world. It looked like the end of their city.

It took the four girls an hour to get back to Chelmsford Street because of the blazing buildings, the fires fuelled by fractured gas mains. They wended their way past miles of hosepipes, and around the enormous craters left by German bombs. They were diverted by the police and wardens many times, as buildings tottered and then collapsed in clouds of dust and flames.

Josie refused to go home to Stour Street, and after Vi called in to see if her family was safe, and had popped down to the Watsons to say that Josie was safe with them, Katie took them all into the Deegan house and put the kettle on. Only their Joe was out there amongst all that carnage and destruction. The raiders had gone, though, so she hoped he, too, was safe.

'Thank God we saved our tea ration,' Katie fussed. 'We all need a good strong cuppa, but there's no sugar, mind.'

'Oh, to hell with the sugar. Let's just have a cuppa,' Vi answered irritably.

The words were barely out of her mouth when again the long drawn-out rising wail of the siren sounded.

'They're back! They're bloody well back! Jesus, Mary and Holy Saint Joseph, haven't they don't enough damage for one night?' Vi was close to tears.

'Well, I'm not moving again until I've had my tea. I'm flaming well worn out,' Katie said grimly, although her heart had dropped like a stone as she thought of her little brother, still out, helping.

As yet, the distinctive drone of the Dorniers could not be heard, but Sarah collected up the blankets, the candles and storm lantern, while Josie took the spirit stove and the cushions off the sofa. 'You two take your tea with you. Go on, we won't be long,' Katie urged her sister and sister-in-law.

'I don't know about you, Katie, but I'm scared to death,' Vi admitted wearily. 'Me nerves have gone this time. Twice in one night, eh? What the hell are our fighters doing, for God's sake?'

Katie shrugged helplessly. 'Drink that tea and then let's get out to the shelter and hope they'll clear off soon.'

They were all exhausted after the long walk home and the terrors of the early part of the evening, yet they were all too afraid to sleep as hour after hour the bombardment went on, and time and again the shelter shuddered. Katie spent most of the night worried sick about Joe, and when he suddenly opened the shelter door, and called out:

'Anyone gorra cuppa for a little 'un?' She nearly burst into tears of relief. Her brother was covered from head to toe in soot; even his face was blackened with smoke.

'Joe! Thank God you're safe! Is our Jimmy all right?' Josie asked anxiously.

'He was half an hour ago. Goin' hell for leather, he was, down Stanley Road.' Joe managed to grin at them all, swig down a mouthful of tea and then he dashed off again.

They were stiff, numb and cold, and at four o'clock and with no sign of the raid being over, Josie began to cry softly.

It was Vi who noticed the way she was holding herself. 'Josie. What's the matter, luv?'

'Just cold and a bit of cramp,' she answered bravely, but her face twisted into a grimace as a sharper spasm of pain shot through her. She knew what lay ahead of her this time.

Katie was instantly concerned. She too knew what was happening. 'Vi, we've *got* to get her back into the house. She may be losing the baby again, and last time— Well, she *can't* stay in here.'

Vi looked stricken. 'Oh, Mother of God! How will we manage?'

'We'll do it somehow, but start praying in earnest Vi, that those bastards up there go home soon!'

Josie didn't protest at the proposed move inside but Sarah did.

'You stay here then,' Katie said sharply. 'If our Joe comes back, send him for a doctor – any doctor.'

As they assisted Josie into the darkened house, they saw the sky was lit up again with the glare of the fires from the incendiaries.

Katie turned to Vi. 'I'm going for Mary,' she hissed.

Vi just nodded and began to grope for the matches.

Outside the heavens were ablaze with red and gold light, and smoke hung heavily in the air. The ground beneath her feet shook, but Katie went on to the Mahers' house. Shouting that it was herself, and that Josie needed help, she managed to find them all huddled under the stairs.

'Jesus, Mary and Joseph, Katie! Get back to your shelter, will you? We're all right,' Mary greeted her.

'No, I think Josie's losing the baby. Oh, please will you come and help? Vi and me have got her into the house and on to the sofa and we've got some oil lamps going, but I don't know what to do! Last time Mam and Florrie coped. I only went in after it was all over.'

Mary didn't hesitate. 'Get back in there, then, I'm on me way. You'll need newspapers, towels, sheets and water, if the mains haven't gone. Oh, God help us all, but is it any wonder she's miscarrying! What a flaming world to bring a baby into. Maybe it's all for the best,' she said, shaking her head sadly as she followed Katie.

When at a quarter past five in the morning the All Clear sounded, Josie had lost her second baby.

Chapter Sixteen

Florrie came around as soon as she could after seeing Fred and the rest of her family off to work and school. Sarah and Vi had gone to the munitions factory, but Katie had stayed at home. Joe was still fast asleep. He was utterly exhausted so she'd let him take the morning off although she intended he should go to school that afternoon.

'Thank God we've still got our lives and a roof over our heads. There's hundreds who've neither this morning, God help them,' Florrie mourned. 'You should see it, luv, well I just can't find the words to describe it. They saved St George's Hall but St Anthony's School, St Alphonsus's and Crescent Church have gone. Roe Street Bus Depot and all the buses in it are wrecked. Ayrton Saunders, that chemical place in Hanover Street, got a direct hit and half the firemen have been sent to hospital from breathing in the fumes. The Royal Infirmary, Hatton Garden, the fish-market, the Electric Station in Highfield Street and the Canada, Gladstone, Brocklebank, Princes, Wapping and King's Docks and all their warehouses are in ruins. God help us, what did we ever do to them to deserve this?' Florrie paused. 'How is she? How's my poor girl?'

'She's ill and weak and frightened. Mary Mayer and Vi and me did the best we could,' Katie said. 'We couldn't find a doctor as they were all busy with people in much worse states. Oh Florrie, I am so sorry.'

The older woman shook her head sorrowfully. 'Oh, me poor girl, God love 'er. Is it any bloody wonder after last night? She was really looking forward to this Christmas, you've all put a lot of time and effort into it.'

Katie's shoulders slumped. 'I know – and things were going so well until last night. Do you think they'll be back?'

'I hope not, luv, but with them devils who can tell.' Florrie climbed wearily up the stairs after her.

Josie was lying down, but as soon as she saw her mother she sat up and burst into tears. Florrie gathered her into her arms and held her tightly.

'Oh, Mam! Mam! What's the matter with me? I keep losing them. You had six and never lost one,' she sobbed.

'Hush now. There's nothing the matter with you, queen. It's not unusual either. Mary Maher lost two before she had their Paddy, and Ellen lost one – stillborn it was. I was lucky, very lucky, and just look at what you've got to put up with. Your husband away and you not knowing when or where or even *if* he'll come back. That's enough worry to make anyone miscarry. Then on top of all that, the raids last night! Half the city in flames and you having to walk home and then they came back. Josie, luv, there'll be dozens of girls and women who'll have miscarried. You won't be on your own.'

Josie raised a tear-streaked face. 'Will there? Will there honestly, Mam? Please don't lie to me.'

'I'm not lying, Josie. Even the Royal Infirmary was hit, and you should see the mess everywhere. The smell of smoke is strong and awful. We should thank God that we were all spared and so were our houses and belongings.'

Josie at last managed a weak but rueful smile. 'We were going to have such a great Christmas, Katie, weren't we?'

'We'll still have a better Christmas than a lot of people in this city. We've still got the food, remember, although I don't know now whether we'll have any meat, we've got our decorations and we've got each other. Except for our Sarah, we've all got someone to worry about and it will take our minds off the worries.'

'That's it. You buck up now, luv. Katie's right. You just get yourself well.' Florrie smiled gratefully at Katie. If they stuck together, the four girls would come through all this. They were good friends still, despite Katie being married to one of the other lot who lived on Netherfield Road. But today, Florrie even felt pity for them, for that area had taken a heavy pounding too. All Liverpudlians were in the same boat, united against Hitler and his death-dealing Luftwaffe.

There was another raid on 23 December but Katie flatly refused to let Josie go to the shelter.

'It's cold and it's damp, and the air's not good either. You're staying here and so am I.'

Vi nodded her agreement. 'We'll take our chances. I heard a bloke on the tram saying if it's got your name on it, no shelter's going to stop it. We'll stay here in comfort, sod them!'

'I passed Hennessey's on Scotland Road, or what was left of it. Mr Hennessey had a bit notice up – CLOSED DUE TO ALTERATIONS. I thought it was – well, funny, like.'

'And brave, Sarah,' Vi replied. 'We'll get through tonight.'

Somehow they all did. No one could sleep because of the thunderous explosions, and Katie was glad now that all their windowpanes had sticky tape criss-crossing them.

This raid marked the last heavy air attack on Liverpool for the year, and despite their tearful prayers for their loved ones at Mass on Christmas Day, they *did* have a good day.

When Georgie got home in January, Josie was up and about and back at work. He'd been horrified, as was every other man on board, at the sight that met their eyes as they came slowly up the river.

'Jesus! I wonder if we've got homes to go to!' he exclaimed, thinking about the tins he had hidden in Stour Street and thanking God he carried his money with him at all times.

When they were reunited, Josie flung herself into his arms.

'Oh, thank God you've made it back safely again! It's been awful, Georgie, especially the raids just before Christmas. They went on and on.'

As she drew away he could see the fear in her eyes.

'What's the matter, Josie?'

She looked down and a tinge of pink came over her cheeks. 'O Georgie, I . . . I lost the baby again. It was the night of the first bad raid, the twenty-first. They came twice in one night, and everywhere . . . everywhere was burning! We had to walk miles to get home because of the hoses and wires and craters and burning buildings. It was terrible. I've spent a lot of time with Katie and Sarah.' To try to hide the guilt and despair she felt, she rushed on.

'Even Joe was out in the raids, as a messenger. He had to ride between the police stations and fire stations and hospitals and God knows where else, as all the phone lines were down. Vinny, Franny and our Jimmy were out as well. The poor kids, they looked terrible some nights, but they've all still gone to school. St Anthony's School got a direct hit and they've got some of the kids from there in their class.'

Georgie was more shocked by the sights he'd seen on the way home, and by learning that his kid brother had been cycling all over the place while a raid was on than by Josie's news. He didn't really mind too much about the baby. It was a rotten world to bring a kid into. Eventually he'd like to have one. Eventually he'd like to be a father and then he'd shower his child with everything. It would want for nothing because boy or girl, it would be Georgie Deegan's heir, heir to all the shops he planned to open – eventually, heir to 'Deegan's Department Stores'. Mam had once asked him why he saved so much. Did he want his name in the papers after he'd died a millionaire? she'd joked. Well, that was just it. With his business interests he *would* be a millionaire before he died. If he survived the bloody war, of course.

'Never mind, Josie,' he said calmly. 'It wasn't your fault, all that bombing. You must have been terrified.'

Josie was so relieved that she clung to him.

'You know, luv, I've been thinking,' he went on. 'What with me being away for so long these days and the danger of more raids, wouldn't it be more sensible to move?'

She looked up at him. 'Move? Where to?'

'To Chelmsford Street with our Katie and Sarah. There's room enough and I'd feel happier. I'd worry less about you if I knew you had company and that if you were expecting, like, and anything went . . . wrong again, you'd all be together.'

Again. It seemed the only word to stand out in the entire conversation. She didn't know yet whether she even wanted to be pregnant *again*. To suffer all that terrible anxiety *again*.

'Don't you think it's more sensible?' he coaxed.

Josie looked around the room that was so neat and tidy. Nothing really belonged to them, except the few little plaster ornaments and the two pictures she'd bought to give the room a more homely and personal look. He was right. She did get lonely and frightened, and what would she do if she were here during a long raid? She didn't know the Bennets that well, even though they shared the same house. She'd die of fright alone here in a raid.

She nodded. 'It is. You're right, Georgie. I'd be terrified here on my own and we do all get on well together.'

'It would save us money too, luv.'

'But I'd have to give Katie something for my keep.'

'Of course, but I meant we'd save nine and six a week on this place. You'll have your wages, and you and our Katie can sort out how much she wants for your keep. She's fair-minded, I'll give her that. You can do whatever you like with the rest. Get some little treat for yourself, luv, you deserve it.' He put his arm around her, his smile magnanimous. There were very few little treats to be had anywhere so Georgie was on safe ground there. But because he'd suggested it, it would keep her happy and she was thrifty so she'd probably save most of it. Then if she did have a baby, she'd have enough put by for clothes and cots and things like that. He also knew Katie wouldn't take too much off her.

'Do you really mean that, Georgie?' Josie was surprised.

'Of course I do, luv, and if we all come through this, we'll have enough to buy our own house. Imagine that. All paid up, like. In a nice area and good furniture too. We'll be the envy of everyone.'

That would keep her happy too, and eventually they *would* have their own house, after he'd made his fortune from the shops.

The look of anxiety had gone from Josie's eyes. He wasn't devastated that she'd lost the baby. She'd enjoy being with Katie and Sarah and their Joe, scamp that he was, and she would have her wages, two pounds ten shillings a week. She'd be able to put quite a bit in her Post Office savings regularly and still have money for the occasional treat he said she deserved. Things weren't so bad at all. She might not even mind getting pregnant again. She'd take care of herself this time, and she'd be with her friends.

Katie could also see the sense in the move, but was suspicious about Georgie telling Josie she could keep her wages. It just wasn't like him at all. It was completely out of character.

'Are you sure? You haven't got it mixed up?' she probed.

'Would I get something like that mixed up?' Josie retorted huffily.

'Does he know how much you earn?'

'Of course he does.'

Katie looked at her sister-in-law thoughtfully. Josie would be safer and happier here. In fact, they'd probably fare better with Josie's skills as a cook and dressmaker – when they had coupons for material. At that moment she saw the way her brother's devious mind was working. He'd have calculated that he'd be saving the nine and six a week rent money, plus whatever Josie used for the gas and electric, which were on meters. He knew she'd give Katie some housekeeping – but it would be nothing compared to keeping up a rented place. She wondered for the hundredth time where he got this mean streak. No one else in the family had it. Still, she wasn't going to upset Josie. In her opinion the girl should be canonised for putting up with her brother.

'What will you buy with the extra money?'

Josie shrugged. 'I'm going to save most of it.'

'In the Post Office?'

Josie nodded. 'And then, when the war's over, I'll have a tidy bit.'

'Well, just don't tell him about it – or if you do, keep some back.'

'I won't tell him until everything is back to normal.'

'God knows when that will be.' Katie's manner was brisk. 'You'd better get him to move your stuff up here then. Do you mind sharing with our Sarah, or would you prefer a bed of your own? I could share with her.'

'No, I'll share. I don't mind if Sarah doesn't.'

'What about when meladdo comes home?'

Josie frowned. 'Oh. Could we . . . could we have your room then? Just for when he's home?'

Katie nodded her agreement. She didn't relish the thought of Georgie back under this roof but if he started any of this 'Head of the Family' business, she'd write to Uncle Alfred. Manchester so far had virtually escaped raids. She wrote, anyway, every now and then to her uncle over there, and received letters back in return. In his last one he'd obviously read between the lines of the security-screened accounts the newspapers carried about the December raids in Liverpool; he told Katie that if things got very bad, the Deegans must all go and live with him until the danger had passed. He presumed Georgie was still on convoy duties and therefore away and she'd written back confirming this.

When Joe came in from school the back way, down the jigger and into the yard, he was surprised to see Georgie sitting on an upturned box, smoking a Woodbine. The dim light of the winter afternoon was already giving way to darkness and it was cold. The first stars could be seen glimmering faintly in the darkening sky.

'Oh, you're home then.'

'That's a nice greeting, I must say! "Welcome home, Georgie, it's great to see you alive and well".' Georgie carefully nicked out the cigarette and put the butt in his pocket. Cigarettes were expensive and rare and he'd picked the wrong time to start smoking. Still, it helped to steady his nerves. He often thought of all the cigarettes he'd got from the B&A. If he'd kept them, he'd be worth a fortune now.

'Well, you're not the only one involved in this war. It's not just *your* war,' Joe flashed back. In fact, after the terrors of the Christmas raids he'd begun to think his elder brother had the right idea. Oh, ships were sunk and men drowned, but not all of them. Not as many as had been killed and injured in their homes. There'd been no battleships to protect *them*, just some searchlights and ack-ack guns.

Georgie could see signs of strain on the boy's face that had never been there before.

'Did I say it was? Anyway, what's up with you? Snapping me head off like that.'

'Nothing. I'm just tired and fed up. There's nothing decent to do. It's no use playing out, you'd half-kill yourself on the bomb sites and the dirty big holes in the roads. I still have homework and I don't think there'll ever be sweets of any kind in the world ever again. Our Katie's a terrible cook and our Sarah's not much better, and if you moan about it all you hear is: "Get it down you. You can't make anything decent with the stuff that's on offer." It's awful, that Woolton Pie,' he said bitterly, scowling. 'It's flaming 'orrible! All sorts of bits of mangy vegetables and runny gravy. At least, our Sarah's gravy is runny. Ugh! It's that Lord Woolton at the Ministry of Food, our Sarah said. He'd be better off giving 'is recipes to the Jerries – that'd soon stop the war!'

Georgie looked at him thoughtfully, then made up his mind. Joe was thirteen. He only had one more year left at school, and after that . . . Yes, he might as well get some experience of life in the harsh world now.

'How would you like some ham for your tea?' Georgie said casually. 'Just you, mind, no one else.'

Joe gaped at him. 'Ham! Who's got ham?'

'I have. I've got other things too. Corned beef, Spam, tongue, tinned salmon and tuna, peaches and pears, evaporated milk, steak and onion pie-filling, jelly, blancmange and custard powder.'

Joe was almost drooling; he could taste the jelly and custard already.

'I got it all in Canada and brought it home, bit by bit, of course. You've got to be crafty, but I need somewhere to put it all and someone I can trust, really trust, to keep an eye on it and even sell it for me.'

Joe's eyes widened. 'That's Black Market! They put you in jail for that!'

'Only if they catch you, and it's the fellers who are greedy who get caught – the ones shifting big amounts. Any ideas on where we could hide it?'

Joe didn't like the word 'we'. It implied that Georgie already considered him a partner in crime. But he'd really love some ham, proper meat!

'There's the wash-house.'

'Don't be so bloody daft. Those three are in and out of there like a fiddler's elbow.'

'No, there's an old wooden box behind a load of rubbish. I don't know what Mam used it for. Not much, because it's got all kinds of things on top of it. Paint tins, rusty Brasso tins, rags and newspapers.'

Georgie got up. 'Show me it before it gets too dark.'

It was already quite dark inside the wash-house, but Joe was scrabbling away in a corner, his efforts causing dust and debris to scatter everywhere.

'For God's sake make less noise, can't you!'

'There you are.' Joe pointed to his handiwork with pride. In the midst of all the clutter and dust was a wooden box, not a very big one, the sort of thing you kept shoe polish and brushes and cloths in, but it was lined with metal so it would be ideal.

'That's great, just the job.' Georgie rubbed his hands together briskly. 'Now, after tea we can bring the stuff up.'

'Who do I sell it to?' Joe was beginning to feel nervous. 'Mrs Maher and Mrs MacCane?'

'Are you round the bloody bend altogether? I'll get the customers. I'll give them a certain time and they'll wait in the jigger. Then you can pretend you're going to the privy, nip out to see what they want, get their money then give them the tins and be back in the house in a few minutes. Simple. Nothing to worry about.'

'Georgie . . . Well, I don't want to get caught. Not like last time.'

'You won't get caught! And last time was your own fault because you were day-dreaming. You didn't have a dekko to see if anyone was watching or coming. You just leaned against the lamp staring into space like a thicko. So it's time you grew up. I'll give you half the profits,' Georgie lied. 'I can keep getting bits and pieces on each trip.'

Joe was still dubious. 'Half?'

'I said that, didn't I?'

'But how am I going to keep that from our Katie and Sarah? They'll want to know where I get money from. I can't hide it in my room because our Sarah's terrible when she cleans, she tips everything upside down, and you know what our Katie's like. She'd batter me and probably chuck me out an' all.'

'God, you're a bloody misery! I'm giving you the chance to earn more money than you'd get from a job, and all you do is whine about those two in there! I'll put it in a bank for you. Keep it safe, then when the war's over you'll have a good bit to start you off, like.'

Joe was still not completely happy, but it was a very tempting offer. 'Well, as long as I don't get caught.'

'I told you, you won't.'

Chapter Seventeen

The new arrangement at the Deegans' house in Chelmsford Street worked well; everyone was happy. The three girls found that by pooling their coupons, they could make things go further and last longer. Josie was an excellent and inventive cook, so meals improved greatly in quality if not quantity. They all took a turn with the housework, but one evening in April 1941 when Katie walked into the kitchen carrying the Ewbank carpet-sweeper she'd just used on the carpet in the living room, she found Josie was clinging to the sink. She looked ill, her face a greyish colour.

Katie dropped the Ewbank. 'Josie, what's wrong? You look terrible!'

'It's all right, really. I always look and feel like this when I'm . . . expecting.'

Katie was taken aback. 'Again?' Trust her brother. Georgie could have had more sensitivity.

Josie nodded.

Katie ran her a glass of cold water. 'Don't you think that maybe it's a bit too soon?'

'No. I want a baby and so does Georgie. It's every man's right to have an heir.'

'I know that, but . . . are you up to it?'

Josie nodded firmly. 'This time I am.'

'Well, this time you're not going to work and that's final. The war effort can do without you.'

'What about my wages?'

'To hell with your wages. Your health, and your baby, are more important.'

'But I'll have nothing to give you for my keep.'

'That doesn't matter. Anyway, when our Georgie comes home I'll prise something out of him, he's still nine and six a week better off, so don't worry!'

Josie sighed. 'Oh, I really wanted to keep on saving up and giving us all the odd treat. They were great, those oranges Da got, and he couldn't have afforded them without my money.' Fred had managed to 'buy' some of the precious fruit that had come in on a ship from a Mediterranean convoy. One of the crates had been broken and some of the fruit damaged. Such things had always been regarded by the dock-workers as a perk of the job and Fred had slipped the money to the Blocker Man as the foremen were called. Florrie had even managed to make some marmalade; not a scrap of the fruit had been wasted.

Katie's expression softened. 'They were. Never mind, at least you've got something in the Post Office already and you'll have us all to keep an eye on you. Your Mam can come round when we're at work and you can have a good natter together. We'll draw up a rota for the housework. You're doing no scrubbing or shoving furniture around to clean behind it or carting coal in, and you're not lifting the wet washing from the copper to the dolly tub either.'

'What am I going to do all day then, Katie?'

'Put your feet up and start knitting. Miss Adaire always has some wool under the counter for valued customers.'

Josie was firm. 'No, I'm not doing any more knitting.'

'Don't be so superstitious, everything is going to be fine this time. I do envy you, Josie. At least you do get to see Georgie . . . be with him. God knows when I'll see Bob again and we didn't even have much time then.'

Josie patted her arm. 'He'll be all right. He'll come through it.'

As April progressed Josie bloomed. She'd got over the sickness and felt much better than she'd done during the early days of her other pregnancies. Each morning she got up at eight o'clock, which was a real luxury compared to six. She helped get Joe off to school, then she washed up, dusted and swept and then went shopping, which invariably took up most of the early afternoon, and then she had a rest before cooking the evening meal. The weather was getting warmer too, so it wasn't too bad standing in queues.

On the first of May, after their evening meal, they were all sitting in a corner of the yard that caught the last rays of the sun. Joe had cleared it for his bike and had dumped the rubbish on top of that which covered the box of tinned food in the wash-house.

'Josie, you're looking great,' Vi complimented her.

'I'm not showing much yet, but it's an easy life. Mam thinks getting up at eight is criminal, almost a sin, and I get plenty of fresh air.'

'Discounting all the soot and muck that's in it,' Katie added.

'Well, soot or not, I could do with some of it myself, working in that stinking place,' Vi complained.

'You could work as a nurse,' Sarah suggested.

Vi raised her eyes to heaven. 'I couldn't, Sarah. You have to be

157

trained and that takes time, and besides I couldn't cope with . . . injuries.' She was about to say 'mangled bodies' but thought better of it. 'Georgie and Jack have been away ages now, Josie. Surely they should be home soon.'

'Lucky you.' Katie twisted the corner of the pocket of her cardigan. 'Sometimes I can hardly credit that I'm married.'

'I'm sorry, I didn't think. Have you had any mail this week, Mrs Goodwin?'

Katie grinned. 'No, Vi, but it's only Thursday. Letters usually arrive on a Saturday. I'm sure the Censor piles them up until he's done a couple of hundred then sends them all out together.'

'Do they have more than one bloke doing it?' Sarah asked.

'I hope so, otherwise no one would get anything,' Vi replied.

'I just thought that *could* be why the mail is so slow arriving,' the younger girl mused.

Just then, Joe came into the yard and went straight into the wash-house. They could hear him rummaging around inside and the sound of things being moved about.

Vi was curious. 'What's he doing in there?'

'I dread to think! He's got all his stuff in there – you know, toy soldiers, comics, football, meccano set, things he wants to keep safe – and I can't blame him, as long as he doesn't start messing with the copper or the pipes or the tap. It's best to ignore him,' Katie advised.

He came out, went back into the jigger and then returned.

'What are you up to now?' Katie demanded.

Joe went cold. The feller was in the jigger and wanted his stuff, and he hadn't bargained on them all sitting in the yard. He'd been terrified as he went into the wash-house, but he hadn't had much choice. The feller might have come into the yard in person and demanded his tins of corned beef, and then there would have been merry hell. He stuffed his hands in his pockets, hoping to disguise the outline of the tins.

'I promised Vinny I'd swop him two of me best ollies for his ciggie card of Dixie Dean.'

'Oh, very generous,' Vi said disparagingly.

'Why couldn't Vinny himself come in and get them?' Katie was suspicious.

'Because . . . I've got them hidden somewhere special. There's nothing wrong with that, is there?' Joe demanded, his face red and angry.

'No, not a thing. Well, go and give him his card, then get in and do your homework,' she nagged him gently. 'We're coming in ourselves soon; it's turning chilly now.'

Joe breathed a sigh of relief as he darted out into the jigger, passed over the tins in return for the money, and then went back inside and up the stairs to his bedroom, the cash clutched tightly in his hand. He was astounded by the prices Georgie asked for, and got. If this kept on he *would* have a tidy bit. Providing he wasn't caught.'

Vi had gone home and the three girls were getting ready for bed when the dismal wail of the siren sounded.

'I thought we'd been lucky for too long,' Katie sighed. 'Sarah, get the blankets and the pillows. I'll go and fetch Joe and the kettle and the stove. Josie, you just see to yourself and don't rush. I don't want you falling downstairs.'

It was eleven o'clock when Joe pushed his bicycle out into the street and started to wheel it up towards the warden's house, wondering if Georgie's stock of black-market tins would survive should a bomb go off near the house. In one way he was beginning to hope they would, because then no one could blame him. He wasn't sleeping well at night now with the threat of discovery and Reform School hanging over him, to say nothing of the raids.

Down in the shelter, the girls tried to keep their minds occupied. They played 'I spy' and other childish games. They sang, but nothing could block out the fear or ease their overstretched nerves. In fact, there were times when Sarah felt she would start screaming and not be able to stop. Only her sister's outward calmness seemed to prevent it. When at one in the morning the All Clear sounded they trooped back into the house, cold and exhausted. Josie insisted that Katie and Sarah went to bed; she'd wait up for Joe. She didn't have to get to work in the morning.

The next day it was clear the damage was heavy, and it took Katie, Vi and Sarah much longer to get to work because of broken and twisted tram-track, cables and pipes, unsafe and still-smouldering heaps of rubble that had been homes and shops the day before. Ten or so hours later they had the same long, tedious journey home, and after a day on their feet.

'God, but I'll be glad to get to bed tonight,' Vi said wearily as they turned the corner into Chelmsford Street.

'So will I, but how long will we be there? Katie's tone was pessimistic.

Her pessimism was well-founded. There was no respite. From ten o'clock until three the following morning, the Luftwaffe dropped hundreds of tons of bombs, incendiaries and landmines, which floated noiselessly down from the sky attached to green parachutes. It was a bright moonlit night. Conditions from the German point of view were perfect, and the city centre was the main target. When they left, Liverpool was once again an inferno.

'There's no way we're going to get out to Kirkby today, Katie, not with all this damage on top of yesterday's,' Vi said when she called, looking tired and miserable.

'Vi, we've got to try. If we don't, they'll have won.'

Vi sighed. 'You can try, luv, but I'm just so weary of it all.'

'All right, stay with Josie for today. It's Saturday tomorrow anyway. I'll go with our Sarah.'

Vi nodded with relief.

When they'd gone, Vi told Josie she was going down to the Pier Head.

'I just need a bit of time to meself, Josie. Time to see with my own eyes what they're doing to us. Time to think, I suppose. Just to get away from work for a day. A day for *me*, Josie.'

Josie nodded. Even cheery Vi had been changed by this war, she thought. When would it ever end?

Vi walked across the cobbled setts of Mann Island, a light breeze lifting her hair. Behind her was a wide swathe of utter devastation. Some buildings, familiar since childhood, were now unrecognisable. The grey sluggish water of the river lay ahead, the morning sun catching the ripples and turning them gold. Some of the dock warehouses were still standing but smouldering, while others were tangled masses of iron girders and shattered bricks.

She stood for a few seconds just staring at the river. It had always been here, she thought, and probably always would be, but because of it and its docks and ships, Liverpool and the Liverpudlians were paying a high price. An extortionate price. She turned and walked down to the Landing Stage, right down on to the wooden platform itself, remembering the last time she'd been here.

It was Katie's wedding day, when the men had gone off to Dunkirk in that flotilla of ships of all shapes and sizes with only one thing in common: bravery and determination. Some of those ships had not come back; they'd never cross the Mersey Bar ever again.

As she gazed sadly to her right, Vi's heart almost jumped out of her chest when she caught sight of them, coming down the Crosby Channel: the first ships of the convoy and their escorts. She'd had no idea they were due in! But as they drew closer she saw with dread how like tired, battered old warhorses they looked. Their hulls were as grey as the waters of the Mersey; many had great streaks of rust down their sides, patched-up gashes in their hulls, rigging missing, decks scoured by sea and wind. And there were gaps in their ranks: the ships and men who hadn't made it back this time.

'Jack,' she whispered. 'Oh Jack, my love. Mary, Holy Mother, tell me he's safely come home to me!'

Motionless, her heart beating steadily now, the prayer running through her head like a song, Vi watched the tugs set out to guide the cargo ships into those docks still capable of functioning. And then, finally, the naval escorts came alongside the stage, as battered as the ships they'd tried so hard to protect from the U-boat packs.

At last, like a dream, she saw Jack coming down the gangway of the *Victor* and she pushed forward to meet him, her arms outstretched, tears streaming down her cheeks.

'Vi! Me own girl! How the hell did you know we were coming in?' He seemed so solid, so normal.

'I didn't,' she said tremulously. 'Something just made me come down here. I couldn't face work today, not after last night.'

Jack looked around and nodded grimly. 'They've been back? Jerry bastards!'

She nodded. 'Two nights on the run. Where's Georgie? Is he all right?' Her thoughts now were for Josie.

'He's OK. Let's just say the devil looks after his own. He'll get a tram from the Brocklebank Dock, that's where they're berthing and unloading, if there's anywhere left to store the cargo.'

'He'll be bloody lucky,' Vi joked. 'There's no trams running down there yet.'

'He'll have to walk then, won't he? Come on, let's go and get a cuppa before we go back home.'

Vi tucked her arm through his and leaned her cheek against his chest, her weariness gone, chased away by joy and thankfulness.

Josie was very relieved to know that Georgie was on his way home, then mortified that she had nothing special for him to eat.

'I wasn't prepared. I'd have gone shopping,' she said, flustered.

'You didn't know, and anyway what is there to get?'

'How did you know they were coming in, Vi?' Now she was getting over the shock, Josie was amazed by the coincidence.

'I didn't know. I just had a funny sort of feeling. I suppose I could have got a bit of something to eat on the way home.'

'You couldn't – I've got the ration books,' Josie reminded her.

'Well, I'm off to see Mam. I'll be back later, Vi,' Jack promised.

By the time Georgie got home, tired and covered in grime, Josie had managed to scrape together enough bits and pieces for a nice savoury pie.

'What a bloody mess!', he cursed, after giving her a perfunctory kiss. 'You should see the state of the dock road. There's more flamin' craters in it than on the moon. There's ships sunk at their moorings, cargo sheds and whole warehouses gone.'

'I can imagine, we've had it bad for two nights running now.' The worry lines between Josie's eyebrows eased and she smiled. 'But you're home now, luv.'

He gave her a more affectionate hug. 'Are you feeling all right?'

'Yes. Yes, I'm great. You were right, it was the best thing to do, move in here. Your sisters spoil me rotten. I stay in bed until all hours in the morning, although after the last two nights I've not had much sleep.'

'With a bit of luck the Jerries'll have packed it in now, just like they did before Christmas,' Georgie replied.

After they'd all shared the pie, they listened to the wireless and then Josie moved her toiletries and nightdress into Katie's room, and Katie moved her things into Sarah's. Georgie was halfway up the stairs when the keening notes of the siren started up.

For the girls and Joe it was becoming a frightening but familiar routine. They gathered up what they would need and went downstairs, followed by Joe, fully dressed and equipped with his tin hat and bull's-eye lantern. Sarah begged him not to go.

'You've done two nights running, Joe. They won't mind, surely?'

'But *I* will,' he told her stubbornly. 'I'm not having me mates saying I'm a coward.'

'Well, come back and report every now and then so we'll know you're all right, or we'll have our Sarah in hysterics,' Katie instructed him, beginning to feel the strain herself.

It was the worst attack so far. Night-fighters brought down sixteen enemy planes, but from a force of five hundred it was hardly noticeable.

Georgie sat with his arm around Josie's shoulder. She was wrapped in a blanket and she clung to him tightly as the explosions came thick and fast.

Joe did call in, looking like a sooty little angel; sweat had made runnels down the grime on his cheeks. He was followed by Jack, who was also covered in soot and plaster dust.

'Georgie, you'd better get out there, mate,' he said hoarsely. 'The whole bloody city's on fire. There's waves of 'em, there must be hundreds of planes – and if they keep this up, the way they're going there won't be a bloody building left standing!'

Georgie disentangled himself from his wife's warm plump arms. He'd come home for a rest, to get away from hours spent with his nerves stretched to breaking point. All he wanted to do was get a couple of decent nights' sleep and now this! He got stiffly to his feet.

Josie bit her knuckles to stifle a cry of protest and watched helplessly as her husband followed Jack. All she could do was pray for his safety.

Just after midnight and with no let up, Vi arrived, out of breath, red-faced and with her hair in curling pins.

'What's the matter?' Katie screamed at her.

'Calm down! Nothing, all right? I'm just so flaming fed up with me Mam and the kids and the carry-on out of them all that I ran around here. Da's out doing his bit with the searchlight battery but every time there's an explosion me Mam screeches like a banshee and then the kids start. It's like a flaming zoo in that shelter!'

'You ran down here in this?' Katie was incredulous.

'I know, I must be mad. I met an ARP feller and he told me we'll be lucky to *have* a city by morning. Lewis's has gone, there's flock and feathers everywhere from the bedding department. Blackler's has burned to the ground, the water main is broken and the firemen couldn't do a thing. The Post Office in Victoria Street, the Museum, the Picton Library, the Lending and the Music Libraries have gone and the Walker Art Gallery's been hit, ditto the Central Phone Exchange. Oh, it just goes on and on.'

Sarah's lip began to tremble and there was terror in her eyes. 'Oh, God! They're going to wipe us out, kill us all! There's hundreds of planes and—'

Vi turned to her, regretting the hysteria her news had set off. She caught the girl by the shoulders and shook her hard.

'For God's sake, Sarah Deegan, don't you start as well! I've come running round here, with all hell breaking loose outside, to escape from screaming, hysterical women, so you can bloody well pipe down as well.'

Katie shot her a grateful look as Sarah's sobs became quieter.

It was five o'clock and daylight before the raid was over, and still later when Joe and Georgie and Jack arrived back. There were cries of relief all round, followed by exclamations at the state they were in. While Katie and Vi made tea and some toast, Josie and Sarah cleaned burns on faces and hands, and then smeared Vaseline on them, listening to an account of the full horrors of the night from two exhausted men and a very shaken Joe.

Jack had gone home to see his parents, and Georgie and Joe were getting washed in the kitchen when Fred, Florrie, Jimmy and the rest of the Watson family arrived.

Josie could see that her Mam had been crying.

'Mam, what's the matter?' she panicked.

Florrie was so overcome all she could do was shake her head silently.

Finally Fred spoke for her. 'We're bombed out, luv. There's nothing left except bits of broken furniture.' He sounded exhausted. He'd been up all night like nearly every man in Liverpool. What had hurt the most, though, was the heartbroken look on Florrie's face as they came up from the public shelter and witnessed the awful sight of their home in complete ruins. It was still smouldering so there was nothing they could try to salvage.

'Oh, Da!' Josie's cry was heartfelt and she turned to Georgie. 'They've lost everything . . . everything!'

'I'm sorry for your trouble, Mr Watson. I really am.'

'They'll have to move in with us,' Josie said swiftly.

'Where?' Georgie looked at her in amazement. 'We haven't got room.'

Josie's eyes filled with tears. 'They've got *nothing*, Georgie! *Nothing!*'

'Well, I've said I'm sorry.'

Florrie drew the remnants of her shattered dignity around her. She wasn't going to beg to the likes of him. They'd sort themselves out somehow.

'Don't upset yerself, luv,' she said firmly to her daughter. 'We'll find somewhere. We'll get sorted, never you fear.'

Josie had been remembering her childhood home. Overcrowded but clean, happy days and memories.

'NO!' She looked up at her husband and defied him for the first time in her married life. 'If they go then I go too, Georgie. I mean it.'

'No one's going anywhere.' Katie turned on her brother. 'You're only here a few days at a time! *I'm* the one who has to be responsible for everyone then and Josie's not leaving this house in her condition. You are all very welcome to move in, Mrs Watson. We'll manage somehow. Times are bad and we've got to help each other.'

All over the city, people were moving in with neighbours, friends and relations. The same was true in Bootle, which had been badly damaged because of its close proximity to the northern docks.

'It's the shipping they're after,' Jack said later, as he and Vi sat on a pile of rubble that had been Vi's home. The Drapers had been lucky; the shelter had saved the family but not the house.

'They've all gone to me aunty's but she'd drive me totally do-lally. Jesus, Mary and Joseph, her and me Mam together! I'd sooner sleep in the street,' Vi shuddered.

'But you *are* going to Katie's?'

Vi nodded. 'God knows we'll be like sardines; all Josie's lot are there, they got bombed out too, but it's still better than me Aunty Mary's. It's losing all my things that's upset me most, Jack. My clothes, make-up, your letters, all my bits of jewellery. Only cheap, mind – Woollies' best, but nice. I've got my identity card and ration books thank God, they were in my handbag and I never leave that behind anywhere.'

'Don't worry, luv, I'll give you some money and coupons for more,' he said tenderly.

'And where the hell am I going to *find* more? There's hardly any shops left standing! I'd have to go to Manchester.' She gave a watery laugh.

Jack fumbled in his pocket. 'I got you this over in Canada.'

Vi opened the little box. Inside was a gold ring with a small diamond and sapphires set on a twist. 'Oh, Jack Milligan,' she gasped. 'It's gorgeous!'

He grinned. 'So, will you?'

'Will I what?' Her heart was hammering against her ribs, but she wanted to hear him say the words.

'Will you marry me, Violet Catherine Draper?'

She smiled, then looked serious. 'I will, Jack, but not till next time you come home.'

He was disappointed. 'Why then?'

'Because I want to try and get organised. Have something to look forward to, feel like a fiancée. Jack, we've got nothing now!' She said urgently. 'Not a stick of furniture or a stitch of clothing, except what we're wearing now. It all went up in flames last night.'

He sighed. He could understand. 'It won't go on for ever, Vi. I love you and I'll give you everything, the best I can afford – always.'

She touched his cheek. 'I love you, too, and I know you'll be good to me, but I want to look like a bride. Oh, not in yards of white satin and a veil. Just something nice and smart. So, let's wait, it's only for a little while.' She grinned. 'After all, I've got to have time to flash me ring about, haven't I?'

Chapter Eighteen

The following night Jack, Georgie, Fred, Joe and Jimmy Watson were out as soon as the first wave of Dorniers was heard. Incendiaries posed one of the worst dangers and people were out now firewatching – putting out the small fires with stirrup pumps before they could take a stronger hold.

Josie, Vi, Sarah, Katie, Florrie and her four girls sat for hour after hour crowded in the shelter as death and destruction fell all around them.

They all heard the shrill whistling that grew louder and louder, aiming straight at them, and they clutched at each other, naked terror in their eyes. This was close, very, very close. Was it their turn, Katie wondered? Was this it? *Oh, Mam! Mam! If you can hear me, don't let this one be for us!* Hail Mary, full of grace . . . she prayed, her arms tightly around a trembling Sarah.

The whole shelter vibrated and the ground beneath their feet moved. Cracks appeared in the concrete base and the blast threw Katie, Vi, Sarah and Brenda Watson across the bunk but their screams were drowned out by the explosion.

Then a complete eerie silence reigned.

'Is . . . is everyone all right?' Florrie's voice asked tremulously from the darkness. She was amazed to find herself alive and uninjured.

'I am. If I can find the matches I'll light the candles again,' Katie volunteered.

'Josie, Sarah, Vi, Norma, Betty and Daisy?' Florrie's voice was steady and had a more authoritative note now.

'We're all fine, Mam, and I know the baby is safe, too.' Josie's voice was also quite steady.

'It must have been next door that got it – Mary Maher's,' Katie said quietly.

'Then let's hope to God that they were in the public shelter. I told Mary only yesterday that they should stop all this nonsense of huddling together under the stairs. The way things are going, it's just too dangerous.'

'But if they've been hit they'll have nothing,' Sarah said sadly.

'They'll have their lives and we've got nothing, Sarah, but we get by,' Florrie reminded her.

'We'll have room for Vinny and Mrs Maher,' Katie said.

'She'll be grateful for that, luv, if they have got hit. You feel so lost and bewildered, not knowing who to turn to or what to do at first. That's how I felt. You just don't believe it and then ... well, probably Ellen MacCane would take the rest, if their house is safe. It's make do and mend for everyone these days, for the time being at least.'

Florrie stood with her arms around Mary Maher as next morning they viewed the pile of rubble.

'Ah God, Florrie!' the woman wept. 'All them years. All that scrapin' to make ends meet an' get a few bits of stuff around yer that yer could call 'ome, an' look at it now.'

'I know, luv. I really do. There's not a thing of any use in what's left of our house, too, and I can't go near it because of gas leaks, and the stink of the broken sewers would turn yer stomach. And now comes the worst bit.' She nodded grimly.

Mary looked at her anxiously. 'What?'

'The traipsing all over the city for new ration books, identity cards, clothes and blankets. Somewhere to stay if you've no roof over your head at all and no one to help put you up. You have to go to the Rest Centres then. It's the docks and the shipping the Germans are after; we just happen to be in the way.'

'Well, their aim is flaming lousy! They must all be bloody cross-eyed like that nasty little git who started this war,' Mary replied with pure venom in her voice.

The increased number in the household annoyed Georgie. Katie had taken it on herself to close the shop and they'd pulled down the window blind and got mattresses on the floor in there and empty fruit boxes for the bits and bobs the Watsons and Mahers had been able to salvage. She'd told him and Jack to look for some pieces of wood, any kind would do, to nail over the huge window. Even though it was taped across, the piece of sheet glass had shattered the night Mary's house was demolished. It had taken herself, Sarah and Vi a long time to sweep up all the fragments and Sarah had managed to cut herself.

The two older women seemed to have taken over the whole household, Georgie thought grimly. Allotting chores, doling out times and turns for washing in the kitchen. All the girls, with the exception of Josie, had gone back to work. It took them hours to get there and to get back, but each day they went on doggedly as night after night without let-up the raids continued.

In number two Husskison Dock, the ammunition ship *Malakand* had been hit and gone up in a series of massive explosions that had hurled pieces of metal for miles and demolished the whole dock and all its buildings.

As more homes were demolished, people went out to the countryside, to Huyton Woods on the estate of Lord Derby, just to sleep, thankful for the warm nights and skies from which fire and death didn't rain down on them. Lorries took them in the late afternoon and brought them back next morning and American canteen trucks kept them supplied with hot food and drinks, courtesy of the citizens of the towns in America that had donated them.

There were now fifteen people living in both the shop and accommodation at Chelmsford Street. Mary and her family had been offered shelter with her sister in Portland Gardens, off Scotland Road. Although that whole area had been hard hit, those who had homes still intact generously offered help to relations less fortunate, even if it meant serious overcrowding.

'It's dead good of her I know,' Mary said, 'but they're only two up, two down and there's five of them already. The place is fallin' down and they've got bugs.'

'Bugs!' Josie shuddered with revulsion.

'Oh, aye, they've had them for years and can't get rid of them.' Mary's tone was very matter-of-fact. People had to live somewhere and not everyone was fortunate. 'The council have tried all kinds of things ter shift them, but back they come. It's something ter do with what the houses are made from.'

'Rubbish is what most of them are made from,' Florrie interrupted. 'They should all have been knocked down years ago. I know women down there who wear themselves out trying to keep the place respectable but it's no use. At least now most of them have been flattened, so the council will *have* to build new ones.'

'So, if yer don't mind, Katie, queen, we'll stay put,' Mary concluded.

'It's a good job we're not often all in at the same time,' Katie had laughed.

After the following night's raid Jimmy, Vinny, Franny and Joe came in tired, dirty and wan-faced as usual, but Mary could tell by her son's expression and stance that they'd been up to something other than the message-running they had undertaken every other night that week.

'He's been up to something, I can see it in his eyes. All right, meladdo, what is it?' she demanded sternly.

'Nothing, Mam, honest!' Vinny was trying very hard to look innocent.

'I can read yer like a book, Vinny Maher. Where've yer been?'

'Yer know where I've been, Mam.' He was indignant. 'With Jimmy and Joe and Franny.'

'Where?'

'Helpin' like we always do, taking messages, and then we was helpin' Georgie.'

At the mention of her brother's name, Mary's suspicions seemed to transfer themselves to Katie, and she scrutinised Joe's face. 'Helping Georgie do what?'

'Firewatching,' he replied.

'You're supposed to be a messenger boy, so why were you firewatching?'

'We were doing both.'

Mary, Katie and Florrie exchanged looks while the three miscreants tried their best to look innocent and earnest.

'What have you got in your coat pocket, Vinny Maher?' Vi demanded, having noticed that all their pockets were sagging slightly. Whatever was in them was heavy. Marbles or possibly ball bearings, she surmised.

'Nothing, just . . . things,' Vinny answered lamely.

Mary grabbed him by the shoulder and shook him. 'Turn them pockets out! Now!'

Beneath the grime all three of them paled.

Vinny made no move so Mary unceremoniously yanked his jacket off and turned it upside down above the kitchen table. A shower of coins, nearly all pennies, but some sixpences and shillings, fell clattering on to the table.

'Right, you as well, Jimmy Watson!' Florrie commanded while Katie stood with her arms folded across her chest and glared at Joe, who delved into his pockets and began to add to the collection on the table top. When all the pockets had been emptied, it was covered in coins.

'Yer thieving little get! Where did it all come from?' Mary clipped Vinny hard across the ear. 'An' don't tell me no barefaced lies, Vincent Maher. Just you wait till yer Da gets in.'

Jimmy Watson was also the recipient of a hefty clout and the same question. He broke down in tears.

'It wasn't my fault, Mam. It wasn't! They're older than me. It wasn't my idea!'

'Where the flaming hell did you get it all?' Mary demanded of Vinny.

'I know where they got it,' Vi interrupted. 'They've been looting

169

gas and electric meters in bombed-out houses.'

Mary and Florrie looked confused but Katie's expression was grim.

'And I've a good idea who put them up to it. You said you were helping our Georgie out, didn't you? And this is the result, isn't it? How much of it did he say he wanted for himself, then?' she demanded.

The three boys looked down, shamefaced. Jimmy and Vinny in tears, Joe just on the brink.

'How much, Joe?' she demanded again.

'Nothing,' he replied sullenly. Georgie had done it again – got him into trouble. He'd foolishly believed his elder brother when he'd said it was easy money and who was there to know about it? 'He said if we didn't take it someone else would.'

'That's just the sort of thing he would say. Right, seeing as you've got no Da, thank God he's in heaven and Mam too, and our Georgie's shoving you off the straight and narrow instead of keeping you on it, when Mr Watson and Mr Maher get in then you'll receive the same punishment as these two. Is that all right with you, Mrs Watson, Mrs Maher?'

Both women nodded grimly. It would be the fathers' broad leather belts with the buckle end for this despicable crime, and then straight off to Father Macreedy for a verbal dressing-down.

Joe stood petrified. He'd often been chastised by his Da and his Mam, but never with the buckle end of a belt. In fact, his Da had never taken his belt off to him. It wasn't fair! He shouldn't have taken any notice of Georgie. Georgie had been lying again when he said they wouldn't get caught. That it was easy money, just lying around. Joe broke down completely.

'I didn't want to do it and I didn't want anything to do with the tins and the fellers that came for them or any of the money! I never wanted to do it! He *made* me! He said—'

'What tins and what fellers?' Katie interrupted.

'The tins in the wash-house.' Joe was sobbing now. He'd thought himself hard after what he'd seen over the last weeks, but he wasn't really. He was just a kid, still at school, tired out and frightened by racing around the dark streets while overhead, enemy bombers dropped their loads and buildings burst into flames or came crashing down. He was doing work and seeing things no lad his age should ever have to see, and now it looked as though he was in deep trouble. He remembered the last time, when he'd been carted off by the police. Well, he wasn't going to keep his mouth shut this time and take all the blame again.

Katie was livid. 'Gerrup those dancers, now. I want the whole story and the truth! Mrs Watson and Mrs Maher have a right to know if their two are involved, but I'll sort you out first, meladdo!' She listened with mounting fury as Joe told her of the whole set-up. Black-marketeering, even in a small way, was still a criminal offence, never mind a moral one. Georgie and Joe could go to jail for it.

'I don't want to go to a Reform School. I'm sorry I did it,' he sobbed.

'In the name of God, will you never grow up, Joe Deegan? Will you never understand that our Georgie's as rotten as they come and deserves to be locked up? But he's not taking this family down with him, oh no! You stay up here while I sort this out.'

How she wished that her husband Bob were here. She seemed to have spent most of her life trying to keep one step ahead of her brother and his immoral, not to say criminal, activities.

When she came downstairs, Vi, Josie and Sarah were helping Mary and Florrie to count up the coins into neat piles, each equalling a pound. They'd decided it would all be taken to the parish priest for him to contact the authorities. Jimmy and Vinny sat pale and tearful in a corner of the room.

She stormed across the living room to the kitchen. 'Katie. Where are you going?' Sarah asked fearfully.

'To the wash-house. I won't be long.' She left all the doors open behind her and when she returned she had her arms around an old box that was obviously heavy. She dumped it on the table and opened it.

'There! Ham, tongue, corned beef, salmon, tuna fish, sardines, peaches, pineapple, evaporated milk, jelly, blancmange, custard powder, tea and coffee, all in tins and right under our noses. Your beloved husband, Josie, has gone into the black-market, it seems.'

'Holy Mother of God! Where did he get all this?'

'He smuggled it home, Mrs Maher. And while we all, including you, Josie, were trying to manage on what little bits of stuff we could get, he had this lot out there, for sale at prices that would make you faint!'

Florrie crossed herself. 'Holy Mother, that's a crime. He could—'

'Go to jail and our Joe could end up in a Reform School – and that fiend couldn't care less,' Katie finished for her. 'What kind of a brother have I got? How can he be so cruel and uncaring? Poor Josie pregnant, and having to stand in queues and make meals out of God-awful stuff! Oh, thank God Mam and Da aren't here.' Katie slumped down at the table, shaking with temper, but her eyes brimming with tears at the shock of it all.

Mary put an arm around her. 'Come on, queen, it's not your fault. Don't go getting upset about a few tins. None of us will say a word, out of respect to yer Mam and Dad, and neither will those two little hooligans either. Their Das will see to them.'

Florrie nodded her agreement, but was deeply shaken. Her poor Josie was married to this creature. 'For better or for worse', it had been, and up to now it had all been 'for worse'.

The women formed a little tableau around Katie and were still trying to calm and console her when Georgie walked in.

His eyes went immediately to the box and the neat piles of coins and then to the faces of the women.

Katie leaped to her feet and physically shoved him backwards into the kitchen. 'Get in there, you! By God, I've got something to say to you!'

She slammed the door behind her and stood with her back to it. 'What kind of a person – no, you're not a person, you're a thieving, lying devil, Georgie Deegan! People are near to starvation, they've lost their homes and everything they own, and you ... you *hide* food, keep it from your own wife even and her pregnant. You've kept it from us, too, your own family – but you get exorbitant amounts for it from strangers!'

Georgie had been taken completely off his guard by her fury but now he had gathered his wits.

'You're talking about a few shillings here and there. With the risks I take, I deserve a bit of a bonus,' he snapped.

She threw back her head and laughed mockingly. Those listening outside heard her clearly. 'A bonus, a bloody bonus – is that what you call it? If you were bringing it for Josie, for us, I could understand. God in heaven, I just can't find the words to describe you! And then, not content with corrupting our Joe for the second time, you get those other little fools to go looting meters in the wreckage of people's homes! You're despicable! Disgusting!'

'Well, if they didn't take it someone else would,' he growled.

'That's no answer and I'll bet Mr Watson and Mr Maher won't see it like that, either. There's going to be plenty of clouts being doled out later and not just to those two little fools. I'd get out of here before they come round, and but for the fact of disgracing Mam and Dad's name and memory, I'd turn you over to the scuffers myself.'

She put her hands on her hips, raking him with a contemptuous stare. 'How much have you saved up now then? It must be close to a hundred pounds, if not more. And how long did you expect your little game with the tins to go on? Well, you step out of line once more, just once, and I'll have you behind bars in Walton. But for Josie's sake and the other good men you sail with and the precious cargo, I'd say "I hope a bloody U-boat gets you next time you go! I hope you drown in the freezing waters of the Atlantic!" You'd be no loss to anyone, Georgie Deegan. Risks! Risks and bonuses! Neither of them are even thought about by Jack Milligan or any of the others. Get out! Go on – get out of my sight now. Get out there with the other men – you might just be able to do a bit of good somewhere!'

He glared at her, a look full of venom, but she was so furious she didn't even notice. Then, wrenching open the back door, he stormed out. She slammed it so hard after him that the panes in the window rattled loudly and then she went back into the living room.

'Sit down, luv, you're in a terrible state,' Mary said. Vi had put the kettle on. They'd heard every word. It was impossible not to.

Katie turned to Josie. 'Oh, Josie, I'm sorry. I'm so sorry . . . what can I say? He's my brother, but I wish to God he wasn't.'

Josie said nothing; she was still stunned. He'd brought all that food home and not even told her. He'd seemed to be really and genuinely concerned about her and the baby, yet how could he be, and still do this?

'Don't worry about her, she'll be all right. I'll keep my eye on her,' Florrie promised grimly.

Katie dropped her head in her hands, her anger spent, replaced by utter exhaustion, and she began to cry.

Vi put her arms around her. 'Cry it out, luv. It's all the tension and the worry and the anger and shame. Cry it out.'

'Oh Vi, I miss Bob so much. I want him here now. I'm sick of coping with everything and putting up with our Georgie. He's done some nasty things in the past, but this is the worst yet.'

Mary patted her arm. 'Listen, queen, didn't we all agree ter say nothing? Yer know yer can trust us, and as for meladdo in the corner there, his Da will sort him out good and proper. We've never had much, we've got nothing at all now, but we've never *thieved* a single thing.' Mary glared at her son who cowered against Jimmy.

'Aye, and it'll be the first and last time that one will touch anything that's not his,' Florrie added fiercely before turning back to Mary. 'Hadn't one of us better go and inform Ellen of what their Francis has been up to? No need to elaborate, like, or say anything about the tins, but she'd go mad if someone else told her.'

Mary nodded. 'I'll do it.'

Sarah had remained in a state of silent horror for most of the time but now she looked at Katie. 'What will we do with all the tinned stuff?'

Vi looked at her still-tearful friend. 'She's got a good question there, Katie. Shall we save it and use it bit by bit, or shall we have a slap-up feed when the men get back?'

Katie managed a watery smile. 'We'll all have a good meal – especially Josie – but we'll save some of it for your wedding breakfast, Vi.'

Chapter Nineteen

After seven continuous nights of German air-raids, the city of Liverpool was in ruins. Half of all homes had been flattened or burnt out, and the docks were in such a state that a casual observer would think it impossible for them to still be operational. But they were. By early evening on 8 May 1941 the citizens of Liverpool and Bootle were wearily clutching the items they took with them to the shelters waiting for the banshee wail of the siren. It never came. Their nightmare ordeal was finally over.

All through that terrible week in May, thousands of civilians had been killed and injured, and everything they owned had gone, but the port had remained working and gradually the ships of the next convoy were loaded then nudged and edged by the tugs out into the river, to the anchorages allotted to them.

No one was supposed to know when they were due to sail, but Jack told Vi and she went down to the landing stage to see him off. The Royal Navy tug *Skirmisher* was waiting for the last men of the escort's crews.

'You're sure you want to wait until I come back, Vi? I mean, we could make a quick dash to the nearest Catholic Church or even Brougham Terrace?'

'I'm NOT going to Brougham Terrace, and we'd never have enough time to get a church and registrar organised. Everything *will* be ready, I *will* be organised when you come back, and I *know* you *will* come back. Here, I got you something.'

He took the small box and opened it. Inside was a silver-coloured chain on which hung a St Christopher medal, along with a cross, an anchor and a heart – the symbols for faith, hope and charity.

Jack took Vi in his arms and held her tightly, burying his face in her soft blonde hair.

'I love you, Vi Draper,' he murmured passionately, but with a catch in his throat.

She couldn't speak, she just nodded and raised a tear-stained face for him to kiss.

'*If yer don't gerra move on, yer'll miss the bloody boat an' then yer'll get cashiered for 'oldin' up the convoy! What's the bloody Service comin' to, that's what I want ter know? In the owld days they'd've 'ad yer flogged before the mast, mate!'*

The reminder, bawled from the deck of the tug, finally made Vi draw away from him. 'Goodbye, Jack, luv. Take care of yourself.'

'God keep you, Vi. It won't be long now,' he called as he ran lightly and easily across the gangplank.

She watched *Skirmisher* cast off and pull away out into the sluggish grey water of the River Mersey, her wake a dirty foamy streak. Right downriver towards New Brighton with its old fort and lighthouse, the ships of the convoy were assembled. She began to count them but stopped at twenty-nine. It wouldn't help; it would only depress her if she began to think how many wouldn't come back. *HMS Victor* looked so small beside some of the lightly armed merchantships, like a toy boat beside the larger Cunarders. They still all travelled at the fastest speed of the slowest ship, which Jack said was infuriating for many captains. Some had put forward the suggestion to the Admiralty that there be 'fast' and 'slow' convoys. The suggestion had been ignored.

Vi brushed away her tears. He *would* come back, she *knew* he would – and for Josie's sake she hoped Georgie would too.

Vi had the money and she had the coupons, thanks to the generosity of her friends – but where was she going to get her wedding clothes? Nearly all the big stores in town had either been demolished or gutted by fire. A few were still in business, like the Bon Marché, George Henry Lee and of course Cripps in Bold Street, but she couldn't afford their prices. She'd intended to go to Frisby Dyke in Lord Street but it too had been gutted.

'It would take all me money and coupons just to walk through the doors of those places,' she joked miserably.

'What about Sturlas?' Katie suggested the department store in Great Homer Street.

'I'm not a snob, Katie, but I wanted something a bit classier.'

'What about Owen Owen's, then?'

'Too expensive.'

'Couldn't Josie help?' Sarah interrupted.

'Oh, I couldn't ask her. She's supposed to be taking things easy.'

'Well, it's not all that arduous to make a dress or something,' Vi said.

'It's the cutting out,' Katie said. 'The bending and stretching, leaning across the table or even having to crawl around the floor if the table's too small – although I could do that for her, get it pinned on and cut out.'

'Do you think she'd mind, really?' Vi questioned.

'Of course not,' Katie said dryly. 'You're marrying a Catholic.'

Sarah defended her sister-in-law. 'Oh Katie, that's not fair! I don't think it was really Josie that wouldn't help with your outfit, it was our Georgie who told her not to.'

'She takes too much notice of him. I'd clock him one if he was my husband, the way he treats her. "Do this, don't do that!" But then I wouldn't have been daft enough to marry him in the first place,' Vi said acidly.

'Hush, she'll hear you,' Sarah hissed at Vi as Josie came downstairs.

'What's the matter with you, Vi Draper? You've a face as long as a drink of water?' Josie said, looking at the unsmiling, anxious little group.

They were still terribly overcrowded, but Mary Maher and Vinny had gone to rejoin the family now staying with one of Jack Maher's relations in Walton-on-the-hill.

'We'll have ter pay to speak ter yer now, I suppose?' Ellen MacCane had laughed when Mary had told her.

'It's not *that* posh, Ellen! It's still only a two-bedroom parlour-house and besides, I'll be comin' down here to do me shopping.'

'Your queuing, more like,' Ellen had retorted.

Vi looked pleadingly at Josie. 'I just don't know what to do about an outfit. The only shops left with decent stuff to sell are the posh ones.'

'I said – well, I wondered . . .' Sarah hesitated.

'She wondered if *you'd* help out,' Katie said forthrightly.

Josie shrugged. 'Of course – but do you trust me? You remember it was Mrs Frost in Sessions Street that did your dresses for my wedding.'

'Well, most of Sessions Street is a pile of rubble now and God knows where Mrs Frost is, so she'll *have* to trust you. But anyway you're great, Josie, you really are! You should do it professionally. You could work from home then.'

'What home? It's like Lime Street Station in here most of the time.'

'It won't always be like this,' Katie said, trying to put an optimistic note in her voice. 'Your Mam and Da will get rehoused and you're here with just your Mam in the day while everyone else is out.'

Josie sat down on the edge of the sofa. 'What did you want, Vi?'

'I don't really know. Something a bit special, though.'

'Rayon is cheap and now it's summer there are bound to be nice flowery prints,' Josie suggested.

Vi pulled a face. 'They'll look . . . ordinary.'

'They won't. Ordinary is all the utility stuff. It's like the civvies' army, we all look the same. Same style, different colours.'

Josie's brow was furrowed in concentration. 'Do you want it to last? Change it around a bit afterwards?'

Vi nodded.

'Moss crêpe, then. It hangs like silk but it'll last.'

'Where will we get that and how much a yard will it cost?'

'It depends on how full you want the skirt.' Josie was really getting down to business now. 'What about a fairly plain dress, with a short skirt with two box pleats in the front, a narrow belt and short sleeves. Padded shoulders of course, and with a bolero to go over it in a darker colour. We could trim the sleeves and the neck of the dress in the darker colour to contrast and even use up the scraps on a hat. With your colour hair, Vi, a lovely pale green with a dark green bolero and trim would look great.'

'Where will we get it?'

'The Co-op on County Road. I saw some from the tram window last time I went with Mam to see Mrs Maher.'

'And how much a yard was it?'

'I couldn't see that far, Vi. The price ticket was too small.'

'Well, it sounds great,' Katie enthused. She fully intended to help Vi with the cost if it was beyond her resources. She'd say it was her wedding present.

Sarah offered Vi the loan of her new shoes that were the very latest fashion. They were made from bleached raffia and canvas and had a high platform sole like those worn by Carmen Miranda, the exotic South American singing star.

'Well, just as long as you don't have to wear a flaming fruit bowl, complete with pineapples, on your head like she does,' Josie giggled.

'Chance would be a fine thing. I've never even tasted a pineapple!' Vi replied good-humouredly.

Because money was tight and they were so overcrowded, there was to be no wedding breakfast on the scale that Josie had enjoyed. The mattresses and other bits were to be removed from the shop and put temporarily into the yard, under the lean-to if necessary. The shop walls were given a fresh coat of white distemper and Sarah was going to make huge bows to decorate them out of pink crepe paper which she'd begged and pleaded from Mr Daly in the newsagent's. She'd also been saving and scrounging silver paper which she was going to stick onto cardboard bell shapes and lucky horseshoes. All were Josie's suggestions. The shop counter would be covered with Molly's best white cloth and the good dishes would be set out on it. They had kept the jelly and blancmange powder, some evaporated milk and two tins of salmon and a tin of ham from Georgie's illegal hoard, so there would be salmon and ham sandwiches for the wedding feast. The rest had been eaten with great relish, although some jelly and custard had been set aside for the kids in the street as a special treat, even if it would only provide a mouthful each.

'You'll have them crawling out of the woodwork, Vi, once they hear about this spread,' Katie joked. 'You'll see relations you haven't clapped eyes on in years.'

'Or didn't know I had. Well, it's just family and friends. You can choose your friends, you're stuck with the damned relations, but to hell with 'em and I don't care if they all get a cob on over it. It's wartime.'

They'd been and bought the material and it was beautiful. 'It really does hang like silk and it looks *so* expensive,' Sarah enthused as she draped it over her arm.

'It was,' was Josie's comment. She, too, had dipped into her savings to help out, although she hadn't minded.

The pale colour was what the sales assistant called 'Eau de Nil' and the darker green was called 'Holly Green'.

'It's more like sage green,' Katie commented meaningfully.

'Oh, don't go and bring that up!' Vi retorted.

Under Josie's eagle eye and her explicit instructions, the material was laid on the kitchen table – previously covered with a clean sheet – the pattern was pinned on to it, and it was then cut out.

'Do we really *have* to cut around these little arrow things?' Vi asked for she couldn't make head nor tail of all the markings.

'Yes, otherwise it won't match up. It will get mixed up.' The pattern had been borrowed and Josie was engrossed in the Instruction Page. Katie raised her eyes to the ceiling. Josie was going to tack it together, then fit it to see how it looked. The dress was to be finished before they started on the hat because, as Vi said, she could easily borrow a hat, but she didn't think Father Macreedy would take kindly to her coming up the aisle in her slip.

They all still had the hats they'd worn for Josie's wedding, but Sarah's was in the best condition. That was to be dyed dark green and Mr Catchpole the rabbit man, who had very kindly come all the way from Kirkby to see if they were all all right, had promised them two beautiful tail-feathers from a cock pheasant.

'With our Sarah's shoes and that little woven raffia bag, you'll look great, Vi,' Katie pronounced.

Sarah sighed longingly. She was twenty now and didn't even have a boyfriend, let alone a fiancé or husband as the others did. She didn't know how to flirt or answer the remarks or compliments from the men at work, most of whom were married anyway, and since the May Blitz the traditional places for meeting boys had been decimated.

Everyone had been allotted tasks because no one knew when the convoy would return. When it did there would be one almighty rush, ending in total chaos if contingency plans hadn't been made. Father Macreedy apprised of the situation, had already called the banns and Registrars were now used to being called out at short notice by Catholic priests, as in the eyes of the Law a marriage wouldn't be legal without the presence of a Registrar.

Florrie, Josie and Katie were in charge of the food, Fred the drink, Sarah, Brenda and Norma the decorations in the shop and Joe and Jimmy had been threatened with such torments that they couldn't even begin to imagine what hell they would be in, if either of them touched a single thing.

'Give them something to do,' Fred advised.

'Like what?' Florrie demanded.

'Send them out on their bikes after school to track down flowers.'

'Flowers!' Brenda exclaimed.

'Aye. They'll not find any florists around here, so they'll have to go further afield. That should keep them busy. Then when they've found one, I'll go out with them and speak to the owner, explain things, like. Then on the big day they can collect the bouquets.'

'I wouldn't trust a bunch of neetles and dandelions to those two,' Vi said in mock horror.

'They've got baskets on the front of their bikes.'

'I know, but they'll probably take it into their heads to go fishing or swimming in the canal at Aintree and then the flowers will wilt and then what'll we do?'

'Meet that worry when it comes,' was Florrie's advice.

The dress and hat were finished and hung behind the door in the room Vi shared with Katie, Sarah and Brenda Watson. And as she lay in bed she looked over at it and reminded herself how lucky she was. Jack would be home soon. She *knew* it, she could *feel* it. The sun would shine, the church would be packed with relations and friends, there'd be the magnificent spread – but just for the select few, now added to by Mr Catchpole's promise of the gift of a chicken that could be cooked, allowed to cool and then carved. Not a single scrap of that would be wasted; even the carcass would be used for a chicken soup.

When she explained that numbers were limited, her Mam started to get annoyed. They were still living with her sister Mary and things were strained.

'Well, I'm sorry, Mam. If she gets a cob on it's tough. There's just no room and not enough food to go around, you should know that. We've been very, very lucky in that department. I'm not even having a proper cake.' The ingredients for the traditional three-tier wedding cake were so scarce that only the small top tier was edible. The other two tiers were made of cardboard painted white and the simple decorations – made by Josie – just stuck on.

'It's all right for you,' Mrs Draper grumbled. 'You don't have to live with 'er! An' what's more, them Watsons are not even related.'

'Mam,' Vi said patiently, 'the whole Watson family have all pulled together.'

'And so would we, 'ad we been asked. And what about your Jack's lot? What's their contribution?'

'Some of the drink.'

'Oh, big mates in Bent's, 'ave they?'

Vi sighed. 'No, not really.' Everything would have been total confusion if she'd left it to Mam. She couldn't even organise her own family, never mind a wedding.

Vi came back from Walton to Chelmsford Street in a disgruntled and irritable mood to find Florrie tidying up. It was more important now she said, because so many of them were sharing. In no time at all the place would resemble a pig sty unless it was done methodically. Vi remembered the way her Aunty Mary's house had looked and agreed wholeheartedly. She began to gather up and fold the newspapers that had been left lying around. They'd be cut into squares and used in the privy or rolled up and twisted into tube-like shapes and used to light the fire – tasks done by Joe and Jimmy.

'You know I'm worried about our Josie, Vi,' Florrie said as she brushed one of the chairs.

Vi was surprised. 'Why? She looks great.'

'Um, but the colour in her cheeks is too high, and her eyes are too bright.'

'She's happy and excited, that's all.'

Florrie shook her head. 'I felt her forehead and it was so hot I've sent her up to lie down.'

Vi looked at Florrie with dawning horror. 'Oh, surely she can't . . . ?'

Florrie pursed her lips. 'I don't know. If she doesn't improve I'm sending for the doctor.'

'Not Dr Birch, I hope. Katie won't have him over the doorstep.'

'No, Dr Askam from Westminster Road.'

Vi bit her lip. Oh, please God, don't let there be anything wrong again, she prayed. 'You don't think she's been doing too much for me? All the sewing, I mean.'

'No, luv, she's done most of that sitting down, and anyway she enjoys it. It keeps her mind off other things.'

'Maybe they'll be back soon. Maybe by the weekend,' Vi ventured hopefully.

Florrie smiled at her. 'Aye, luv, that would make you happy, but our Josie – well . . .'

'I know. He's not much of a catch, is he?'

Florrie's expression hardened. 'He's the most tight-fisted, selfish, arrogant pig I've ever met, God forgive me. Where does he get it from, Vi? Certainly not Molly or Bill, although I remember Molly once telling me she had an uncle on her mother's side who was a right reprobate. Maybe Georgie's a throwback to him.'

'Could be he'll change after the baby's born,' Vi said hopefully.

'And pigs might fly!' Florrie answered grimly.

It was tea-time when Florrie ushered the portly figure of Dr Askam up the stairs to the room Josie shared with Norma, Sarah and herself. The pains had started half an hour earlier.

After examining Josie gently, he turned to Florrie and drew her aside. 'This is the third?'

Florrie nodded. 'It is.'

'I want her in hospital, Mrs Watson, so they can keep an eye on her, but not Stanley or Walton. She must go to the Women's in Catherine Street.'

'Oh, she's not going to lose it again, is she? God help her, she'll be broken-hearted. She was doing so well, you see.'

'I know, I see from her notes that she lost the last one during the Christmas raids.'

Florrie nodded. 'But she came right through the May Blitz fine.'

He nodded. 'I'll send for an ambulance, if you will get her things together?'

Florrie sat holding her daughter's hand. The small battered Gladstone bag that held Josie's clean nightdresses and few toiletries was packed. Vi and Katie sat on the bed and Katie held Josie's hand.

'It just might be for the best, Josie. They probably have ways of stopping . . . things.' She hoped she sounded convincing.

'They might know why it happens,' Vi added.

Josie's eyes were round with fear and luminous with tears. 'I know.' She tried to sound confident, but a small voice deep inside her told her that she was going to lose this baby too.

Florrie was sitting in the silent tiled corridor. They wouldn't let her stay with Josie even though she'd protested.

'But I'm her *Mam*! She *needs* me!' she pleaded, but to no avail. A doctor, a nurse and a midwife were with Josie, she couldn't be in better hands she told herself, but at half-past midnight they came to tell her that Josie had lost her third baby. They sedated Josie and gave Florrie a cup of strong tea with plenty of sugar in it and she wondered dazedly where they'd got the sugar from to be doling it out like this.

She was still sitting there half an hour later, just staring at the wall and wondering why Josie should be so unfortunate when she herself had been so lucky. Could it, she wondered, have anything to do with Georgie?

'Mrs Watson. Mrs Watson.' The gentle tapping on her shoulder and the quiet cultured voice made her look up. It was the doctor who'd been with Josie since she'd been admitted.

'Yes?'

He sat beside her. 'Her husband is, I believe, away on convoy duty?'

Florrie nodded. She was very, very nervous but she *had* to ask. 'I was wondering, Doctor, whether it could be something wrong with him?'

'I very much doubt it. We just don't know why some women have trouble and others don't.'

'I had six myself, all alive and healthy thanks be to God. She's the oldest.'

'Have you any idea when her husband will be home?'

'None, but I for one won't be upset if he doesn't make it back.'

He looked shocked.

'I know it's a terrible thing to say, sir, but I wish she'd never married him.'

He ignored her remarks. It wasn't his wish or intent to become embroiled in family quarrels. 'Well, when Mr Deegan finally arrives I wish to see him urgently.'

She looked at him questioningly.

'She can't go on like this, Mrs Watson. Another pregnancy may cost her her life, that's what I have to tell him. Have you any idea how he will react?'

'No, but I don't think he'll be heartbroken though. He's too damned selfish for that!' Florrie replied bitterly.

It was the second week in July when the battlecruiser *HMS Defiant* passed the Bar Lightship, leading the convoy into the safe waters of the Mersey. The docks had been hastily patched up, transport was running more smoothly again and horses and carts were lined up waiting for the precious cargoes to come ashore. Petrol was still in very short supply and reserved for ambulances, fire engines and the like, so many of the carters, or 'haulage men' as some of them now preferred to call themselves, had put their vehicles in storage and gone back to the original mode of 'horse power'.

Vi and Florrie stood together on the landing stage, Vi's heart pounding with joy as she recognised the *Victor* and Florrie's dropping like a stone when she caught sight of the familiar outline of the *Ascania*.

183

'You stay here, Vi, luv. You wait for him. I'm not going to spoil your day. I'll ask at the Dock Office where *he's* coming into, and I'll get a tram.'

Vi laid her hand on the older woman's arm. 'Thanks, Mrs Watson. Take him straight up to Catherine Street and let that doctor talk to him before he goes home.'

Florrie nodded sombrely as she turned and walked towards the magnificent domed building of the Mersey Docks and Harbour Board.

'Where's Josie?' Georgie asked as he stepped off the crew gangway and caught sight of his mother-in-law.

'She's not well. That's why I'm here, and why we've to go straight up to the Women's Hospital in Catherine Street. The doctor wants to see you urgently.'

Georgie stared at Florrie with dislike. Bossy, nosey old bat, always giving out her orders. He'd never liked her.

'Is Josie in hospital?' he asked curtly.

'No, not now. She's at home.'

'She's lost it again, hasn't she? That's what you've come to tell me.'

Florrie nodded.

This was a great homecoming, he thought. Christ, he could do with a drink. On the way home they'd been hit by a bomb from a lone enemy plane. The damage was slight as luckily it had just skimmed the stern before exploding. Only four men had been injured by the blast, which in itself was a miracle, but it had shaken him. And now this.

'I need a drink.'

'You can have a drink on the way home. You're not going to speak to any doctor smelling of drink, Georgie Deegan,' Florrie snapped at him. Not a word about Josie's health or state of mind had he uttered.

He followed her across the Pier Head to the tram-stop in a black mood of frustration and rising anger.

They didn't speak on the tram on their way home from Catherine Street. To the explanations and instructions the doctor had given, Georgie had said nothing. Not a single word. When asked if he understood fully he nodded abruptly, thanked the doctor and turned and left, leaving Florrie to bid the man a more civil farewell.

She knew she would have to have it out with him before they got home, so as they alighted on Stanley Road she caught his arm and pushed him towards a narrow alleyway that led to the jigger at the back of the shops.

'I know you're disappointed, lad, but Josie's heartbroken, and she's the one who has had to go through it three times.'

He turned on her. 'What the hell's the matter with her? I didn't understand all the technical stuff he was spouting. I want a child! I want a son! It's my right.'

'It *is* your right, but if it's not *God's will* then there's nothing we can do.'

'*God's will!* Don't make me bloody laugh! It's *her*. She's useless. She's pathetic!'

Florrie was barely controlling her temper. 'I wouldn't blaspheme if I were you, Georgie Deegan. You're all in the palm of His hand when you're at sea, aye, and the men of the escorts too. And if you tell her she's useless or pathetic I'll swing for you, so help me God! They can stick me in Walton Jail and I won't care. My girl's been to hell and back three times, and it's NOT her fault!'

'I'd be better off without her. What use is she at all?' he repeated bitterly.

Florrie lost her battle to control her rage. 'Then why the hell did you marry her in the first place?' she yelled.

'If you must know, I was in a bit of trouble with the scuffers and needed her to cover for me, and marrying her was the bloody price *she* asked!'

'You used her! So that's all you wanted her for – an alibi!' The sound of Florrie's hand striking his cheek was like the crack of a rifle, and not having expected it, Georgie stumbled backwards.

'May God forgive you, Georgie Deegan, because I never will – and if you've any ideas about belting me or our Josie, you'll have Fred and all his brothers to deal with.'

With that she turned and walked away from him, leaving him furious and with his cheek livid with the mark of her hand.

As soon as he walked into the house there seemed to be a general scattering of people in all directions. But there, on the bottom stair, blocking his path, stood Katie.

'Mrs Watson told me what you said.'

'So? What's it got to do with you?'

'She's my friend and you're my brother, God help me. Josie is ill and she's upset, so don't you dare upset her even more by saying wicked things like you said to her Mam.'

He pushed past her and she glared after him. Stupid, interfering bitch of a sister, he thought savagely.

And then he forgot his sister in contemplation of his wife. Josie did look ill, he thought as he opened the bedroom door. There was no colour in her cheeks or her lips, and her eyes were full of tears. There seemed to hang over her the dead look of utter failure. And this time he'd bragged so much to his mates on board about *his* kid and all he was going to do for it. He'd even bought a fluffy toy animal of some sort, to reinforce his boasts, and it hadn't been a cheap one either. His disappointment and pity were very real, but they were not for Josie. They were for himself. As he'd told her Mam, he'd only really married her to keep himself out of jail. At first he'd felt a sort of affection for her; she was pleasant and easy to get along with, and she catered willingly to his every wish, but lately she'd begun to irritate him and their love-making had only been for one purpose, on his part anyway. He wanted a child that he could pass his business on to, a child he could mould to his will and rid of all Josie's stupid sentimentality. The physical side of marriage to Josie now didn't seem to have much charm, and he doubted that either of them would miss it. Desires could easily be quenched in the whorehouses of the city or those in Quebec or Montreal. However, it was a grievous slight on his manhood to be childless, and that was something that would matter more and more as time passed, because Georgie was determined to come through this bloody war and make a fortune, even if it was only to spite both Josie and Katie. With money came power, and he'd use that power to keep them both in their places – and to hell with Bob Bloody Goodwin and his Orange relations!

The happiness, laughter and disorganised chaos of Vi's wedding preparations pushed Georgie and his moods into the background. Josie was up now and all the activity seemed to cheer her. The colour was returning to her cheeks and she was eating a bit more.

Vi, who'd heard from Katie what Georgie had said to Florrie, had deliberately made a big show of asking Josie's advice about everything, and today she was trying on the whole outfit for Josie's scrutiny and approval. All the younger girls had been thrown out of the bedroom, with just Josie and Katie being privileged to a preview.

'Now, is it right?' Vi said anxiously, mincing about. 'Have I got the hat on at the right angle, this time?'

Josie nodded.

'So, how will I manage my bag and the bouquet, if I ever get it and it's not half-dead?'

'Just tuck your bag under your arm tightly and that leaves your hands free. It's easy.'

'And don't worry about not getting the flowers. Our Joe and Jimmy Watson have been promised a shilling each to get back here with them in record time so they won't wilt.'

'Well, we certainly put up with enough complaints before they found that place opposite the school at Warbreck Moor.'

'We don't even know what kind or colour they'll be.'

'Oh, Vi, stop complaining,' Katie yawned. 'You'll have flowers! There's a war on, remember.' It was becoming such a familiar catch-phrase that they all laughed.

Vi shook her head. 'I'll do something to make a show of myself, I know I will.'

'Vi, you won't! What can you do?'

'I'll drop my bag, or knock my hat off or trip over something. I can feel it in me bones. You weren't like this, either of you.' Vi clenched and unclenched her hands nervously.

'Oh yes I was – and so were you, Josie Watson. You were worse than me, in fact. Do you remember your Aunty Imelda chucking Brenda and Norma out and into Jimmy's room so you could have a few minutes with your Mam? It's a wonder we all came out looking respectable, we were so cramped.'

Josie smiled as she remembered. It had been a happy day but then she'd thought Georgie loved her.

'Well, thank God I'm not going to me Aunty Mary's, I'd be that airyated I'd probably end up belting someone!' It had been decided that Vi would get dressed and go from the house she now looked on as home, although not for much longer.

'Will you get on all right with his Mam?' Katie asked hastily. She'd seen the tears start in Josie's eyes.

'I'll have to. There's no room for Jack here as well. Mrs Milligan's all right really. A bit bossy, mouth a bit like a parish oven, but if she thinks she can walk all over me, she's in for a shock!'

'But you will come round to see us?' Josie pleaded.

'Of course – try and stop me. Jack'll be away again soon after, and it's back to work.'

Josie nodded. 'Back to work for all of us.'

'When you're well enough, luv.'

'Oh, I'll be fine. I've got to do my bit for the war effort after all, haven't I?' She managed a smile, but neither of her friends would ever know how much she envied them or the pain she had to hide from them.

PART TWO

Chapter Twenty

It was dark now when they came home from work and dark when they left in the morning.

'I hate November,' Katie said with feeling.

'I know. Foggy and freezing cold,' Vi answered gloomily.

Her wedding day seemed so long ago. July had been a glorious month, at least weatherwise. The church had looked beautiful, even though flowers were in short supply. Vi had come up with the idea of using a lot of greenery with just a few brightly coloured flowers for contrast. Little did the Parish Priest know that the lovely boughs and sprigs of oak, horse chestnut and beech that transformed the high altar had all been 'borrowed' under cover of darkness and passed through railings of Stanley Park. There had been candles and music. The boys in the choir had sung like angels, even if they neither looked nor behaved like angels outside the church.

Everyone had admired her outfit and asked where she'd got it. Vi had made sure that Josie got all the credit.

'It's just like silk the way it 'angs, isn't it, Mary?' Ellen MacCane nodded her approval, dismissing from her mind the fact that a lot of people thought green an unlucky colour for a wedding. In the middle of a war it seemed daft to even think like that.

'Dead gorgeous, yer look like the Princess Elizabeth,' Mary Maher replied.

'If only I had her money!' Vi'd laughed, but she had been brimming with contentment with what had turned out to be a wonderful day. Nowadays she often picked up the framed photo of Jack and herself and looked at it with pleasure and longing.

'I suppose we can look forward to Christmas,' Vi said, wistfully.

'These days there's nothing special about Christmas at all,' Josie sighed.

'Why don't we do what we did last year?' Katie suggested. Was it only last year that they'd gone to the Empire, and sat through the bombs? she thought. It seemed a lifetime ago, belonging to another world. They'd thought things were bad then. They'd had no idea how much worse they would become that May . . . But it didn't do to look back into the past; it only brought heartbreak.

At least from his letters she knew that Bob was all right. He complained about the terrific heat in the day and the bitter cold at night, and the sandstorms after which everything was covered, sometimes buried, in sand. He wasn't too keen on the snakes and scorpions, either. She'd had to ask Joe about what scorpions were, and had paled when he told her their sting could kill. Still, she wouldn't have minded a bit of sun and sand right now as the icy November wind stung her cheeks and made her eyes water.

'Back to the Empire? That's too much like tempting fate! I'm not going near the place until the war's over,' Vi declared forcefully.

'All right then, let's go dancing.'

'Where?'

'The Grafton's still going strong. They've patched up the roof. Oh, come on, we all need *something* to look forward to, to cheer us up. A sort of pre-Christmas outing,' she urged.

'I haven't got anything to wear,' Vi complained.

'God Almighty, Vi Milligan! I've never met anyone who moans so much about clothes. I wouldn't mind, but you've got more than us three put together!'

'That's what we could do,' Sarah suggested. 'Make do and mend, like that column in the newspaper tells you to do.'

'If you took notice of half the things they suggest, you'd look a right freak and the fellers would run a mile.'

'Oh, come on, Vi. You were always the one with the bright ideas,' Sarah urged.

'I suppose we can swop things – we're all more or less the same size. I could wear my white blouse with your blue wool skirt, Sarah, and you could borrow my pale green dress.'

'That's your good one – your wedding dress.'

'No one would know that now, would they? I mean, there's no big pictures on the advertising hoardings saying "This is Vi Milligan's wedding dress". Josie, what have you got?'

Josie shrugged; she wasn't really interested. She said little these days. She wasn't a single girl like Sarah who could go out any time to any place with anyone. She was a wife, but not a wife like either Katie or Vi. They had husbands who were away in the front line, and who adored them. She was . . . nothing. Not a sweetheart, mother or even a widow. All life consisted of now was work, and most of the chat there was depressing to listen to.

Georgie had been home a couple of times since her last miscarriage, and they'd shared the same room, the same bed . . . but she'd turned her back on him and hugged the edge of the mattress. There was hardly any conversation between them now either.

'Josie, you're miles away again. Did you hear what I said?' Katie asked.

'Yes, but I'm not going to the Grafton.'

'Why not?' they all chorused.

'Because . . . well, what's the use?'

'It's only a night out. Some of the girls in our room are going to the State Ballroom. Apparently that's where the Yanks who drive the canteen lorries go. But we're not looking for fellers or anything. Well, at least Katie and me aren't. Look – it'll do you good. Take you out of yourself,' Vi persisted.

Eventually Josie agreed. What harm could there be in it? She might even enjoy herself! After all, she was only twenty-one, even though sometimes she felt about forty.

There was a great deal of swopping and changing and putting on and taking off of beads and earrings, and parading around the bedroom in each outfit before the Saturday night they'd agreed on. It would be mid-November so that did make it near enough to Christmas, they told themselves. Joe was going with Vinny and Franny to stay at Florrie's with Jimmy, as all four lads were now split up and didn't get to see each other very often. For Christmas Day lunch (such as it would be) Katie, Sarah and Vi had been invited with Josie to Florrie's. Very reluctantly, Vi had to decline. If Jack wasn't home she couldn't leave his Mam on her own, she being a widow. And if he was home they'd still have to have their dinner there.

Vi had spent half an hour doing Sarah's hair in a new, glamorous upswept style. Vi herself, when not working, copied the film star Veronica Lake's hairstyle – turned under like a pageboy's but parted on the left and let fall to cover the right side of her face. Her Mam had told her plainly that she'd blind herself with all that hair hanging in her eyes. Katie had no trouble with the upswept curls, as her hair curled naturally, and Josie just kept to the style she wore every day – a series of rolls round her face which both Katie and Vi said made her look about fifty.

'She's just like a shell these days,' Vi said to Katie on one occasion.

'I know and no wonder, stuck with our Georgie for the rest of her life. It's not exactly something to look forward to, is it?' Katie answered acidly.

The Saturday night arrived and they were all a little excited as they got off the tram in West Derby Road and crossed over to the Grafton Ballroom that still showed clearly the scars of the Blitz. It was in darkness from the outside, but inside, the place was full of light and colour and warmth and laughter. They gave their coats in and tucked the tickets in their purses, then went into the Ladies to touch up their make-up and hairstyles. The cloakroom was crowded.

'That's the only thing wrong with this place on a Saturday night,' muttered Katie. 'I'd forgotten. Half of Liverpool is in here.'

'It looked as though half of the Army, Navy and Air Force are out there as well,' Vi added.

'Well, at least we won't be wallflowers then.'

'We might, as soon as we start flashing the wedding rings.' Vi looked meaningfully at Katie and winked.

'Oh, no! We're not taking them off.'

'You can't do that!' Sarah's eyes were round with concern.

'I was only joking, but I bet there's quite a few here who've left their rings at home.'

With a great deal of pushing and shoving they managed to get a table on the ground floor not too far at the back. The dance floor was already crowded, and as Vi had said, every man was in a uniform of one kind or another.

There wasn't much in the way of drink to choose from, so they agreed to make what they had got last by just sipping it slowly.

They were all asked to dance, but as Vi had prophesied, the wedding rings once noted, and husbands enquired about, concluded any further dances. One sailor did ask Vi up again but she smiled, thanked him and told him he'd be better off with someone he could walk home.

Sarah fared much better because, as Vi had predicted, she looked much older and far more attractive with the new hairstyle and Vi's pale green dress.

'That feller's asked her up four times now,' Katie remarked.

'Which one?' Vi peered through the crowd. The band was playing a waltz and the prisms of light that fell on the dancers from the huge revolving glass ball in the centre of the ceiling looked pretty and exotic but rather obscured the view.

'Him in the RAF uniform. The fair-haired one.'

Vi craned her neck to get a better view.

'She's really attractive, our Sarah, but she's so timid and shy. She'd run a mile if a bloke tried to kiss her – and she's twenty!'

'How do you know? I bet she doesn't when Mr Right turns up,' Vi countered.

Josie pulled a face. 'As long as she doesn't end up with a Mr Wrong.'

'Oh, stop it, Josie!' Katie said. 'Look, that Marine is coming over. Get up and have a twirl with him, and for God's sake, smile! You're supposed to be enjoying yourself. It's not every night we're out, done up to the nines and with Joe Loss and his orchestra to serenade us.'

194

'And no bloody bombs either, thank God,' Vi added.

Katie virtually pushed Josie to her feet when the young Marine did ask Josie to take the floor with him, but she noticed that her sister-in-law looked bored and hardly said a word to him.

Sarah was having a great time. She didn't feel shy at all, which was very unusual for her. Her attentive dance partner was called Duncan Kinross, and he was a Scot, from Glasgow. He was stationed somewhere near Liverpool, he couldn't tell her exactly where, of course, but he belonged to Coastal Command. She knew that meant Woodvale near Southport or Sealand near Chester, probably Woodvale. It would have taken hours to get from Chester to Liverpool. He'd have had to set out in the afternoon.

'I live in Kirkdale,' she volunteered. 'It's not far away. My Mam and Dad are dead, our Georgie – my brother – is on the convoys, our Joe's at school but he was a messenger in the Blitz, and we all have to work in munitions. We did have a shop, but it's been too difficult getting supplies of fish so had to close it.'

'But you'll open it again when this show's over?' He smiled down at her. She was very pretty. Young and with a naive charm which made a refreshing change, he thought as he looked around him.

'We might.'

'Is that your sister, the dark-haired girl?'

'Yes, and the other girl, not the one with the blonde hair, is my sister-in-law.'

'But you're not married or anything, are you, Sarah?'

'No.' She looked down at her feet and blushed as he squeezed her hand. Duncan was nice, a bit older than herself, probably about Georgie's age, but she'd heard that there were no old men in the Air Force, except Air Marshals and the like. It saddened her to think of all the handsome young men who had died in the Battle of Britain, and the bombing raids on German-held countries like France, Belgium and Holland. They had been so brave and dashing, just like the generation of heroes who'd fought and flown before them in the Great War. She'd heard someone on the wireless say that. She looked up at him. Yes, he was just like them, but she pushed the grim sentiments from her mind.

He made her laugh. He said the funniest things and she loved his accent.

'You're very pretty, Sarah. I'm surprised no one's snapped you up.'

'I just don't go out much and I . . . I've always been a bit shy.'

'But not with me?'

She smiled up at him. 'No, I'm not with you, Duncan. I know it sounds daft but I feel I've known you a long time.' She felt so reckless. She'd never said anything like that to a boy or man before.

'Maybe we met in another life,' he teased. 'Do you believe in reincarnation?'

'I don't even know what that is.'

'Living more than once. When you die, you come back as someone or something else.'

She looked puzzled.

He laughed. 'Maybe I was someone terrible.'

She entered into the spirit of the thing. 'Like who?'

'Oh, Henry the eighth.'

'He wasn't terrible. He was a King.'

'Och, he was awful! He kept cutting off his wives' heads!' He'd startled her, he could see, so he laughed again reassuringly. 'I'm only joking, lassie. Not all of them, just two.'

She'd never been called 'lassie' before but it sounded nice. She smiled up at him and he gently brushed back a curl from her forehead.

'Can I walk you home, Sarah?'

'Well, I did come with the others, but I don't think they'll mind.'

'Fine. That's settled then.'

Katie had been watching her sister closely. 'She certainly seems to be doing a lot of laughing and talking,' she commented thoughtfully.

'Well, maybe she's finally copped off,' Vi remarked. 'And he's dead handsome too, and RAF. I wonder if he's a pilot?'

'I shouldn't think pilots come here. He's probably air-crew, a gunner or a navigator.'

'Or maybe he just fixes the engines. They wear posh uniforms too when they're out.' Josie's voice held a sharp and slightly sneering note.

Vi and Katie looked at each other.

'Well, his job doesn't matter. He seems to like her and she seems to like him,' Vi said quietly.

For the last waltz they played 'Goodnight Sweetheart' and as he drew her close and her cheek rested against Duncan's, Sarah thought she'd never felt so happy in her life. Everything was forgotten – all the misery and fear and privations.

At the end of the evening, Duncan escorted her back to their table and they all stood while the National Anthem was sung.

'I'll wait for you just outside the door, Sarah,' he promised, giving her hand a squeeze.

'Go on and wait with him, I'll fetch your coat,' Vi offered.

Katie frowned at her. 'Come and get your coat first, Sarah, or you'll catch your death of cold in that dress.'

As they joined the queue for the coats, Sarah stood beside Josie who looked as bored and listless as she had been all night.

'What did you do that for?' Katie hissed at Vi.

196

'Do what?'

'Tell her to go off with him. I wanted to talk to her first.'

'About what? God Almighty, girl, she's twenty years old, not a kid of sixteen.'

'I know that, but he's the first bloke who's shown a real interest in her and you never know, she could get carried away with it all.'

'Oh, don't be so bloody miserable! You sound just like your Mam, do you know that, Katie Goodwin?'

Katie ignored her and turned to Sarah. 'You're to be in by midnight.'

'Or you'll turn into a pumpkin,' Vi interrupted. 'Stop treating her like bloody Cinderella.'

'All right, we'll get an earlier tram, so you can have more time to chat to him,' Katie conceded as Vi raised her eyes to the heavens.

'He's very nice, Katie. I don't think he'd – well, take advantage of me.'

'I wouldn't be too sure of that. They're all the same – men,' Josie said bitterly.

'Oh, God! Hand me your ticket, Sarah, and yours, Katie. Josie and I will get the coats while you give her a sisterly talk and you, Josie Deegan, can stop being so miserable and putting the mockers on everything.'

After they'd alighted from the tram, Sarah and Duncan walked slowly along a blacked-out Stanley Road. He had taken her hand and pulled it through the crook of his arm.

'Is she very strict?' he asked.

Sarah smiled. 'No, not really. I suppose it's because she feels sort of responsible for me, with Mam and Da being dead.'

'Aye, I can understand that. Has she been married long?'

'No, but he's in the Army with Monty in Africa and they only had a two-day honeymoon. That was ages ago.'

'She was lucky. Some people don't even get two days.'

She thought he sounded a little bitter. 'Have you . . .' she hesitated then summoned up her courage ' . . . have you got a girl, in Scotland? A fiancée?' She really didn't want to know but felt she had to ask. Katie certainly would.

'No, no fiancée. I've a sister about your age, but not half as pretty though.'

They stopped beneath the unlit street-lamp on the corner, a lovers' tryst since time immemorial, and Duncan took her in his arms and drew her gently to him.

'Sarah! My bonny wee Sarah.' He kissed her forehead. 'Does no one ever call you Sally or Sal?'

'No, Mam wouldn't let them.' She could feel the colour rushing to her cheeks.

'Then I won't either.' He kissed her full on the lips and she felt so dizzy she thought she was going to faint. She clung to him, her hands locked around his neck. The feel of his lips, the closeness of his body was having a strange effect on her.

It seemed a long time, a very long time before he drew away from her.

'Will I see you again, Sarah?'

She could only nod.

'When – tomorrow? I'm on duty until the afternoon but we could go somewhere later. The cinema, perhaps?'

She ducked her head. 'I'd like that, Duncan.'

'Will I call for you? It does take me quite a while to get into Liverpool, so it might be late.'

'I won't mind that and we needn't go to the pictures; we could go on the ferry instead. Have you been on the ferry yet?'

'No, and I can't say I've been to Liverpool and not been on the famous ferries now, can I?'

'They're not that famous.'

'They are too. For their service at Zeebrugge in the Great War, the King said they were to be called the *Royal Iris* and the *Royal Daffodil*. The ferries went to Dunkirk too, didn't they?'

She nodded. 'It used to be so nice before the war, especially in summer.' She sounded wisful.

'It will be again, Sarah. The war won't go on for ever. I'll call for you at eight, then.'

She nodded again and then did something so out of character that, a few hours earlier, she would never have thought herself capable of it. She reached up and kissed him on the mouth, then she turned and ran quickly up the road, her heart singing. They'd all always skitted her about 'Mr Right' – well, now she'd found him. She knew for sure she was in love, hopelessly in love, with Duncan Kinross.

'And he's calling for you tonight at eight?' Vi was very interested as they finished their meagre lunch. She often called around after work or weekends. Things were rather strained between herself and her mother-in-law at present. Vi said Jack's Mam was cleaning mad, a bit like Florrie. Jack's Mam had told Vi she was one of the untidiest people she'd met in a month of Sundays. It didn't augur well for an amicable co-existence.

'Here's the lunch-time post. I'm going down to Mam's – I'll bring Joe back with me.' Josie had her coat and hat on.

'You don't *have* to, Josie. He's big enough and daft enough to find his own way,' Katie said.

'It's no trouble.'

Katie nodded. She could understand Josie's feelings. Both she and Vi with their loving husbands, and now Sarah looking as though she were walking on clouds, hardly hearing a word anyone said to her . . . Yes, Josie was better off with her Mam and sisters for a few hours.

'I got a letter from Jack this morning, in the early post,' Vi said when she'd gone, 'but I didn't want to say anything in front of Josie in case she hasn't had one. Does your Georgie ever write to her?'

'Not often. He says he hasn't got time, the liar. Weeks and weeks at sea and he's no time, my foot!'

'Well, they'll be on their way home now.' Vi looked at the envelope Katie was holding. 'That looks very official.'

They both stared at the buff-coloured envelope bearing the ominous initials *HM War Office*.

'Go on, open it. Get it over with. Just staring at it isn't going to make the contents any better,' Vi advised solemnly.

Katie ripped it open and scanned the lines of neat typing, then her face lit up. 'He's coming home! My Bob is coming home, Vi! Oh God! He's been injured in the shoulder, but not too badly, apparently.'

'When? When?' Vi asked, jumping up and down with excitement for her friend.

'It doesn't say.'

'It never bloody does!'

'They can't tell you for security reasons, you know that. But he's on the Hospital Ship *Conway Castle*.'

Vi was looking around the room. 'Where's last night's *Echo*?'

'Why? It won't say anything in that. You know as well as I do that shipping movements are never given out.'

'You're right – but it won't be long, though. How far is it from North Africa to Liverpool? Where's your Joe's atlas?'

Pushing aside the dishes they opened out the atlas on the table and traced with their fingers a route from Gibraltar, up the coast of Spain and Portugal.

'They won't go near the French coast, so they'll have to cut across and up the Channel, then the Irish Sea . . .'

'The Channel Islands are occupied so they might go around the west coast of Ireland.'

'No, that's too far and they've got U-boats to face, either way they come.'

'Surely to God they won't attack a hospital ship? You can't possibly mistake them, they're painted white and have a damned big red cross on each side and sometimes on the funnel as well.'

Katie bit her lips and shrugged. The Germans seemed to be capable of anything. 'They attacked and sank the *City of Benares* with all those kids on board.'

Vi's lips tightened into a thin line. She'd forgotten about that, and the *Lancastria* that had been bombed off the French coast. Over 2000 people, mainly women and children, had died. The worst tragedy in their maritime history, Mr Churchill had called it. Yes, Katie had a right to be worried.

Neither of them could work out the scale of the map, but they assumed it would probably be only four or five days before Bob arrived home. Clutching the letter to her, Katie closed her eyes. Her husband was coming home! In less than a week he'd be here, in this very room and safely in her arms. When she opened her eyes, Sarah was sitting looking at her with exactly the same expression of joy and love on her face. Katie turned to Vi who was wiping away a tear.

'What's wrong?'

'Nothing! I'm just so made up for you.'

Katie's smile dimmed a little. 'Maybe it's as well Josie's gone to see her Mam. I don't think she could bear to see us all so happy.'

It was Joe who managed to find out, by what means Katie never discovered, that the Union Castle Line ship *Conway Castle* was due into Gladstone Dock on Friday, 21 November. Katie sent a message into work with Vi, to say that she needed the day off. She didn't trust Sarah with the message; her younger sister was so lost in her dreams she didn't seem able to concentrate for very long.

Trembling with excitement, Katie had a good wash, arranged her hair prettily, put on her best navy skirt and the navy and white jumper Josie had knitted for her, then her good coat and hat, and dabbed a few precious spots of 'Evening in Paris' behind her ears. She headed for the tram-stop in a flurry of longing, tinged with a little apprehension. Would Bob have changed at all, she wondered.

The ship had docked by the time she arrived and the seriously injured were being brought off on stretchers, accompanied by the girls and women of the Queen Alexandra's Nursing Corps. A fleet of ambulances was lined up, ready to take them to the various hospitals in the city.

The walking wounded helped each other and there were dock-workers on hand too, as well as wives, mothers, sisters, sweethearts, cousins and in fact whole families. As she pushed her way forward, she caught sight of Bob at the top of the gangway. His right arm was in a sling, but his left one was around the waist of another soldier whose leg was heavily bandaged. As a nurse stepped forward to help them both, Katie caught her arm.

'Oh, please! Let me help him, he's my husband.' The woman

smiled as she and a docker took charge of the man with the leg wound. Katie threw her arms around Bob's neck, tears covering her cheeks. Tears of sheer joy and happiness.

'Oh, I've missed you! I've missed you *so* much! How's your arm? What exactly happened? Does it hurt badly?'

He laughed. 'Will you give me time to draw breath, Mrs Goodwin!'

She laughed with him and guided him solicitously towards one of the sheds that was being used as a clearing station. She took his kitbag and he put his good arm around her shoulder and when the Nursing Sister in charge had given him instructions to see his doctor or go to the Out-Patients of his local hospital, and asked him if he had everything he needed, Bob said joyfully: 'I have now, Sister, thanks. This is my wife!'

Later, much later that afternoon, Katie made a pot of very weak tea and took it up to the bedroom, wishing it was stronger and that they had sugar to put in it.

'I'm not an invalid, luv.'

'Yes, you are. Now shut up while I talk to you.'

He sipped the tea, made a face and then pulled her towards him again.

'Stop it! Our Joe'll be in soon, I'll have to get dressed. You've got an excuse, you're injured, but there's no excuse at all for me to be running around in my camiknickers in the afternoon.'

When Joe came bounding up the stairs like a baby elephant, Katie was decently dressed and sitting on the bed holding Bob's good hand. He'd be home for a bit, he told her – until after Christmas at least.

'I told yer, Katie, didn't I?' Joe said triumphantly. 'I said it was today.' He had hundreds of questions he wanted to ask Bob – Georgie didn't ever have much to say and to Joe, sailing backwards and forwards across the Atlantic seemed pretty tame compared to real fighting with tanks and heavy artillery.

'It's "you" not "yer" and don't go overtiring him. I'd best go and get some tea on the go, as they'll all be in soon.'

Bob looked across at her and smiled. There'd be time to talk later. Plenty of time.

For Josie and Vi the weekend brought the news that the aircraft of Coastal Command were escorting the convoy in. Duncan had told Sarah as much – he wasn't supposed to, he said, but Sarah's family and friends had husbands on those ships. For Vi it meant huge relief and enormous happiness; for Josie nothing but an empty, joyless feeling that deepened into misery when Georgie actually landed.

Duncan Kinross had taken Sarah out, or they'd stayed in and just talked and listened to the wireless, every night since they'd met at the Grafton. All about her, Josie was surrounded by happiness and relief and laughter. Now, as she lay at the edge of the bed, listening to her husband's heavy breathing, tears of despair slid down her cheeks. What did she have to look forward to in life, even after the war? In fact, it would be even worse then. He'd be home every night. If only . . . if only she'd managed to carry the last baby to full term, she'd have had *someone* in her life who would love her – and maybe Georgie would have been different, too. All she got from her Mam was that she'd taken her vows; she must stand by them. They were sacred promises and she should be grateful her husband was alive and well and would provide for her. There were plenty of young girls who'd envy her that, girls far too young to be widows and many with babies to bring up, alone. And that was it. The sum total of it all. He would *provide* for her. Food, shelter, clothing and warmth but nothing else. Nothing at all.

The atmosphere in Chelmsford Street was strained to say the least. Josie and Georgie hardly had a word to say between them, and Bob and Georgie communicated only when it was unavoidable. And the sleeping arrangements had had to be altered too.

'It's terrible, Vi, it really is. Our Sarah says she doesn't mind sharing with our Joe, but I feel it's not decent.'

'Decent! There's whole families sharing one room and have been since long before the war. When was *that* ever decent? Anyway, Sarah's not on the same planet as the rest of us most of the time.'

'I know, and Bob's rigged up a sort of curtain affair to divide the room so they can both have a bit of privacy, but Bob and I feel we can't even *talk* to each other in front of my dear brother, and poor Josie looks so miserable all the time, so downtrodden.'

'I'll agree with that. God forgive me for saying this, and me with a husband in the Navy, but the best thing for Josie would be if that bastard didn't come back. Oh, I know he's your brother and all . . .'

'I've wished it myself, Vi,' Katie interrupted. 'I've even told him so. And to make matters worse, things aren't good between Bob and his family.'

'Still not speaking? No sign of even a twig of an olive branch?'

Katie shook her head. 'Nope. He's written all the time he's been away, but he's never had a single letter back in return. It's as though they just don't want to know anything. He won't go round there and he doesn't want me to either, but I'm going to see his Mam and if she won't talk to me, I'll leave a note, just to tell her how he is. Surely she *must* be worried. Probably the rest of them won't let her write or come around; they all sound awful. But he's her only son!'

Vi sighed. 'I've never really understood it all. It's just a different way of worshipping the same God. It's not as if he's from one of those pagan religions that have half a dozen gods and goddesses.'

'Our Joe says it's all part of history. All to do with some king or two kings and some old battle in Ireland.'

'Well, they've not been much help, have they, staying neutral.'

'You can't blame them for that, Vi. They suffered enough under us for hundreds of years, and there are Irish lads in the Army and Navy.'

'Another of your Joe's little gems of history?'

Katie nodded. 'You know, Vi, he really should have gone to a better school. I feel I've denied him a future.'

'He didn't want to go, and who knows anything about the future? Live one week to the next, is my motto.'

Katie sighed. 'I'm just dreading Christmas, I really am. Our Georgie's flatly refused to go to Florrie's. Joe wants to go, at least he'll have Jimmy, but at the same time he wants to go to the Mahers' or the MacCanes'. They've both asked him.'

'It's nice to be popular,' Vi commented sarcastically.

'Bob won't go and visit his lot, so I can see us all landing up at Florrie's and leaving our Georgie on his own.'

'Serve him right.'

'The only one who's happy is our Sarah,' Kate finished.

'I'm not looking forward to it either,' Vi said. '*She's* doing all the cooking and organising, you'd think I was two years old – and the way she fusses over Jack when he gets home! She won't let me do a thing for him, and yet he's my husband. I could clock her one, I really could.'

'Ever since Mam died,' Katie said quietly, 'every flaming Christmas seems to be worse than the last. I've got this awful feeling that I'll hate Christmas for the rest of my life – and that's wrong, Vi. It *is* Christ's birthday.'

'I know, and I bet He's looking down on us all and thinking what a waste of His efforts we all are! A nice way to celebrate His birthday, one half of the world trying to kill the other half.'

Katie stood up. 'Well, I'd better go and face the old battleaxe. At least that will be something out of the way. Maybe I can persuade her to meet him somewhere on the sly. She *must* want to see him.'

'I'll walk to the bottom of Everton Valley with you,' Vi offered.

'It's a deal,' Katie grinned.

It was like many areas of the city now, Katie thought as she walked along Netherfield Road. There were gaps where homes and shops had stood not long ago, now pieces of wasteland, still covered with rubble.

Other buildings were blackened by smoke; some windows were still boarded up, the rest taped over. In two houses she passed, displayed prominently in the front windows were lilies made of wax and dyed orange, and fretwork plaques bearing the sentiments *No Surrender* and *God Bless King Billy*. It wearied her. Surely all this had gone on for too long? Now that the country was fighting for its life, couldn't old battles be forgotten?

She knocked sharply on the door of Bob's former home and waited. She could feel eyes watching her from the surrounding houses. A small, plump, neatly dressed woman with grey hair opened the door.

'Mrs Goodwin, I'm—' That was as far as she got.

'I know who you are! You're that bloody Papist bitch that married our Bob. You and your kind used your wiles on him. Your rosaries, your novenas, the plaster idols you worship – you turned him from his Protestant beliefs and his family.'

'I married him because I love him,' Katie said quietly, refusing to be drawn into a row to explain that she did not worship plaster idols. 'I don't care if you approve or not, but you *are* his Mam and I'd have thought you'd care something about him. He's written to you, I know that, and we've all been through hell in this city. Don't you *want* to see him? Don't you *care* how he is? My Mam, God rest her, didn't approve either, but she liked Bob for the kind of person he is. She didn't hate him just because he was a different religion.'

The woman stared back implacably and Katie knew she was getting nowhere. 'He's home. He's been wounded in the shoulder but it's healing and he's well. If you want to see him, you know where we live. This is from both of us.' She held out the note.

Mrs Goodwin took it and very deliberately tore it up and threw it in her face. The scraps of paper floated around her then fell to the ground like confetti. A few clung to her coat and she brushed them off. She was trembling now with anger but she wasn't going to show it.

'And how will that help? How will you explain, Mrs Goodwin, why you've turned on your son? Why your love for him has changed to hatred? And you'll have to, when you stand before God on the Last Day – and who knows when that will be? Will next May bring another Blitz, or will it come next week? Then you and your family will be judged and will go hand in hand straight to Hell!'

She'd already turned away before the door was slammed shut. She held her head high and her shoulders back as she walked away. She knew full well that venomous looks were being directed at her from behind curtained windows. The curses and obscenities shouted at her she ignored, but by the time she arrived home she couldn't hold back the tears.

'She . . . she tore it up and threw it in my face,' she sobbed.

Bob took her in his arms, his face set in harsh lines of anger. 'We tried, luv, and you were brave just to go and see her. I'll never forgive her, and I never want to see her or any of them again.'

She looked up at him. 'But Bob, she's your *Mam!*'

'And you're my wife and in time we'll have our own family and to hell with them all.'

Jack and Vi came around later that evening, ostensibly to try and sort out *something* cheerful for Christmas, even if it was just everyone going to the pub for a drink on Christmas Eve before family duty took over on Christmas Day.

Vi looked closely at Katie as they walked into the crowded front room. 'Not all sweetness and light, I take it?'

Katie shook her head.

'I didn't expect anything else from *that* lot!'

'Whatever we decide to do, can Duncan be included?' Sarah pleaded. 'I mean, he's so far away from home and I know they try to make the best of things, but it's not the same as being part of a family.'

'He should be glad he's not part of *this* family,' Josie said tartly.

Georgie glared at her.

'The more the merrier,' Vi said cheerfully.

'I don't like that Scottish feller,' Georgie said grimly. 'There's something about him I just don't trust. He's got shifty eyes and his talk's a bit too pat.'

'Takes one to know one,' Vi muttered.

Everyone else but Sarah ignored him.

'How can you say things like that?' she burst out heatedly. 'He *hasn't* got shifty eyes! You don't know him, our Georgie. You're just jealous because he's in the RAF.'

'Don't be thick, Sarah. He's no Wing-Commander or Squadron-Leader, is he – and you're right, I don't know him, but maybe I'll make it my business to find out more about him.'

'Why don't you just mind your own business and leave them both alone – or can't you bear to see anyone happy?' Katie snapped.

'*Him* – happy!' Vi's tone was scathing. 'That's a laugh. If they gave out medals for being mean, miserable and devious he'd be loaded down with them.'

Georgie's face turned a deep shade of red. 'I seem to remember *us* giving *you* a home here not long ago.'

'I paid my way, and don't you start on me, Georgie Deegan, or you'll soon find you've picked on the wrong one.' Vi turned to Josie. 'God Almighty, luv, how do you put up with him?'

Katie could see all the makings of a first-class row, but before Josie could reply that she had little choice, Bob hushed them all into silence. There was something coming over the wireless, something important.

They all listened to the precise, clipped voice of the newscaster as he announced that over three hundred Japanese planes had, without provocation or warning, attacked and destroyed the American Naval Base at Pearl Harbor. Nineteen ships had been badly damaged, as had two hundred planes – but two thousand four hundred people had been killed, and it was expected that many more would die from their wounds.

Jack and Bob exchanged glances.

'That's it then. The Yanks have been helping us with arms and steel and coal and food, but they'll be fighting alongside us now,' Bob said quietly, putting his arm around Katie's shoulder.

'Or maybe we'll go out with them. Hong Kong, Singapore, Burma, India, New Zealand and Australia – they're all in the Empire,' Jack added. 'To say nothing of the French Colonies out there.'

Georgie said nothing. He'd be glad to see the pair of them sent out East, particularly Bob Goodwin.

Chapter Twenty-One

Georgie hadn't got all of his wish. Bob was still at home convalescing, but the *Victor* had been taken off convoy duty and sent out to the Far East.

It had been a very strained Christmas but at least New Year 1942 was better. Katie and Bob along with Sarah and Duncan and Jack and Vi went into town on New Year's Eve.

Even then Jack knew there were changes afoot, though they'd heard nothing definite. The one thing he did know was that there was another convoy being assembled, but the *Victor* didn't appear to be part of it. Usually they were kept busy helping to load stores and ammunition, but not this time. He'd said nothing to Vi; there would be time enough when there was something definite to tell her.

To celebrate the New Year, the six of them went to 'The State' on Lime Street, and on the first stroke of the Town Hall clock at midnight, everyone surged into the street, spilling across the road and on to St George's Plateau, to kiss each other and sing *Auld Lang Syne*. At the far end of Lime Street, by Commutation Row, revellers heedless of the cold were splashing about in the Steble Fountain, while the police looked the other way and were occasionally kissed by girls who had had rather too much to drink. Some smiled back; others, more conscious of their dignity, ignored them. There were no church bells because of the war, but there was the usual cacophony of whistles and sirens from the ships in the river.

'You're sure you're going to be all right? I mean, I don't want you getting that shoulder hurt with people bumping into you and shoving you,' Katie had asked Bob before they left the house, a frown of concern creasing her forehead.

'I'll be fine, luv, really.'

'Put a red cross on the sling, it'll stand out more,' Vi suggested as a joke, but the others seemed to think it was a good idea.

'Should we have asked them to come? I mean, I feel awful leaving poor Josie. Even our Joe's gone to Mary's.'

'God, Sarah, don't you think we've put up with him for long enough? I was hoping that the gorgeous chicken Mr Catchpole brought us – that man is a saint – would choke our Georgie!'

'Why hasn't he gone and got himself an allotment and grown some veg,' Bob said. 'It's what I'd do if I were home more often like he is. There's not much skill needed to grow spuds and carrots.'

'Him do extra work? Go and dig and plant and water? You've got to be joking,' Katie answered scathingly.

'I did feel sorry for Josie though,' Vi added. 'I couldn't stand to see the look in her eyes before we left.'

'Oh, I know, but at least she had the guts to tell him she was going to her Mam's on Christmas Day with or without him.'

'Oh, aye, but she'd never have done it without you and Sarah backing her up.' Sarah was far more outgoing nowadays, but when Duncan wasn't around, she was still afraid of her brother.

'Well, it would have served him right to have had to stay on his own. He certainly tried hard enough to put the mockers on the whole day!'

In that respect, Georgie hadn't succeeded. His complaints had been ignored by Florrie, Fred and the entire family. Since the entry into the war by the United States, men, machinery and war materials were coming ashore in Liverpool in ever-increasing numbers. And although attitudes were starting to become a little strained between the Allies, when the first American soldiers had seen the war-torn state of Liverpool, they'd been horrified and sympathetic. They'd brought with them unlimited quantities of luxuries, from stockings to fruit and cigarettes, and these were generously shared.

'They'll have the women throwing themselves at them for nylons and chewing gum,' Georgie had remarked nastily, but everyone had ignored him, much to his annoyance.

'Katie, can I sleep on the sofa?' Duncan asked as their party emerged into the dawn of 1 January 1942, after a marvellous night at 'The State'. 'It's a helluva long way back to Base and I'd probably end up falling asleep by the roadside.'

'Ah, God, will you listen to him. Wouldn't he tear at your heart-strings,' Vi made plucking movements with her hands.

'Of course you can. Will you have to go back early tomorrow – today?' Katie corrected herself.

'Aye.' He sounded dour and disgruntled.

'There's another convoy being assembled,' Jack announced. As normal, nearly all conversations seemed to revolve around the war, one way or another.

'Careless talk costs lives,' Sarah said, primly quoting the propaganda warning. Posters bearing that slogan could be seen everywhere.

'Who's going to hear us in the middle of the night?' Vi asked.

'Walls have ears,' Sarah answered neatly with another slogan.

'There's also a rumour that the two Cunard *Queens* will be running a shuttle service bringing troops here. They reckon the *Queen Elizabeth* can take fifteen thousand men at once!'

'Aren't they worried they'll get sunk?'

'They're too fast, Sarah. There's not another ship that can keep up with or outrun them.'

'But there's planes that can,' Duncan informed them.

'Isn't that what your lot are supposed to do? Go out and make sure they don't get bombed?' Bob asked.

'We do, but we've only got a limited range. Still, it's the same for the enemy fighters and bombers. They'd have to attack them in mid-Atlantic – and that's too far for them. When they get within range, so do we.'

The general mood had suddenly become gloomy. 'Then let's hope all these extra troops will get it over with sooner,' said Katie.

'Well, that certainly killed the light-hearted conversation,' Vi remarked. 'Let's have a sing song, or by the time we get back we'll be suicidal.'

'We'd better shut up before we get back, though, or the neighbours won't be very pleased, and neither will Georgie and Josie.'

'Did you *have* to go and mention them, just when I was starting to feel lively again?' Vi chided.

They parted company with Joe and Vi on the corner of Fountains Road and Stanley Road, and tried their best to be as quiet as they could entering the house in Chelmsford Street. Katie fetched the pillows and blankets and quilt off Joe's bed, and Duncan said he'd be as snug as a bug in a rug on the sofa.

'Don't mention bugs around here, there's people not too far away who have to live their whole lives in a constant battle with them,' Katie warned as she went upstairs.

Although Sarah was tired she couldn't sleep. She kept thinking of Duncan downstairs on the sofa. It was the first time he'd stayed, the first time they'd slept under the same roof. She wished it was in the same bed. He never spoke much about what he did, and never talked about the future at all, but then she'd heard all fliers were superstitious like that. She knew he was air-crew and that the planes of Coastal Command didn't go on dangerous bombing raids, but there was always a risk from enemy fighters.

She was dozing off finally when she heard the creak on the landing. The board had been loose for ages; Joe was supposed to have fixed it. She sat up as the door opened quietly.

'Sarah! Are you awake?' Duncan hissed.

'Hush! You'll have them all awake.' She got out of bed and went to the door.

'I can't sleep.'

'Neither can I.'

'Shall we . . . just talk for a bit?'

'Not up here! I'll come downstairs. Our Georgie would kill us both if he saw us up here, and besides, it's warmer down there with the fire in the range. Let me go first. I know all the creaky places on the landing and stairs.'

As she silently crossed the landing and began to descend the stairs, Sarah felt uncomfortable. She only had a nightdress on; she'd forgotten her dressing gown. Her cheeks burned with embarrassment.

When they got into the living room she sat down on the sofa and tucked her bare feet under her, while Duncan sat beside her wrapping the quilt around them both. It was warm and peaceful down there. The house was quiet, the street silent now too.

'Isn't this restful,' Sarah said dreamily. 'Peaceful, like. I mean, you could almost imagine there wasn't a war on or that there is a special little world, just for us.' She turned and smiled at him. In a way she was thankful for the war. She'd never have met him otherwise.

'You look so beautiful in the glow from the fire, and we do have our own little world, Sarah.' He gathered her to him and kissed her and she responded eagerly, easily slipping into the warm, solitary and magical world his kisses evoked. There was just the cotton of her nightdress and his shirt between them, and she could feel his heart beating.

'Oh, Sarah! My sweet, precious little lassie.' He was gently caressing her breasts and she made no move to stop him, but clung to his lips.

He gently eased her down on the sofa and took her face in his hands. 'Sarah, do you love me?'

'You know I do,' she breathed.

'I want you so much, Sarah. I want to love you. I want to make you mine. Can you understand that?'

She nodded. Her emotions were betraying her, shutting out the voice of reason and that of her conscience, eating away at her resolve, her fear of everything. She wanted him, too! Even if only for this night. They'd get married, in time, when the war was over. She knew they would, if he lived through it. It was that thought that made her respond to his touch, his kisses, and the strange but exciting urges that claimed her. Once she cried out, but he instantly covered her lips with his own. He didn't want anyone to hear them, and she was so very special.

It was back to work next morning for everyone. New Year's Day was

210

not a national holiday like Boxing Day, and there were many who turned up with the most awful hangovers.

Katie felt sickly herself as they walked to the tram-stop. Too much to drink and not enough to eat, she thought. She'd been unable to face anything this morning, except a cup of weak tea.

'You look like death warmed up,' Vi said as she joined them, and both she and Katie dropped behind Sarah and Josie, leaving Sarah to regale Josie with some of Duncan's funny sayings.

'I feel it. Too much to drink.'

'We didn't have much, though. Let's face it, there *wasn't* much to be had. Could it be, er . . . something else?'

Katie stopped dead. 'I never thought of that! I can't be, Vi. I know I'm always late these days, but I've always been erratic, ever since the May Blitz. In fact, I don't even think about getting pregnant.'

'Well, it's about time you did.'

'Vi, if I am, Bob and me will both be made up, but how would I tell Josie?'

'Don't. At least not until you really have to. Until you're showing so much you can't get away with it. She's going to feel terrible, so why make it any worse by telling her yet?'

Katie nodded. Vi was right. Josie would be awfully upset, but . . . the more she thought about it, the happier she became. A baby – hers and Bob's first baby. Oh, she couldn't wait to get the news confirmed, and if it was true, to tell him. She wouldn't raise his hopes until she'd seen Dr Askam; it wouldn't be fair. She started to hum to herself as the tram trundled along the icy rails, its trolley shooting out blue sparks at the junctions of the overhead wires.

'Well, you certainly seem better,' Josie commented.

Katie took an exaggeratedly deep breath. 'I am – it must be the good cold fresh air,' she replied smiling, jumping lightly onto the platform of the tram.

She went to see Dr Askam that evening before going home. To Josie's questions she answered that she'd managed to cut herself at work before the holiday and what with all the poisonous stuff around there, wanted to get it checked. She had, of course, washed the cut immediately but it was just as well to be wise. She prayed Josie or Sarah wouldn't ask to see this imaginary cut or demand to know why she hadn't mentioned it before now, but they didn't.

When Katie arrived home, Sarah took her meal from the oven and put it on the table. Katie wasn't hungry, however. She just wanted to tell Bob her news. She was bursting with happiness and her eyes were sparkling.

'You look very pleased with yourself tonight,' he said, smiling when she walked into the front room.

She glanced over to see what Josie was doing but she was in the kitchen. 'I want to talk to you, as soon as I've had this. Upstairs, though, it's private,' she whispered. She bolted her meal down and then took her plate into the kitchen and washed it herself. 'I'm going to get changed, Josie,' she announced. 'I think our Sarah and Duncan are going out and he's staying the night on the sofa – again.'

'Well, it's an awful long way for him to get back. The Base is about fifteen miles away and all in the pitch dark and freezing cold,' Josie replied sympathetically.

Bob was already sitting on the bed waiting for her. 'Now what's all this secrecy about?'

'I – we're – going to have a baby! You're going to be a dad, Bob Goodwin.'

The smile spread right across his face and in an instant he'd swept her up in his arms. 'Oh, that's great luv! When? Why didn't you say something sooner?'

'I didn't think about it. I've been so erratic since last May. It was Vi who made me realise this morning, that's why I went to the doctor's on the way home.'

'When is it to be?'

'In August.' She hugged him.

'You see, Katie – we'll have our own little family. I told you we would.'

'I know. There's only one thing worrying me and that's, how am I going to tell Josie? I'll feel so cruel. Vi says not to tell her until I've really got to, when I'm showing.'

He looked serious. 'I think she's right, luv. Why upset that poor girl before we have to. Now lie on that bed, Katie Goodwin, and I'll put a pillow under your feet.'

She laughed. 'You'll do no such thing! Dr Askam said pregnancy was not an illness, it's a perfectly natural state and should be treated as such. Just use commonsense for the first months. So no fussing – and besides, Josie will notice it. Anyway, you're the one who's supposed to be the invalid.'

'It's nearly healed now, luv. I think when I next have to go before the Army Doctor he'll find me fit to return to my Regiment.'

'When are you due to see him?'

'At the end of this month.'

'Oh, no! You've not been home long.'

'Long enough by Army standards,' Bob said grimly.

When Vi called round later with Jack, Katie could see she was upset, even though her friend was trying hard to conceal it.

'I was just thinking, Bob, doesn't she look well? You should have seen her this morning, a right hangover she had then.' Vi winked, doing her best to put on a show.

'She looks great to me, but then she always does – and I didn't see her this morning. I was still asleep.' He grinned back at Vi.

'Oh, aye, he lies in bed all day, like King Tut,' Katie laughed.

'I've told her to make the most of me. I don't think they'll leave me hanging around here for much longer.'

Katie looked closely at Vi. There were tears in her eyes.

'Longer than me, Bob,' said Jack quietly. 'I'm off to destinations unknown at the weekend, although it's rumoured we're to join up with the Yanks in the Far East. The Yellow Peril seem to be swarming all over the place out there. I was talking to some Yankee sailors – "doughboys", they call them, God knows why – and they reckon it's all to do with the Jap religion. That feller, their Emperor, Hirohito, they think is God. Apparently it's a great honour to die for him, and they'd sooner commit suicide than be taken prisoner.'

'Religion again,' Katie said in disgust. 'There's always religion in it somewhere.'

'Don't get bitter, luv,' Bob soothed quietly.

'Well, are we going to the pub or not?' Vi asked, changing the subject.

'I'll just get my coat and hat.'

'I'll get them,' Bob offered solicitously, but his wife shot him a warning look.

Katie turned to her sister-in-law. 'Josie, get your coat on luv and come with us. What's the point in staying here moping?'

Georgie had gone to see a mate he sailed with, saying he was getting fed up with them all and having Vi and Jack calling in at all hours. And to make matters worse, his orders and ship had been changed. The next convoy he would sail with would be to Russia, Murmansk to be precise, with supplies for the Russians who were in a desperate plight. Worse even than themselves. His ship now would be the *Montroyal*, a Canadian Pacific ship. They didn't have as far to go, with the endless width of ocean to cross, but they were too near to land and it was freezing all the time. Everyone dreaded the Arctic convoys. Thanks to this latest turn of events, Georgie was even more irritable than normal.

Josie refused to go to the pub and when they'd all left she sank down wearily. She knew Katie was pregnant. She wasn't a fool. All that talk of hangovers. Oh, why was life so unfair?

She turned on the wireless to hear Tommy Handley and the rest of that crowd in *ITMA*. It was very funny, if you were in the mood for it, she thought, bleakly. Well, she might as well tidy up a bit and have a cup of tea before Georgie got home. Not that he'd have much to say to her when he did.

She put the kettle on the hob, tidied up the papers, plumped up the cushions on the sofa and straightened the colourful rag rug in front of the range. There was a scrap of paper just sticking out from beneath one corner and she bent down to pick it up, tutting slightly. Katie never used the Ewbank properly, just a quick up and down the carpet and things were never moved to be cleaned behind or under. Her mother wouldn't approve, Josie thought ruefully. But it wasn't just a scrap of paper, it was a whole envelope, addressed to Rear-Gunner Duncan Kinross, RAF Woodvale, Southport, Lancashire. She turned it over in her hand. He must have dropped it from his pocket last night, and it had somehow got under the rug. Curiously, she drew out the two pages of small, wavering writing and then sat down suddenly on the sofa. Duncan Kinross was married. He had a wife called Fiona and a little boy of two called Angus.

Chapter Twenty-Two

Josie waited until Bob and Katie got back. She'd sat rigid for hours trying to come to terms with the shock, praying that Georgie wouldn't be home early or Sarah and Duncan either. They'd gone to the pictures together. He'd seemed so nice, so utterly plausible, but now that she thought about it, he'd hardly ever spoken of his home. Sarah would be heartbroken, but she'd get over it. At least she wasn't tied to him by marriage for the rest of her life. Her heart went out to Fiona Kinross up in Glasgow and her little boy. Duncan had probably been writing to her, tender letters telling her how much he loved and missed her and Angus, and how miserable he was, with not a single word about what he did in his spare time here.

Katie and Bob were both laughing when they came in and their happy faces, the look in their eyes, tore at Josie's heart.

'I thought you'd have gone to bed,' Katie said. 'Is there any tea in that pot?'

'Katie, I think you'd better read this, then have the tea. I found it under the hearth-rug when I was clearing up.

Katie looked questioningly at her as she took the envelope. Then she read the letter.

'Oh, my God! I don't believe it!'

'What is it? What's wrong?' Bob was all concern. His wife's face had turned pale.

'He . . . he's married and with a little boy!'

'Who?'

'Him! That bloody two-timing heartless, faithless, bastard Duncan Kinross!' Katie passed the letter to Bob who also scanned the lines, his expression becoming grim and angry.

'Where are they?'

'Gone to the pictures. They'll be in soon,' Josie replied.

'I don't believe the flaming nerve of him – the barefaced cheek! He's become almost one of the family. Oh God, our poor Sarah!'

'She'll know now how I feel, how unhappy and miserable I've felt for months, years, but she's lucky!' Josie burst out passionately. 'She's not married to him. That poor girl up in Glasgow is.'

Katie sat down, her face still pale with shock. It was unbelievable, utterly incredible.

In a moment of compassion, Josie reached out and took her sister-in-law's hand. 'So you see how lucky you are, Katie. Me, Vi and now Sarah all heartbroken for one reason or another.'

Katie looked at her uncomprehendingly.

'I *know*,' Josie said gently. 'I can see it in your face. I'm not a fool. You're expecting.'

'Oh, Josie! I wasn't going to tell you yet. I didn't know *how* I was going to tell you.'

Josie squeezed her hand. 'Katie, you can't let this upset you.' She looked up at Bob.

Bob looked worried. 'No, Josie's right, Katie. She knows, don't you, luv, what shock and upset can do.'

Josie nodded.

'Go on up to bed and I'll bring you some warm milk,' Bob urged. 'I'll see to Sarah and meladdo when he arrives.'

'Oh Bob, it's not Sarah's fault. How could she have known? Duncan took us all in. She's going to be broken-hearted. Send her up to me.'

'I'll bring her up, when it's time,' Josie promised. 'Between us we'll have to try to do our best and comfort her.'

Katie's eyes flashed with anger. 'That lying swine!'

'That's just what I *don't* want you to do – start getting angry and upset. Josie, take her up to bed, will you?' Bob pleaded.

Sarah and Duncan were laughing happily as they came in, but when Sarah saw Josie's face and Bob standing with his hands behind his back by the range, her laughter died.

'What's wrong? What's happened? Is it our Joe? Is it Katie?' Her eyes darted from one to the other.

Josie didn't reply but Bob held out the letter to Duncan. 'This is yours, I believe. You must have dropped it.'

Duncan looked at the letter and then at Bob and his eyes narrowed.

'You've read it? You've read my private mail?'

'When it's left lying on *our* floor and when it concerns *my* sister-in-law, then yes, I've read it. Now you should let her read it too. The rest of us have, you lying, cheating, conniving bastard!'

Sarah looked from Bob to Duncan in horror. She'd never heard Bob talk like that to anyone. 'Bob! Duncan! What's wrong?' she begged.

Josie spoke before Bob could open his mouth. 'Sarah, luv, he's been fooling us all, lying to us all. He's married. He's got a wife called Fiona and a little boy called Angus. Oh Sarah, I'm so sorry.'

Sarah just stared at Josie. She couldn't take it in. 'No! You're wrong, Josie. Duncan isn't married.' She turned eyes wide with shock and bewilderment towards Duncan. 'You said there was no other girl, no fiancée, when I asked you.'

'I suppose I lied by omission, Sarah. There wasn't a girlfriend or a fiancée, but there is a wife – Fiona.' He reached out for her but she backed away.

'No! No! You said you loved me. You said you always would.'

'I do, Sarah, and part of me always will. You're . . . ' He struggled to find the words. He did love her, in a way. He'd been homesick, and fed up when he'd met her and it had been so good to be welcomed into a family, although he could sense that Georgie didn't like him and maybe even suspected something. But he hadn't intended to deceive or hurt her.

'Touch her and I'll kill you,' Bob said quietly but his tone was full of menace.

Josie had her arms around Sarah who was still staring at Duncan although now the tears were falling rapidly down her cheeks. She made no attempt to brush them away.

The two men were evenly matched, of the same height and build and age, but Duncan knew that Bob's rage would be the deciding factor. He stepped back.

'I'm so sorry, Sarah, more than I can ever tell you.'

'Take your letter and get out! You've a long walk home and I hope you freeze to death on the way.'

'NO!' Sarah shrieked, as Duncan turned and made for the door. 'No! Don't leave me! I love you!'

He looked back at her, as Bob and Josie tried to restrain her. 'Just remember that I *did* love you, Sarah. My posting's been changed anyway. I'm going away, down south to join the crew of a Lancaster for bombing raids.'

'I won't wish you luck,' Bob growled. 'Bastards like you deserve to die. Now get out before I break your neck.'

Duncan left without another word and Josie took a half-hysterical Sarah upstairs. Bob rooted in the cupboard of the dresser and brought out a half-bottle of brandy, kept strictly for medicinal purposes. He knew from his experiences that you shouldn't give alcohol for shock, but he discounted it. Poor Sarah would need something to help her sleep and there wasn't anything else.

Joe was standing at the top of the stairs, yawning and looking confused.

'What's going on, Bob? What's all the yelling, and why is our Sarah screaming and crying? She woke me up.'

'Go back to bed, Joe. Sarah's upset. We all are. That Duncan feller's married and with a kid, but not a word to anyone and that includes Georgie, do you hear me? It's important, Joe. It's not kids' stuff. This is the grown-up world, so promise?'

Joe solemnly promised and went back to the room he shared with Sarah. He had a feeling he wouldn't be sharing it with her tonight.

As Bob went into the bedroom, he saw that Sarah had thrown herself on the bed, her face buried against Katie's shoulder, while Josie sat on the edge of the bed and stroked her hair. She was sobbing as though her heart would break.

'We'd better think up something quickly. Georgie will be in any minute now. Thank God he's late.'

'I wish to God he'd never come back,' Josie said bitterly. 'But I'm not having him ranting and raving at her the state she's in.'

'We'll just have to say he's given her the push. That he's going off down south to join a Lancaster crew. At least that bit's true.'

'Is it? I'd never believe a single thing he said ever again,' Josie snapped.

Katie shook her head. 'It doesn't make her look good, does it, just being dumped. I know – we'll say he's had emergency orders to leave tomorrow, and that's why she's so upset. Bob, I won't have her humiliated in front of our Georgie.'

He nodded. 'Here, Josie, make her sip this. She'll have to have something to calm her down. She can sleep with you, Katie, luv. I'll share with Joe.'

'I'd sooner Georgie shared with Joe,' Josie said. 'Katie shouldn't be upset.'

'Oh Josie, we're all upset!' Katie answered.

'I hope that bastard "gets it" over Germany.' Bob's voice was as cold as ice.

'No, don't say things like that. Think of – well, think of the other lives involved.'

Sarah was a little quieter now, but occasionally huge racking sobs shook her. She wanted to die. She couldn't believe she'd never see him again. She couldn't believe the lies he'd told her. She *wouldn't* believe that he didn't love her, that he'd just *used* her. If she believed that she'd go insane. But he'd said he loved her so often, even before he turned and left he'd said it, so it really *must* be true. Maybe he didn't love his wife. Georgie didn't love Josie. Then the tiny spark of hope died. He might leave his wife, but there would be no way he'd desert his little son.

Bob went downstairs to wait for Georgie. He wanted no more confrontations, no more shouting and yelling.

He didn't have long to wait.

'I thought you'd be in bed,' Georgie muttered sourly, hanging up his overcoat and muffler.

Bob could see he had been drinking. He'd never pay for more than one drink, so he assumed the 'mate' he'd been to see had had a bottle of some kind in the house.

'I waited up for you,' Bob said, pleasantly. 'You'll be sharing with Joe tonight.'

'Like hell I am.'

'Sarah's upset. More than upset, actually. She's all broken up.'

'What's that swine done to her? I'll lay him out if he's touched her!'

'Look, Georgie, calm down. He's done nothing. He's just been posted down south, that's all, as of tomorrow.'

'Is that all? She's up there having hysterics, turning the whole bloody household into Fred Carno's Circus and all because meladdo has been posted somewhere else?'

Bob held on to his temper, fighting to sound calm and normal, affable even. 'Yes, but you know what these women are like, Georgie. And Sarah's very sensitive.'

'Soft, more like. There's plenty of other fellers. She's young and not bad-looking, so what's all the bloody fuss for?'

'Well, she loved him, I suppose, and when women are in love . . . ' He left the sentence unfinished.

'You've got a point there. When they're in love, they're a bloody pain in the arse. I suppose we'll have her whinging and mooning all around the place now. So I've got to go and share our Joe's room, eh?'

'Just for tonight and I think we can put up with a bit of weeping. She'll get over it.' Bob changed the subject. Seeing as his normally obnoxious brother-in-law was being reasonably pleasant, he might as well make the most of it and give Katie and Josie time to get Sarah asleep.

'When are you off then, Georgie?'

'Soon – too bloody soon. The weekend, probably.'

'Same as Jack.'

Georgie thought how he'd wished the two of them to the back of beyond. He'd had no idea then that it would be himself and Jack Milligan who'd be going, leaving Bob Goodwin behind at home.

'I've heard it's murder on those Arctic convoys,' Georgie shivered. 'You're always cold, the ice builds up on the masts and makes the ship top-heavy, and the storms have to be seen to be believed, or survived, so Bert told me. Then you've got the bloody U-boats and you're within range of their bloody planes for most of the time. The Atlantic's beginning to look like a picnic.'

'Well, the Russians are having a hell of a time. They're far worse off than us, and if anything will stop the Jerries from getting to Moscow, their winter will. God knows how they live in a country like that.'

'Bloody Bolshies!' Georgie spat out. 'I'm not dead pleased about risking my life for people who bloody well murder their King, Queen and all their kids too. That lad was only eleven and he was ill, poor little perisher. They're as bad as the bloody Jerries.'

'Aye, you're right.' Bob would have agreed with Georgie that black was white, as long as it kept him quiet. There was no movement now from upstairs so he thought he'd risk it. 'Well, I can't see them leaving me here for much longer either. It's more or less OK now.' He flexed his arm. 'And I've a good idea where they'll send me.'

'Oh, and where's that, then?'

'Out to the Far East, like Jack. We'll swelter while you freeze. What a bloody world it is.'

'It's not the world, it's the bloody people in it, lad,' Georgie said sagely as he climbed the stairs.

Bob switched off the light and followed him. It was the nearest he'd ever had to a normal, amicable conversation with his brother-in-law. Drink obviously mellowed Georgie.

Sarah's head was thudding; her eyes were so swollen she could hardly see and her throat was raw. Both Josie and Katie said she must stay at home. She couldn't go into work looking and feeling like that. Questions would be asked which would only make her break down again.

'Why, Katie? Why did he do it?' she pleaded.

'Who knows, luv. Maybe he was lonely, being away from his family. Maybe he only *thought* he loved you. These things happen sometimes.'

'No! No, he did love me, Katie, he said he did.'

'Oh Sarah, it wasn't love. It was infatuation.'

'No, I knew it was love. I loved him and you once told me that you've got to fight for things in this world, if you want them badly enough. I've *got* to see him again, Katie! I've *got* to!'

Her sister took her firmly by the shoulders. 'NO, Sarah. You will *never* see him again. It's over. It's finished. When I told you you had to fight for what you wanted, I didn't mean fight for someone else's husband and father. Think of that poor little boy, Sarah, even if you can't think of the pain Duncan has caused his wife. If she ever found out, there'd be no contest. He'd deny everything. Put him out of your mind, luv. It's over! He was cruel – no decent man or one who really loved you, would deceive you like that. And remember – Georgie doesn't know and he never will, but if you try to go sneaking off to see him, he'll definitely find out, and then there'll be murder.' She drew her sister's head down on her shoulder as the sobs shook Sarah's slim body again. Oh, why had this happened to Sarah? She was so sensitive, quiet and shy. She was one of the least able to fight back or indeed bounce back. Why couldn't she have found someone like him, but single? No, not like him, someone like Bob or Jack. She thought about Bob. She'd had to fight for him. She'd had to fight the religious bigotry and the hatred on both sides, yet they were happy. That's what she'd meant when she'd told Sarah to fight for what she wanted. But Duncan Kinross wasn't worth fighting for.

That day, Bob said he'd talk to Sarah, sit with her and listen to her, and Katie knew he was probably the best one to do this at the moment. Of course, Georgie would be there but he wouldn't give a hoot for Sarah. In fact, he'd probably make himself scarce all day to avoid both of them. The mellow mood Bob had said her brother was in last night would have worn off.

'Where's your Sarah?' Vi asked as they met on the corner. Vi, too, looked miserable, Katie thought.

'For God's sake, Vi, swear to God that what I'm going to tell you you won't breathe to anyone – and I mean *anyone*.'

'Mother of God, what's she done?'

'It's not what *she's* done, it's him.'

'Duncan?' Vi queried.

'I found a letter belonging to him – he must have dropped it and it got under the rug.' Josie's voice was flat and unemotional.

'The swine's married and he's got a little boy, too,' Katie finished.

Vi was speechless. Her mouth opened and closed but no words came out and her eyes were wide with disbelief. 'You . . . you . . . mean . . . ' she stammered, then found her voice. 'The bloody two-faced, two-timing, lying, cheating—'

'Calm down,' Katie hissed. 'People are looking at you.'

'The cheek! The bloody barefaced cheek! I can't believe anyone would be so hardfaced – and after the way you've all been so good to him.'

'Neither could we believe it, but our Georgie doesn't know.'

'Well, that's something. Oh God, poor Sarah! She's so sweet and trusting.'

'Maybe this will teach her a lesson about men.' Josie's tone was curt.

'Oh, go on, Josie, that's right, rub it in. Just because you made a bloody mistake don't go and crow over her.'

'I wasn't,' Josie snapped back.

Katie glared at them both. 'Oh, stop it the pair of you! All we can do is try to help her as much as we can and hope she gets over it.'

'At least he's left this neck of the woods,' Josie said.

'Has he?'

'He's been posted down south, Vi.'

'Katie, you don't think – well, that she'll be so devastated that she'll do something stupid?' Vi's voice was filled with fear. Sarah had been so besotted and she *was* terribly upset and sensitive.

'Oh, Jesus, Mary and Joseph! I'd not thought like that. Thank God Bob is at home with her, and perhaps by tomorrow he'll be able to talk her into coming to work.'

'She does know suicide's a sin?' Josie added with a worried look on her face. It was a sin she herself had been almost tempted to commit in her lowest moments.

'Yes, and so is getting married in the Register Office, living in sin and having a baby that the church will look on as illegitimate, but it didn't stop me because I love Bob so much.' Katie looked very anxious. 'Oh, we'll just have to try and watch her, Josie.'

They'd reached the tram-stop and could see one approaching. It was only a few yards away, its hooded headlights piercing the darkness. Another day doing a boring job, Katie thought drearily, and with the added worry of her sister's misery. She didn't feel as though she was walking on air today. She'd almost forgotten about her own baby.

Chapter Twenty-Three

In February 1942, Singapore fell to the Japanese; in March the first heavy raids of the Lancaster bombers began on the German-controlled industrial towns in France and Holland, and on the Krupps factory at Essen in Germany itself.

In February, too, both Georgie and Bob left Liverpool. Georgie was bound for Murmansk, Bob for Burma. Vi had received her first letters from Jack in Colombo, Ceylon; he described the place as 'Paradise'.

'Oh, it's all very nice being in Paradise,' Vi moaned as they walked, heads bent against the icy wind towards the tram-stop.

Josie had trotted out all the usual platitudes as Georgie left. 'Take care of yourself. Make sure you've something on your head and wear gloves or you'll get frostbite.' She'd tried, with an emptiness in her heart, to be a dutiful wife.

Georgie ignored her. They were kitted out with all the necessary gear, so he didn't need her useless advice. At least these trips didn't take as long as the Atlantic convoys, but he wished he'd been transferred to a Mediterranean one. They were just as dangerous – because although the British held the Rock and controlled the Straits, Allied ships were always within range of enemy planes, but if you were unlucky enough to be sunk, at least the water was warm! On the run up to Murmansk, you died almost within seconds of being submerged. The bitterly cold water often caused such a shock to the body that the heart stopped instantly.

'Will you try and write, this time?' Josie had asked.

'I'll try, but the postal service is diabolical. Letters can lie there unattended to for months. Those bloody Bolshies don't care a fig about the mail.'

So she'd resigned herself to hear nothing, to get no letters at all.

Katie and Bob's farewells were, of course, totally different. The night before he went, Bob held his wife in his arms all night long. 'I never want to let you go, Katie,' he murmured. 'Both of you!'

Katie had once again taken a look at Joe's Atlas; this time, her husband was going to the other side of the world – and that was a long, long way away.

'I'll go to Mass,' she promised, snuggling up to him in bed. 'I'll say the Thirty Days' Prayer as well, just so you'll come home safe and well to me . . . us.'

He smiled down at her. 'You can't bribe God, luv. It's not a question of "If I do such and such, then You have to give me such and such". Just pray that things go well and that it will be over soon, and promise me you'll take care of yourself?'

'Stop lecturing me,' she replied, laughing, before drawing his head down towards her, her lips eager for his.

The following morning in the bedroom she kissed him and held him tightly, fighting back the tears. They agreed that there'd be no emotional farewells in front of Josie and Sarah.

Life was just one long, dull, meaningless round of repetitive chores, Sarah thought drearily. The light had gone from her life entirely. There was nothing to look forward to, and now, three months after Duncan's traumatic departure, she willed herself not to look back any longer.

Night after night, day after day, she'd remembered everything they'd said and done together. The places they'd been, the songs they'd sung. Now she wouldn't even go into town or down to the riverside because it was all too painful. She seemed to have spent all these weeks in a waking nightmare. Would the pain, the longing, the humiliation *ever* go away?

Josie and Katie had been wonderful but the best thing was that they'd kept it from Georgie. She knew she couldn't have borne his rage. There were days when she thought she could stand no more of this dire existence, but she hadn't the courage to take her own life. Not the physical courage to slash the blade of Georgie's razor across her wrists or hurl herself under a tram or bus. Nor the courage she would need to face God. It was a Mortal Sin to take the life God had given you, and to die in Mortal Sin was to go straight to Hell. Whichever way she turned, there was no way out. None at all!

As the first buds appeared on the trees in the parks and gardens, and the daffodils began to open their golden trumpets to a warmer sun and a milder wind, Josie once again saw her husband leave for another trip to Murmansk. It was with heartfelt relief that she and Katie watched him slouch down the street and turn the corner, out of their sight.

'Well, thank God for that! I'm sick of listening to him. He's like a flaming gramophone record that's got stuck: "You don't know how lucky you are"!' Katie began to clear away the breakfast dishes. It was a Sunday, but they'd willingly foregone their lie-in to get Georgie away. They were all due in work for the late shift.

'I don't blame our Sarah for not getting up.'

'She is up, Katie,' Josie said quietly.

'Since when?'

'Two hours ago.'

'Where is she, then?' Katie was puzzled.

'She's upstairs now, but since six o'clock she's been up and down to the privy, being sick.'

A plate dropped straight from Katie's hands and smashed on the floor. 'Oh no, Josie! She's not . . . she can't be! Tell me she's just got a stomach upset.'

'She's pregnant,' Josie said baldly. 'I can tell.' Josie sat down at the table and dropped her head in her hands.

'Oh, my God! What are we going to do, Josie? What will everyone think? At least *he*'s not around any more and hasn't been for a while.'

'That only makes it look worse, Katie. Everyone will be saying he'd got what he wanted and cleared off.'

Katie nodded, biting her lip. Not only was she shocked that Sarah had been so foolish as to let Duncan Kinross make love to her, but they'd clearly taken no precautions. Sarah wouldn't have known about such things anyway, but he would. 'Oh, Josie what am I going to do?' Katie groaned. 'Mam will be turning in her grave, she was respected so much. Oh, stupid, silly little madam!' Another thought struck her. 'Georgie! How am I going to tell him? He'll go absolutely mad.'

Suddenly, Josie burst into tears. Stepping over the broken crockery, Katie instantly went to her and put her arms around her. 'Oh, Josie! Josie! I forgot about . . . you.'

Josie's shoulders were shaking. 'He'll blame us both, I know he will. He'll say we've brought all this shame down on the family. That it's our fault for not keeping our eye on her. You know how he'll carry on and . . . and . . .'

'And what?'

Josie looked up at her. 'What's the matter with me? Sarah can get caught the very first time but me . . . ' She turned a tear stained face towards Katie. 'I'm so miserable! I'm so bloody miserable and now this. There's nothing to look forward to any more, nothing.'

Gently Katie smoothed her friend's brown hair and made shushing, soothing noises but she knew Josie was right. What was there for her to look forward to? Georgie? Oh, poor Josie and poor, silly Sarah.

Neither of them heard Sarah come into the room, but the sight of Katie comforting a weeping Josie brought a choking sob into Sarah's throat.

Katie looked up and so did Josie.

'Sarah, sit down,' her elder sister said quietly, indicating the sofa.

Sarah knew what was coming, but she didn't care. She felt too ill and miserable, and frightened, too.

'You're pregnant, aren't you?'

To Sarah's relief, her sister seemed more upset than annoyed. She nodded.

'How many months? Have you been to see the doctor?'

'No, and I must be . . . ' she paused, to control herself, ' . . . three months.'

'Oh Sarah, you little fool! You poor little fool.' Josie's words were harsh but her tone wasn't.

Katie sighed. 'There's no use ranting and raving now. The deed is done.' The germ of an idea had implanted itself while poor, barren Josie had been comforting her and it had swiftly grown. *Why not*? she thought. There was no law against it.

'I want to ask you both a question,' she said now, 'and I want you to think hard before answering.'

They looked at her questioningly.

'Sarah, will you give your baby up for adoption, to Josie?'

There was a deep silence as the two girls looked at each other. Then slowly Sarah nodded.

'Yes. Yes – I'll give it to Josie and Georgie.'

There were tears of astonished joy in Josie's eyes. Wordlessly, she looked from one sister to the other. In a few seconds, her whole world had changed from a place of darkness to one with a bright and gleaming future. Her depression melted away in a burst of radiance.

'Oh, Sarah! Sarah! It will have everything, everything and it will have so much love. Your child will be so . . . so precious,' she whispered at last.

'And it will be family, or part-family,' Katie said, smiling. This seemed the perfect solution to a nightmare situation – but would it in time cause friction between Josie and Sarah? She hoped not. In time, Sarah would meet someone else, get married and have more children. The slate would be wiped clean. No one outside the family would know. Of course, they'd swear their Joe to secrecy, when the time came. Their close neighbours were scattered now, but Florrie would have to be taken into their confidence. and then there was Georgie . . .

Josie had obviously had the same thought. 'What about Georgie?'

'To hell with our flaming Georgie. All he's interested in is himself and anyway, apart from the immediate family, to all intents and purposes it would be his. You just leave our Georgie to me!' Katie said grimly.

★ ★ ★

Sarah had her pregnancy confirmed; both Josie and Katie went to the doctor's with her and they explained their plans to him. He nodded, considered the matter then agreed that it was probably the best solution, although he had reservations. When Sarah had actually held the child in her arms, would she be as willing to give it up? Only time would tell.

Katie herself was begining to show now and the baby had 'quickened'. She'd had a fainting spell at work, and the nurse on duty had told her not to worry, it often happened when the baby moved for the first time. She'd placed both her hands on her stomach in wonderment. It had moved. It was starting to move around, this precious little life that she was carrying. She'd write and tell Bob immediately.

Katie had received two letters so far, which Vi said was a miracle. Bob was well, it was hot and steamy, the people were friendly, he loved her and hoped she was looking after herself and his son or daughter. He wasn't allowed to say much more and neither was she. It was awful to try and pour your heart out when you knew everything was going to be read by a civil servant. Censorship was such an invasion of privacy even though everyone knew it was vitally necessary.

The house in Chelmsford Street was a much happier place these days than it had been for a good while. Sarah was less lethargic and depressed, and Josie had begun to knit and cut up old sheets and hem them for cot sheets. She intended to make a patchwork quilt for the cot, and was busy scrounging bits of material from everyone. The only thing that secretly nagged at her was how Georgie would react? It was all very well for Katie to say she'd handle him – although Josie honestly *did* believe her, but Georgie was so strong-willed. Yet oh, how she wanted this baby and she'd be with Sarah all the time it was growing within her. Just yesterday Katie had taken her hand, then Sarah's and placed them on her own rounded abdomen. They'd felt the movement within and had looked with wonder at each other. For Sarah it was a novel and slightly apprehensive feeling, for Josie it was pure joy. If Georgie objected then this time she'd fight him, for this was worth fighting for. She'd have someone to love, who would love her in return. She'd have a future.

So far, Joe had been told nothing. He knew something was going on but he thought it was all to do with Duncan Kinross and Georgie and Bob being away. Women were daft that way. Always worrying and crying over stupid things. And besides, life had changed for him. He'd left school now and thanks to the reference Mr Peel had given him, he had a job with prospects in the General Post Office in Victoria Street. He received two pounds a week – a wage he considered an absolute fortune, and Katie only took seven shillings a week for his keep. He had also bought his first proper suit. It had cost four pounds and eight shillings which he was paying off each week. It was utility, of course, with no turn-ups and narrow lapels, but a really snazzy shade of navy blue, and he had two good shirts and ties and a pair of black shoes for best, not boots. He only wore boots for work now. When he got more coupons and he'd finished paying his five shillings a week off the navy suit, he was going to buy another suit. He fancied himself as a real sharp dresser and now used Brylcreem to smooth down his unruly hair.

He'd made some new mates, although Vinny worked with him and they often saw Franny, who was a junior clerk in one of the shipping offices. Now he had more things to think of than weeping and wailing women. He'd begun to notice that not all girls were spiteful, bossy, scruffy little cats; some were very attractive indeed, and there was always a good film on at one of the many cinemas in town. Oh, life was great at the moment. Of course, if the war went on for another four years he'd be called up. He'd opt for the RAF, he decided. Girls thought it was classy: you got known as one of the 'Brylcreem Boys'. But surely it wouldn't last *that* long. It would be three years in September since the war began.

At the beginning of May, Georgie arrived home unannounced and looking as miserable as sin. Josie had told Katie and Sarah that she would speak to him first and then, if she needed support, she would call them in.

He'd had his meal, unpacked and was just settling down with a cigarette and a copy of the *Echo* to catch up on the news, when Josie said she wanted to talk to him. Seriously. Katie and Sarah had disappeared upstairs and Joe was out.

'Bloody hell, Josie, I've not been over the doorstep more than a couple of hours and you start. What the hell's the matter now?'

'Put that paper down and listen and I don't want to hear a word out of you until I've finished,' she said firmly. Start as you mean to go on, Katie had said, and so far she was covering her nervousness well.

Georgie looked at her in amazement.

'Sarah is expecting a baby in October.'

He opened his mouth but before he could speak she rushed on: 'There's no use in getting all airyated about it. We've talked about it and we know what we're going to do. It was Katie's idea and it will save face all round and . . . be the best thing for Sarah and me – us. Sarah's agreed to let us adopt her baby.'

Georgie looked as though he'd been punched hard in the solar plexus. He didn't utter a sound for quite a while but then the dark red flush of anger came flooding into his face. He threw down the paper and the cigarette went into the fire.

'If you think I'm going to have that . . . that brat of *his* and pass it off as mine, feed it, clothe it, educate it, then you're bloody wrong! You get that idea out of your head now, Josie – do you hear me? Do you understand?! NO! NO! NO!' The last words were roared and Josie shrank back away from him, her resolve faltering.

Katie was down the stairs first. She'd expected this and had been poised on the landing in readiness.

'And you get *this* idea into your head, Georgie Deegan. This "brat" as you call it, is your niece or nephew, whether you like it or not! You've given Josie nothing over the years – absolutely nothing. No love or affection. No sympathy or understanding. No money even, unless it was prised out of you! And I know that Mam asked the doctor at the hospital if all Josie's miscarriages had anything to do with you. You'd not thought of that, had you? Oh no, it was all Josie's fault. There couldn't possibly be anything wrong with *you*! But is there? Maybe you should go to see a doctor. Maybe it's God's punishment for all the rotten, crooked things you've done in your life. So, to spare having our Sarah's name dragged through the mud around here and your . . . capabilities questioned too, Sarah will go away, we'll say it's for her nerves, and she'll eventually give Josie the baby and it will be done all legal. The child will be family!'

Sarah now faced him with a determination fired by Katie's attack. 'I want her to have it. I don't care about you. This baby is Josie's – I'm just carrying it for her.'

He rounded on his sister. 'You little whore. Don't you stand there and tell me what *you* want. You slut! You trollop! It's on Lime Street you belong! I suppose you were rolling around this floor with that . . . Scottish pig. And no doubt begging for more while we were all asleep in our beds.' He was livid, not only with Sarah but mainly with Katie, for casting doubts on his ability to father a child. Who else had she told? That Vi Milligan who had a mouth like the Mersey Tunnel? And Florrie Watson and that tribe and Mary Maher and Ellen MacCane. Half the bloody neighbourhood would know by now and be sniggering behind their hands at him. Well, there was no way he was going to have that – and no way was he going to bring up Duncan Kinross's bastard!

'You three bloody bitches, you're all in this together, aren't you? You've made all these plans behind my back while I've been away. Well, all your scheming's been for nothing because it's not going to happen!'

Katie faced him, white with fury, her fists clenched tightly. 'She's not a whore and you know it. Our Sarah made one mistake. One, and many's the drink you accepted from him. You stop these plans, Georgie Deegan, and by God I'll see to it that it's known in every parish and pub in this city that you're not capable of fathering a child that lives!' It was all a lie, of course, she'd never do that – but it was the only weapon she had. She could already hear Josie's quiet weeping and Sarah's sobs as they clung together.

'Go on then, tell them! You probably have already, so it doesn't bloody matter, does it? I'm not having it! I'm *not* having that bloody little bastard in this house. She can go away and not come back, the flaming little whore!' he yelled and then stormed upstairs.

Katie was shaking. She'd been sure the threat of such humiliation would work but it hadn't. She went and put her arms around both Josie and Sarah. 'Take no notice of him, I'll think of something else. I always do. I know how his mind works. I'll find a way.' Her tone was determined but in her heart she felt desolate.

After the scene in the evening, Georgie lay awake all night fuming. As if he didn't have enough to put up with, without those three conniving, immoral bitches! That's what they were – immoral. Well, if there was any more of it he'd have Father Macreedy round to the house. Katie was beyond the pale of the Church, but the parish priest would soon sort the other two out. What a homecoming! What a sodding bloody homecoming!

It was the early hours of the morning when he had the idea. He smiled grimly into the darkness, unaware that Josie lying beside him was still awake too, her tears falling silently, her pillow soaked with them. She told herself she'd be strong, she'd be resolute, but she hadn't been. Oh, she and Sarah had a lot in common. Neither of them were brave enough or clever enough to stand up to him.

She'd known that Katie had been lying about it being his fault, but she'd stood up to him, totally unafraid, her dark eyes flashing with an anger that matched Georgie's. No one could have had a better champion, sister-in-law and friend. The only shred of hope she had left was that Katie would find another way to defy him, a new strategy to persuade him to co-operate.

You could have cut the atmosphere with a knife the following morning. Even Joe noticed, but after a few half-heartedly cheerful remarks that had fallen decidedly flat, he gave up and went gratefully off to work.

Georgie waited until he was sure they'd all be well on their way to work, then he put on his jacket and cap and left to get a tram to Scotland Road. He had a vague idea where Doreen MacNally, Josie's distant and disreputable cousin, lived. She was Mickey Mac's mother, or had been, and not a very good one either, so he'd heard. He asked at a house in Cartwright Place and was told she lived in Number Seven Court, just around the corner.

This area had been hit worse than their own. It had always been a slum, but now it was worse, if that was at all possible. Number Seven Court had a flagged yard with a gutter running down the middle of it, choked in places with debris. The houses had been built around three sides and looked decidedly unsafe. A lad of about five, bare-footed, in ragged trousers and jersey, was sitting on the step of the first house.

'Where does Mrs MacNally live?'

The child pointed to a house in the corner.

The door with the paint peeling was open and the combined smells of rotten vegetables, dirty washing and urine made him baulk with disgust, but there were some things that had to be endured. He hammered loudly on the door, which shuddered on its hinges and seemed ready to collapse under his fist.

Finally, a woman answered it. She was fat and blowsy, her hair uncombed and peroxided but with the black roots showing. There were the remains of heavy make-up on her face which made it look raddled. She clutched a flowered but dirty dressing gown around her and smelled anything but sweet. A cigarette dangled from the corner of her mouth.

'What's up with youse, la! 'Ammerin' on the door at this hour in the mornin'?'

'Are you Doreen MacNally?'

Her eyes narrowed, almost disappearing into the folds of flesh. 'Who wants ter know, like?'

'Me. I'm Josie Watson's husband. Your Mickey came to our wedding. I was sorry to hear about . . . him,' he added, thinking she might look more sympathetically on his request.

'Oh, yeah, thanks. 'E was a right little bleeder at times though, snot-nosed little get, but 'e was me lad. I gorra nice letter offen some officer feller. Well, seein' as yer family, yer'd better come in.'

He couldn't stand here in the hallway and talk to her, yet he didn't really want to go in either. He had no choice. He was ushered into a dark, cluttered and smelly room. There was everything in it. A brass bed – unmade and strewn with clothes, armchairs, a table, cupboards, chests of drawers, stools – and every surface was littered. The smell of cheap perfume, stale cigarette smoke and beer were the most prevalent pongs. He tried not to show his disgust. A girl of about sixteen or seventeen was sprawled in an armchair, a cigarette also in her mouth. Her long dark hair was matted and her large brown eyes were narrowed with suspicion, but with a good wash and decent clothes she'd be very attractive, he could see that. There was an oriental look about her in the high cheekbones and almond-shaped eyes fringed with thick dark lashes. She'd probably inherited that from her father, whoever he had been.

'This is our Joanie, me girl. Well, yer 'aven't come all the way 'ere just to say yer sorry about our Mickey, nor after all this time. So, what can we do yez for?'

He'd taken off his cap, an habitual gesture of respect but one that was lost on Doreen. He twisted it round in his hands. 'It's a bit . . . delicate.' He looked over at Joanie who was blowing smoke rings and appeared to be taking no notice whatsoever.

'Oh, don't yer mind 'er. She can keep 'er gob shut an' she's sixteen, goin' on twenty-six, if yer get me.'

'Well, it's about our Sarah, my youngest sister . . .'

'In the club, is she? Gorra bun in the oven? Some Yank, was it? It usually is. I've told 'er over there ter watch herself with them Yanks. 'Ere terday, gone termorrer an' all for a few pair of nylons or fags. Don't sell yer favours cheap. I've told yer that offen enough, 'aven't I, Joanie?'

There was a shrug in response.

'No, not a Yank. A feller in the RAF. Turned out he was married with a kid in Scotland.'

'Bastards, the lot of them! Get their birrof fun then bugger off.'

'I don't want her life ruined. She's a good girl – quiet and shy, like. He was the first and she believed him. We all did.'

''Ow old is she, then?'

'Twenty-one.'

'Twenty-one! An' it was 'er first? The first feller she'd ever 'ad?'

'Yes, what's so odd about that?' His voice was cold.

'Christ, she 'ad fellers touchin' 'er up when she was fourteen! What do yer do, lock 'er in at night? Purra gob on any feller who looks twice at 'er?'

He was disgusted. 'Look, can you help or not? Do you know anyone? Someone clean and reliable, like?'

'It depends if yer've got the money – an' if yer want clean and reliable, it'll cost yer more.'

'How much?'

'Fifteen quid.'

He was taken aback. Fifteen pounds was extortionate but then he nodded. It would be worth it.

'Up front.'

He got out his wallet and passed over a single white five-pound note.

'Are yer deaf? I said fifteen.'

'How will I know this person will get the money?'

'Yer bloody suspicious, ain't yer! She'll gerrit. We're not like that round 'ere, norrover things like this.'

'Then you'll get the other ten when I've got a name and address and a date and a time.'

She shrugged her fleshy shoulders. 'All right. I'll send our Joanie down with a note and yer can give 'er the rest of the cash. After that it's all down ter youse. Where do yer live?'

'Chelmsford Street. It's the empty shop there – she'll have to come around the back, down the jigger. And in the afternoon.'

'Did yer get that, Joanie?'

The girl nodded.

'She'll be down termorrer then.'

He nodded and turned away. At the door he thanked her and with relief walked out into the comparatively clean air. This would settle things once and for all. There'd be no need to bring in the Clergy. He'd have no trouble with Sarah. He'd always been able to bully her into anything. Once he got a date, time and place he'd think up some ruse, something plausible. Oh, this time he'd settle the three of them once and for all. Nor could any of them report him to the police. Doreen, Joanie and the woman they would approach would all swear blind they knew nothing, that they'd never even met each other before. And Sarah wouldn't dare open her mouth. Abortion was illegal; she'd go to jail and neither Josie nor Katie would let that happen, so they'd keep their mouths shut as well. He straightened his shoulders and walked resolutely up Cartwright Place to Scotland Road. He had no qualms of guilt that according to his faith what he had just arranged was a sin, or that he would be forcing Sarah to commit a heinous sin also. It was the most practical course to take and that's what mattered.

Chapter Twenty-Four

The atmosphere in the house was unpleasant, to say the least. Sarah had become silent and withdrawn again. Josie wore an expression of mute misery and Katie looked depressed and tired. She'd lain awake racking her brains for a reason to force her brother to let Josie take Sarah's child.

Georgie had waited impatiently for two afternoons, but when there was no sign of the girl, he began to think that Doreen MacNally had cheated him out of five pounds, and the more he thought about it, the more furious he became. He couldn't go to the police. He'd have to explain why he'd given a complete stranger, and such a disreputable one who was probably known to them already, a large amount of money. She'd deny it anyway and so would the girl.

When on the third afternoon, a Saturday, there was still no sign of Joanie, he made up his mind that first thing in the morning, he was going down to Number Seven Court to confront the blowsy old harridan. For the past few days and nights his temper had been foul.

'What the hell's the matter with him Josie?' Katie said after Georgie had snapped her head off in reply to a simple question.

'I don't know. Maybe he's lost some money,' Josie said sarcastically. 'We all know that's the only thing he cares about. But then he's never in the best of moods to start with, these days, is he?'

'Do I have to come with you to the pictures?' Sarah begged. The three women were due to go out, but she felt too miserable. Since the confrontation with her brother, all her plans, the simple hopes she'd had for the future, were shattered.

'Yes, it'll cheer you up a bit,' Katie told her, then dropped her tone to a whisper. 'We all need cheering up. I could still murder him, but I'm searching for something – *anything* – to force him to change his mind.'

Georgie glowered at them from over his *Echo*, it carried the first news of the four-day-long American and Japanese naval battle of Midway Island which had Vi worried sick.

'We might see something on the Pathé News about Midway,' Josie said.

Katie looked concerned. 'That could be a blessing or a disaster for Vi.'

Georgie suddenly lost his patience. He was fuming, his mind dwelling constantly on that five pounds.

'If you lot are going out, will you flaming well go! A man can't read the paper in peace in his own home because he's surrounded by cackling women!'

'We'll go when we're ready,' Katie snapped back while Josie shrugged and went through into the kitchen, followed by Sarah and Katie.

Joe, too, was going out that afternoon and was thankful that now they'd gone he could get into the kitchen to put the finishing touches to his toilette in the mirror. The girls had been gone only minutes when Joe heard the backyard door open and peering through the window he saw a girl come into the yard. She had long straight black hair that fell loosely over her shoulders and dark almond-shaped eyes. Her skin was a light olive colour. She wore a pretty summer frock with large white daisies on a pale blue background, and the same wedged canvas and raffia-type shoes that Sarah wore. She stood staring at the back of the house, and he thought he'd never seen anyone as beautiful in his whole life. He almost tripped over the leg of the chair as he rushed out into the yard, straightening his tie.

'Who're you?' he asked before realising it sounded a bit bald and not exactly the way to speak to a girl who would haunt your dreams. 'I mean, I haven't seen you around here before.'

'Is this where Georgie Deegan lives?'

Joe nodded. God, he hoped Georgie wasn't fooling around with her. She looked too young, for a start, only a few years older than himself.

'Can I help? I'm his brother, Joe. His *younger* brother,' he stressed.

She smiled radiantly and he stepped back, a little dizzy. She was utterly gorgeous.

'Yer might. Is he in?'

'Yes, but—'

'I just brung a note from me Mam. She sent me down.' She looked around. 'It ain't bad round 'ere, is it? Is the shop yours?'

'Oh, aye, yeah. We shut it because of the shortages and everyone being away or out at work. But we'll open up again when the war's over. It used to be a little gold mine when me Mam was alive. I've got a position in the GPO – white-collar, like, with good prospects.' He hoped he sounded sophisticated. He wanted to impress her.

'Are yer going out, like?'

Joe took the note she held out. 'Nowhere special,' he lied. He'd arranged to meet Vera Summers from Dart Street to go to the pictures. But he'd stand her up. She wasn't important, not beside this beauty.

235

'Will yer show me around, like?' She gazed straight at him, her dark eyes suggestive, her full lips parted a little. She ran the tip of her tongue slowly over her bottom lip. This one would be a real soft touch, she could see it and these Deegans seemed to have money. If she played her cards right she could con him into anything. Maybe even buying her clothes and jewellery.

Joe tried not to gape and stammered that he'd love to 'show her around' then maybe they could catch the main feature at the Astoria on Walton Road, with fish and chips to follow.

He was rewarded with another dazzling smile. 'What's yer name?'

'Joe. Joe Deegan. What's yours?'

'Joan MacNally, but me friends call me Joanie, so you can an' all.' She reached out and touched his tie, letting her fingers brush the skin of his neck. 'It's dead nice, that tie.'

At her touch he felt a shiver run down his spine. 'I'll just nip in an' get me jacket. Don't go away.'

'I won't. An' don't forget to give the note to your Georgie,' she called after him.

Joe ran into the living room, snatched up his jacket from the back of the chair and thrust the single sheet of paper at Georgie.

'This is for you. I'm off. I won't be late.' And he had gone.

Georgie was so surprised that he didn't utter a word, just stared after Joe until he heard the backyard door slam, then he looked down at the grubby piece of paper. He unfolded it. *Mrs Ada Bushell, 12 Juvenal Street, 2.30 Friday afternoon.*

Bloody hell, Joe must have got it from that Joanie . . . Never mind – at least she had arrived, that was the main thing. His money hadn't been spirited away. He was thankful that all the women were out.

He read the note again with some annoyance. Friday. He was sailing next Saturday, very early too. Why the hell hadn't the lazy old bitch moved herself, asked this Mrs Bushell sooner. He'd wanted to see that Sarah would be all right, physically at least, and to see the look on the faces of the other two when he announced that there was no longer anything to be scheming and planning for. If he was going to be paying out fifteen bloody quid, he wanted at least to get some satisfaction out of it.

When they arrived back he had it all worked out. They were smiling about something, probably the film.

'Did it say anything about Midway?' he asked.

'The Japs lost three aircraft carriers and about a dozen other ships, some of them battleships. The Yanks won but Vi's still worried. The fighting was heavy and went on for four days.'

'At least we won. That'll teach the bloody Nips.' He paused.

236

'Sarah, I've been to see Father Macreedy.'

She looked down and the colour flooded into her cheeks. There was a general silence.

'We've fixed it all up between us,' he went on smoothly. 'There's a home for fallen women, fallen Catholic women, run by the Sisters of Charity. It's over the water, on the Wirral. I've got the address and the Mother Superior is expecting us at half-past two on Friday afternoon. Father Macreedy phoned her there and then.'

'I don't want to go – not yet!' Sarah felt suddenly terrified. She looked wildly to Josie and Katie for support.

'It's not up to you when you want to go. It's all been arranged,' he said in a voice of steel.

'Will we be able to go and visit her?' Katie demanded, feeling utterly defeated. What Georgie'd arranged was now the only option left for Sarah if she wanted to retain some dignity and a chance of a future and maybe eventually marriage.

'I suppose so. I don't think they lock them up,' Georgie replied sarcastically. It was obvious they were already beaten, and his confidence surged.

'She'll not get much charity out of that lot,' Josie remarked, defiantly outstaring her husband. The misery she'd felt, the awful disappointment was being replaced by hatred.

'There's no need for either of you two to stay off work. They're expecting me to take her over.' His voice smug, gloating.

Sarah was in tears and Georgie turned on her.

'Oh, grow up, Sarah, for God's sake! You have to pay for your pleasure and suffer for your sins.'

'May God damn you for a bloody hypocrite, Georgie Deegan!' Katie cried.

Georgie decided to be patient and a little accommodating. Katie was a pain, and she just might take it into her head to follow them. 'Sarah, if you don't like the look of it, we can come home and we'll find somewhere else.'

'Oh, that's very generous of you. I suppose she could go to the one in Gambia Terrace and we could announce it in the *Echo* and the *Catholic Herald*. Tell the whole of the bloody city,' Katie replied.

Georgie ignored her. Sarah was drying her eyes. 'And I've thought up a reason. It's because of her nerves, and Dr Askam has suggested she stay in the country for a while.'

'We'd already thought of that.'

'Then great minds think alike, don't they?' he answered his wife nastily before returning to his newspaper.

There could be no further discussion on the matter as Joe came in whistling and looking like the cat that got the cream.

'Well, someone's dead happy. Where've you been, meladdo?'

'The Astoria. It was a great film – a Western.' It had been a Western but he hadn't seen much of it. They'd sat in the back row and Joanie had been more than willing to let him kiss and stroke her. She was three years older and much more experienced, and when her hand had slid across his leg and upwards towards the fastening of his fly, he'd thought his body was going to explode with ecstasy. God, she was beautiful and he wanted her and she'd sort of promised that he could do anything he wanted to her, but she liked a feller to give her nice things in return. Scent, bits of jewellery, maybe even a handbag or shoes or stockings. Her Mam wouldn't mind, she was easy going like that. He was seeing her tomorrow night and he was going out in his lunchtime to buy her something. Probably a bottle of scent, the biggest he could find.

'Who did you go with?' Georgie's voice finally penetrated the dreamy cloud of elation.

Joe shrugged. 'A girl. I met her at the Rialto last weekend,' he lied. He had the distinct feeling that Georgie wouldn't approve of Joanie at all. And what was all that nonsense about a note? Joanie wouldn't tell him what it was about and he certainly wasn't going to enquire further. Georgie liked to keep his business strictly private. It was probably only something stupid anyway.

Before they went to work the next Friday, Josie and Katie sat with Sarah in the bedroom she shared with Joe.

'Look, he did say if you didn't like the look of it you don't have to stay. There are other places, not in Liverpool,' Katie stressed.

'And for all their strictness, the Sisters of Charity aren't that bad,' Josie added, wishing she'd never made the disparaging remark in the first place. She'd only heard about them from gossip. There were other religious orders that looked after girls who had 'fallen', and as long as you were repentant and quiet you were treated well.

'You will come and see me on Sunday? You promised,' Sarah pleaded.

'Of course we will, won't we, Josie. We'll bring Vi, she should liven the place up a bit. She hasn't had a letter or a telegram or heard on the wireless that "The Admiralty regrets the loss of . . . " so she thinks the *Victor* and Jack are all right. Oh Sarah, you don't think we'd let him dump you there and never come and see you, do you? You know we will, as often as we can. I feel so useless, so furious with myself. I *should* have thought harder, planned better to make him see things our way.'

'Stop it, Katie. You did everything you could,' Josie said firmly.

They both kissed Sarah and left her sitting on the bed with her small case beside her. She heard the front door slam behind them and burst into wretched tears.

'We'd better get going if we're to be there on time,' Georgie called upstairs, an hour or so later.

Reluctantly Sarah looked around her; she'd never felt so desolate in all her life. She wouldn't see this room or this house for months and months. And she *wouldn't* think of Duncan at all.

They walked in total silence down the road and caught a tram, but she went ahead of him up the aisle and found a seat by the window. That way she wouldn't have to look at anyone. Just the familiar streets and shops that she wouldn't see either for a long time.

When they reached the stop at the end of Scotland Road and he got up she looked startled.

'Why aren't we going to the Pier Head?'

'I've a bit of business to attend to around here first. Come on, give me the case.'

She handed it over and followed him, again in silence. They walked along Scotland Road until they came to Juvenal Street and Georgie turned the corner.

Sarah hung back.

'Well, come on.'

'Can't I wait here? I don't like the look of that street.'

'Don't be such a bloody snob, and no, you can't wait here. The bit of business concerns you.'

Again she followed him down the dusty pavement where flies hovered and settled on the rubbish in the gutter. She was beginning to feel very anxious now. What could concern her around here?

They stopped at a house and Georgie rapped smartly on the brass knocker. It looked quite smart compared to some of the other houses, Sarah noticed. The brass was shiny, the step brushed, the curtains and windows clean-looking.

A tall, thin woman dressed in a blue and green print dress opened the door. She looked very respectable, formidable even.

'Mrs Bushell?' Georgie asked.

She nodded.

'This is my sister, Sarah.'

The woman looked closely at Sarah and then at Georgie.

'Will you be staying?' she asked him.

He coughed and shuffled his feet. 'Er . . . I don't think—'

'Right then. Come back for her at about four o'clock then, with a taxi.' The instructions were issued in a forceful tone.

Before Sarah could understand what was happening, Georgie had pushed her inside the house. Mrs Bushell shut the door and taking her by the shoulders, guided her towards the stairs.

'No! Stop it! What's going on? Why am I here? I should be going to the Sisters of Charity.' Sarah was totally confused and afraid.

'Now, look, luv, I know it's not a pleasant experience. It can be frightening the first time, but don't worry. I'm very experienced. I was a nurse and everything is very, very clean.'

Sarah still didn't understand. 'What won't be pleasant? What's frightening?' She was aware that someone else had come into the hall; maybe it was Georgie back to say it was a mistake. She half-turned but Mrs Bushell pulled her back.

'Come along now, luv, it will all be over in a few minutes, then a rest and you'll be as right as rain by the time your brother comes for you at four.'

Sarah backed away. 'I don't understand. I'm not supposed to be here. I . . . was going to the nuns.'

'Well, there won't be any need for that now, will there? You can get on with your life again. No baby, no worries.'

Suddenly Sarah understood, and clinging to the newel post tightly she began to scream. She kept on screaming until someone pressed a foul-smelling cloth over her face. She fought hard but gradually she lost strength and then finally all awareness.

When she came to, she felt sick and dizzy and there was a dull, dragging pain in the pit of her stomach. She tried to sit up but was pushed gently back by capable hands and the face of Mrs Bushell loomed over her.

'That's it. It's all over now, luv. You just lie still, I'll bring you a cup of tea and then you have a doze until your brother comes for you. A couple of days' rest in bed and you'll be fighting fit again. Ready to go back to work for the war effort.'

The walls of the room, whitewashed and bright in the sunlight, blinded her and she closed her eyes. She slipped in and out of consciousness until Mrs Bushell arrived with the tea. The chloroform had worn off and now she realised what they'd done to her, this woman and Georgie. She refused the tea and tried to get up again, tears of misery, despair and shock streaming down her cheeks.

'Lie down.' The woman's voice had turned harsh. 'It's not good for you, all this silly throwing yourself around.'

Sarah felt the anger and hurt bubble up inside her. 'You killed my baby! You killed my baby! You . . . *bitch*!' she screamed. She'd never called anyone such names before, but the tirade of abuse stopped when Mrs Bushell slapped her hard across the mouth.

'Stop that noise! Do you want the whole street to hear, and the scuffers as well? You'll get us all arrested and then we'll go to jail – and

I can tell you, you won't like it one little bit in Walton Prison!'

Too ill, too shocked, too beaten to continue the fight, Sarah lay down and turned her face to the wall. Georgie and this woman had killed her baby. He'd lied about the Home and the Sisters of Charity. Oh, why hadn't she suspected something and run away from him? Run home or to Mary Maher's or Ellen MacCane's? Or even into the nearest church; he wouldn't have dared to follow her and have to confront a priest. But it was too late now. Georgie had set all this up. He'd killed the baby she would willingly have given to Josie and himself. Katie would have murdered him, had she known what he had planned. She lay sobbing quietly, the pain in her abdomen as nothing compared to the pain in her heart.

Time passed. She was able to walk downstairs and into the cab Georgie had waiting. She never looked at him or Mrs Bushell, who gave him some instructions in an undertone. She didn't speak or look up during the entire journey home and when they arrived, she went straight upstairs and lay on the bed in Katie's room. This is what it must feel like to be dead, she thought as she stared at the cracks in the ceiling. There were no emotions. Just darkness in her mind and an emptiness in her body.

She must have gone into a deep sleep, because when she awoke it was dark outside, but Katie and Josie were sitting beside the bed.

'He—' she began but her emotions overwhelmed her completely.

'Hush, luv, we know,' Josie comforted her, her own heart breaking. She'd lost three babies through miscarriage and had never wavered in her faith in God. Now she'd lost a fourth who would have had just as much love showered on it, and it too had been taken from her. Ripped from Sarah's body by some so-called nurse, and thanks to Georgie's malice and selfishness.

'May God blast him to hell for all eternity! The liar. The bloody murderer!' Katie could hardly control herself. It was obvious that Sarah hadn't heard the almighty row that had raged downstairs, because Katie was certain the rest of the street had.

Both women were depressed anyway when they came in. There had been an accident further down the room in which they worked. A girl filling a shell with gunpowder had been taken away in an ambulance, screaming horribly. The shell had exploded in her face.

'Did everything go all right?' Josie asked her husband dully. 'Sarah decided to stay, then?'

'No, she's in bed. We never went there.'

'So what happened then? Why did she change her mind, or did you change it for her?' Katie demanded, alerted to trouble by the look on his face. It was smug – too cocky by half.

'She's had an abortion,' he announced with a sneer. 'I arranged it. Cost me fifteen quid, too. There never was a home for fallen women.' He laughed harshly. 'I didn't go to see Father Macreedy.'

It took a few minutes for the news to sink in, then Josie's face distorted with horror; she couldn't speak, the words just wouldn't come out. She felt they were choking her. She clung to the back of a chair to steady herself. An abortion! No baby! No baby for Sarah, no baby for herself.

Katie's voice broke the silence.

'You murderer!' she screamed. 'You bloody murderer! You're evil, that's what you are, Georgie Deegan – evil! You killed your own niece or nephew. Thank God Mam and Da aren't here because I tell you now, Da would have broken your neck. *You're* the one who's not fit to live! You're . . . scum!'

The same surge of furious rage swept over her as the day, long ago, when she'd attacked him before. There were cups and two plates on the table and without hesitation she snatched them up one by one and hurled them at him. The first plate missed him but the second caught him on the cheekbone and a cut spurted blood on his face. The cups hit the wall and smashed. Josie was screaming and crying but Katie didn't notice. A red mist seemed to be dancing before her eyes. A red mist of rage.

'You've cut me! You've bloody cut me!' Georgie roared, putting his hand to his face.

'I wish to God I'd killed you because you deserve it. Yes, look at your hands, there's blood on them, all right. Not only your blood but the blood of the little innocent baby you murdered today – and no matter how hard you try, you'll never wash that off!' Katie's voice was low and passionate, a terrible note of warning in it. 'That baby would have had all the love in the world. I wouldn't like to be you when you have to stand before God and explain that away. "Thou shalt not kill." What answer will you give Him and his angels?'

He lunged towards her but she held her ground.

'Touch me,' she whispered, 'and you'll not raise a hand to anyone ever again because I'll go straight to the police and then to Father Macreedy. You know what they do to murderers, don't you? They hang them, and I'll be outside Walton Jail cheering, the day they string you up, because you're not going to get away with this.'

He'd regained some of his composure. 'You run blabbing to the police and I won't go down alone. I'll take our Sarah with me. She was the one who had the abortion.'

'She knew nothing about it. You lied to her, you deceived her, you probably physically forced her.'

'You'll have to prove it.'

'We would because both Katie and I would back Sarah up,' Josie cried. Oh, how she hated him! He'd deliberately taken a life, but he'd also deliberately set out to deprive her of a child.

He looked from one to the other. 'And who'd believe you? Three women living on their own, a pregnant unmarried girl and me away. Me, the head of the family. A sober, respectable man away facing the dangers of the Arctic convoys. You'd all certainly want to get rid of it. *I'd* be the one they'd believe. You wouldn't, so sod you! Sod the bloody lot of you! I'm sailing tomorrow so I won't have to put up with you – any of you!'

'Don't bother coming back, Georgie. Now get out! Pack your stuff and get the hell out of this house,' Katie yelled at him, the red mist coming over her again.

'I'll be glad to. At least you get some peace at Bert's, it's not a bloody lunatic asylum. You're mad, all three of you!'

When the door slammed shut behind him, they all clung together and cried. Josie, for the loss of the child she would have loved, and her chance of a worthwhile future. Katie, from anger and guilt that she'd proved incapable of saving the life of the poor little thing that would have been her niece or nephew, and cousin to the child she was carrying.

It was Josie who pulled herself together first.

'Sit down, Katie, I'll make us a cup of tea. You shouldn't be getting into such a state, it's not good for you.'

'Oh God, Josie, he's a devil, isn't he? I just don't understand how he can be like this! How could he have done something so terribly wicked?'

'Should we go up and see her?' Josie's blotched and tear-streaked face was full of anxiety.

'We'll have to calm ourselves down first, I reckon. God knows what kind of a mental state she's in. Why did I ever believe him? Why didn't I check with Father Macreedy? I should have insisted I went with her.'

'Katie, stop it,' Josie said tiredly. 'You can't blame yourself.'

'Mam warned me about him,' Katie wept quietly. 'And she asked me to take care of Sarah and Joe.'

'Where is Joe, by the way?'

'Out with some girl, I suppose. The least he knows, the better.'

They drank their tea and then washed their faces and went up to sit with Sarah until she'd woken up and begun to cry.

'He's gone, luv. He sails tomorrow, so we won't see him for a while,' Josie soothed, but Sarah wouldn't be comforted. She screamed and sobbed and pummelled the pillow and thrashed from side to side. Her face was distorted and red with pain, her eyes overbright. Despite all their efforts she showed no sign of calming down, so they decided to take it in turns to sit with her through the night.

When Joe came in at about eleven on that Friday night, Katie was dozing in a chair.

'What have you been up to, meladdo?' she said, waking up. 'You've got a stupid grin on your face and your best shirt-collar is covered in cheap lipstick.'

The grin vanished. 'What's up with you? You've got a right cob on. Have you been rowing with our Georgie again?'

'Yes. He's gone to stay with that Bert and he sails tomorrow, thank God.'

Joe raised his eyes to the ceiling. They were always at it, those two. Like cat and dog ever since he could remember. He didn't want to think about them. He wanted to think, to dream, about Joanie. She was wonderful. She promised him a paradise of passion for a pair of real gold earrings and he was going to get them for her. He'd start saving up.

'Don't make a noise up there,' Katie warned him. 'Our Sarah's in my room, she's not well. Josie's sitting with her.'

Joe nodded and went up the stairs.

By five o'clock the next morning, Sarah was delirious. She'd developed a high temperature and was sweating profusely. Then she began to ramble. Nothing coherent. Names, places. Sometimes she just cried out for Molly or Duncan. Josie and Katie sponged her down continuously, but they were both very worried.

'At least there's no blood. She's not haemorrhaging,' Josie said, a note of thankfulness in her voice. She remembered only too well the bright scarlet tide that had flowed from her, and the almost unbearable agony.

'God knows what kind of a filthy place he took her to. Josie, we'll have to get the doctor,' Katie decided.

'How can we? He'll *have* to call in the police, it's his duty.'

'But she's ill, Josie.' Katie was scared.

'I know, but we could end up as accessories and what use would that be to her? He'll have sailed. We don't know where he took her or anything and he'd deny everything. You heard him.'

'Then get your Mam, Josie. Please, let's hurry.'

'Mary Maher's nearer.'

'She's not family.'

'Does it matter? Look, I'll go for Mary and you ask Joe to go for Mam.'

Katie bit her lip but nodded.

★ ★ ★

A pale and apprehensive Joe went on the delivery bike to Norris Green while Josie waited for the first tram to Walton. Mary arrived first, followed by a tight-lipped and anxious Florrie.

'Dear God in heaven, who did this to her?' Florrie demanded.

'Mam, I've already said we don't know. He told us all a pack of lies and then took her somewhere himself. She didn't even know about it.' Josie's voice was choked with emotion.

The two older women looked at each other. They'd seen births, deaths, miscarriages and once or twice the results of an abortion when girls and women had risked their lives, driven by desperation to seek out those who performed these illegal operations.

'There's no blood,' Florrie said.

'There might be inside, if . . . if it was a knitting needle,' Mary said, shuddering at the thought.

'Mam, what can we do?' Josie asked. 'We can't just leave her like this. She doesn't even know who we are or where she is.'

'What time was the convoy leaving?' Florrie asked.

Joe had been standing at the open door eavesdropping. Sarah was ill, very ill, and he was afraid.

'They were departing at four o'clock,' he spoke up sheepishly.

'How do you know for sure?' Mary demanded.

'Joanie told me. She knows fellers off some of the ships.'

Florrie turned on him. 'Joanie? Joanie MacNally?'

Joe nodded.

'You've taken up with that little tart!'

'She brought a note for our Georgie. That's how I met her.'

Florrie closed her eyes and clutched the bedpost to steady herself. Now it all fell into place. 'He went to Doreen Mac,' she told the others in a faint voice. 'That dirty trollop. Katie, we'll have to get a doctor now. Anyone that she knows or has suggested is bound to be—' Florrie just shook her head. She was about to say 'a dirty butcher' but thought better of it.

Again it was Joe who went on the bike for Dr Askam. Katie had writen a short note of explanation and they all knew what his reaction would be. One of anger.

'Doctor, can I have a word before you see her?' Florrie asked as she let him in.

He nodded curtly and removed his hat.

'None of the girls knew a thing about this, not even Sarah herself. Georgie lied to them. He told them she was going to a Catholic Home over the water to stay with nuns, but he'd arranged . . . this . . . with a woman I know to be a filthy, diseased old whore, if you'll beg pardon me using such a word to you, sir. When the girls got home from work, young Sarah was in bed. It was all over. The one to blame is Georgie

Deegan, my poor Josie's husband, God help her, and he sailed with the Russian convoy this morning. He's gone off and left them all to face the music.'

He nodded his acceptance and understanding, and then went quickly upstairs.

He asked a few questions, took her temperature, examined Sarah's stomach and abdomen gently and shook his head.

'What is it?' Katie asked fearfully.

'Puerperal fever. It usually only occurs after childbirth, sometimes after an abortion, and I'm almost sure there is some form of internal bleeding. She should go to hopsital, but I doubt if . . . ' He didn't finish.

Both Mary and Florrie shook their heads sadly. They'd seen women die from this fever after childbirth and Sarah was in no state to undergo surgery to see if the internal bleeding could be stopped.

'Will you have to inform the authorities?' Josie asked, although he could see she was begging him not to by the fear in her eyes.

'Yes. It's more than my professional life or my ethics are worth not to, but I'll stress in writing that you all had no knowledge or intent to terminate this pregnancy. When will your husband return, Mrs Deegan?'

Josie shook her head.

'Never, I hope,' Katie said bitterly.

'Unfortunately, abortion is very hard to prove and therefore to get a conviction. No one ever knows anything. No one will collaborate or confirm, names, times etc. It's very difficult. If I had my way, every backstreet abortionist would be publicly flogged and then hanged.' Dr Askam's anger was barely controlled. He took off his coat and rolled up his sleeves.

'Ladies, you'd better get some rest, especially you, Mrs Goodwin. Mrs Watson, if you would be so good as to bring me some boiled tepid water and towels? All we can do is make her as comfortable as possible. I shall give her a sedative to ease the pain and distress.'

Mary looked at him questioningly. 'Sir, is it time for us to get the priest?'

He nodded. Young Sarah Deegan wasn't long for this life.

Mary stayed with the doctor. While Josie went for the priest, Florrie insisted that Katie at least lie on the bed with her feet up, even if she didn't sleep, and then she caught Joe by the shoulder and pointed downstairs. 'Down there, meladdo. I want a few words with you about Joanie MacNally!'

It wasn't the parish priest who came, but Father Murray, who Mary thought was a much kinder man. She'd set everything out in readiness, working quietly as the doctor gave Sarah an injection then bathed her face. Outwardly he was calm and in control; inwardly he was seething with frustration and the sheer tragic waste of life. She was so young.

Josie had explained the circumstances on the hurried way back from the presbytery. Like her mother before her, Sarah was anointed and Father Murray stayed until the end, as did Doctor Askam who wrote out the Death Certificate. For Cause of Death he wrote: *Puerperal Fever*.

Sarah died peacefully at half-past seven with Katie, Josie and Joe at her bedside, while downstairs Mary and Florrie gripped their rosaries tightly and prayed to the Mother of God to keep the Angel of Death away from this house. The visitations had become so frequent of late.

Chapter Twenty-Five

It was a simple little ceremony. The Mass was low-key, attended only by family, close friends and neighbours, and then Sarah was buried in the same grave as her father and mother in Kirkdale Cemetery.

It wasn't the right sort of a day for a funeral, Josie thought. The sky had no right to be so blue, nor the sun so warm on their backs. The trees and grass and flowers in the cemetery were all so fresh and colourful. This was a beautiful summer's day when it should have been cloudy and raining. That would have been far more appropriate.

The night before, Katie had sobbed for hours in Vi's arms as all the half-buried grief for both Bill and Molly was resurrected and added to that for Sarah.

'Oh Vi, how I wish we'd never gone to the Grafton that night. Then she'd never have met Duncan and she'd still be alive now. It's my fault! She's dead and it's my fault!'

'Katie, stop tearing yourself apart with guilt. None of it's your fault. It just happened. If it's anyone's fault it's that bloody Duncan's and your Georgie's, but they'll pay one day, Katie. God will punish them.'

'But that won't bring her back. Oh Vi, it's awful to see her lying upstairs, so white and cold. I keep expecting that in a minute she'll open her eyes and ask where she is, but she won't. She won't ever speak again!'

'I know, Katie. I know.' Vi wept herself, feeling utterly useless. There were no words in the world to comfort her friend. She'd had a letter from Jack that morning saying he was safe and well. It had been a bit dangerous at times, but they'd come through and sent the Japs running for home with half their fleet sunk or damaged beyond repair. Her joy and thankfulness had had to be repressed, though, because of the terrible tragedy of Sarah's death.

Katie raised a tear-stained, blotched face. 'And the worst thing is, Vi, I can't even tell Bob how or why she died, not properly, because of the Censor. They'd pass such information on to the police.'

This war had robbed them all, Vi thought sadly. Not only of the presence of their menfolk but also the support and comfort needed at times like this.

There was no formal funeral tea, the girls were too upset. Florrie, Mary and Ellen had clubbed together to get them a bottle of Tonic Wine, and there was tea and some egg sandwiches for which the women had used up their weekly ration, but as Mary said: 'They can all do without at home for once. It won't 'urt them.'

To Katie's surprise, Uncle Alfred came over from Manchester. Josie had written to him, just a brief note informing him of the death.

He took Katie aside after she thanked him for coming. It was so kind of him, she said.

'No, it's not. I feel I should have taken more of an interest in you all. It's a terrible, terrible shame. A tragic waste, and I should have kept a better eye on you .'

'He *made* her go to that place. He took her himself. He's done some awful things, Uncle Alfred, but I'll never forgive him for this.'

'There is no possible chance of taking out proceedings against him, then?'

She shook her head. 'We've been over all that, and no, it's not really feasible.'

'Well, then you must concentrate on yourself, my dear.' He smiled kindly at her. 'Do you know. I'm quite looking forward to being a great-uncle! You will let me know when it happens, won't you?'

In the middle of the Arctic Ocean, Georgie Deegan lay in his hammock and tried to sleep, but the pitching and rolling, and the protesting of the metal plates of the *Montrose*'s hull made it impossible.

He should have been used to it by now, he thought. This was summer and the voyage was longer because they had more clear water between them and the ice edge, which was always much further south in winter. The Powers That Be claimed that although the journey was longer it was less dangerous, but what the hell did they know, sitting in London in their nice cosy offices? It was Archangel this summer, a port far into the waters of the White Sea and therefore considered safer. Murmansk was their winter port. Although it wasn't cold, not compared with winter temperatures, it never really got dark at this time of the year and once, Bert had dragged him up on deck to see the Aurora Borealis, the Northern Lights, when the sky was shot through with lights of every colour. It had been stunning.

They were only moving at a snail's pace and Georgie wished to God they'd get a move on. They'd passed the North Cape, so there were three or four days yet to go.

His mind wandered. He wondered how Jack Milligan was faring out East. He'd sooner sweat than freeze any day, he thought.

He spent another half-hour of restlessness before deciding to get up, get dressed and go up on deck. Maybe the cooler temperature would clear his head. If he stood in the lee of the boat deck no one would notice him. He put on a few layers of clothes and found his reefer jacket and cap.

Out on deck, the change in temperature was a relief from the stuffiness of the crew quarters, and Georgie leaned back against the superstructure and lit a cigarette. There were thirty-three ships in the convoy, including his own, and their shapes were visible in the sepia-toned half-light. They were strung out over the grey churning sea and he could see quite clearly the outline of *HMS Raleigh*, one of their escorts. As he stood watching the grey-painted cruiser, he saw a flash of light and then another. *Raleigh* was sending out a signal in morse. He'd mastered Morse Code on the long days and nights on the Atlantic. He began converting the flashes and length of spaces into letters, then words. And then he felt his stomach turn over. The message *Raleigh* was flashing read:

ENEMY FLEET AHEAD. READY TO ATTACK. SCATTER.
GOOD LUCK. GOD SPEED.

His heart pounding, Georgie saw *Raleigh* fall back and begin to turn sharply to starboard. God Almighty! The whole bloody German fleet must be waiting for them up ahead if the escorts were falling back and turning away. A silly childhood saying floated briefly through his mind: 'Those who fight and run away, live to fight another day.' God help them all, they were well in range of enemy aircraft too. By scattering they'd stand very little chance at all, especially the slower ships. He felt the vibrations of the screws increase as they began to turn faster and then pick up speed, turning to port. They were on their own now.

During the days and nights that followed, the tension crackled through the ship. With binoculars they scoured the skies for enemy aircraft. They adopted a zig-zagging technique at times and then abandoned it for a faster, straighter course. Once in the far, far distance they saw a huge billowing column of thick black smoke rising into the clear bright air, and knew that at least one tanker had been hit. The rest of the ships in the convoy were so scattered they were not to be seen even through binoculars or on radar. He thought, once or twice, about what Katie had screamed at him, about facing his Maker. He was scared, in fact he was terrified, but his faith was in the captain and senior officers of the *Montrose* and no one else.

They hadn't seen a single enemy plane or ship and wondered, had they just been fortunate, or had there been some massive cock-up by the Admiralty, as they finally sailed, unscathed, into the White Sea and on to Archangel. It was only later – much later – that the crew of the *Montrose* found out that they were one of only four ships which had reached the port safely. The rest had been picked off one by one as soon as they'd scattered. The Admiralty had got it wrong – again! Convoy PQ-17 had been doomed almost from its time of sailing. Twenty-nine ships were lost in all, with their crews and cargoes. Even in summer, no one survived long in these Arctic waters.

It was in Archangel that he received the message, sent by wireless at huge expense and some hefty string-pulling by Alfred Deegan, that told him that his sister Sarah was dead and buried.

He was deeply shocked by the brief but succinct wording, and knew immediately that they all blamed him and not that bastard Kinross.

SARAH DEAD AND BURIED. TRAGIC LOSS. A HEAVY BURDEN FOR YOU
TO CARRY. ALFRED DEEGAN ESQ.

Those at home were heartsore of switching on the wireless and hearing the words, 'The Admiralty Regrets'. The loss of the ships in the convoy seemed unending. Josie tried not to wish that the next ship named would be the *Montrose* because then so many other innocent men would die as well as *him*. She felt guilty that she hoped he never came back, then she could make a new life for herself. It was something she wrestled constantly with in her mind. And each time she went to Confession she begged forgiveness and promised not to think such things ever again. But she couldn't help it; the thoughts crept invidiously back and refused to be dislodged or banished.

Katie felt she had broken her promise to her Mam but from now on she was determined to look after Joe.

'I know Mam had a talk to him, just before Dr Askam arrived,' Josie said after Katie had voiced her intentions.

'But he still goes out.'

'I don't suppose we can stop him.'

'Oh, I wish Mam and Da were here, Josie.'

'Look, I'll get Mam to come round again and we'll all have a go at making him see sense.'

Katie nodded thankfully, and massaged her aching back. Thank God for family, she thought, and tried hard to smile.

* * *

251

Florrie arrived the following evening, and Joe was told he wasn't going anywhere tonight.

'I've made arrangements,' he protested.

'I don't flaming well care. You're stopping in tonight, Joseph Deegan. Some things have got to be sorted. I promised Mam I'd look after you, and our Sarah. I didn't do very good for her, so . . . ' She left the sentence unfinished.

Joe sat down. He was still stunned and upset by the death of his sister and the manner in which she'd died. It had all been so quick and he too felt a little guilty. He'd taken the note from Joanie, after all. She must have known there was a risk of Sarah dying, but she'd never said a word.

'Listen, soft lad, she'd have given it to your Georgie if you hadn't been there,' had been Vinny Maher's comforting reply to his outpourings. Joe wasn't really supposed to talk about it to other people, but Vinny Maher could be trusted. He hoped Vinny was right. He'd already had one warning from Florrie Watson about Joanie, but everyone had been upset that day and he was sure she hadn't meant all she'd said.

Josie had explained to her mother how Katie was blaming herself for everything and was determined that Joe was going to make something of himself, of his life. Florrie was in total agreement. It was what Molly would have wanted. The college education had been sacrificed but his future needn't be.

Florrie settled herself on the sofa between Josie and Katie.

'Right, meladdo. I want to ask you a few questions and then I want you to listen while I tell you a few facts,' Florrie started. She'd noticed that Katie looked tired and drawn. The poor girl was getting near her time and she didn't need all this worry.

'Are you still going out with Joanie MacNally?'

Joe shrugged, not wanting to commit himself totally before this inquisition really got underway. He could see they were all serious.

'Well, you must know. Yes or no?' Florrie demanded sharply.

'Yes.'

'How often? Is it just a casual thing or have you any plans to "walk out" together as they used to say in my younger day?'

'I don't know.'

'You don't know flaming much, do you?' Katie interrupted, her nerves taut as piano-strings.

'Is it serious?' Florrie persisted.

Oh God, this was awful, Joe thought. The three of them sitting there on the sofa facing him, like three Stipendiary Magistrates. He just hoped that Vi Draper wasn't coming round too. 'I . . . I . . . like her,' he tried to explain. 'A lot.'

252

Florrie's eyes narrowed. 'And have you bought her any little gifts?'

'A couple. A bottle of scent, a brooch and some earrings – from Woollies,' he added. He was still desperately trying to save up for the gold ones she wanted; he was even going without his lunch.

Florrie nodded her head sagaciously. 'In return for favours rendered, no doubt. Like mother, like daughter. Now you just listen to me, Joe Deegan, and you take notice because I'm going to say what your Mam would have said if she'd been here. Get rid of that Joanie Mac. Get shut. She's nothing but trouble and always will be.'

Florrie paused; there was no nice way around this.

'She's family, unfortunately, but I have to tell the truth. Her Mam's a whore. A real one, or used to be. We all disowned her. Up and down Lime Street every night and in and out of jail. God knows who that girl's father is – or Mickey's either, for that matter.'

Joe was stung. 'Joanie's not a . . . one of them.' He couldn't bring himself to say the word.

'Oh yes she is, and if you think otherwise then you're as thick as a docker's butty! Oh, maybe she doesn't always demand money, but she gets something in return. Ever since she was fourteen she's been at it, and probably before that even. She's been with half the crews of half the ships that dock here and you know how many that is.'

Florrie paused again. It wasn't easy to shatter a young lad's dreams.

'You said she knew some fellers off the ships in Georgie's convoy, didn't you? Didn't you ask yourself *how* she came to know them, Joe? I don't want to have to say these things to you. There's hundreds of lovely, decent girls in this city, so why in God's name did you have to pick her? If she's not full of disease now she soon will be, and she'll pass it on to you, and when someone else comes along who takes her fancy she'll be off. She'll dump you. There's plenty of good-looking, well-off Yanks coming through the Port now and it won't be long before she latches on to one of them. She won't give you a second thought. In a few days she'll even have forgotten your name.'

Everything she was saying was true, but he didn't want it to be true, especially about Joanie and other fellers, so Joe just blanked it out of his mind. She'd said she loved him. *Him* – not anyone else. She'd even said that after he'd bought her the earrings and she'd become 'his', she'd consider looking at rings. When she'd said that he couldn't believe such happiness existed. She wasn't a whore. She *wasn't*! Her Mam probably was, but not Joanie. His Joanie.

'So you'll give her up,' Florrie said. It wasn't really a question.

Joe looked at the three women. They just didn't understand. Florrie was old and old-fashioned, too. Josie seemed to do whatever her Mam or Katie told her to do and Katie, well, she must know what it was like being in love. Or maybe it was a different kind of love she felt for Bob. It couldn't possibly be the same as that he felt for Joanie.

'Joe, I promised Mam I'd look after you. You've to stop seeing her. She's no good and in the end she'll only hurt you,' Katie begged.

'Joe, I know what it's like to love someone so much that you feel miserable if you don't see them, speak to them, hold them just for a day. But look where it's got me.' Josie spread her hands in a gesture of despair. 'Take notice of Mam and Katie. Give her up! You'll meet someone else, I know you will.'

But I'll never meet anyone like Joanie. The words sprang to his lips but he could see they would do no good. Slowly he nodded although he had no intention of giving her up. He loved her. He adored her. He worshipped her. They were forcing him to tell lies. From now on it would have to be secret meetings; he'd have to think up excuses, make some plans with Vinny and Franny to cover for him. But he wasn't going to give her up.

At the end of the month the survivors of convoy PQ-17 were flown home from Russia by the RAF, leaving the captains and skeleton crews to bring the four ships home. The plane journey was a long, cold, bone-shaking and terrifying experience. None of them had ever been in a plane before and this was a transport craft so there were no seats, no concessions to comfort of any kind. They all sat on the floor, their backs to the fuselage, swathed in blankets, most of them praying that after surviving the terrors en route to Archangel, they'd arrive home in one piece.

'If God 'ad wanted us ter fly, He'd 'ave given us bloody wings,' Bert shouted to Georgie over the noise of the engines.

'And if He'd wanted us to spend our lives going backwards and forwards across the sea, he'd have given us bloody webbed feet,' Georgie yelled back.

He wasn't sure what kind of a welcome he was going to receive when he got home, *if* he got home. Would it be the police? The parish priest? Josie, Katie, Vi and a deputation of neighbours?

He hadn't meant Sarah to die. He'd paid over the odds to that bloody woman because he'd believed her to be efficient and clean. The house and indeed Mrs Bushell herself had given that impression. He felt guilty about it. All he'd wanted to do was to preserve some dignity for the family and to give Sarah another chance, an opportunity to make a decent marriage and have a respectable life. Now she had no life at all and he was partly to blame. Only partly, he told himself firmly. There was Kinross's involvement, the cause of it all. Nor had he actually performed the act. He'd gone over it in his mind. They wouldn't, *couldn't* have reported it to the police . . . surely?

No, Georgie wasn't looking forward to the reception at all – when he did get home.

They'd discussed it and agreed on the best strategy. It was useless to yell and bawl and hurl recriminations, abuse and accusations. All that would achieve would be to upset themselves. No, they would ignore him. He would face a wall of silence. They would behave as though he didn't exist at all.

His reception surprised and unnerved him. He hadn't expected cries of delight or even words of thankfulness, but this . . . this was so unexpected. So unnatural. There were no words of abuse or condemnation. It meant that they considered him beneath even that. It meant they despised him.

They spoke to each other and to Joe. They made arrangements, asked questions and carried on in a totally normal way amongst themselves. He didn't seem to exist. There was no summons from the clergy but there was from Dr Askam, in the form of a blunt note written by Katie and left on the table. The doctor wanted to see him this evening at 8 p.m. sharp.

'Is it about our Sarah? Does he want to hear my side of it?' He was almost pleading.

She just stared at him for a few seconds, her dark eyes full of contempt, her gaze never wavering, then she turned away without a word.

A woman with a young lad was just leaving when he arrived at the surgery in Westminster Road and the receptionist announced him.

'Sit down, I won't keep you long,' Dr Askam ordered, indicating a straight-backed wooden chair. 'You know the circumstances of your sister's death, I presume?'

Georgie nodded.

'Puerperal fever and internal bleeding was what I wrote on the Death Certificate.'

'She wasn't meant to die! I never meant to harm her. I paid over the odds, fifteen pounds, to that bloody woman because . . . because . . .'

'Because she was supposed to be experienced and clean? It's what they all say, and no amount of money can justify a murder – two, if you count your sister's death.'

'But I didn't mean it?'

'You tricked her into having an illegal abortion which you arranged and paid for, and you didn't *mean* it!' Dr Askam's voice thundered around the room and seemed to bounce and echo from the walls and ceiling.

Georgie shrank back in the chair, suddenly wondering what was going to happen next? Had it been a trick? A set-up? Would the scuffers come bursting through the door having heard all?

'I took an oath,' the doctor's voice was calm now, icily so. 'It's a long time ago now. I was a young man. It was the Hippocratic Oath. Do you know what that means?'

Georgie didn't so he just shook his head.

'It's an oath taken by doctors to adhere to certain standards and ethics and to save life. But if you were lying there on the floor in front of me, fatally injured, I would have to think very hard about my choice. Whether to break and therefore dishonour that oath and let you die, or to keep it and minister to you.' He paused and picked up a pen, gripping it so tightly his knuckles showed white.

'I think I'd probably let you die – delirious and in agony as she did. Now get out of my surgery and my sight! Find yourself another doctor, if you can!'

Georgie was trembling when he got outside. Everything was going wrong, so very very wrong. He didn't even know yet what he'd be ordered to do next. Would he stay on the convoys or would he be made to go into the Royal Navy or the Army and fight?

He leaned against the wall of a house for a moment to pull himself together. There was no one to turn to, not even Bert. Bert thought Sarah had been killed in a light air raid and he was a devout man, in his own way, and would probably turn against him too once he knew the real circumstances. He was alone. Totally alone and it wasn't pleasant at all.

Chapter Twenty-Six

Joe looked over his shoulder again. He knew no one was following him, but someone on a passing tram might have seen him as he turned into Cartwright Place. Even though it was now evening, the stifling heat of the August day seemed to be trapped in Number Seven Court. It enhanced the stink of dire poverty so that it seemed to hit you forcefully and almost made you gag. He took out his handkerchief and wiped the sweat from his forehead. In his pocket he had a box in which were the gold hooped earrings Joanie had set her heart on. And now, well . . . now ahead of him lay the 'paradise' she'd promised.

The curtains were drawn across the window and the room was in semi-darkness. God, it was a dump, he thought. It stank to high heaven; neither of them must ever even attempt to clean up a bit. You'd think at least her Mam might do a bit. It was *her* home.

Joanie was half-sitting, half-lying on the bed, wearing what looked like some kind of bright blue satin dressing gown, with birds and flowers in garish colours embroidered on it. There was no sign of her Mam.

She smiled lazily up at him. 'I didn't think yer were goin' ter show up.'

He felt his insides turn to jelly.

'Where's your Mam?'

Joanie shrugged. 'Probably blind paralytic drunk somewhere. Some feller she knew years ago turned up an' they went out. So, I'm 'ere on me own, like.'

He sat gingerly on the bed beside her and took the box from his pocket and handed it to her.

She sat up, an excited gleam in her dark eyes. 'Yer got me them! Yer really got me them!' She took the earrings out and put them on, throwing back her wild mane of blue-black hair and exposing her throat and the slight rise of her breasts beneath the robe.

''Ow do they look?'

'Gorgeous, Joanie. Like you.' He could hardly get the words out.

'Well, I promised yer somethin' in return, didn't I?'

He swallowed hard as she let the robe slip down over her shoulders.

257

She wore nothing beneath it; she was entirely naked. She reached out and took his hand and placed it on the warm, slightly moist skin of her breast. For a few seconds he was unable to move but she laughed and drew his head down to her nipple.

'Yer do know I love yer, Joe, don't yer?' she said as she slid under him.

'I . . . I . . . love you, Joanie!' he managed to gasp, her part in Sarah's death forgotten. She was driving him mad. Her hands were all over his body, stroking, searching, and he didn't care if everyone in the whole house heard his cries as she took him into a world of white-hot passion.

He stayed as late as he dared, but he could hardly drag himself away from her. She was insatiable and he'd have promised her the whole world. All she wanted instead, she hinted, was maybe a nice gold chain for around her neck, to go with her pretty new earrings. She ran a finger down the length of her throat to between her breasts. Or maybe she'd wear it around her waist like some Arab women did. She raised her buttocks off the bed and circled her waist with her hands.

'Oh God, Joanie! Don't do things . . . like that.'

'Why not? You've 'ad me four times ternight an' yer thought it was great. I love yer.'

Suddenly Joanie looked around the room. 'I 'ate this bleeding dump! I 'ate this sodding Court! I want nice things and a nice 'ouse like you've got.' She turned to him again and began to undo the buttons of his shirt which only seconds before he'd fastened with fingers that shook. 'Every night could be like this, Joe. Iffen we 'ad somewhere . . . nice.'

'Joanie, I've got to go.'

She pouted and lay back on the bed. 'So go then. Sod off – I don't care,' she said petulantly.

He was trembling with indecision. 'I'll get you a chain, I promise.'

'When?' The gleam was back in her eye, the sulky look gone.

'As soon as I can, in about a month.'

She looked at him calculatingly. 'A month! We could all be dead an' buried by then. Them bloody Jerries could be back an' it would be like the May Blitz all over again.'

'All right, I'll get the money,' he conceded pathetically. 'Our Georgie owes me some – I'll get it off him.'

All the way home he tried to think up valid reasons to tell Georgie why he wanted his money. His share of the bit of blackmarketeering? That would probably buy her a couple of chains, but what about when all that was gone? She loved nice things. She hated living the way she did, but he couldn't afford to rent somewhere even if there was somewhere in this half-demolished city to rent. He couldn't get married without Georgie or Uncle Alfred's consent. Their Katie had gone over Georgie's head and appealed to Uncle Alfred, but he couldn't even do that. He'd never ever get it from Uncle Alfred, not after what Florrie Watson had said about Joanie in his hearing.

He didn't care what they said. Maybe it was true that she'd been with other men. She'd driven him wild tonight so she was certainly no innocent, but he didn't bloody care. She'd got into his heart and soul and he just wanted her for the rest of his life. He'd *have* to get the money or find a solution – somehow.

When he got in, Georgie was fumbling with something which he immediately put into one of the dresser drawers. The wireless was on low. Josie and Katie had gone to bed.

'Your face is like a turkey cock. Have you been running or something?'

'It's hot out there, in case you hadn't noticed. Stinking, bloody hot.'

'Stop swearing, I won't have it,' Georgie snapped.

Joe went into the kitchen and washed his face, then he came and sat on the edge of the sofa, facing his older brother. 'You know that . . . er . . . money?'

Georgie looked up. 'What money?'

'The money we got from selling the black-market stuff. Well, I need my share of it. I'd like to buy someone some nice presents.'

Georgie grinned. 'Got a bit of skirt in tow, like?'

Joe was relieved at the smile. 'Yeah, sort of. So I need a bit of cash.'

'Well, you can't have it yet.' In fact, Georgie had no intention of ever giving Joe any of it, if he could help it.

'Why not?'

'I bought War Bonds with it,' he lied.

'What the hell did you buy them for?' Joe was outraged, seeing his dreams slipping rapidly away.

'That's very patriotic, isn't it? I bought them to help pay for this bloody war like hundreds of other people have. So you see the money's tied up.'

Joe stared at him in disbelief. He'd not get his money for years and years and by then, Joanie . . . He *had* to have money and soon.

Georgie quickly dismissed the subject from his mind. He wasn't happy at all. He'd received a letter instructing him to go to Portsmouth next week to join *HMS Delphinium*, a 'Flower'-class Corvette. His days in the Merchant Navy were over.

Upstairs, Katie tossed fitfully. She was exhausted. The room was still warm, the air heavy and she wished her pregnancy was over. She couldn't take much more of this heat. It was midnight, according to the hands on the alarm clock whose face took on the red glow of the little lamp that stood beside the statue of the Sacred Heart on the chest of drawers. Both she and Josie had come upstairs together. They were both tired and had no wish to break their silence with Georgie.

The first pain came ten minutes later, and she gasped and clung to the headboard until it passed. There was no use waking Josie yet. It could take a long time; some babies took hours and hours, so Florrie had told her – and besides, it would remind Josie of her own fruitless agonies and she wanted to spare her sister-in-law for as long as possible.

An hour later, her hair and nightdress drenched in sweat, she dragged herself to Josie's room and collapsed on the bed.

'Katie?' Josie sat up, still half-asleep.

'I've started, Josie. About an hour ago.' She nearly bit through her lip trying to stifle the pain.

'Oh God! Let me get you back to bed, then I'll send that useless sod down there for the midwife and the doctor.'

'Joe?' Katie gasped.

'Don't worry about him. He's in and probably fast asleep.'

Josie ran downstairs and into the living room.

'Katie's started with the baby,' she said brusquely to her husband. 'You can help me get her back to her room and then go for Miss MacCormack and Dr Askam.'

'I'm not going anywhere near that bloody man.'

'Oh, yes you are! Do you want Katie's and the baby's blood on your hands as well as that of Sarah and her baby?' Josie turned away as reluctantly Georgie rose and followed her.

After Joe had gone to bed looking totally dejected, Georgie had taken the tin box out of the drawer. He had sold one of Mam's chains and made a good bit on it, so he had removed the tin from its usual place, wedged between the bricks in the narrow chimney of the bedroom fireplace. He could never remember a fire being lit there even in the coldest winter. It was wrapped in canvas and then the rough box he'd made from some asbestos sheeting he'd found on a bomb-site. Just to be on the safe side. Because he knew Josie would go to bed early he managed to get it downstairs and under the armchair where it went unnoticed, hidden by the fringed valance around the bottom.

He'd sat in the chair all night and when he was sure Josie would have settled, he went meticulously through the box, trying to evaluate the price of each piece. Joe's appearance had taken him by surprise and now, when he'd only just retrieved the box, he heard Josie running down the stairs and had yet again to hastily stuff it in a drawer.

Now he followed her upstairs and between them they got Katie back to her own room. She gripped Josie's hand as another contraction began and tried not to scream.

'For God's sake, Katie, yell the bloody house down if you want,' Josie urged.

Georgie had turned rather pale as he watched his sister's bloated body thrash about in pain.

'Go and get the flaming midwife and the doctor!' Josie yelled at him. He needed no second telling. There'd been too many tragic pregnancies in this house.

The noise had woken Joe from a very shallow, disturbed sleep. He lay for a few minutes listening to Katie's groans and Josie's cries of sympathy and encouragement. His mouth felt dry and it was too hot to sleep yet he was exhausted. He was half-demented trying to think up some way of getting money. He had his watch, he could sell that, but it wouldn't be enough. His head was thumping with the heat and the search for a solution to his problem. Trust Katie to have her baby tonight.

He went downstairs and got himself a glass of water, then went over to the top dresser drawer for the aspirin. He picked up the long narrow strip of tablets, each individually enclosed in its own little paper pouch and then he noticed the box. He'd seen it before but couldn't remember where or when.

In a moment of curiosity, he prised open the lid and forgot about the aspirin. Mam's jewellery – of course! Georgie must have kept it well hidden all this time. He must take it away with himself each trip. Joe quickly removed a pair of heavy drop earrings, two chains and a thin bracelet of solid gold in the shape of a snake with garnets for eyes. Mam had had a passion for gold. She'd only ever worn it when she went somewhere special, which wasn't very often, but she'd said it was an investment as well as a luxury. If paper money lost its value, gold didn't. Well, why shouldn't he have some of it? He had a right. It didn't belong entirely to their Georgie.

Joe hastily stuffed the items into the pocket of his pyjama jacket, put the box back in the drawer, tore off an aspirin, picked up the glass and went quickly upstairs to his bed. He'd get no sleep, of course, what with the noise of Katie and Josie, and the plans now whirling around in his head . . . but he had day-dreams aplenty to keep him occupied . . .

Katie felt as though the pain would never end. It seemed to be tearing her body apart. She clutched Josie's hand so tightly that it was red and swollen.

'Josie, get an old towel or piece of sheeting that you can tie to the bedpost. Your hand is very swollen,' Miss MacCormack instructed.

Dr Askam gently examined Josie's hand. 'I'm afraid something might be broken. Just a small bone. I've seen it happen often.'

The midwife nodded her agreement and Josie went to get a towel. Her hand was painful but she'd not really noticed it until now. She'd been going through every pain, every contraction, with Katie. Before the doctor had arrived, Katie had hissed to her, her face working with emotion: 'Josie! You don't have to stay with me. I don't want to hurt you, being like this. Bringing back the memories.'

Josie had smiled reassuringly. Her friend could be tough and hard, but she was thoughtful and sensitive too.

'Don't even think about it, luv, I'm staying put,' she replied firmly, but she *was* thinking about it. At least, with the blessing of God, Katie should have a healthy living child at the end of all this agony.

'Bob! Oh, I want Bob! I can't stand this for much longer!' Katie bellowed.

'And a fat lot of use he'd be, Katie Goodwin, I can tell you. I've seen strong men pass out, fall in a heap on the floor when they've inadvertently become involved with a birth. Isn't that so, Doctor?'

Dr Askam agreed and then looked at Katie, then the midwife and nodded. He was quite happy to let Miss MacCormack take charge. He would be there if she needed help, which he very much doubted. She was a very experienced and capable woman.

'All right now, Katie. Not long and your Bob will be the proud father of a son or daughter. Now, when the next contraction comes, bear down as hard as you can.'

The midwife had barely finished speaking when Katie grabbed the towel tied to the bedpost.

'Push, Katie! Go on, girl!' Josie encouraged.

'Come on, Katie, you're nearly there. Push,' Miss MacCormack said firmly, but it was the authority in the doctor's voice she responded to.

'Mrs Goodwin, bear down hard! Hard! That's not hard enough! *Push!*' Then his voice died away, and Katie fell back exhausted and in a lather of sweat. The midwife held in her hands a baby boy.

'A good night's work, Miss MacCormack,' Dr Askam smiled.

'You've a fine healthy son, Katie. I'm just going to cut the cord.' She held the baby upside down by its heels and gave it a slap on the back. The room was instantly filled with robust wails of protest.

Dr Askam exchanged another glance with the midwife. 'Mrs Deegan, while I attend to Mrs Goodwin, could you see to Baby?'

They both knew of Josie's history of miscarriages. The young woman had been incredibly strong under the circumstances and neither of them wanted her to start to shun or resent this baby and its mother.

Gently Josie took the baby and under the supervision of Miss MacCormack, wiped the mucus from its nose and mouth and bathed away the blood from the tiny scrap of humanity and wrapped him in a large soft white towel. Her heart was so full. If only . . . Oh, if only . . . ! She placed the tip of her index finger gently against the soft, downy little cheek and immediately the tiny mouth turned towards it and he looked up at her for a few moments before closing his eyes again. His eyes were blue but all babies were born with blue eyes, they would change soon, maybe to brown like Katie's or green like Bob's. A child of her own would do that, at the first touch turn its head and look for food and security. Sarah's child would have too. It was with great reluctance that she passed him over to his mother.

Katie looked down at him. The gruelling hours of labour had been worth it; he was beautiful.

'And do you have a name for him?' the doctor asked, smiling.

'Oh, yes. He's to be named after his Da. Robert. But while he's little we'll call him Robbie.'

They all smiled.

Later, as Josie sat exhausted yet unable to sleep, the sun burst over the slate-grey rooftops, turning the whole panorama of the sleeping city to gold. Katie and little Robbie slept. Joe and Georgie too were asleep but while they slept a plan had been growing in Josie's mind. Her husband had eight more days before he left for Portsmouth. Was that long enough to father a child? She hated him. There was nothing, not a single shred left of the love she'd once felt for him. After holding Katie's baby in her arms, though, she knew that without a child of her own she had no future. She might as well commit the Mortal Sin – just go down to the Landing Stage now and step over the chain and into the water of the Mersey. It would be quick, there was a terrific undertow at the Stage. She was fully prepared to risk her life for a baby – for what kind of a life was it anyway? The hardest part would be to put up with Georgie's attentions and indeed, having to make the first overtures, but she'd do it. Oh yes, she'd do it. Even if she had to act like a tart, like little Joanie MacNally, she'd do it!

When Georgie went off to Portsmouth, everyone sighed with relief. Katie had written to Bob and Uncle Alfred, and Vi to Jack, and Joe seemed to be in a world of his own. No one had had much time to notice him and for that he was grateful, for Joanie filled his mind, night and day.

As Josie watched her husband walk down the street and turn the corner, she thought of all the nights when she'd bitten her tongue and clenched her hands so tightly that the nails had made deep indentations in the palm of her hand. Her first overtures had surprised him, particularly as she barely spoke to him during the day, but then he'd turned to her night after night and had not found her unresponsive.

Josie had concentrated her mind on one thing only. The way she'd felt when she first held little Robbie in her arms. They were not nights of wild passion, Georgie had thought. Their love-making had never been like that and in the past, exhaustion, tension and fear had played a big part in him being almost celibate. The knowledge that he was now part of the Royal and not Merchant Navy, had obviously changed her attitude, he decided, and he found that the physical and emotional efforts involved in love-making eased the tension, lessened the fear and allowed him to fall immediately into oblivion. Josie just prayed it had all been worth it.

Vi came round every day after work, and was never tired of nursing Robbie. She longed for Jack to come home. He'd been away many months now.

'Will they ever get home leave?' Josie asked.

'I don't think so; it's too far away. Even if they get wounded they are taken into hospital in Australia or India.'

Josie smiled and Vi and Katie exchanged glances of understanding.

'Well, at least one of us is happy. Glad to see the back of him, Josie? And speaking of God, what are you going to do about having the baby christened?' Vi asked.

Katie frowned. 'Bob said he didn't mind what I decided to do, so I was hoping that Father Murray or Father Dempsey would do it. At least they're not so bitter as Father Macreedy.'

'Do you want me to speak to one of them – ask them to pop in and see you?'

'Oh, would you, Vi? I've written to Bob's Mam, telling her she's got a grandson and that his name is Robert William, so no one can ever say I didn't let them know. Now it's up to them.'

'Maybe his middle name will have some effect. You know they go on and on about "King Billy" and all that,' Josie said.

Katie smiled. 'Maybe, but I didn't choose it for that reason. It was Da's name. They don't have the monopoly on it.'

Josie sighed. 'Oh aye, I'd forgotten.'

'Mam would have been made up with him.'

'She would, but don't go dwelling on things like that, Katie girl, or you'll get miserable.'

'Vi's right. Lots of women get really miserable and depressed after a baby, so I've heard,' Josie added.

'Will you both be godmothers? I'd like our Joe to be the godfather. There's no one else.'

'It's a bit unusual having two godmothers, isn't it?' Vi mused.

'Well, I want you both. I don't want to have to pick and choose.'

'I only said it was unusual! I'll call around to the Presbytery on my way home. Maybe one of them will come tomorrow.'

Katie fed and settled Robbie in the crib beside her bed. He was a good baby, sleeping for six or seven hours a night as well as daytime naps and so she had plenty of rest. She was still under the doctor's orders and Josie did nearly everything, no matter how much she protested.

'You know the lying-in time is two weeks! Do you want to make yourself ill? What will happen to him then? What if you have a problem feeding him? You'll have to give him National Dried Milk and mess about with bottles and teats, that's what.'

'Josie, I feel great. Honestly I do. I'm sure it's not necessary to be stuck in bed for two weeks. How ever did your Mam and mine manage to keep a household going?'

'Relatives, friends, neighbours and the rest of us kids, that's how,' Josie answered firmly, before going over to the baby and tickling him gently under his chin.

Vi called in on her way home the next day and they could tell by her face that something was wrong.

'What's the matter?' Josie asked.

'I went round to St John's. Mrs Conlon showed me in and I saw Father Murray and explained things. Then he got all serious-looking and excused himself. He was gone for ages, at least ten minutes. I thought he'd forgotten me, but then in comes Father Macreedy with a face like thunder and I knew what he was going to say.'

'So?' Josie interrupted.

'So I got in before him. I said, "I can see by your face, Father, that you don't want Robbie Goodwin over the step of your church, let alone anywhere near your font, or his mother either, so I've wasted your time and mine. Good evening," and I let myself out. I wasn't nasty or disrespectful in the way I said it, so he can't complain. Anyway if he does and Da starts on me, he'll have Jack to contend with when he gets back. I'm a grown-up married woman now. Not a kid.'

Josie looked from Vi to Katie with apprehension.

Katie looked calm but she was hurt. Deeply hurt. What had this child ever done except to be born? She looked across at the statue in front of which the little red lamp burned. She knew for certain He wouldn't take this attitude, He had said so. 'Suffer little children to come unto me' was what He'd said, but His priests obviously thought otherwise. 'Will you do me another favour, Vi?'

'Of course I will. What is it?'

'Will you go to see the vicar at St Athanasius's, just off Fountains Road and tell him I would like my son to be baptised there, into the religion his father was baptised in.'

They both looked shocked. Josie's eyes were round with amazement.

Vi was the first to recover. 'You mean it, don't you? You're not just threatening?'

Katie's chin jerked up. 'No, I'm not threatening, and yes, I *do* mean it. If my own lot won't baptise him then we'll go to someone who will. My son will be a Christian and that's all that matters to me.'

Chapter Twenty-Seven

November. Winter was on them again, Katie thought as she pushed Robbie, well wrapped up, in his pram along Stanley Road. She remembered how her Mam had always hated November and the little rhyme she always repeated glumly.

No sun, no moon,
No night, no noon,
November.

It was their fourth winter of war and still no sign of it ending. There were now daily heavy bombing raids on all German-occupied countries and Germany itself.

'Give them a taste of their own bloody medicine,' Vi said.

She thought of Duncan Kinross and wondered was he still flying over Germany in his Lancaster bomber, or was he dead – like Sarah.

The convoys still sailed in and out of Liverpool, but Captain Johnny Walker and his hunter-killer destroyers were taking a heavy toll on the German U-boat packs, so at least the merchant ships were safer. There were battles going on in Africa and all over the Far East. No, there still wasn't much to hope for in the future, and another winter of shortages lay ahead.

As the cold wind stung her cheeks and made her eyes water, Katie thought of Bob. At least he would be warm. Too warm, as he always said in his letters, although she hadn't had one for a while now. Oh, she knew what the mail was like, especially coming from the Far East, so she was determined not to worry.

He'd been so overjoyed about his son. She smiled into the teeth of the raw wind. His words had just tripped over each other, making no sense really, and she'd had a photograph taken of Robbie and herself and sent it to him. He must have received it by now.

She bent over to tuck the blankets more securely around the baby and make sure the thick apron, which acted as a wind break, was hooked securely to the hood. Robbie was thriving despite the shortages and when he was weaned, she, like so many other mothers, would willingly give him the largest portion of her rations.

By the time she'd stood in various queues and had returned home with her few purchases, Katie felt frozen to the marrow. She unlocked the door of the disused shop and manoeuvred the pram through the entrance. She kept it in here because it was warmer and drier than the lean-to in the yard and she always brought it into the living room to air for an hour before she put him in it. With her shopping bag over one arm and Robbie in the other she went through and was surprised to see Josie sitting hunched in a chair close to the fire.

'What's the matter? You look awful. Did they send you home?' She dumped the bag on the table and began to unwrap the blankets and shawls that swaddled Robbie.

'They told me to come home and I had a rotten journey. It being between shifts there were no workers' buses. I had to get the train to Aintree and then wait ages for a tram.'

'Do you think it's flu or something?' Katie was concerned.

Josie shook her head. She hadn't been sure, not really sure until today. 'Didn't I tell you once that I always look and feel terrible when I'm expecting?'

Katie sat down suddenly on the sofa, still with her hat and coat on and still holding a bonneted and mittened baby.

'Oh, Mother of God, Josie! You can't be! You're not supposed to—'

'I know that, but I am,' Josie interrupted. 'And I hated every single minute of it. It was disgusting. Sometimes I felt as though I was going to be sick, or scream or go hysterical, but I *had* to do it, Katie. I've got no life, have I? I go to work, I come home, we listen to all the news, which is mostly bad, then go to bed and I could just see things going on like that . . . for ever.'

Robbie had started to whimper which claimed Katie's attention. She finished taking off his layers of clothes and gave him his dummy. She usually only used it for dire emergencies as Florrie had told her if she let him have it constantly it would cause his mouth to become misshapen. But this *was* a dire emergency.

'I'm going to be extra careful,' Josie said quietly, trying to smile. 'I'm not going back to work.'

Katie looked at her. 'Oh Josie, you know what the doctor said.'

Josie nodded. 'I still don't care. I want – *need* someone in my life. Someone who will love me. Surely you must be able to understand?'

Katie nodded slowly. She couldn't envisage a life without Bob's love or Robbie. Oh, why hadn't Georgie let Josie adopt Sarah's baby? Sarah would be alive and maybe enjoying life, and Josie would have been happy and fulfilled, but that had been too much to ask of him. Now because of him Sarah was dead and Josie was risking her life.

'Vi will probably call round,' Josie said now. 'She's on my shift.

When I'm not waiting for her at the gate, she'll ask and find out I've come home.'

Katie sighed. 'I'll put the kettle on, we both could do with a cuppa.'

Josie held out her arms. 'Give him to me, he's really crabby today.'

'I think he's started teething,' Katie said distractedly as Josie took Robbie and began to rock him gently in her arms. Some of the colour had come back into her cheeks and Katie had to smile at the little scene. Who was she to be telling Josie she was mad?

Vi did call – with Florrie in tow, much to Josie's surprise. 'Mam!' she said, as her mother marched through the door.

'Blame me, Josie,' Vi said, holding her hands out to the warmth of the fire. 'The only other times I've seen you look so awful was when you were expecting.'

'When did you see me?'

'When you came back from the toilet. I was at that end of the room but you didn't see me, and when we knocked off and you weren't waiting, I knew you'd gone home and why.' Vi gave a half-smile and a shrug. There were times when she, too, wished she was pregnant but with Jack so far away and for God knows how long, she would have to wait. She could understand Josie's feelings.

'Josie, is it true?' Florrie demanded, her face lined with worry.

'Yes, and please don't start on me, Mam.'

'Jesus, Mary and Joseph! "Don't start on me"! You fool, Josie! You know what the doctor at the hospital said. Any more of these miscarriages could kill you.'

Josie burst into tears and Katie put her arms around her.

'She knows that, but what has she got to live for or look forward to? Putting up with our Georgie for the rest of her life? *I'd* risk my life too, if that was all I had for a future.'

'Oh, Josie! Josie!' Florrie wrung her hands helplessly. She could see Katie's point of view. She could imagine what life with Georgie Deegan would be like and she sympathised, but she was shocked and worried sick. There were enough people dead and dying in the world without her daughter deliberately courting danger.

'But how did you put up with him, when you hate him so much?' Her mother was upset, confused.

Josie looked down at her hands and began to twist her wedding ring around. 'It wasn't easy, but when you want something desperately, you'll put up with almost anything.'

'What am I going to tell your Da, Josie?' Florrie pleaded.

'Tell him Georgie's my husband "until death do us part". There's no other way out, and this baby – my baby – will have all the love and care and attention in the world.'

'And what if something happens to you?'

'Then . . . ' Josie faltered.

'Then I'll bring it up with Robbie,' Katie interrupted quietly, although if anything did happen to Josie, she knew Florrie would willingly take the child. After all, she would be its grandmother.

'Oh, in the name of God! Can't we look on the bright side?' Vi cried. 'Everything might go like clockwork and everyone will be safe and well and happy.'

Josie smiled at her. 'I think I'd better start the Thirty Days' Prayer.'

'And I can see us all being traipsed up to Fox Street for the special Novenas.'

'Well, she's certainly going to need all the help she can get, Vi. The first thing to do is go and see Dr Askam.' Florrie was brisk and practical now. She was over the initial shock, but the worry would be with her constantly. 'But you'd better be prepared for a real dressing down, my girl.'

Josie sat with her mother at her side while all the risks and complications were explained to her. Dr Askam didn't mince his words, but in the end he promised that if it was in his power, he'd do everything to see that this time both Josie and her baby would thrive.

Apart from the sickness, which she knew would pass, Josie had never felt so happy since her wedding day. She was so sure, so confident that this time everything would be all right. She had plenty of rest, she took the tonics the doctor left on his weekly visit which her Da insisted on paying for. She found it a joy to watch Katie with Robbie, and Georgie was far, far away. She wished him no harm now. Gone were the bitter thoughts, the sinful hopes that something awful would happen to him to release her from her predicament. Some of the hatred had abated. She'd written, of course, but what kind of a reply, if any, she would receive she didn't know. Nor did she really care. This was *her* baby and she was determined that she was going to be around to bring it up. Georgie could do what the hell he liked. She didn't care.

When the reply came, surprisingly quickly, everyone was dumbfounded. He was overjoyed. Made up. Over the moon. Now he felt there was something worth fighting for. A peaceful and better world for *his* child to grow up in.

'He's gone round the bend. Right round the flaming twist. It must be the heat out there,' Katie said as Josie read out the letter to herself and Vi.

'Isn't there some saying about the sun and mad dogs?' Josie asked.

'It's a song, Josie. "Mad dogs and Englishmen go out in the midday

270

sun" – but it's the only explanation I can think of,' Vi confessed, equally amazed.

'He says it will want for nothing. It will have the best of everything and he's got big plans now for the future.'

But he hadn't mentioned that Josie too would enjoy all these benefits, or play a part in his big plans, Katie thought as Josie continued to read. Typical!

'Where's he going to get the money for all these things?' Vi demanded.

'Oh, he's got money all right. He always has had, and he's got Mam's jewellery, if he hasn't sold it by now,' Katie replied bitterly.

'He says if it's a boy, the plans will be even grander as he'll have an heir.'

'God – aren't we using some fancy words. Did I miss something? Has he been knighted or given a seat in the House of Lords and no one told me?' Vi asked sarcastically.

'Josie, I don't want to sound like a killjoy, but don't let all this play on your mind. Don't let him put pressure and worry on you,' Katie advised.

Josie folded up the letter and put it back in the envelope and placed it on the table. It wouldn't be read again. In fact, she might well consign it to the fire. 'No, Katie, I won't and anyway, God knows how long it will be before he comes home. My baby will really love its Mam by then. It won't even know who Georgie is.'

Katie and Vi exchanged glances. Josie seemed so calm in her attitude. Maybe this time she *would* carry the baby full-term and have no complications or after-effects.

'Have you heard anything from Jack, Vi?' Katie asked. Georgie's reply had come very quickly indeed.

'Not for a good while. The Navy is worse than the Army, except in the case of Georgie Deegan's mail, that is. But I've written and told him the good news, Josie.'

The yard door slammed and Joe came through the kitchen and into the living room. He looked at the three girls and grimaced. The house was always full of bloody women, not to mention his noisy Cousin Robbie.

'I met Archie Creswell halfway up the road and he gave me this. He said it was his last call and he was dead glad he'd seen me, he could go and get his tea now.' Joe threw an envelope on the table and went upstairs.

The three girls looked at each other. The envelope was a dark beige colour and of the type used for official letters.

'Oh, God!' Vi exclaimed.

'Turn it over, luv. Who is it for?' Josie asked quietly.

Vi's heart was in her mouth. It concerned either Georgie or Bob, and she knew which one she hoped it would be. The colour drained from her cheeks and she bit her lip. It was for Katie. With an unsteady hand she held it out to her friend and watched the fear creep into the dark eyes that only a few minutes ago had held amusement at Georgie's unexpected attitude and her own caustic remarks.

Josie too was watching her sister-in-law closely. Oh, not Bob! He didn't deserve to die. Georgie did. It would have been a sort of justice in a way for all the terrible things he'd done. But not Bob! He was so cheerful, caring and gentle, and honest as the day was long. She looked at Robbie and tears pricked her eyes. Oh Lord, please don't let him be dead, for Robbie's sake.

Katie opened it slowly, her mouth dry. She held her baby son tightly in the crook of her arm as she read the brief message. Then she hung her head.

'Katie, in the name of God what is it?' Vi pleaded.

'He's missing.'

Hope leapt in both Josie and Vi's hearts.

'It doesn't say "Dead" or "Missing Believed Dead" or anything like that?' Vi pressed.

Katie shook her head as she reread the telegram. 'No. Just "Missing".'

'Not even "In action"?' Josie asked.

'No, nothing like that.'

Vi seized her hand and squeezed it hard. 'Then that's good, pet, honestly it is. Nelly Nolan who lived next door to us in the old house, she got a telegram like that and her Dan is a prisoner of war. They wrote and told her that he's alive and reasonably well. She's always sending stuff for Red Cross parcels. She half-starves herself to save it.'

Katie held her little son close to her, silent tears falling on the soft reddish-brown hair. It was so like his Da's, she thought. Oh, please God, let him be safe. I won't mind if he's a prisoner somewhere or injured, or even if he's lost an arm or a leg. I won't even mind if I have to nurse him for the rest of his life. Just keep him safe. Oh, Holy Mother of God, let him come home to see his son. Let my baby still have a father when all this is over.

Josie and Vi sat comforting her, bolstering up her hopes, something they knew they would have to do for a long time to come, until Joe finally came down and asked was there going to be anything to eat tonight or what?

Vi stood up, her eyes full of indignation. 'You've got the same amount of tact and thoughtfulness as your flaming brother, Joe Deegan!'

Josie began to get up but Katie wiped away her tears and passed

Robbie over to her. 'No, stay there, Josie. I'm fine now. Really I am.'

Vi looked at her closely. 'Are you sure? I can stay and cook meladdo here some tea, although why the hell someone of his age can't see to himself I don't know, especially as he brings in a flaming telegram from the War Office and chucks it on the table and then does a disappearing act.'

'I'll get a meal going, Vi. I'm over the shock now and I've things to keep me busy.'

Vi turned to a crestfallen Joe. 'If it's of any interest to you at all, Bob's missing.' She gave Katie a quick hug. 'I'll call in tomorrow to see you, luv.'

When she'd gone, Josie glared at Joe as Katie went into the kitchen and began preparing a meal.

'Why is everyone taking it out on me?' he demanded indignantly.

'We're not, but you could have read who it was addressed to, and handed it over properly, not just flung it down and then waltz upstairs. Go and tell your sister you're sorry and think about her feelings a bit more. One selfish, thoughtless brother in this family is enough.'

Joe looked chastened; he liked Bob. He hadn't even looked at the envelope, really; he'd been so wrapped up in other things.

He had managed, with great stealth and agility, to take another gold bracelet from the tin box that was still lying in the dresser drawer. He'd hoped that, with the household being in such a turmoil, with people visiting to see the baby and that bossy midwife, Miss Mac-Cormack, always in and out and ordering people around, that Georgie wouldn't have had time to check the contents of his tin box. His hopes were violently dashed, because the day before he was due to leave for Portsmouth, Georgie had collared him.

'All right, you thieving little get,' he rasped. 'Where's the stuff you pinched?'

'What stuff?' Joe tried to act the innocent but the bright red flush of guilt crept over his face.

'You know bloody well what stuff. Mam's gold. There's two chains, a pair of earrings, that snake bracelet and another heavy gold one missing. You couldn't get your hands on your money, so you took the jewellery instead. Well, I want them back!'

'I . . . I haven't got them,' he stammered.

Georgie's expression became very grim. 'Have you sold them or pawned them?'

'No! I—'

'You've given them to that tart, that whore Joanie Mac, haven't you? Oh, I've heard all about you and her. People see things, hear things and talk about them.'

He became defensive. 'She's not a whore! Her Mam is – *was* – but Joanie's not. You put my money into those bloody Bonds, you never asked me first, and anyway, I've as much right to Mam's things as you have. They're not *all* yours! They're our Katie's and mine too – and they would've belonged to our Sarah an' all!'

'God stiffen you, you stupid little sod! I'm the oldest, everything's mine. A lawyer would back me up on it.'

'It's *not* all yours – and if you go on about it, I'll tell our Katie what you said and she'll go mad.'

'You tell her and I'll break your bloody neck, lad. I want every bit of my property back. You can just go round there tonight and get it all.'

'I won't! I gave it to Joanie!'

'Then I'll go.'

His temper had flared at the thought of how Georgie would treat her. 'And I suppose you'll take the scuffers with you? If you go near Joanie I'll be straight down to Westminster Road Police Station and tell them about you. About all those lies you told that CID feller about the Pitch and Toss games, and about the black-market tinned stuff and about . . . about our Sarah.'

When Joe began his series of threats, Georgie looked at him scornfully. The police weren't interested in petty things that had happened years ago, and anyway, they couldn't prove a thing. But Sarah was different. He didn't know just how much Joe knew. It could be a great deal, since he'd taken up with Joanie. She might have told him names and places, and if she did think something of Joe, or if she saw an end to the lavish gifts, she'd be more than willing to grass on him.

'Well, just you keep your thieving hands off things that don't belong to you,' Georgie snapped, and pushed Joe away from him.

Joe grinned to himself. He'd fooled him. He still had the wide heavy gate bracelet that was worth a fair bit of money. Maybe enough to pay for a room in a better house for Joanie to live in. That's what she seemed to want now. All mention of rings had been abandoned but he didn't mind too much. They had plenty of time. They were young. In fact, he wasn't sixteen yet, far too young even to be conscripted.

When he reached Number Seven Court that evening, Joe was soaked. It had started to rain just as he'd left the house. Ostensibly he was going to meet Vinny and Franny in town to go to an ARP lecture in Blair Hall.

The room was overly warm, with a fire roaring halfway up the chimney but it was just as untidy, dirty and smelly as usual. Joanie was putting on lipstick in front of a speckled and misty mirror on the wall, bending over the clutter on top of a chest of drawers. She wore a thin clingy bright green dress and the firm rounded shape of her buttocks was clearly visible. He was thankful there was no sign of her Mam. Sometimes she was in, sometimes not.

Joanie turned around.

'God, yer soaked!'

'I know, it's chucking it down out there.' He took off his cap and overcoat and shook them briskly and droplets of water hissed as they fell into the hearth or onto the burning coals. 'I'll put them over a chair in front of the fire,' he said, 'then they'll be dry by the time I've got to go home.'

Joanie glared at him. 'I thought we was goin' out? You said you'd take me to the pictures or dancin' or to a pub for a drink an' a birrof a laugh!'

'It's no use going out there, honest. We'd get soaked. It's nice an' warm in here.' He sat on the edge of the bed and patted it, smiling up at her.

She threw the lipstick across the room and dragged off the gold earrings that had belonged to Molly. 'Youse never take me out! All we do is stay in 'ere, in this . . . bloody kip, an' youse know I 'ate it! It's bad enough in summer but it's bleedin' worse in winter. Yer can't even gerra wash. The bloody water's froze solid!'

He got up and took her in his arms. 'I know you hate it here, and I've got plans for you.'

The anger and resentment left her face. 'What plans?'

'I'll tell you them later.'

She twisted out of his embrace. 'No, I want ter 'ear them now.'

Joe sighed. It had been a rotten day and now it looked as though she was going to be awkward.

She'd thrown herself on the bed and lay staring at the cracked and discoloured ceiling, her arms folded behind her head.

He sat beside her and gently stroked her breast, feeling the thrill, the passion surge as it always did.

'Before our Georgie went away, I got something off him.'

'So?'

'A bracelet.'

She turned her head towards him, her eyes narrowed. 'I've gorra bracelet already. The one like a snake.'

'No, this is different. It's worth a lot of money and I'm going to sell it and then get you a place of your own so you can move out of this dump.'

A slow smile spread across her face and she leaned towards him. 'Honest? A place of me own, like?'

'Yes. With the way things are it might only be a room, but in a nice house,' he added hastily, seeing the smile fade. 'And I can get you some nice bits of furniture too,' he promised lavishly.

'An' can we go out, an' will yer buy me some dead classy gear an' all?'

He couldn't do all that. What did she think he was, a bank manager or something? With whatever he got for the bracelet he could afford maybe six months' rent on a room, but not much else. He'd save up for the 'bits of furniture' he'd promised, but there was no hope of new clothes. He felt as though his heart was sinking slowly towards his stomach, he was so afraid he'd lose her.

'Yeah, it'll be Christmas soon. I'll buy you an outfit.'

Now her dark, almond-shaped eyes sparkled. 'When can I 'ave this room an' a new outfit, then? Next week?'

'Joanie, it's . . . it's just not that easy. I'll have to look in the paper at the adverts and these days there aren't many of them and you've got to get round there quick before someone else does. It might take weeks.' He was trying to sound rational, grown-up and yet optimistic.

She rolled over onto her stomach, away from him, her face to the wall. 'I 'ate you, Joe Deegan, I bloody do! Yer promise me all them things an' then yer say I can't 'ave them.'

'I didn't say that, Joanie, I didn't!' He pleaded. 'I promise I'll get you them as soon as I can, honest to God I will.' He reached out and touched her shoulder and she turned back towards him.

'I 'ate being disappointed, Joe. All me life I've been disappointed. Me Mam was always doin' it. "I'll get yer this, Joanie, if yer good." Or, "Yer Uncle Fred will buy yer a dolly iffen yer good" an' then Uncle Fred would 'ave gone an' there was never no dollies. I've 'ad that many bloody uncles I lost count.'

'I won't disappoint you, Joanie, you know that. I love you, I really do, and I want you to have nice things. Everything you've asked me for you've got, haven't you?'

'I suppose so.' The sullen grudging tone was still in her voice. Then she smiled the lazy sensual smile he loved and slid her arms around his neck. Everything would be fine now, he thought. He'd sell the bracelet tomorrow and really get cracking to look for a room. He'd ask Vinny and Franny to help. They thought he was great – the real experienced, dead smart feller who had sex nearly every night. Real sex, not just fumbling and groping in back jiggers, but on a bed and with no clothes on at all . . .

He sighed dreamily and began to kiss her, moaning with delight as her clever pointed tongue darted out and into his hungry young mouth.

★ ★ ★

It was still raining, Vi noticed miserably as she got off the bus that ran from the factory to the bottom of Everton Valley. She'd get soaked if she walked or soaked if she stood and waited for a tram. It wasn't much of a choice. She made up her mind. She'd walk down Archer Street onto Westminster Road and across to Tillard Street. At least that way she'd keep reasonably warm.

She was a few yards from Pobjoy's, the jewellers and pawnbrokers on Walton Road, when she saw Joe go into the shop. His cap was pulled well down and the collar of his coat was turned up around his ears, but she still recognised him. Now what was that little fiend up to? Katie had enough on her plate as it was. She stepped into the dark doorway of 'Ted's Fruiterers', the shop next door, and waited. It wasn't a long wait.

Joe looked sullen and annoyed as he slammed the shop door behind him.

Vi stepped out. 'Right, what are you up to now, Joe Deegan?'

Joe jumped nervously. Vi was the last person he'd expected to see. He had to gather his wits and quickly. 'I was just looking at . . . something.'

'What?'

'Er, a bit of jewellery.' He stuffed the bracelet that they'd only offered him five guineas for further down into his pocket.

Vi noticed. 'What have you got in your pocket?'

Joe panicked. 'Nothing! Nothing!'

Thinking he'd been pinching something, Vi grabbed his arm tightly. 'You've got something in your pocket that you don't want me to see. Have you been nicking things?'

'No! No!'

'God Almighty! Hasn't your Katie got enough on her plate already? She'll kill you if you've been thieving, so she will! Now let me see what's in your pocket.'

He felt so defeated. Five flaming guineas he'd been offered for something worth at least ten, and the feller had been suspicious too and had asked some awkward questions. He slowly withdrew the bracelet.

'Where in God's name did you get that?'

'It was me Mam's. Our Georgie's got all her other stuff. He gave me this.'

Vi was furious. 'If he wanted to give it away, then why not give it to Katie or Josie?' She clipped him sharply across the ear. 'You're getting more and more like him every day. A nasty piece of work. You pinched it, he didn't give it you. He wouldn't give you last week's bloody *Echo*.'

'Ah God, Vi, don't tell our Katie, please? I've got as much right to it as he has. Look, I've got a girlfriend and she likes me to give her things. All girls like presents, don't they?'

'Not when they've been pinched, they don't.'

He tried a different approach. 'I really love her, Vi – you can understand that, can't you, you being married an' all. She lives in this terrible house. In just one dead-grotty room and I thought I could sell this and get her a decent place, and that's the truth,' he pleaded.

Vi's eyes narrowed as she scrutinised his face. Then she made up her mind. 'OK. Quick, let's run, there's a tram coming!'

Joe could hardly believe his ears as she grabbed him by the arm and they ran for the tram. She wasn't going to tell anyone. She was great sometimes, was Vi. It was only when they'd sat down and he looked out of the window that he saw they were going towards town. Then she asked the conductress for two to Scotland Road and he realised she'd duped him.

They walked in complete silence down the road. Or rather she marched him down the road, her hand gripping his arm like a vice. Oh God! he thought miserably, everything was going wrong today. He'd had a rotten day at work, the Chief Clerk had been on his back from the minute he'd set foot in the place. He'd not sold the bracelet, he was wet and cold and hungry, and now she'd guessed that he'd been talking about Joanie. He twisted abruptly, ready to run like hell back up the road, but she'd anticipated this and was quicker. She caught him by the ear and twisted it hard, just as Katie had done years ago.

'Oh no, you don't! Me Aunty Mary's got four little brats, remember. I'm used to dealing with lads.'

'Ah, eh, Vi! Let go, you're hurting me and I look such a fool!' he cried.

'You *are* a fool, Joe Deegan. A right flaming idiot. What did Josie's Mam tell you about Joanie MacNally, and she wasn't lying?'

'She was! Joanie loves me, she really loves me! That's why she wants to clear out of here, live somewhere decent.'

'Set up on her own, more like, you bloody fool.'

They'd reached the Court and Vi cursed as she stepped on something slimy and smelly. 'Jesus, Mary and Joseph what a dump!'

'You see?' Joe pleaded.

'It's a good job I can't or I think I'd be sick! Which one of these glorified pigsties does she live in?'

Joe indicated the house and then the door and Vi hammered hard on it. There was no light at all in the hallway.

Joanie's voice called out, wanting to know who it was.

'Open the bloody door and you'll find out, won't you, Joanie?' Vi yelled.

There was movement and some scuffling inside and then slowly the door was opened an inch.

Vi kicked it and it swung inward out of Joanie's grasp.

'Aye! Who the 'ell are youse?' Joanie demanded. She wore only a creased satin slip and her hair was wild and tangled. Quite clearly, over the girl's shoulder, Vi saw a man lying on the bed. He was an American, judging by his underwear, his haircut and the gum he was chewing. She caught a glimpse of a uniform jacket hung on the bedpost.

Her temper, already simmering, boiled up. 'The bloody debt-collector, you little whore!' She lashed out and slapped Joanie hard across her right cheek. 'That's for my best mate,' she yelled, and as the girl's head jerked sideways she made a swipe at the other side of her face. The sound of the slap echoed around the hallway. 'And that's for what you've done to him!'

Vi stepped back and Joanie saw Joe standing there, his face ashen, his eyes riveted on the GI sprawled on the bed who was watching them with mild amusement.

Before Joanie could move or even open her mouth, Vi snatched at the chain she wore around her neck. It broke and Vi pressed it into Joe's hand. She guessed it had belonged to Molly Deegan.

'Gold's too good for a whore. You should know that, Joe Deegan. You should have given her brass. Brass for a brassy little tart!'

Joe still stood paralysed but he jerked back as Joanie slammed the door in their faces and began to scream abuse and obscenities at them from behind it.

Vi put her arm around him; she was shaking but her anger was being replaced by pity.

'Come on lad, she's not worth it. I know that right now it's killing you, it's tearing at your guts and it'll go on for a while, but you'll get over it. You'll find someone else. You *will*, Joe. It'll be like the way you felt after your Mam or Sarah died, but it'll get better. Time will help, Joe. It will, I'm not lying to you.'

He let her lead him back out into the dark, dank Court and knew he'd never come here again. He hardly heard the words she was saying, trying to comfort him. Joanie hadn't been expecting him tonight. He'd told her he was going to get things moving and she'd encouraged him. She must have told that feller to come around or maybe she'd just picked him up. He never really knew what exactly she did in the day. She'd never loved him. She'd lied to him. All the things Florrie had said and he'd refused to believe, were true. They'd been true all along but he'd just closed off his mind.

A sob rose in his throat and made him shudder. She must have been laughing at him behind his back to that fat old cow of a Mam, Doreen.

Maybe they'd even planned it together. He'd lied to Katie and Josie over and over. His soul must be black with lies. He'd stolen his Mam's jewellery and given it to Joanie. More sins to stain his soul. He'd stayed away from Confession because of all the things they'd done together. Things that should only be done after you were married. Misery, shame and guilt descended on him. Was Vi right? Was he becoming like Georgie? He was so confused and upset he didn't know where he was or what time it was or where he was going.

Vi just put her finger to her lips as she led him into the kitchen where Katie was preparing the tea. When he'd gone upstairs looking like a zombie, she turned to her old friend.

'Don't say a word to him, Katie, not tonight or maybe even not at all. He's had a shock, a terrible shock. He's devastated, the poor stupid lad. That Joanie Mac has been playing him for a fool and he's just found out.'

'Joanie Mac? But he gave her up, ages ago.'

Vi shook her head. 'He didn't. The poor lad was besotted with her. She had him wrapped around her little finger.'

Katie was mystified. 'How did you know? And how did he find out about her making a fool of him?'

'Because I followed him,' Vi said evasively. 'Then I dragged him down there and she opened the door to me. She was half-naked and with a feller – a Yank, by the look of him. I belted her twice across the face, the little whore! He'll stay away from her kind now, luv. He's learned a bloody hard lesson tonight, believe me – so don't even let on you know, no matter how hard it might be – and don't tell Josie, eh?'

Katie sighed. 'I won't, Vi. And thanks, for everything. You're a great mate, do you know that?'

'I do try, luv. Oh, I just wish this bloody war was over and we could all get back to normal.' There was no way on earth she was going to tell Katie that her Mam's jewellery had ended up adorning a common little whore like Joanie Mac. Joe's broken heart would mend in time, but Katie would never forget the loss of her Mam's jewellery or Joe's part in it.

Chapter Twenty-Eight

It had taken Joe a long time to get over Joanie Mac, Katie mused, watching nine-month-old Robbie sitting in his pram waving a rattle and gurgling at the sparrows and starlings which landed on the yard wall. The May sunlight was warm so she'd pushed the pram into the yard. She could keep an eye on him while she did the ironing. Poor Joe had moped around for weeks, hardly eating, dragging himself to work, sitting staring into space and refusing all offers from Vinny and Franny to go out. It had been so hard not to hug him and say, 'It's all right, Joe. I know how you feel, but you'll get over it.' But she had kept her own counsel as Vi had instructed.

'He won't thank you for it later on when he's over it. He'll only feel more of a fool and it will always be there between you.'

Gradually she noticed that after Christmas he started to pick up. Vinny and Franny began to come to the house to call for him. The night she heard him laugh – a proper hearty guffaw – she sighed with relief. They were all mates again, off out looking for a bit of a gas. She thanked God for it. It was one less worry.

Since she'd had the telegram, there had been no further news of Bob. She'd written letter after letter to the War Office pleading for information, but although they replied courteously, they could tell her nothing more. It was seven months now. Seven long, dreary, heart-breaking months. She'd refused to believe the worst could have happened to him. She *wouldn't* give up. She *couldn't* give up. He was alive somewhere, she knew it.

Vi and Josie had been pillars of strength, even though Vi was worried sick about her Jack. They'd heard on the wireless that there had been terrible typhoons and tidal waves in the Malacca Straits, and she hadn't had a letter for months. They'd decided that Georgie had suffered their cold silence for long enough. In a way it had been a relief, at least there was no longer the strain of keeping their wall of silence; in many ways their relenting had made for a happier household.

Josie was nearing her time now and had really blossomed. They were all so relieved that there had been no miscarriage, and Josie looked so healthy, complaining cheerfully that she had no right to look so well, she got hardly any sleep as the baby kicked like a footballer. They laughed about which team would have him, Liverpool or Everton, if it was a boy.

'The post,' she announced now, coming into the kitchen.

Katie looked up from the ironing. 'Anything for me?'

'No, but there's one for me and it's OHMS.' She didn't really care a great deal about the contents; wished rather it had been good news for Katie, instead of something to do with Georgie.

'Open it. Staring at it's not going to do any good.'

Josie ripped it open, scanned the lines and then pursed her lips.

'Wouldn't you just believe it. He apparently got a minor leg wound and it won't heal. It's turning into something called a "Tropical ulcer" which won't go away because of the conditions out there – the heat and the humidity, whatever that is.'

'So?' Katie prompted.

'So he's coming home. Wouldn't you just flaming well know it! The devil certainly looks after his own. Everyone else goes to hospital in Australia or New Zealand, but oh no, it's too hot for what Georgie Deegan's got. He gets sent home! Oh, God! Well, I'm not looking after him, Katie, and you're not waiting on him hand and foot either. You've enough to do.'

Katie nodded. She had no intention of doing anything for her brother. It was only a minor leg wound, after all.

When Vi called round that evening and they told her the news she nearly hit the roof. 'The jammy sod – the lucky swine! Oh, wouldn't it make you sick! I'm dead sorry, Josie, I can't help it.'

'Don't be sorry, Vi, I wish he wasn't coming home either. I wish they would ship him off to Australia and keep him there for ever!'

'Does it say when?' Vi asked, still fuming.

'Not an exact date. They'll write with that when they know, but in about three weeks.'

'There's no bloody justice in this world at all,' Vi said grimly.

Joe came downstairs all clean and spruce in his good suit, shirt and tie.

'Out gallivanting again, are we?' Vi commented, pleased that he'd got over Joanie Mac.

He grinned. 'Sort of. Sis, I wanted to ask you something.'

'What?' Katie looked at him closely, waiting for him to speak.

'Can I bring a friend home?'

'Your friends are always around here,' she answered, puzzled.

'No, this is a girl.'

Vi grinned. 'What's her name and where does she live?'

'It's Lucy Wade and she lives in Denbigh Street off Rice Lane. In

Blessed Sacrament Parish.' That was a respectable area, Katie thought with relief. 'Of course you can', she said. 'It's your home the same as everyone else's. Just let me know, that's all I ask, so I can have the place and myself tidy. If you want to bring her to tea, she'll have to take pot luck.'

'Oh, she won't mind that.'

'I like her already. Oh, and by the way, your dear brother will be home soon too.'

'What!' Joe looked aghast.

'Georgie, with the luck – I won't say of the Irish because that would be insulting every Irishman and woman – got a bit of a leg wound. He probably fell over his wallet or something stupid like that, but it won't heal because of the heat, so he'll be home in about three weeks,' Katie informed him.

'You don't look very pleased,' Vi commented.

Joe shrugged. He didn't want to offend Josie or upset her by saying that Vi was right. Life had looked up and he didn't want to be reminded about Joanie Mac. He'd put the chain and bracelet safely in a box at Vi's instigation and this had been given to Josie for safekeeping with an edited version of events. Josie would hand them straight to Katie and with a bit of luck they'd hear no more about it.

For the rest of the evening Katie felt unaccountably miserable. Worry nagged at her the way it did during the dark hours of the night. At least during the day she had things to do to keep her busy and so relieve some of the strain and stress.

She'd write to the War Office again tomorrow, she decided. Maybe some new information might have come in to them. She wasn't relishing the thought of Georgie coming home. He'd start ordering everyone around, doing his 'I'm the Head of the Family' bit and he'd be under their feet all day too and for God knows how long. Maybe they'd get lucky, and he'd be taken into hospital here. That would be great.

Ten days later, Georgie came in on the *Aquitania* that was acting as a hospital ship. Katie had left Robbie with Josie and gone to meet him, much against her will but someone had to go and Josie just couldn't do it; she was over her time as it was.

He looked quite well, she thought, lightly tanned and neat in his uniform. She pushed her worries about Bob to the back of her mind and went forward to greet him.

'I suppose I should say "Welcome Home",' she said gruffly as he disembarked, his kitbag over his arm.

'Oh, that's a lovely way to greet anyone, isn't it?' he said waspishly. 'Where's Josie?' He hadn't expected a brass band and a great turnout, but he'd at least have liked a few people to meet him.

'At home minding Robbie. She's overdue as it is, so there was no way she was coming down here.'

He had to lean heavily on her shoulder to walk. Glancing around at the stretcher cases and those with bandages around their heads or their eyes, she looked up at him.

'I suppose they all think you're a bit of a fraud?' She jerked her head in the direction of the line of ambulances.

'I don't bloody care *what* they think. This ulcer hurts like hell and it won't heal. It's running with pus all the time.'

She shuddered. 'I hope it's not infectious, I've got our Robbie to think of.'

'It's only a bloody ulcer, not TB,' he said exasperatedly. 'Where are you going?'

'For a taxi. You can't go home on the tram like that.'

'I hope you've got the fare.'

'Oh, nothing changes, does it! Yes, I've got the flaming fare.'

'Have you heard anything more about Bob?'

She shook her head. She didn't want to talk about it with him.

'He'll be all right. Those places out there are all jungle; he'll have got separated from his unit or something, and he'll turn up eventually. I've heard that the natives will hide anyone who's not a Jap. They seem to hate the little yellow swine more than we do.'

That raised her spirits. 'Will they really hide people?'

'That's only what I've heard, it's not Gospel, like.'

'Have you brought any dressings with you or have you got to see the doctor or anything?' she asked.

'I have to go to the School of Tropical Medicine, up by the Royal Infirmary, as soon as possible.'

'Will it need dressing every day?'

'I suppose so. It was done every day on the ship.'

Katie felt sick with revulsion. 'Well, Josie can't do it. She can't bend.' He hadn't even asked how Josie was yet.

'I can do it myself. You just said she's near her time. Is she looking all right? What does the doctor think?'

For the first time he was actually showing some interest, Katie marvelled.

'She looks great, but she gets very tired. Dr Askam is looking in today actually, and the midwife comes each morning, just on the offchance. It's got to be any day now.'

'And I'll be home.' He sounded smug and self-satisfied.

'Which is more than Bob was when I had our Robbie.'

'Well, don't go blaming me for that! And, I'm sorry he's . . . well, that you've not heard anything further. I really am.'

She nodded briefly in silent gratitude. He *was* alive, she knew it in her heart. 'Vi hasn't heard from Jack; the *Victor* may have gone down. They said on the wireless that there have been typhoons out in the Malacca Straits.'

'They'd have announced it if it had. You know: "The Admiralty Regrets . . ."'

That's what Katie kept telling Vi. She changed the subject. 'When your ulcer finally gets better, what will you do?'

'I'll have to be careful that I don't bang or knock it, so I won't be going back. I'm thinking of opening up the shop again, when my ulcer is healed.'

'You'll have to get some kind of transport to get to market, and there's still not a lot of fish coming in – no one knows from day to day how much so you have to go down on the off-chance. And you'll have to go and see Mr Catchpole.'

'Da's cart is still in the yard around the corner, and I can get a horse. I can even sell the manure as fertiliser.'

'God, you never change. Money, money, money. Grab, grab, grab!'

'It's not for me,' he said stiffly, 'it's for my son or daughter.'

'That makes a change. I hope you haven't gone and set your heart on a son, and will upset Josie if you have a girl?'

'I'd like a son, but as long as it's healthy I won't mind a girl. With the right guidance, she could marry into a good family. One with money.'

'Jesus, Mary and Joseph!' she said as she helped him into the taxi cab. 'It's not even born and you're talking about marriage!'

Back at Chelmsford Street there was a strained greeting between himself and Josie. He gave her a peck on the cheek and she said, 'Welcome home,' in a sepulchral tone. He was amazed she looked so well but she *was* enormous.

'Er, it's not going to be twins, is it?' he asked, hopefully.

Katie cast her eyes to the ceiling. Even with something like this he wanted more than anyone else had.

'Not according to the doctor or midwife. Isn't one enough?' his wife replied tartly.

When they'd settled him, neither woman wishing to see the wound on his leg or hear about his experiences, to their relief the doctor called.

'Home is the sailor, I see?' he commented acidly.

'I've a note for you and one for the School of Tropical Medicine,' Georgie announced. 'They're in my kitbag.'

Katie went and fetched the one for the doctor. When she returned he was asking Josie questions and looked concerned. He was ignoring Georgie so Katie just put the envelope by his black Gladstone bag which was on the table.

'Everything *is* all right?' Josie asked anxiously.

'It's perfect. I just wish this baby would decide to put in an appearance soon, that's all.' Dr Askam smiled at her. Bringing babies into the world was far better than ministering to those who were leaving it, even though it was a far from perfect place for a baby to be born into. He always had a look at little Robbie Goodwin too and asked Katie if there was any news and if she needed something for her nerves. The reply was always the same. A firm shake of the head but genuine thanks for the offer. She hadn't given up hope and probably never would. She was a determined young woman and he had a lot of respect for her.

'Well, call me night or day, when that little imp decides to make its debut. Good afternoon.' He smiled at Josie and picked up his bag and put the letter, unopened, into his pocket.

Georgie felt aggrieved. Although the man's, 'Good afternoon,' had been affable enough, he had a sneaking feeling it wasn't meant to include him.

Georgie was woken during the night by Josie's groans and the throbbing in his leg. It had been a restless, troubled sleep.

He fumbled to put on the bedside lamp. 'Have you started?'

'Yes, I think so. Get Katie.'

'I can't walk very well.'

'Then call her,' Josie snapped.

Katie came dashing in response to his shouts, rubbing the sleep from her eyes. 'You've started?'

Josie nodded.

'Right, I'll get Joe up. He can go on the bike to fetch the doctor and Miss Mac. Georgie, you'd better move yourself. Downstairs if possible, or either my room or our Joe's if you can't.'

'You'll have to help me.'

She glared at him. Still as self-centred as ever. 'Scoot along on your backside, it won't hurt you for once.' She turned back to Josie. 'Right, let's get you more comfortable.'

Josie smiled up at her. 'You'd better get an old towel, Katie, and tie it to the bedpost.'

'God, I'd forgotten that.' She smiled ruefully. 'I nearly broke all your fingers, didn't I?'

'Will you stay with me?'

'Of course I will, but we'll need someone to boil water and that big brother of mine is useless, whinging on about his flaming leg. I'll send for your Mam too. She'll kill me if I don't.'

Everyone arrived within fifteen minutes of each other and to Georgie, who had got himself downstairs and was being totally ignored by everyone, the living room was like a lunatic asylum.

Miss MacCormack instantly ordered boiling water and Katie hurried into the kitchen. Dr Askam told Joe it was no use him going back to bed, he must be ready to dash down to the end of the street to the public phone box to call an ambulance. If there were complications, Josie would have to go to Oxford Street Maternity Hospital. Florrie refused to leave her daughter and put a very dozy Norma on standby to go back home to fetch her Da, whether things went to plan or not, and in the meantime to make tea for them all. It looked as though it was going to be a long night.

Surprisingly, though, it wasn't – and no complications arose, either. Josie's cries of agony had sent shudders through Georgie, Joe and Norma, but by the time the first bright rays of sunlight broke over the city that May morning, Josie had been delivered of a very healthy and quite perfect little girl.

She was tired but as Miss Mac and Florrie washed her down, combed her hair and changed her nightdress, she felt deliriously happy. Dr Askam had washed his hands and was unrolling his shirtsleeves as Katie cleaned the baby and dressed her in a fine wool vest, a soft new nappy and a white cotton gown that almost swamped her. Then she wrapped her in a hand-knitted shawl of soft white wool and passed her over to Josie.

There were dark circles of tiredness under Katie's eyes but she beamed down at her friend. 'You did it, Josie! This time you really did it. Oh, I'm so happy for you and she's beautiful.'

'Thank God and His Holy Mother.' Florrie too was smiling. Her prayers had been answered. Josie was fine and her new granddaughter was, as Katie had said, perfect.

'Hadn't someone better go and tell the happy father?' Miss Mac suggested, without much enthusiasm. She had no time for Georgie Deegan either.

'I'll go,' Katie volunteered. 'After all, he *is* my brother – unfortunately.'

Georgie was sitting in the armchair by the range. He looked tired and anxious, and for a brief second Katie felt sorry for him, but then it passed.

'You've got a lovely little girl,' she announced. 'She's healthy and perfect, and Josie is all right, too. Tired but ecstatic. Congratulations. At least you were here and you'll see her grow.' She paused sadly. 'Bob's never seen Robbie.'

The tiredness seemed to leave him and his shoulders straightened. 'Can I go up? Will our Joe give me a hand?'

'Yes.' Katie turned to Joe. 'Then you'd better try and get your head down for an hour or two before you go to work.'

Nothing could dim Josie's happiness, not even the sight of Georgie looking as proud as punch, as though it was him who'd done all the work, suffered all the pain.

'She's fine,' she said softly. 'Look.'

He sat on the bed and very, very reluctantly Josie passed the baby over for him to hold. She watched him closely and saw not joy or shining love in his eyes, but pride, arrogance and the gleam of obsession.

'I'm going to call her Olivia Florence,' she stated flatly but firmly. He was going to have no part in this. It was *her* choice.

'They're not saints' names,' he replied.

'Then we'll add Mary after your Mam.'

'She'll have the biggest christening St John's has seen in years.' He looked malevolently at Katie, who outstared him. They'd had a terrible row over Robbie being baptised into the Church of England. 'She'll have the best education, go to university, become a doctor or a lawyer. Yes, a lawyer. A barrister, maybe even the first woman judge. Attitudes will have changed by then. Aye, that's what she'll be. A powerful woman. A barrister.'

'Don't you think that's reaching for the stars? People of our class don't go to university or become barristers, and anyway she's barely an hour old.'

'Oh, I've been making plans for her for months now, and why the hell shouldn't she be a barrister? If we've got the money.'

'And have we?' Josie asked quietly.

'We have and we'll save too. I'm going to open up the shop again when this leg's healed. The Navy won't want me back.'

Josie sighed. She was too tired now to argue, but he wasn't going to take over and run Olivia's life the way he seemed to think he had every right to do. She'd risked her life to have this child and that meant she was more *her* child than his.

'Right then, everyone has had their say, seen the baby, so I'll just get Mrs Deegan and Baby comfortable.' Miss Mac made rapid gestures with her hands to signal that it was time to clear the room.

Dr Askam had put on his hat and coat but now he went over to the bedside. 'Well done, Josie. She's a little beauty, just like her mother, and I suspect she'll be a fighter too, just like her mother.'

Josie smiled up at him. What a lovely thing to say. Georgie hadn't even given her a peck on the cheek or said, 'Isn't it great?' or, 'How do you feel now?' She closed her eyes and let the sleep of exhaustion claim her. She didn't want Georgie to kiss her ever again. But all she'd been through to have Olivia had been worth it.

By the end of July, in the dry English heat, Georgie's leg had almost healed and Olivia had had her lavish christening. Where Georgie got all the food from no one knew, except Joe, who'd flatly refused to have anything to do with the proposition his brother had put to him. His own money was safely in War Bonds. He had a good job and his new girlfriend Lucy came from a respectable family who'd welcomed him. He loved her in a totally different way from the infatuation he'd felt for Joanie. His life was too good to spoil. Georgie could make his own arrangements, and he told him so.

'He goes on and on about what *he* wants for her, what *he's* going to do for her. I'm going to scream at him soon, Katie, I am!' Josie complained.

The two women were sitting with their babies in the back yard, enjoying the sun. Katie could see Josie meant it. She too was fed up listening to her brother and having him under their feet all day.

'Do you think we should go back to work?' Josie said suddenly. 'I've been thinking about it a lot, although I'll miss Olivia terribly.'

'How the hell can we do that?'

'Mam will look after Robbie and Olivia, she's already promised she will. She knows Georgie's driving me mad and it will get Olivia away from him.'

'What if he refuses?'

'I don't care. Look, Katie, I can't stand the sight of him.'

'Well, if you feel that way I'll ask Vi to see Mr Parkinson about going back. But are you really strong enough, yet. It's only been two months – and what about feeding her?'

'I'll put her on the bottle,' Josie said matter-of-factly. 'I've seen other babies fed on National Dried Milk and they're thriving.'

'Your Mam's not going to be happy about this, Josie,' Katie warned her. 'I can tell you now.'

'I know, but she understands the way I feel about *him*.'

Florrie didn't raise too many objections, however.

'Every little helps, I suppose. This damned war seems to have no end and if you've made up your mind, Josie, then go back. You know that both Robbie and Olivia will be fine here with me. In fact, they'll probably both get spoiled to death by your Da and our Norma and Brenda.'

'Thanks, Mam.' Josie hugged her mother gratefully.

'You just take care of yourself,' was Florrie's parting admonition.

Vi called in a day or so later to say that Mr Parkinson would be only too pleased to see them back.

'Back? Back where?' Georgie asked.

'At work. In munitions. For the war effort,' Katie answered.

'Some of us are still interested in what's going on and have husbands who are still fighting,' Vi added acidly. But at least she now knew Jack was fine. *Victor* had taken a battering from the weather but had managed to limp back to Colombo for repairs. She'd been so relieved when she'd got his letter. There still hadn't been any word about Bob, though, and as time passed, it was getting harder and harder to keep Katie's spirits up. But she still had an unshakable belief that, one day, he would come home. It was the waiting that was difficult, that was all. Maybe it would do her good to get back to work.

'Who's going to see to Olivia and Robbie and me?'

'Florrie is going to mind the children, and you can mind yourself. For the past week you've been going on and on about the shop. Well, *do* something instead of just talking,' Katie answered.

He glared at her. This was her idea, he knew it, and as usual she'd made all the arrangements without consulting him. Well, he *would* open the shop and he damn well *would* make it pay. He'd sell anything he could lay his hands on to get it redecorated and stocked up. The first thing he'd done as soon as he had had the bedroom to himself for half an hour, was to check that his money and the jewellery were still in their hiding place. They were. He continued to fume about the things Joe had given to Joanie Mac, but now the rest of Molly's jewellery would go to Olivia, when she was old enough to wear it.

He shrugged. 'I can see you've got it all arranged.'

'That's right,' Katie shot back.

Next morning he picked up the post. There were only two letters. One was addressed to Josie, with a Manchester postmark. From Uncle Alfred, no doubt. The old chap had come for the christening and had given Olivia a silver cup, engraved with her name and date of birth. It was solid silver, Georgie knew, because he'd examined the hallmarks. It was exactly the same as the one Uncle Alfred had sent for Robbie, although he hadn't attended the service.

The buff-coloured envelope was official, addressed to *Mrs R. Goodwin*. He turned it towards the light. It wasn't a telegram, it was too bulky and it hadn't been brought by a boy on a bike. Was Bob Goodwin dead? Had they found his corpse, or was he still alive? If he opened it and Bob was dead, he could always say he knew what it contained and wanted to break it more gently than in some offhand way by a snob of an officer. But what if he was alive? Georgie hesitated only for a second, then he opened it and scanned the lines of neat copperplate writing from a Major who had been in charge of Bob's lot.

Apparently Bob had been wounded in the shoulder and separated from his unit. He'd been found and hidden by the natives who had nursed him back to health. He'd remained with them for an incredible six months before the Japs had discovered him. He was now a Prisoner of War but had managed to get a message via a Burmese woman who came to the camp to do the washing for the guards. She'd told him that all the men in the village had been executed as a punishment for hiding him.

Georgie finished reading the letter and stood for a while thinking of all the times his sister had confounded his plans. She'd shown him up by going over his head to Uncle Alfred for permission to marry a bloody Protestant, and having Robbie baptised one too. She'd accused him of being responsible for both Mam and Sarah's deaths. She'd implied he was a coward because he'd stayed in the Merchant Navy – and what about all the names she'd called him over the years! She'd only yesterday talked Josie into going back to work, and had organised for Florrie to see more of his child than he would.

Georgie's mouth twisted into a sneer and his eyes narrowed into two hard, grey flints. He wouldn't tell her about the letter. Let the bitch stew. Let her go on worrying and wondering, she deserved it. He put the letter in his pocket and went upstairs quickly to hide it in the box with his roll of white five-pound notes.

Chapter Twenty-Nine

It looked as though the end was finally in sight, Josie thought as she sat on the bus on Monday evening taking herself, Katie and Vi home from the factory. She should feel elated, but she was so tired, so very tired. Since Olivia's birth her periods had become heavier and heavier. They drained her, and a couple of times she'd had to stay off work and rest in bed. She knew her Mam was worried about her, but she wouldn't let them call the doctor out, nor would she go to see him. It was just a female problem – something she would have to put up with. She had Olivia and that was all that mattered.

The rays of the setting sun tinged the fields and hedgerows with gold; they hadn't reached the houses of Fazakerley yet, one of the city's most pleasant outer suburbs.

The Allied Forces had crossed Europe, liberating country after country. German towns and cities like Hamburg, Essen and Dresden had been bombed and left in ruins, as had so many British cities. And now Berlin itself was being overrun by Russian and Allied soldiers. The guns would fall silent any day now. Katie sat beside her, tired and also silent. There had been no further news of Bob. He was still Missing. Katie, though, was still grimly firm in the conviction that he'd come home. In the seat behind, Vi sensed her mood. It was two years now since that first official letter, and still no word. Vi feared the worst. Even the good news of Allied victories all over Europe and in the Far East didn't seem to help, and how could they, when both she and Josie had their husbands home?

Jack had come home for good in June last year. He'd been wounded when a lone German plane dropped a bomb which had caught the *Victor*'s stern, before the plane itself was blasted from the skies by the guns of a warship close by. He'd suffered a broken leg and collarbone, and minor burns.

It had happened last year on D-Day, the huge assault by the Allied Forces on the beaches of Normandy. The *Victor* had sailed for home from the Far East in the early spring of 1944, and when they arrived, she went down to Portsmouth to see him. They had a wonderful week together, before he'd had to return to his ship. Then she heard he'd been wounded on D-Day and was in hospital in Southampton, and she'd made the seemingly endless journey down there. They wouldn't let her bring him home, he was in no fit state to travel so far, and Vi had had to bow to that decision. But she was waiting at the barrier at Lime Street Station when the hospital train had pulled in. Jack was on crutches then; his shoulder had healed but the leg was more serious.

'I'll only have a bit of a limp, so they tell me,' he said when they got home and she'd made a cup of tea.

'Was it very bad?' she asked. She'd seen the film of the landings on the Pathé News in the cinema, and it looked like chaos, but as someone at work had said: 'Never mind that, it bloody well worked.'

Jack nodded. 'The bloody weather didn't help, it was awful. Rain, wind and a heavy swell. Some of the poor blokes drowned before they got ashore. See, the landing craft couldn't get into shallower water and the blokes' packs dragged them down. Most of the others were seasick and some were literally shit-scared, Vi.'

She put her hand over his; he seemed far away in a world of memories in which she had no part.

'But there was one bloke there I think I'll always remember,' Jack said in a choked voice.

'Why?'

'Because he was so quiet, so calm. A nice feller he was too, well-spoken, probably from a good family. He sat and sketched some of the lads on the back of envelopes, as though nothing was going on at all. They were good pictures, too. He was an artist in civ life. Ormesher his name was. Joe Ormesher. Told me he had a wife and a baby daughter at home. He showed me snaps of them. A bonny little thing, the kiddie was, called Marie Lynda. I don't know what happened to him. I lost sight of him when they got into the landing craft. He said he'd been to Communion – they had a Catholic chaplain with their lot – and I got the feeling that he knew he wasn't going to make it. He was their Intelligence Officer, non-Commissioned, of course. And then that bloody bomb caught us.' He stopped and closed his eyes.

Vi shook her head sadly. She knew so many had not made it further than the beach, especially the American lads on 'Omaha'.

When Jack first went round to see Katie and Josie, Georgie was in the shop, but he came through to the back to moan about his leg. They all wished he hadn't, for a row nearly broke out after Jack, finally goaded to breaking point by Georgie's self-pity, said, 'You had an easy war, mate.'

Vi looked out of the bus window unseeing as the reel of recent memories flashed before her inner eye like a personal Pathé News.

The bus had reached its destination and they all stood up to get off.

'Thank God for the end of another shift. At least we're winding down now,' Vi yawned as she jumped off and waited for Katie and Josie. But when Josie stepped from the platform, her knees suddenly buckled and she crumpled to the pavement. Instantly Vi and Katie pulled her up and held her.

'Josie! What's wrong?' Katie cried.

'Just a bit weak – faint, like.'

'You're a terrible colour,' Vi added. 'Look, put your arms around our shoulders and we'll carry you, it's not far.'

'What's up with her?' Florrie demanded when Katie and Vi half-carried Josie into the little house on Chelmsford Street. She'd given Robbie and Olivia their tea, and had undressed, washed and got them ready for bed. Now she was worn out and didn't want any more worry.

'Just a bit faint, Mam,' Josie whispered.

'She's exhausted. I think she should go to bed and we'll get the doctor,' Katie advised.

'No, I'm fine. Don't drag him out. I'll have something to eat and an early night.'

'You'll go to bed now,' Florrie said firmly.

'All right, Mam, but I don't need the doctor.'

'It's time for Olivia to go to bed anyway. I'll bring her up to give you a kiss in bed before she goes down.'

Josie smiled and held out her arms to give her little daughter a cuddle now. Olivia would be two next week.

Katie took off her coat and swung her son around in her arms. 'Have you been good for Nanna Flo?' she asked, using the pet name Robbie called Florrie.

He nodded vigorously, chuckling uproariously.

'Then we'll play for a bit before you go to bed.' He would be three in August and he'd never even seen his father. Oh, she hoped to God it would all be over soon as everyone was saying and then they'd *have* to find out where Bob was. One way or another.

Georgie came through the shop. 'What's the matter with her?' he said, nodding at Josie.

Florrie glared at him. 'She's worn out, that's what's the matter with her. Working all day, with a baby to see to, and don't think I don't know that she helps you out in the shop from time to time.'

He was stung. 'Only when I'm having my tea.'

'Well, she's going to bed now, she's in no fit state to stay on her feet.'

Georgie was annoyed. He'd wanted to get some money out from his hiding place in the bedroom. Now that the Allies had reached Berlin the war would be over any day now, and people would start using cars and vans and lorries again. The days of the horse and cart were over.

He knew of a decent lorry that had been laid up for the duration, and could get a good deal on it now. But he had to get in quick with the cash, because other people were having the same ideas. Now, with Josie and Olivia in the room he couldn't get at his money.

'Isn't she going to have something to eat first?' he asked, trying to sound concerned instead of irritable.

'No,' Josie answered, wishing Georgie wouldn't call her 'she'. 'I really don't feel like anything. In fact, I feel sick.'

'Right then, I'd better get back and shut up shop.'

Two hours later Josie and the children had gone to bed and Florrie had gone home. Katie was trying to read the newspaper while Georgie sat and gnawed at his fingernails. If he didn't get the cash round to Billy Smythe by tonight, someone else would. Finally he decided he'd have to risk it. He'd be as quiet as a mouse. He just hoped the box wasn't wedged in too tightly because he would make a bit of noise getting it out.

The room was quite light. The curtains were closed but the evening was still bright – the blackout curtains had long since been removed. He stared hard at his wife and was relieved that she seemed to be in a deep sleep. Olivia lay in her cot, her little thumb in her mouth, fast asleep. He crept over to the fireplace and crouched down on his heels, then cautiously put his arm up the narrow chimney. His fingers closed over the box and he gave it a gentle tug. It didn't move and he cursed silently to himself. He gave it another pull and it dropped an inch. He twisted his hand around until he could draw the box down slowly. It was never locked; there was no need for it to be. It had always been safe. He took out the amount of money he needed and closed the lid. Now all he had to do was replace it quietly.

He'd almost completed the task when Josie stirred. He gave the box a final shove.

'Georgie?' Josie asked sleepily, raising herself on one elbow. A dull dragging pain in her abdomen had disturbed her.

He hastily shoved the money in his pocket and stood up. 'I just came up to see if you were both all right.'

'What time is it?'

'About half-past seven. Go back to sleep, luv, you need the rest.' He was relieved when she lay down again. He closed the door quietly behind him and breathed a sigh of relief. He could go round to Billy Smythe's now.

Josie lay trying to sleep but the ache had become worse and seemed to have spread to her back as well. What had Georgie really been doing in here? He wasn't thoughtful enough to come up to see if she was all right . . . He'd been kneeling in front of the fireplace, or at least she thought he had.

Gingerly, she threw back the bedclothes and sat on the edge of the bed. She'd go and get some aspirin for the pain and a cup of warm milk; maybe then she'd be able to sleep. She looked across at Olivia and smiled. The baby looked so lovely when she was asleep, like a little angel, and everyone said that she resembled her Mam rather than Georgie.

She thought again about what he'd been doing in the bedroom, and crept over to the small fireplace, trying not to wake her daughter. She looked at it carefully. There were dirty fingermarks on the green-painted grate, which hadn't been there yesterday, when, as usual on a Sunday she and Katie had given the whole place a good going over. It was probably why she was so tired today. But what had he been up to?

She looked up the chimney but could see nothing. That was unusual because it meant it was blocked. She put her arm up and her hand came into contact with something solid. She pulled and a box, made of grimy, discoloured asbestos fell into the hearth. Olivia twitched and gave a little cry, then fell asleep once more. Josie breathed again. So *that's* what he'd been up to. This was where he kept his money and the rest of Molly's jewellery.

She opened the clumsy box to reveal the tin box inside it. Then she opened that. The gold earrings and chains gleamed softly in the half-light, and folded neatly beneath them was a wad of five-pound notes. Josie forgot all about the dragging ache as she slowly counted the notes. She'd heard the yard door slam, so knew that Georgie had gone out. When she'd finished counting she sat on the floor astounded. God in heaven! There was two hundred and fifty pounds there! You could buy a whole shop or a house with that. He'd been saving or swindling people, or both, for years, obviously. No wonder he'd been able to pay for all that black-market food for Olivia's christening, *and* the gold bracelet engraved with her name that he'd bought for her first birthday last year.

She recalled that Katie had said he wanted to enlarge the shop, make it into some kind of department store; he definitely had the capital to do it. During his time in both the Royal and the Merchant Navy, Georgie had hardly spent a penny. When she'd moved in with Katie they'd lived on what she earned. He was barely ever home . . . Suddenly, the typing on an envelope in the box caught her eye. *Mrs R. Goodwin.* What was he doing with a letter addressed to Katie.

Josie opened the letter and read it, and then she leaned her head against the footboard of the bed. The wicked, wicked swine! There were no words bad enough to describe him and what he'd done. For two whole years he'd let his sister suffer. Let her agonise day and night over Bob's fate. It was more than cruel – it was true evil. What right had he in the first place to be opening other people's letters?

Were there others? She rummaged through the box but could find no more. She counted out one hundred and twenty-five pounds and folded them up. Then she closed the box and put it back. It was money she was entitled to, she reasoned. 'And with all my worldly goods I thee endow,' she muttered grimly. The only reason he had so much was because she'd worked. She'd give it to Katie with the letter, as a token of compensation – although nothing could ever fully compensate for what he'd done. 'Oh, God forgive me, but I wish he'd not come back!' she said quietly. Then she got up and went downstairs.

At the sound of her step, Katie looked up from the paper. 'I thought you were asleep, luv?'

Without a word Josie handed her the money and the envelope and sat down.

'What's all this? Where on earth did all this money come from?'

'Georgie had it hidden in a box with your Mam's jewellery, up the chimney in our bedroom, but never mind the money. Read the letter, Katie.'

Josie watched the expressions and emotions that crossed Katie's face in rapid succession – the disbelief followed by sheer joy, followed by anger as what her brother had done to her sunk in.

'I'll kill him for this, Josie!' Her voice was low, toneless, and it terrified Josie. Usually Katie yelled and shouted at him. This was much more frightening.

'You'd only go to prison or be hanged, and he's not worth it,' Josie pleaded. 'It's a pity the Germans didn't do it for us. But luv, at least it proves Bob's alive. He's not dead! And the way things are going, he'll be home soon. The British have taken Rangoon!'

Katie threw her arms around her sister-in-law and they sobbed with joy and relief.

When she'd recovered a little, Katie immediately dashed round to tell Vi the news. That led to more tears, more prayers of thanks, more incredulity and anger at Georgie's actions. When she got back, Josie was still up, curled in an armchair with an old coat covering her, staring at Georgie with hatred. Her husband had only just come in, and hadn't noticed her expression. He was too busy feeling pleased with himself now that he was the proud owner of a small lorry. It was a start, though. A real step in the right direction for the future, he'd gloated to himself all the way home.

Josie just stared at him, and he was beginning to feel uneasy. What the hell was the matter with the stupid bitch? And now Katie came in with a face like thunder.

'You bastard, Georgie Deegan. I just can't find the words to describe you!' She waved the letter at him. 'You opened my letter.

You kept it! I'm sure there's a law against that and I'll find out and get you prosecuted.'

Georgie said nothing but a flush crept over his cheeks.

'For two whole years you've said nothing; you've watched me live on a knife-edge!' She flung the letter at him. 'I'll never ever forgive you for this.'

Suddenly, he saw the money in her hand. 'Where did you get that?'

She laughed. 'Josie gave it to me as a sort of "compensation".'

He rounded on his wife. 'That's my money! You gave her *my* money?'

Josie stood up. She hated him so much now that she wasn't afraid of him any longer. 'It's mine to give: I've earned it. We lived on my wages and Katie's goodness while you hoarded every penny you could get your hands on. Oh, you're a miserable excuse for a man, Georgie Deegan! I was such a fool to have married you! Katie and Bob can use that money for whatever they want.' She turned to Katie, 'Buy a shop, luv, start with one and expand. Buy more, that's what *he* intended to do. He had two hundred and fifty pounds up there and for all we know, he may have more stashed away somewhere. He's got your Mam's jewellery, too.'

Katie was speechless with fury, but she cried out in shock as Josie suddenly slumped to the floor, unconscious. She bent down beside her and tried to lift her up, but as she did so, she saw the bright red stain on the carpet.

'Go and get an ambulance!' she screamed at Georgie. 'Go on – get a move on! Run to the bottom of the road.'

They took the haemorrhaging girl first of all to Stanley Hospital, but the doctor there said she needed a specialist in gynaecology, so she was next taken to the Women's Hospital in Catherine Street. Katie stayed with her. Georgie was told to go and get Florrie and Vi who would look after the children.

Josie was conscious when she arrived at the hospital and Katie held tightly to her hand.

'Why didn't you say something?'

'I didn't know. I had pains, but nothing too bad. The curse has got heavier but I didn't worry about it.'

'Then they took her into a ward and Katie had to wait outside in the corridor. Everything was so jumbled up, so confusing. The letter, the money, now Josie. She dropped her head in her hands and began to cry. A nurse brought her a cup of tea. She was still sobbing when Florrie arrived.

'Come on, Katie, luv. Pull yerself together.' Florrie put her arm around her shoulder.

'Oh, one minute she was fine, the next she was on the floor and there was all the blood.'

'What's gone wrong?'

'I don't know and no one will tell me. I've asked everyone I've seen passing.'

Florrie stood up, her mouth set in a grim line, the light of battle in her eyes. 'Right, where is she?'

Katie pointed to a door that led into a side ward.

Florrie marched straight in without even bothering to knock.

Her appearance drew cries of surprise, annoyance and outrage from the sister, the doctor and the consultant.

Florrie ignored them all. 'I don't care who any of you are, I'm this girl's mother and I want to know, right this minute, what's the matter with her.'

Before such a determined onslaught, silence prevailed.

'Well?' she demanded.

The doctor came over to her. 'She's started haemorrhaging and we don't know why. She's told us her periods have been heavy lately.'

'They have. We've had to prop up the bed sometimes.'

'Has she any children?'

'One, a little girl, she's nearly two.'

The older man, the consultant, was studying a file. 'But she had three miscarriages before that, and was told she could never have any more children – that another pregnancy would put her life in jeopardy. I'm afraid she'll have to have an emergency operation. A rather serious one, to take away the entire womb and ovaries. In medical terminology, it's known as a hysterectomy.'

'And will she be better after it?' Florrie asked. Her fierceness had evaporated and her voice trembled with worry.

'We don't know. Now, if you would mind leaving, we will do everything we possibly can. Is her husband here?'

'No, and it's his fault anyway. He's utterly useless. If there had been any justice in this war, he'd have been killed and someone else's son would have been spared.'

They all looked at her horrified. 'You don't know him,' she said, defiantly. 'Josie won't want him here.'

Sister bent over Josie. 'Would you like your husband to come and wait?'

Josie felt very weak and dizzy. 'No, I don't want to see him. I want my Mam and Katie, my sister.' She didn't continue. Katie had become more of a sister than all her natural sisters were.

'Then you may have a couple of minutes with the patient before we get her ready, that's all,' the consultant said firmly.

Florrie went to the door to call Katie. There was dread in her heart.

299

They never usually let you near a sick patient before an operation.

They both bent over Josie to hear her words. She looked so pale and drawn that Katie's heart dropped like a stone.

Josie looked up at her. 'Katie, if anything goes wrong, will you watch Olivia for me? I don't want him to rule her life.'

'Oh Josie, you're going to get better,' Katie said tenderly. 'You'll be right as rain after this operation. Of course you know I'll do everything I can. I won't let my brother rule the roost.'

'Mam, will you take her? Don't leave her with him. He can't look after her.'

'Josie! Oh, Josie, luv, don't talk like that. Katie's right. You'll be just great, they're very good in here. Very clever. But you know I'll take her. *He* might be her father, but I'm her Granny.'

There was no time for anything more; they were shepherded firmly towards the door.

Katie held on like grim death to Florrie's arm as the poker-faced sister told them to go home and come back in the morning. There was absolutely no use their waiting – and besides, it was against hospital rules. They must come between ten and eleven, visiting hours.

'I'll be here at half-past eight, and you and your flaming Visiting Hours and Rules can go to hell, you hard-hearted bitch!' Florrie shouted. 'That's my daughter in there. I carried her for nine months and gave birth to her. I suppose you're an old maid, so you won't and can't understand the bond between a mother and her daughter.'

The sister turned abruptly and walked away, her cheeks burning with rage. She wasn't going to stand and take abuse from such a common woman.

'Will we come early?' Katie asked as they waited for the tram home.

'Just let them try and stop us!'

Katie leaned heavily on the older woman. She was utterly exhausted. It was hard to believe that so much had happened in the space of one evening. But Bob was alive – she must cling to that good news.

They arrived at the hospital at half-past eight and were grudgingly allowed to sit in the white-tiled waiting room where the smells of carbolic and ether permeated the air and reminded Katie forcefully of the day her Da had died. She shivered at the memory.

'I hate hospitals,' she whispered.

'I do myself. I wonder how much longer they're going to keep us stuck here?'

The staccato tapping of a sister's sensible shoes echoed down the corridor and preceded her actual appearance.

'Mrs Watson, Mrs Goodwin, Doctor will see you now.'

'I'd like to see my daughter, please?' Florrie's tone was quiet but firm.

'Doctor wishes to see you first,' was the not-unkind reply. This was a different kind of nurse from the one last night, Katie thought as they followed the woman.

It was the same doctor though, and he looked tired and defeated.

Florrie knew immediately. His expression was enough. 'Oh, my God!' she cried, her hand going to her throat.

He looked incredibly sad. 'Mrs Watson, I'm . . . I'm so sorry but we couldn't stop the haemorrhaging. The hysterectomy should have been performed much, much earlier. Her doctor should have informed us. She died at six o'clock this morning. We were about to send the police to inform you.'

Florrie shook her head in disbelief. 'She refused to see Dr Askam. She said it was—' Then she broke down. Katie wrapped her arms around her, silent tears falling down her cheeks. In the space of fourteen hours she'd found out that her husband was alive, but she'd lost a sister-in-law and friend who had become very dear to her. Sorrow shut out all her joy.

They got a tram home and wept silently all the way, the other passengers looking at them with pity, saddened that the war had obviously claimed yet another victim, and with victory now in sight.

For the next few days, every one in Chelmsford Street was in such a state of shock that they didn't notice the underlying air of excitement and relief elsewhere. It was nearly over. Any day now the end would be declared, people told each other. The dim-out would soon be lifted, the boys would soon be home, every one of them a hero.

Florrie stuck to tradition, and Josie was brought home to lie in the bedroom where her daughter Olivia had been born. That was the only happy event that had occurred in there, Katie thought. Mary Maher and Ellen MacCane and their families all came to pay their respects, as did other neighbours, friends and relations. For Florrie and Fred, Katie and Vi, Joe and Lucy there was real sympathy and heartfelt words of comfort and regret. For Georgie only a limp, half-hearted handshake and no words of comfort or condolence.

Joe and Lucy knelt beside the coffin with the rest of the family as Father Macreedy led them into the Litany of Prayers for the Dead, commencing with the *De Profundis*. Josie had become so much a part of Joe's daily life that she'd been almost like a real sister. As he knelt by the coffin, fighting back the tears, he remembered both his Mam and Dad, and poor Sarah. Lucy, her rosary in her hand, took his hand and gave it a squeeze. He turned to look at her. She was so different, so very different from Joanie.

301

The grief and tension in the house were so great they almost crackled around the living room like electricity. Georgie had said hardly anything, which Father Macreedy mistakenly interpreted as a sign of deeply felt but hidden grief.

'And have any arrangements been made about the little one?' he asked Georgie in a soothing but concerned tone.

'I'll be bringing her up, Father,' Florrie stated firmly.

Georgie glared at her. 'Oh no you won't. You'll turn her against me – all of you! I've got money . . . '

'We know, you worked my girl to death to get it,' Florrie interrupted angrily. 'Now *you'll* have to work to provide for this child.'

'I said I've got money! She'll have a nanny, go to private schools and have the best of everything.' Georgie's voice had risen an octave.

'Everything that money can buy, except love!' Florrie answered bitterly.

'She'll have that too.'

Katie joined Florrie in her condemnation. 'From you? You're incapable of loving anyone but yourself. You'll just use her as a way to boast. "Look at *my* daughter, she's better than any of yours!" An object to show people, a testament to your own selfish pride, that's all she'll be. You won't love her the way Josie did. Josie lived for Olivia. Her world revolved around that baby and she risked and finally sacrificed her life for her.'

Georgie rounded on her, stung by her accusations. 'She's *my* daughter!'

'By birth maybe, God help her, but no one would want her to be like you in character or nature, Georgie Deegan.'

Florrie took a pace forward towards Georgie. 'Over my dead body will you pay a stranger to bring her up. She's *my* grand-daughter!'

Father Macreedy was horrified. 'In the Name of God, have none of you any shame? Any sensitivity? A poor young woman is lying upstairs, dead before her time, and you are all tearing each other to pieces and with such venom! God forgive you all.'

They all fell silent, but both Katie and Florrie knew the battle wasn't over. Not by a long way.

After the funeral, and after most people had gone home, Katie went upstairs to pack her case and Robbie's. She'd been born here in Chelmsford Street, she'd lived here all her life, but now she was leaving and taking Robbie with her. No matter how strong the ties and memories were, and it *was* a wrench, she wouldn't stay another night under her brother's roof. It had been different when Josie – and Sarah – had been alive. She wasn't putting up with him on her own. No, they would stay with Vi and Jack until Bob came home, and now it seemed as though they were only days away from peace. She'd also packed all Olivia's things and left the case on the landing for Fred to collect.

'Where the hell are you going?' Georgie demanded as she entered the living room with a suitcase in one hand and a sleepy Robbie on the other arm.

'We're leaving. We're going to stay with Vi.' She turned to Florrie. 'Olivia's things are packed. I've left the case on the landing.'

Fred instantly rose.

So did Georgie. 'You're not taking her.'

'And who is going to see to her until you find a posh nanny for her?' Katie demanded. He'd assumed that she would stay on here. 'You try and stop her grandparents taking her and I'll call the police. You were responsible for killing Mam and Sarah and Josie in one way or another. You tampered with my mail and that's a criminal offence. You let me nearly go out of my mind with worry for two years, not knowing if Bob was alive or dead – and that's just the tip of the iceberg. I'll never, ever forgive you, Georgie Deegan.' Her dark eyes blazed. 'And remember this day as the one I cursed you. You'll die alone. Alone and with no one to care, or even shed a single tear for you.'

'Olivia will,' he yelled defiantly. Who the hell did she think she was? But superstition sent a shiver down his spine.

She laughed, an ugly brittle sound. 'Don't kid yourself. If she's like you, and if all your grand plans work out and she becomes a lawyer or a judge, do you think she'll want you around? You, a working-class ex-seaman from Kirkdale? She'll run a mile and she'll be wise to do so. She'll probably go to London, and she'll make damned sure you don't follow to embarrass her! *If* she's like you, that is, and not her poor gentle, caring mother.'

'There'll be no danger of her growing up like *him* – I'll make sure o' that,' Florrie promised. 'Go and get the case, Fred. Lucy, luv, pass Olivia over to her Granny and if you make one move, Georgie Deegan, you'll have Fred and Jack to reckon with.'

'And me, too,' Joe added suddenly. Georgie had been responsible for him meeting Joanie MacNally and nearly ruining his life, and now he knew that Katie was right about Mam and Sarah.

Katie faced Georgie again, even though she could see the fury that was consuming him. 'Go on, go ahead and make your fortune,' she goaded him. 'It's all you've ever been interested in – money. It's an obsession and I hope it makes you happy, because everyone who knows you hates and despises you.'

Jack took her case and Vi shepherded her towards the door while Florrie and Fred followed. Joe took Lucy's hand and drew her to her feet.

'Shall we go for a walk? The air's cleaner outside.'

She smiled, took his hand and suddenly the room was empty.

Georgie looked around him. Well, he'd show them! He'd bloody well show them all. He'd make enough money to buy back his daughter. To give her all the things he'd promised. He wasn't having her growing up in some overcrowded two-up, two-down terraced house and let run wild. He'd bloody show Katie Deegan that she wasn't always right!

On the morning of 13 May 1945, Vi woke Katie by jumping up and down on the bed.

'It's over, luv! It's really over!' she cried.

Katie sat up. 'Is it? Is it official?'

'Yes, Mr Churchill's going to make a speech on the wireless this afternoon, but the party will have started by then.'

They hugged each other, laughing and crying at the same time. After six long years in which their city had been half-demolished, when they'd survived on rations that kept them above starvation level – just – and their husbands, friends and relations had always been in danger, and their way of life, their traditions, had been changed beyond belief, it was over.

They got dressed, and taking Robbie with them, walked down to Florrie's house. Already people were running up and down the streets laughing, hugging and kissing each other. The heavy black cloud that had hung over all of them for those six interminable years had gone. Women were tacking up strips of red, white and blue bunting, Union Jacks were being draped over bedroom windowsills, the traffic was barely moving and from every church in the city, bells rang out triumphantly, the sound rising into the clear air, into a pure blue sky from which death and destruction would never again rain down, and in which only friendly aircraft would be seen.

All Josie's sisters and young Jimmy were out in the street when they finally arrived. They'd been hugged and kissed by half the neighbourhood and were flushed and laughing as Norma dragged them inside.

'Oh, I can't believe it! I can't believe it!' Vi cried, hugging Fred, then Florrie and then planting a kiss on Olivia's chubby pink cheek.

Florrie's smile held sadness. 'My poor Josie. If only she could just have had a few more weeks.'

Fred placed his hand on her shoulder. 'Come on, luv, today is for celebrating and thanking God that it's all over.'

'I know, but I keep thinking of all the mothers and wives and sisters whose men won't be coming back, because they are buried in foreign lands or in the sea. Those women will have nothing much to celebrate today.'

Her words sobered them for a few minutes until Norma said, 'Oh Mam, don't be such a misery! Mrs Keefe wants to know who's going to organise the street party?'

After that the festivities got well underway as tables, chairs and benches were dragged out into the street. Women were gathering together to discuss just how and where they were going to find food, never mind party fare.

There was a break in all the activities in the afternoon when they grouped around the wireless to hear the Prime Minister inform them that the war in Europe would officially be over at midnight, although Japan remained to be subdued. The voice that was now so familiar and that had kept their willpower and spirits up over the last terrible years finished with the rousing words: 'Advance Britannia! Long live the cause of freedom! God Save the King!'

'Don't worry, Katie, luv, the way MacArthur and his troops are going out there the Japs can't last long. The Yanks raised their flag on Iwo Jima three months ago, and they haven't stopped advancing since. They're bombing Tokyo now,' Fred said cheerfully.

'Oh, go on, the pair of you! Go out and enjoy yourselves, I'll see to the kids. I'll have Sadie Keefe and Lizzie Flannagan down here any minute now. Fred, has anyone got a piano left in one piece, do you know?' Florrie asked, her mind already turning to the future with enthusiasm, the sorrow she would bear for the rest of her life, put away for this one day.

The bells rang all afternoon and into the glorious May evening, and crowds of laughing, singing people thronged the city and all the main streets. Uniformed servicemen were hoisted on shoulders and carried along. Parties were going on everywhere, and the Licensing Laws had been abandoned for the day. Even the police were seen dancing, singing and being kissed by girls and women. Pianos had been dragged into the street, and bottles and even barrels of beer appeared miraculously, and the closely packed little streets rang with the strains of 'Land of Hope and Glory', 'Rule Britannia', the National Anthem and then on to 'Roll Out the Barrel', 'Nelly Dean', 'Show me the Way to go Home', 'Pack up Your Troubles', 'We'll Meet Again' and all the favourites that would forever be known as 'the wartime songs'.

Dusk was falling when Katie finally took Robbie home to Vi's. He was so tired he could hardly keep his eyes open.

'He's absolutely dead beat and so am I myself,' she said to Vi, who was still skipping and dancing along with Jack, both of them decidedly merry.

Suddenly they all stopped and looked at each other. One by one, the street-lights that had survived were coming on. After six years, The Blackout was over.

Jack touched Katie on the shoulder. 'He'll be home soon, girl. They can't hold out for much longer in the East.'

She smiled up at him. 'I know, Jack. I'd never given up on him.' She stroked Robbie's cheek. 'Look, look at the pretty lights, Robbie. Liverpool Lamplight! The war is over and your Daddy's coming home!' He *would*, she knew he would . . .

Epilogue

December, 1994

It was a miserable day, of grey skies, bare, dripping trees, and needle-fine drizzle. In fact, quite suitable weather for a funeral, Katie thought. Such a contrast to the lovely spring day, nearly five years ago now, when she'd stood and watched Bob's coffin being lowered into the ground. His death had broken her heart but not her spirit, and they'd had so many good years together after he'd come home, emaciated but still cheerful from his time in that hell-hole of a prisoner of war camp.

Today the skies seemed to be weeping softly for the young woman who had just been laid to rest, Katie's niece, Olivia Florence Mary Deegan, QC. A career girl flying home after a short holiday on a flight that was doomed. A flight that had ended in disaster. The 747 had broken up on impact as, in dense fog, it had suddenly lost height and ploughed into the bleak Pennine mountainside. There had been no survivors.

There was a sadness in Katie's heart for her niece, but none at all for Olivia's father. She stared at her eldest brother across the gaping mouth of the grave. Never a tall man, but always stocky and strong-looking, Georgie Deegan seemed to have shrunk. His shoulders were bent, his head bowed. He stood alone on the opposite side of the narrow chasm. Olivia had meant everything to him, but that knowledge did nothing to soften Katie's heart towards him. There were too many years of bitterness, too much hatred between them for that.

The drizzle was turning to sleet and the wind was keening.

'Mother, that's it. It's over, come back to the car. You're getting soaked.'

Katie looked up at her son with pride. Robbie was the centre of *her* life now. Bob, too, had been so proud when Robbie had graduated, and even more so when he'd become a GP. She remembered how proud Georgie had been of Olivia, though his driving ambition for her, the pressures he put on her, had meant she'd taken refuge many a time with her warm and welcoming Aunt Katie. In character, Olivia had resembled her mother, not her father, and by the end of her short life

307

Olivia had resented him almost as much as her mother had.

Katie adjusted her smart black hat with the veiling that covered most of her face. At eighty she was of a generation that believed that the black of mourning was a sign of dignified respect. She was still a small, slight woman, very smartly dressed, but her appearance had deluded many people into thinking she was frail and gullible when in fact she had a will of iron. Her back was unbowed, her dark eyes sharp and intelligent. She looked towards her oldest and dearest friend, Vi, in a wheelchair now after a stroke. She'd had the stroke two years ago, when Jack had literally dropped dead from a heart attack at her feet. Now her eldest daughter, Denise, did everything for her. Their eyes met, and there was still a spark of the old Vi visible.

Just for today, Katie had discarded the hated stick. She'd been forced to use it after a fall last year that had resulted in a broken hip, but she would never let *him* see that she was making concessions to the relentless march of time. When she'd felt the need, she'd leaned on the arm of her daughter-in-law, Marcia, a tall, slim woman in her late forties, impeccably dressed as always. On her other side stood her grand-daughter Elizabeth, an art student. There was a special bond between them, for Elizabeth had inherited many of her own character-istics.

Behind her, bare-headed in the wind and sleet, a few paces behind their father, stood her grandsons, Richard and James. A smile hovered around Katie's lips. Oh, she'd done well. The pleasing success of her business apart, she had a close, affectionate, caring family around her while her brother Georgie Deegan couldn't muster a single friend or relation. He stood alone.

'Grandma, you'll catch pneumonia – we all will.' Elizabeth's voice was full of concern and urgency.

Katie smiled at her. 'Just a few more minutes, luv. There are things to be said.' She looked steadily at the priest whose head was bent either devoutly in prayer or to hide the fact that he too was cold and wet.

Her voice broke the uncomfortable silence. 'Isn't there something in the Bible, Father Bradshaw, that says "As ye sow, so shall ye reap"?'

He looked up and nodded. He hoped they weren't going to stand here for much longer. The sleet was soaking into his surplice and soutane, and was dripping from his biretta down the back of his neck. The icy-cold weather conditions appeared to have no effect on Mrs Goodwin whatsoever, although she looked frail.

'I thought so.' Her gaze shifted now to her brother. It was almost fifty years since the blackout had ended, and that beautiful golden lamplight had once more bathed the streets of Liverpool in its glow. She remembered that day. She also remembered her curse, that in the end he'd be left alone in the world.

'So, now you've gathered your harvest, Georgie Deegan,' she said strongly, before them all. 'It's a bitter one, but one you deserve. Your sins are legion. You stole from your own mother. You killed our Sarah as surely as if you'd held the knife. You encouraged our Joe to steal and cheat before he had sense to refuse and marry Lucy . . . No thanks to you they're doing well now out in Australia. Do you remember my curse, Georgie?'

'Mother-in-law, for God's sake!' Marcia hissed, seeing the look of horror on the priest's face.

Katie laughed, a harsh brittle sound from the past. 'For *God's* sake, Marcia! Oh, that's rich. Look at him! He's a liar, a cheat, a hypocrite, a thief and indirectly a murderer.' She paused, ignoring the looks of shock and horror. 'Poor Josie. She was so lonely and felt so guilty and useless until she had Olivia. It's her I'm thinking of now. It's only pity I feel for *him*. What's he left with? Nothing worth having.'

Katie turned to her son. 'I'll go now. I've no more to say to him.'

Georgie Deegan stared at her with unconcealed hatred. He was a proud man and she'd said publicly that she pitied him. That he had nothing. 'You're a liar, Katie!' he said strongly.

She turned back. 'Am I? The truth hurts, but knowing that I feel sorry for you hurts more, doesn't it?'

They all moved away towards the waiting black limousines, and he stared after the small figure in the centre of the group, which seemed to form a protective barrier around her. He had no one now. She was comfortably off but she hadn't pursued money the way he had. That had been his downfall. Money and possessions had been his gods. He shivered as the cold wind buffeted him but he stood and watched the cars leave. Her prediction had been accurate. He *was* alone, and when he died, which couldn't be long now, he'd have to face his Maker and give account of his life. Even when she'd been young, Katie had always been straight and honest, caring, courageous and charitable. But now she'd won the final battle in the long war that had raged between them for almost all their lives. She could forget him now, and get on with living and enjoying the family she loved and who would always love her.